THREE
PRINCES

THREE PRINCES

RAMONA WHEELER

TOR®

A TOM DOHERTY ASSOCIATES BOOK
NEW YORK

THREE PRINCES

A Tor Book
Published by Tom Doherty Associates, LLC
175 Fifth Avenue
New York, NY 10010

www.tor-forge.com

Tor® is a registered trademark of Tom Doherty Associates, LLC.

Library of Congress Cataloging-in-Publication Data

Wheeler, Ramona Louise, 1952–
    Three Princes / by Ramona Louise Wheeler. — 1st ed.
        p. cm.
    "A Tom Doherty Associates Book."
    ISBN 978-0-7653-3597-5 (hardcover)
    ISBN 978-1-4668-2631-1 (e-book)
    1. Egypt—History—19th century—Fiction.   2. Alternative histories
(Fiction).   I. Title.
    PS3623.H445T48 2014
    813'.6—dc23

                                                            2013026232

Tor books may be purchased for educational, business, or promotional use. For information on bulk purchases, please contact Macmillan Corporate and Premium Sales Department at 1-800-221-7945, extension 5442, or write special markets@macmillan.com.

First Edition: February 2014

Printed in the United States of America

0 9 8 7 6 5 4 3 2 1

Contents

THREE
PRINCES

PROLOGUE

THE WHEEL OF DARKNESS TURNS

Year 1877 of Our Lord Julius Caesar

"THE WHEEL of Darkness turns far above us, far above the top of the Sky itself. The Wheel of Darkness bears the Moon upon its immortal brow just as the Inca wears the Moon Jewel upon his living brow. The Wheel of Darkness wears the Face of the Moon as a mask. The great Peoples of the Four Quarters climb the mountains to the top of the world. We build upward to the heavens, yet the Wheel of Darkness turns beyond our reach. For two thousand years, the temples atop the Pyramids of the Moon have fed the power that turns that Wheel, yet we cannot touch the Moon."

Emperor Inca Viracocha Yupanqui XII interrupted this familiar litany with an impatient tapping of his gold-covered fingertips upon the arm of his throne.

Ihhuipapalotl, High Priest of the Qurikancha, lost his place in his memorized speech. He covered by bowing his head until his forehead touched his bended knee. When he looked up, Ihhuipapalotl said, "The launch failed, Glorious One."

"Did *anything* work?" Inca Yupanqui said petulantly. He was old. He did not have time for failure.

Ihhuipapalotl hesitated. "This one did not blow up, Glorious One. It just . . . fell over."

CHAPTER ONE

LORD SCOTT Oken sharpened the focus of the opera-eyes so that a particular pair of legs filled the frame. She was the tallest woman on the stage, and to Oken's eye, she was Golden Hathor with all her graces, a joy to behold. Certainly, there was not another pair of legs so exquisite, white thighs shaped by riding wild Cossack ponies as a child. In his better moments, Oken regretted the power he had over her intentions. In other moments, he simply had to admit that he loved his work.

His attention was interrupted by a knock on the door to his private viewing booth. It would be unseemly for a man of his rank to leap at an interruption.

The dancers sank into their final pose amid a swirl of silk and pearls. The gentle knocking became more insistent. The booth was small and carefully secured, so Lord Oken had only to turn in his seat to unlatch the door behind him.

The theater manager peered around the door, with only his self-important face and fashionably trimmed beard visible. He reverently held out a velvet cushion with a leather scroll-case. The gold-wax seal was the explanation for the manager's excited decision to interrupt a dance scene. Oken took the case, thanking him with a casual word. The manager gave such a deep bow that he had to retrieve his top hat with a sudden snatch, and he retreated, struggling to balance his hat and the cushion while bowing as he backed away.

Oken shut the door and latched it. He sat, looking down at the golden seal on the case, feeling the familiar tug of duty and awe invoked by that familiar and historical icon. The Queen of Egypt was thousands of leagues away at Pharaoh's Palace in Memphis, yet she could ensnare him with such a simple gesture. The blare of brass instruments striking up the final strains sounded, but he did not look up.

Oken unclipped his watch fob from its gold chain, a small, enameled-gold Watch It Eye. He tapped the snake coiled in the inner corner of the Eye and the cover opened, revealing a magnifying lens. The signs of tampering on the gold-wax seal were slight yet unmistakable: indentations in the bottom edge. Someone had read the Queen's message, then skillfully resealed the case.

Oken closed the Eye and returned it to the chain, then broke the seal and unrolled the scroll. He raised it to his nose and sniffed gently. The unique incense of Pharaoh's Palace was faintly present, evoking the majesty and wonder of Memphis. He was an agent of the Egyptian Empire. That thought had more power over him than the lure of those long, long legs.

The presence of Lord Scott Oken is requested at the palace in Memphis, for a presentation to Pharaoh Djoser-George. Life! Health! Courage! On Famenoth 30, commencing at 8 of the clock.

The handwriting was Lady Khamanny's formal secretarial hand, signed with the hieroglyphic signet of the palace. Underneath it, however, was a simple sentence in the Queen's familiar hand: *We are counting on you to be there to dance with us, Scott, since poor old Dozey says his knees just won't take the strain! Sashetah Irene.*

Oken returned the little papyrus roll to its case and slipped it into an inner pocket, resettling his jacket around the stiff shape with a graceful shrug. He was smiling.

A reply to the Queen's message could wait until morning. Oken returned to his close-up view of the stage.

HE LEFT his fur-lined overcoat in the booth. The manager would send it to the embassy hotel. Street carriages were heated, and Natyra kept her apartment unusually warm. She claimed she did so because she could spend more time in the bathing pool in the center of her bedroom. "Water, it keeps my body ready for the next dance!" Oken believed, however, it was more likely that she preferred being nude. This thought kept him warm as he climbed the nine stories to her apartment via the back stair, unheated and unguarded, lit only by small and ancient windows admitting the streetlights.

Natyra Arkadyena Solovyova lived in a great, round room in the sky above Novgorod, at the top of a stone tower in a western wall of the royal palace. Her sponsor, the grand vizier of all Oesterreich, Nevski XXI, was generous. Her room was as luxurious as any in the main halls of the palace, where the vizier and his many wives lived. It was also quite private, in its remote tower above the city.

Lord Oken found the door at the top of the staircase also unguarded, as he had expected. He removed his left glove and rested his fingertips against the touch-points of the ornate figure in the central panel. The hidden circuits in the silver inlay responded only to bare skin. Oken felt, rather than heard, the slight tremble as the panel activated; then it divided down the center and silently slid apart. He had to bend his head down and to the side as he stepped through the portal that had opened in the door. He was taller than most.

There were candles everywhere in her apartment, in silver and alabaster candlesticks. He could smell the soft, warm-wax scent of candles that had, until only moments before, been lit. The dying smoke made a sweet, mournful fragrance that told him the candles had burned while she awaited his arrival. He had known that they would not be lit when he walked in.

Oken asked her about it once. She told him someone (she would never tell him who, or when or why) had used candle flame to hurt her, badly. She showed him the pale scar still lingering on her sweet white breast. Whoever it was had used her own candles to burn her until she screamed her throat raw and confessed to things that she had not done and had never thought of doing until those ideas were put into her head. She had adored candles and candlelight from the first time she had been carried—small and helpless, and loving of the arms that held her—into a temple ceremony of the divine Neith, she of the wick and the lamps. Natyra's first dances on temple stages had been to this ancient divinity. Natyra loved candles, the waxy scent, the yellow orange glow, the simple magic of light and heat that arose from string and wax and oil. She could not let that night of torture turn her away from her divine guide, but she could never bear to have anyone share them with her. She lit candles only when alone.

Oken, upon hearing this sad confession, had gotten up from her bed and taken a fat green candle from the mantel and set it on her nightstand. When he lit it, he saw her face go pale and her lips tremble. She held her chin up, still proud, yet a cloudy fear touched her green eyes.

He did not touch the lit candle. He held his hands out beside it, with the firm, tanned flesh of the backs of his hands and wrists close to her.

"Burn *me*," he said to her, firmly. "Burn *me* with the candle."

Natyra shook her head. He could see the candlelight gleaming in her eyes and on the smooth, polished skin of her shaved head.

"Do it."

She stared at him, gauging his conviction, then took the candle and dripped hot wax onto the backs of his hands.

He winced.

He let her drip more wax, until he saw something fierce and clean shine in her perfect face. With a cry of alarm, she put the candle back into its holder and pushed it away. Oken blew out the flame, watching her face in the sudden twilight. He used a bit of ice from his drink to chill the wax on his hands until it was brittle and fell away.

Natyra had tears in her eyes as she kissed his hands then, the soft, unburned insides of his wrists and his palms. They never spoke of it again. She did not light candles when he was there, but she trusted him.

Her trust hurt Oken more than the mild blisters on his hands. He was testing a theory, doing his job. What truly mattered was that he discover the identity of her contact in Novgorod, in the palace of the grand vizier of Oesterreich, who was leaking vital information to Bismarck in Turkistan, the only nation in open resistance to Egypt's embrace.

THE TAPESTRY that concealed the hidden entrance to her apartment was drenched with the fragrance of incense, oils and candles. Oken was familiar now with that mingled scent of smoke and time and he felt his pulse quickening.

He paused with the corner of the tapestry's fabric in one hand, gazing around, adjusting to the dim light. At the far side of the room, tall windows looked out over Novgorod. City lights created an orange glow in the night sky. Opposite the tapestry was a fireplace, originally built to burn whole trees at once, radiating warmth into the room from the complex flutings of a steel radiator. White peonies filled the mantel, masses of them in crystal vases set between miniature lotus columns.

Oken could see the gold and silver threads of the tapestry's design reflected in the mirror above the mantel, making the divine faces of Isis and Osiris shine softly in the darkness. They seemed to be smiling down benignly at his face, reflected in the mirror as well. For an instant he felt himself to be a part of their eternal scene. He pushed the feeling aside to focus on the moment. However lovely the scene, this moment was not benign. He was here on a mission, weaving lies in search of a truth.

Natyra's pale form was outlined by blue radiance as she floated comfortably in the bathwater with an ivory headrest supporting her slender neck and shaved head. She raised her glass to him in salute when he stepped into sight.

Oken strolled slowly toward the glowing pool and her magical presence. He circled the pool so that he could see every curve in the water, then he stopped beside the ivory headrest. The blue radiance emphasized the pattern of veins in her throat and breast. Her eyes were deeper green in this light, large and luminous, gazing up at him with sultry promise.

He dropped to one knee beside her upturned face. "My mum spent a lot of her wealth to make sure that I had a proper appreciation of classical art. You are a classic, and I do appreciate perfection."

"My compliments to your dear mum," Natyra whispered.

"My mum would not like you," he whispered in return.

"Good." She reached up and drew his face close to kiss him.

Oken was careful not to let the cuffs of his jacket get wet. He tasted vodka and hints of absinthe along with her incomparable sweetness.

"Join me." She gestured toward the pool.

"Your bed would be more comfortable."

"I am comfortable here." She waved her hand once slowly through the glowing water so that inviting ripples swirled over her creamy flesh.

"Yes, you are, but I've had my bath already."

"Silly boy. You will need another bath when I am done with you."

"I certainly hope so."

"I am tired from the dancing. The hot water, it makes me relax." A slight pout in her voice suggested Oken was going to give in to her.

"I can make you relax," he whispered.

Natyra stretched lazily in the water, arching her back so that the pearl white mounds of her breasts rose out of the pool, sparkling with water drops.

Oken sighed. This was his favorite suit and he was on very good terms with the tailor. He did not want to get it wet. It was silk. Then he remembered the scroll in his pocket. He sat back on his heels.

"I'll meet you there." He stood up.

Natyra's scrunched up her forehead, and she let her glass drop into the bath.

Oken stepped back, smiling down at her, then strolled over to the canopied bed. He settled onto it, bracing himself on hip and elbow and stretching his long, lean legs out across the silk quilts. He lazily undid the buttons of his jacket, thinking not of Natyra but of the royal wax seal on the scroll calling him back to Memphis to dance with the Queen of the world.

"You are a tyrant." Natyra stood up in the pool. "You did not even give me a towel."

"Do you need one?"

She pouted at him more firmly as she climbed out of the bathing pool and took a towel from the warming rack. She let it trail dramatically behind her in one hand as she stepped slowly toward the bed with the exaggerated grace of the stage. Droplets of water rolled down her perfect flesh, tracing the rise and fall of her muscles as she moved.

Natyra was forty-eight, almost twice Oken's age. She always made sure that her lovers saw her only from the distance of the stage or in the twilight luxury of her private apartment. Oken was less mindful of her age than of her ageless perfection. He marveled at the good fortune that had brought him here. Were their ages reversed, he doubted she could have been more beautiful. She wore time better than most women wore youth.

She swirled the towel around and draped it across his hip as she knelt on the bed. "You must dry my back."

Oken sat up, pulling her to him as he pushed the towel to the floor. She put her arms around him, stroking his thick hair as she kissed him. The bare curve of her skull fit his hand perfectly. Oken knew, whatever else happened, he would remember that curve of bare skin against his palm for as long as he lived, and not just because of his perfect memory.

She teased his teeth with the tip of her tongue, and Oken stretched her out on the bed.

There was a thunder of fists pounding on wood from behind the huge tapestry covering the far wall, then a crashing thud, and the corner of the tapestry was thrust aside as a man in uniform burst into the room. "Natyra!" he shouted when he saw them.

Natyra sat up as though stung, her eyes wide.

The man looked as big as a bear—not a big European bear, but some giant, golden animal from the deep, wild woods of Rusland, towering over everything and everyone, sleek and enormous. Even his blond mustache was waxed into giant curls. His bushy brows were drawn down into a fierce *V* of anger over his raging blue eyes.

Oken recognized him at once, with some surprise, as General Vladimir Modestovich Blestyak, in command of the vizier's royal horsemen guard, and the last person Oken expected to see in Natyra's apartment. Blestyak was a lowbrow from a famous family, never seen out of uniform and never seen when anything important or dangerous was happening. Oken was more curious than alarmed by his noisy entrance. He made himself remain still, ready to leap in whichever direction this invasion demanded.

Blestyak bellowed as he stalked toward the two poised on the bed. The size of his rage and his volume made his words incoherent. Even so, Oken picked up at once that the general was not happy about the "Egyptian pig" in Natyra's bed.

Natyra reared up, defiantly nude, to stand between Oken and the general. She placed her hands on her hips and lifted her chin with regal disdain. "How dare you come in here uninvited!"

The general spat out a torrent of words, accusing Oken of being a spy for the Pharaoh. The sight of those perfect breasts, however, made the intensity of his rage falter. He hesitated before taking another step toward her. He repeated the accusation at a lower volume.

Natyra, speaking in the same language, reminded the general that he was also a spy. In Trade Speak she added haughtily, "Irrelevant! He is invited to be here—*you* are not!"

Oken had faked ignorance of the native tongue. He had just received his reward for the ruse. General Blestyak was not on the embassy's suspect list. He was considered to be something of an idiot, fit only for horses and royal stables. Natyra's single sentence, however, made pieces fall into place. The royal stables were part of the palace compound, with access to the entire grounds. The royal family worshipped their horses. The stables were temples to Epona, sacred ground. Blestyak was in a perfect position to observe anything happening there. His obscurity even made sense. Who would notice him?

Oken made himself lie still, resting back on one elbow, a hand draped across his hip. He let his gaze drift as if the glorious view of Natyra from behind were more important than a raging giant.

Blestyak's step faltered again as he looked back and forth between the lovers. "I will have this pig arrested!"

"I will have *you* thrown out!" Natyra stamped once with her foot.

"That's one big bear." Oken spoke lightly, pretending to be entertained by the interruption. "What's he shouting about? Does he plan to join us?"

She turned her head to glare at Oken. "Do not be impertinent."

"Good." Oken made himself relax back against the pillows. "I don't much like animals, not in bed." He waved the general out as he would dismiss a servant. "Make him go away, *milya* Natyra."

Blestyak recovered his rage, flinging himself at Oken with a roar.

He landed on the bed with such a crash that the solid wooden frame creaked ominously. Oken, however, had neatly rolled away. He leaped to his feet as the general raised himself up to scramble after him.

Oken was glad that he had not yet taken off his jacket. He sprang around the bed to where Natyra was just regaining her feet. He picked up the towel and draped it around her shoulders like a dinner cloak.

Blestyak also regained his feet and was coming around the bed with an incoherent string of curses. Giant hands stretched out to grab Oken.

Oken kissed Natyra lightly on the tip of her nose, feeling, as he had from the first, a strange jolt when so close to her green eyes. "I'll be back," he said, knowing it was a lie. His work here was done.

He turned aside as the general reached them, thus Natyra intercepted Blestyak's assault. Both of them fell heavily onto the bed, with the general's arms tangled around Natyra's long limbs. Oken sprang away, running toward the secret exit behind the tapestry.

The general moved with surprising swiftness, untangling himself and snatching up giant handfuls of the carpet with a fierce jerk. Oken went down. He rolled as he fell, and he came up just as Blestyak's fist came down on the side of his face.

The buzzing in Oken's head nearly drowned out Natyra's scream. He tasted blood.

Even Oken's eidetic memory recalled only a blur of pain and pounding fists in the next few seconds. His best training in martial arts could only keep him moving fast enough that the general could not kill him, not all at once. Natyra's angry screams penetrated like darts in the fog.

There was an abrupt explosion of shattering crystal. Blestyak fell heavily across Oken, pinning him to the carpet.

Oken had a glimpse of Natyra's nude form standing over them, holding the broken remains of the vase she had just smashed over the giant general's giant head. White peony petals clung to the droplets of water on her arms and legs like stray feathers. She held that crystal weapon raised, prepared to hit Blestyak again if he stirred.

"Is he dead?" she whispered.

Oken could see the flutter of veins pulsing in the general's forehead as blood spilled down across the huge face. Petals were caught in the hot, red blood. "No," he managed to gasp. "Get him off me." Then the lights vanished, and the world fell silent and still.

LIGHT AND sound returned with stunning cold.

Oken found himself lying on a mound of snow beneath a clear black sky of northern stars. His first thought was to regret that he had left his gloves on Natyra's bed. The next was to hope that the blood staining the snow was not his own—at least, not all of it.

He tried to sit up, thought better of it, and settled for lifting his head enough to see beyond the bloodied snow. He was lying on the frozen drift at the base of a stone wall. He recognized the wall. He had been carried to the side entrance of his hotel. The Egyptian Embassy was across the street. He checked his jacket pocket with trembling fingers. The case was still there. He shook it, hearing the slight rattle that said the scroll was inside.

His body ached with the fierce cold and bruising and the hard, sharp pain of fractured ribs. He rolled off the snowdrift and into the road. Pain gave him the strength to pull himself up to his feet and he staggered over the pavement to the embassy building. His legs gave way as he reached the huge windows. The building's automatic security system would alert the guards inside. He lay huddled around the pain, waiting for them to find him. It was time to leave Novgorod. He had accomplished his mission and his best suit was ruined.

CHAPTER TWO

LORD OKEN arrived in Memphis under an Egyptian sky transformed into a chill midnight by the garment of Noot, brilliant with stars. The Memphis cityscape glittered from horizon to horizon, spread out for leagues below the coach station perched on the outer rim of the elevated highway. Distant lamps glowed in windows and on street corners, creating pools of light in the darkness. Temple flags fluttered high above the maze of rooftops, orchard trees, and courtyard walls. The Nile was just visible, a broad, shimmering ribbon glimpsed between buildings and trees. Blue navigation lights gleamed along the shore.

Oken stepped down from the coach, letting the other passengers surge past him toward the warm glow of the station interior. He had felt a profound impatience during this last stretch of the journey. The night pouring past the coach windows made him keenly aware of his eagerness to return. The sharp, sweet air of Egypt filled his lungs with a delighted intoxication. He had been born in the foggy world of Mercia, but Memphis was his home. He was glad to be back.

The journey had been swift, just two weeks by coach to cover the leagues between Novgorod and Memphis, giving him occasion once again to appreciate the complex system of Caesar's elevated highways that covered Europe. Rusland was exciting, but the deep cold of winter chilled more than his bones. He rested his hand briefly on his side, wincing. His bones barely had time to knit on the journey. He could not stretch without feeling the dull ache under the wrapping of bandages.

The charm of the night hour made him decide to walk. Drivers were plentiful, waiting in the station. Oken wanted to feel and to taste his return to Memphis more directly. He had admired the pristine snowbanks laid over Novgorod like a velvet quilt. He had enjoyed the layover in Athens, filthy, noisy streets ripe with smells and delicious human intrigue. Memphis, however, was a temple, solemn, stone-cut, clean, and eternal. Melodious, deep-throated bells pealing forth the hours and the days wove a pattern of timelessness. The night sky above Egypt was the color of eternity.

Oken went into the station and told the agent to send his luggage ahead to the west wing of the professors' hall at Thoth's Manor. The acolytes in the reception foyer would take it up to his apartment. His luggage would arrive before he did, which would give Professor-Prince Mikel Mabruke advance warning of his homecoming. Oken did not want to surprise his friend. Mik might have company. Oken certainly hoped Mik had company. Mik was used to company. His recent retirement have given him, at last, time for company.

Oken set off for the staircase that spiraled down to ground level on the city side. His destination was clearly visible. The twin towers of the Galileo Observatory and the pylons of Thoth's Manor rose above Memphis, dominating every view. The highway skirting the city was a pale white presence in the night fading behind him as he descended the many steps.

Once at street level, he was surrounded by restaurants and nightclubs catering to travelers coming in from the coach station above. Spinglass lights flashed and beckoned with a rainbow of colors, inviting him in for the usual variety of services and entertainment.

The streets were not busy. A few people strolled here and there, weary travelers just arriving and young folk on the prowl for anything offered by the night. Laughter and music spilled from opened doors.

Oken walked on, guided by memory and by the flags of Thoth's Manor riding high over the city.

He crossed through a residential neighborhood, street after street of vertical, multistory houses pressed up against each other. The tops of palm, sycamore, and cypress could be seen from the courtyards within, and flowerpots circled the base of every corner streetlamp.

Hand painted on these housefronts were wildly innocent designs showing the personalities of the owners, family identity tattooed on the skin of their homes. Every kind of art could be found here: ancient hieroglyphics painted alongside Celtic maze designs, Danish realism, and Spanish surrealism. In these neighborhoods the house art was as well known as the family's name. These were people proud to be in Memphis, even as part of backstreet life. Banners fluttered above the doorways, leftovers from this or that festival. Music and laughter floated gently through open windows and from the inner courtyards. Occasionally a hire-carriage or a private vehicle went silently past Oken on gusts of air, stirring the dried sycamore leaves piled up against the curb.

The perfumes of gardens carried on the night breeze told him he was approaching the Uptown District, the ancient estates of Memphis overwhelmed by the sprawl of Thoth's Manor on one side and the shifting Nile on the other. Caesar and Cleopatra had counted the original families of these estates as friends. The Sacred Couple had walked in those courtyards. They had been carried along these very streets in litters made of the finest Lebanese cedar, resting on the shoulders of Roman guards. Altars, artwork, and architecture had remained unchanged here since those days, living tribute to the parents of civilization and of enlightened life.

There were bigger, flashier estates north and south of Uptown and across the river, as far as the sandstone hills around Lake Fame. Here, however, along these narrow streets, Old Memphis enfolded him within the timeless atmosphere of her antique and gracious architecture.

Oken had arrived in Memphis just fifteen years earlier, shortly before his twelfth birthday, a new and very nervous student at Caesar's Royal Academy of Political Reality. His parents were both descendants of Caesar's children with Queen Cleopatra, which made Oken royalty born of royalty, family lines nineteen centuries unbroken. By Caesar's royal decree, royalty born of royalty were to be educated only by Caesar. Oken's entire family had been educated in the Caesarian System, although one or the other of his three older brothers was more likely to inherit the throne of the Spate of Mercia in the Britannic Isles than he was. Oken knew he would always call Memphis home, no matter who he was or where he had been born.

More than a lifetime of changes had swept through him and around him during his years at school. Memphis herself was utterly unchanged, changeless, with only the patterns of leaves against the sky and thickened branches of the sycamores lining the avenue to show that time had any hold here. This might have been his very first stroll through these streets fifteen years ago. The delicate night breezes carried identical wafts of incense and the perfume of flowers, the fragrances of roses and lilies, mint and sandalwood, jasmine, honeysuckle, and the sweet purple scents of lavender and myrrh. Fountains splashing sang gentle, wordless tunes of constant delight. These ancient estates were a shield against time. Elsewhere, the world wheeled forward on aqueduct highways and on the spreading sails of Quetzals floating through the skies. In Memphis, time paused, pleased with this eternal moment.

The avenue wound on between the high walls of estates gated by painted pylons, temple-fronts-in-miniature proudly displaying the names, generation upon generation, of the venerable Memphite families who had lived and died behind those antique stone walls, in the cool shade of towering date palms, and sycamores, and cypresses. Family names dating back to Caesar's day were the bottom row of names on the pylons, originally hand painted in hieroglyphics by master artists whose names themselves were legend. The hieroglyphs were carefully maintained, restored as needed by schools of artists who kept the ancient techniques alive and thriving. These families were the elite among the elite. Their names were registered in eternity, names spoken with hushed awe and respect everywhere, names like Rokhmyr, Djoser, Orkon and Rae-Imhotep.

Memphis was the capital of the world. All roads led to Memphis. On most maps, they did. Oken walked down those midnight avenues, feeling the timeless presence of millennia of history. At twenty-seven, Lord Oken was too young to be jaded by the magnificence around him. He felt the thrill of association with the grandeur of such ancient lineages and ageless beauty.

The first time he walked these streets, at age twelve, Oken had met a group of giggling, sloe-eyed beauties wearing silk wrap-dresses in butterfly colors. Layers of curls framed their girlish faces. Their bronzed-golden skin looked richer than Greek coins. Their lips were painted red as berries. They surrounded him and his bodyguard, jingling their golden bracelets and laughing, whispering to one another in a rapid, joyful-sounding language Oken did not know. One of them had been brave enough to reach out and stroke Oken's curly hair. The others squealed and whisked her away, their girlish laughter drifting back to him on the incense-flavored breeze. Oken could feel the heat in his face, the internal fires that had flared at her brazen touch.

His bodyguard, a kindly old soldier who yearned to be back in his misty homeland of Mercia, was trying to frown. The little beauties, however, had taken hold of his heart as well.

"Do they live here?" Oken made his voice light to cover the sudden fires. "Do they live in these estates?"

"Aye."

"Mum hopes I will find a wife from one of these Uptown estate-families in Memphis." He hesitated. "The one who touched my hair was quite fine, you know."

The old man laughed, the hearty laugh of an elder at the foolishness of the young. "Those were servant girls—mademoiselles. They were ladies' maids out on a holiday! Your mum would not like them a bit, mark my words, lad. She wouldn't let them clean her boots."

Oken's face burned then, more fiercely in shame than desire. "How do you know that? You're just an old soldier!"

"That I am. A servant knows a servant when he meets her. The ladies who live here, the fine ladies your mum craves, would never walk these avenues without a full guard and a retinue of attendants." He warmed to his narrative. "The ladies your mum craves mostly dress in white, old-Egyptian white, so that the gold and jewels that cover their bare arms and ankles and their fine, long necks shine out the better—those girls there wore their own hair. You should know that no fine lady of Old Memphis would ever wear her own hair! Bare, clean skulls to put expensive wigs on, wigs with diamonds wove into the braids. No—those girls were mademoiselles. Your mum would have my bottle on toast if I let you mingle with them!"

He was greatly pleased with this revelation, nodding as he walked beside Oken.

Oken risked a glance over his shoulder at the group of girls. The one who had touched his hair, leaving a burning impression on his skull, was at that moment looking back at him.

"You mark my words," the old man said then, "your mum is a child of Caesar's line, and you'll win no arguments with her."

"I am also a child of Caesar's line."

"You're a lad. Your mum is always right."

The memory of Natyra intruded on Oken's reminiscing. "My compliments to your dear mum," she had whispered from out of her radiant pool.

Oken strolled on, his hands in his pockets, breathing in flower-scented memories. The old soldier was retired in his beloved Mercia, with a lovely Greek widow whom he met one night beside the Nile. "A servant knows a servant when he meets her."

He wished the old man luck. Oken was no longer a "lad." He could walk the streets at night alone now. He was his own body-guard, trained by Caesar's best.

"Hoy there, mister!" a voice hailed from out of the night.

Oken stopped. He saw a Memphis city constable in the uniform of white trousers and a short-sleeved ostrich-leather waistcoat with lapels and gold braid. The constable was standing in the light beneath a corner lamppost at the intersection Oken had just passed.

"You're out late, sir." The constable walked toward Oken with measured, unhurried strides. "Are you lost?"

"No, constable." Oken stood quietly as the man approached. "I've never felt more at home. I just returned from a tour of Europe. I missed Memphis. I missed the air, and the lights."

Oken held out his hand when the constable reached him. "Lord Scott Oken." His signet ring and the silver torque around his neck backed his words. "Of the Mercia Spate. And you?"

The constable took Oken's hand with a firm grip. "Constable Mathias of the Uptown Station, but from north of the Mersey myself, sir."

"Constable Mathias," Oken said in echo. "I know Redfield and Evanstead of the Uptown. I don't think I've met you before."

The invocation of the names of his superior officers took the stiffness from the man's stance. "Just out the academy, sir. Only my second night on patrol, truth be known. They've pulled out every man jack in the corps on account of some royal fella got himself nicked. Pharaoh set us out hunting for him, so new men get to pull extra duty. Extra pay, if you get my meaning, sir."

"Well, I'm not the man you're looking for, but I'll walk with you, if you like. I know these streets. I can introduce you around."

"I'd not mind the company, truth be known. These old places seem thick with ghosts and old names, if you get my meaning, sir."

"Indeed, Constable Mathias, thick with ghosts and old names."

"Are you headed home, Lord Oken?"

"The Ibis Road Gate. I have rooms on Campus." Oken realized then how eager he was to see his friend, Prince Mikel Mabruke. Novgorod had been Oken's longest assignment outside of Memphis since Mabruke retired. Oken had been away for months. The story of this adventure would have proper resonance and context once shared.

"A fine spot, sir," Mathias said, respect clear in his voice. "The view from those tower rooms must be quite the thing."

"If you like, Constable." Oken had a sudden impulse. "You should walk up with me, and watch sunrise over the Temple of Hathor Ascendant. There's no finer view of dawn in all the world."

"A worthy invitation, sir, but I'm on duty until noon. By rights I can walk with you only as far as the guard post at Ibis Gate."

"Good enough, Mathias, and spoken with a proper sense of duty. Come up for supper, then, and watch the Sun set over the Temple of Ptah-Sokar. My friend will be happy to meet you." Professor-Prince Mabruke, Oken's mentor in espionage, had taught the necessity of maintaining good relations with officials of public authority. Many difficult explanations could be avoided by knowing what to say to whom.

"That be most gracious of you, sir." Mathias was a rough-hewn fellow, sandy-haired, with layers of dark freckles. He kept a big-knuckled hand resting on the handle of his nightstick, peering into the night from side to side in steady watch as they strolled up the avenue toward the Ibis Road.

Oken had the nagging feeling that there was a question he should ask, but the night was peaceful and still, with only the fragrance-laden breezes stirring. He was grateful for Mathias's simple company without need for conversation.

Ibis Gate was in sight at last. Mathias was making a polite

comment about the emptiness of the road at this hour of the night when two figures, half-stumbling, emerged from a side alley, hurrying in the direction of the gate and the guard station there. Mathias unclipped a metal torch from his belt, excusing himself to Oken, and strode after them, shining the beam over them and ordering them to halt.

Oken leaped after him in abrupt impulse, not out of concern for crime or criminals. To his complete astonishment, Oken recognized those two men.

One was a security officer from the Campus Guard, Sergeant Aaron Wast. The other was, quite impossibly, Oken's mentor and best friend, the very person whom Oken was most eager to see, Captain-Prince Mikel Mabruke of Pharaoh's Special Investigators, Retired. Even in the dark night, Oken was certain.

He ran. The men were in trouble. Wast could barely walk, and was being half carried by the tall, thin figure of Mabruke, who was himself clearly struggling to go on. They moved with a weary determination that spoke of grave danger.

Constable Mathias called to them again to halt, yet they stumbled on more quickly as if alarmed to be discovered.

"Mik!" Oken called loudly. "Mik! It's me, Scott!"

He caught up with the constable. "That's Professor-Prince Mabruke!" he shouted as he ran past him toward the two men. "He's in trouble!"

Mabruke stopped, turning his head to peer at Oken running toward him. "Scott?" he whispered in clear astonishment. He stumbled, with Wast nearly slipping from his grasp.

Oken took the weight of Wast as he caught up with them, putting an arm around the man's shoulders despite the pain of his half-healed ribs. Mabruke put a hand on Oken to steady himself. He was breathing heavily.

"Red Hand," Mabruke gasped, his voice a barely audible croak. "Too many."

Oken could smell the iron-sharp tang of fresh blood on Wast. The man was barely conscious, only a lifetime of fierce discipline keeping him on his feet.

"The Red Hand!" Mathias said in disbelief as he caught up to them. "Here? In Thoth's District?"

There was no more notorious criminal syndicate in Memphis, perhaps in all Egypt, but the university district of Egypt's capital city was believed to be too well patrolled to permit their activities. The young constable's hesitation was understandable. The Red Hand League was an organization as old as Memphis, claiming descent from the Hittite kings of Egypt ousted three millennia ago, a ruthless order of criminals ruled by the deadliest impulses, justifying their crimes with ancient rituals and corrupted gods. They believed that their stone knives and obscene rites granted them powers that put them above the law, above decency, above civilization itself.

Mabruke pointed with a shaking hand to the alleyway from which he had just emerged.

"Call for help, Mathias!" Oken said.

Lord Oken's rank was too important to ignore. Mathias took the whistle that hung on a steel chain around his neck and blew a series of loud blasts, a coded pattern that would alert other officers within hearing.

"The hounds!" Oken said to him in command. "Call out the hounds!"

The constable blew a second series of blasts. At that same moment, black-clad figures surged out of the alleyway, running toward them. Mabruke backed away, dragging Oken and Wast with him.

Before the men of the Red Hand could reach them, however, the great hounds that lived in the guardhouses beside the gates along the street burst forth in response to the constable's whistle, baying their challenge. They had been called, and they were well-trained animals, huge beasts, black and brindled and gray, wearing leather harnesses studded with spikes. Each hound knew Mabruke personally. They knew his scent and remembered the kindness he had shown them. They also knew the scent of human blood. From up and down the street, they ran to him, gathering around Mabruke. The dark night was suddenly filled with their voices.

Booted feet were heard running toward them from farther up the road. The guards at Ibis Gate were also responding to the call.

Vicious howls rose from the hounds as they attacked the attackers. They screamed like women when hurt. The night was rent by their voices in triumph and in pain.

Seconds later the yellow uniforms of Thoth's guardsmen broke like flames against the shadows in the dark street, sparked by the gleams of white teeth and flint blades.

Oken held Wast with one arm and Mabruke with the other, dragging them away from the chaos. Wast was fading quickly. Oken hefted him over one shoulder, blanching for breathless seconds under the stab of protest from his rib cage. The pain was almost as sharp as the stab of fear he felt when he saw the expression on Mabruke's face. Something terrible had happened to him. Oken had perhaps arrived too late. He put his arm around his friend's waist and hurried him away from the brawling mass of hounds and men.

Guards from Thoth's Manor were pouring out onto the road, some on foot, some on horseback. An armored vehicle with gun ports and fiercely brilliant spotlights came roaring out of the main gate.

The eternal night froze over this bloody tableau.

Oken clung to his friend, step by step, staggering under the limp weight of the man on his shoulder. He lost sight of the kindly Constable Mathias, who had volunteered to lead him safely through the nighttime streets. Oken focused on the blue security lights around Ibis Gate. His single thought was that he had to get to those lights.

* * *

ACOLYTES POURED out as they reached the gate, surrounding them, murmuring gentle reassurances. Mabruke and Wast were taken from Oken by practiced, confident hands and swiftly carried away. Oken found himself being ushered inside.

Once the doors shut behind them, the sudden hush and stillness was overwhelming. He had just awakened from some terrible nightmare. Nothing that had just happened was real.

There was blood on his hands, on his clothes. That was real. He mumbled thanks to the acolytes and hurried after the crowd of young people who were carrying Mabruke and Wast away down a side corridor toward the Sakhmet Healing Station deep in the front wall of Thoth's Manor.

Emergency sakhmeticians, wearing the light blue, high-collared uniforms of their guild, met them on the way. They were pushing a pair of beds on cushioned wheels. Wast and Mabruke were placed on these, then immediately hurried away. The temple acolytes followed, with Oken at their heels.

Tense minutes passed as this parade hurried through the late-night silence of empty corridors, until they reached the lobby of the emergency sakhmetical facility. Nurses and sakhmeticians closed in around the beds with hasty exchanges of jargon that Oken only half understood. "Dehydration," "blood loss," and "intravenous fluids" rang ominously in his ears. In the desert climate of Memphis, dehydration was always serious and often fatal.

Oken's attention was interrupted by a youngster tapping his shoulder. One of the acolytes had brought a tray with a set of steaming washbowls, soap, and towels. "If you would care to wash? It is not safe to let someone else's blood dry on your skin, sir."

Oken looked down at his hands, then gave the boy a shaky smile. "A good thought, my young friend."

"The water has a purifier, so you will take no harm from anything in the blood."

"Will it clean the blood off my 'jacket?" Oken swirled his hands in the heated water in the bowl.

"No, sir. Cloth must be cleaned in other ways."

Oken realized that the interruption had not only cleaned his hands but also calmed him. He rinsed and dried carefully, struck by the realization that the touch of warm water on his skin would always carry a lingering trace of the blue radiance of a bathing pool in faraway Novgorod. That was one of the compensations of a well-trained memory.

He thanked the boy for his assistance.

Another group of emergency sakhmeticians rushed into the lobby then, disrupting the scene with noisy calls for assistance and hurried instructions. Apparently the staff were prepared for the recovery of a kidnapped nobleman and his bodyguard. Equipment had been waiting on standby. The staff were not so prepared for the number of casualties from the unexpected battle that had erupted between temple guards and the agents of the Red Hand in pursuit of Mabruke. More than a dozen men, as well as five hounds, were being brought in on stretchers. Four more hounds were "walking wounded," still on their feet but bleeding from cuts on their muzzles and backs.

The beds with Wast and Mabruke were smoothly wheeled away to side rooms as the wounded and staff members filled the lobby.

Oken saw that one of the most severely wounded was young Constable Mathias. Indeed, the stillness of death lay on his bloody and battered form. Oken absorbed this with dismay, then hurried after Mabruke.

There was only one nurse left beside Mabruke's bed, working at a side table with a silver heating tray, measuring herbs into a carafe of steaming water. She looked up when Oken came in, gave him a slight, professionally concerned smile, then continued her work. She did not protest his presence at Mabruke's side. Oken stood beside the bed, looking down at his friend.

Oken felt helpless, something he had not experienced since child-hood. Mabruke's dark skin, normally as shiny and purple black as ripe Nubian plums, was almost yellowish green. His lips were dry and cracked, bleeding in one corner. His long limbs, usually as gracefully posed as a dancer's, were slack, lying limply in awkward positions, as though he could neither feel himself nor move according to his will. Worst of all, his long-fingered, beautiful hands, his most expressive and elegant hands trembled, plucking listlessly at the air as though trying to find themselves. His fingernails were broken and torn, almost as if the man had tried to dig through solid stone with his bare hands. Mabruke had never gone unshaven in his life, so the length of harsh, graying stubble covering his scalp, his cheeks, chin, and throat was a shock. The ordeal had lasted for days.

Oken had never seen anyone look so lost. He put his hand gently on his friend's shoulder and softly called his name. "Mik? Mikel. Are you in there?"

At Oken's touch and the sound of his voice, Mabruke's eyes flew open. The change in him was immediate. Energy and life woke in him. His large chestnut eyes devoured the vision of Oken bending over him, searching his face. Mabruke's hands steadied at once, gripping Oken's wrist. He was weak; that was clear. He was not defeated. That was also clear. His cracked lips parted as he tried to speak.

The nurse leaned over from the other side of the bed, lifting Mabruke's head. "Drink this slowly," she said calmly. "You are severely dehydrated."

The glass held green, sweet-smelling tea and a glass straw. "Drink slowly," she repeated, putting the straw to his lips. "This will restore you," she went on encouragingly. "Let it rest on your tongue and be careful swallowing."

Mabruke obeyed, his eyes closing slowly as he sipped the tea.

Oken watched anxiously, focused on his friend's face. He kept his hand on Mabruke's shoulder. Mabruke's hand rested on Oken's arm, drawing strength from him.

"Professor-Prince Mabruke has been missing for several days," the nurse said quietly to Oken, without looking away from the glass of tea she held. "Pharaoh has had every man on the force out searching for him since yesterday morning. We feared the worst."

Oken held himself still against the keen aftermath of panic. What would have happened to Mabruke if he and the constable had not chanced to be there at that moment? Could Oken have summoned the guards and the hounds as swiftly without Constable Mathias and his whistle? The mystery of destiny was beyond him. Oken felt himself snared in its web, with only Osiris as his guide. The hounds who had saved their lives were the scions of Anubis. Mabruke's years of attention to the guard animals housed in the neighborhood of Thoth's Manor had before been a mystery to Oken. Now he felt he understood one thing: Captain-Prince Mikel Mabruke knew how to plan. Mabruke had made a point, years earlier, of introducing Oken to each one of the hounds guarding the estates surrounding Thoth's Manor. Mabruke had carefully given names and lineages as though introducing two human beings, two friends of his who had not met before. He knew Oken would remember them by sight, as the hounds would remember Oken by scent.

A young man opened the door to the room enough to stick his head in, and called the nurse. "Sara, we need every hand we can get out here. Can the gentleman spare you?"

Sara looked at Oken. "He should finish the tea, sir, then he should sleep. Can you hold the glass for him?"

"Of course." Oken said. Mabruke smiled encouragingly at her and nodded.

"He will recover," Nurse Sara said reassuringly as Oken took the glass. "He was found in time."

Oken watched in concerned silence as Mabruke slowly finished swallowing the tea; then Oken refilled the glass. With great relief, he noted that color was returning to the man's face.

"You have a new scar," Mabruke whispered, gesturing weakly toward Oken's cheek.

Oken touched the thin line of newly healed skin. "Fractured ribs, too. Both solid evidence of the success of my assignment in Novgorod."

Mabruke drank half the glass in a single swallow. His strength was returning. He sank back and waved it away. "Enough." His voice was just above a whisper, yet he spoke steadily. "Was it Antonyev, as I predicted?"

"Not even close."

Mabruke raised an eyebrow in query.

"Blestyak—General Vladimir Modestovich Blestyak of the vizier's horse guard."

"Never heard of him."

"Exactly."

Mabruke lay his head back on the pillow, and fell instantly asleep.

"I knew you'd be impressed." Oken dimmed the lamp and went out.

OKEN SLOWLY climbed the spiral stair to Mabruke's apartments at the top of the Professors' Hall West, feeling, at last, the weariness of the journey and the desperate nature of his journey's end. Arriving in Memphis had carried him through such a variety of changing emotions that he felt empty, a weariness beyond sleep. In the hallway at the top of the stair he stood quietly, breathing in the silence, the sweet, familiar scents of incense, coffee, and meals lingering from the day.

Before he could reach into his vest pocket for the key to his own suite of rooms on the top floor, the door was flung open. There stood old Yadir, Mabruke's maternal grandfather. Mabruke's mother had been a dancer in the temples when discovered by the King of Nubia.

Her parents were much loved in the court. Yadir seemed smaller than Oken remembered; perhaps memory had been made grander by Oken's regard for the old man. Yadir had once been as tall as his grandson. Age had curved his spine. Yadir and his surviving wife, a faded Teutonic beauty named Helga, had visited Mabruke years earlier, and stayed as unofficial butler and enthusiastic cook to take care of Mabruke, and to manage the staff. Mabruke preferred to keep his loved ones close at hand, and Oken could not imagine the place without the elderly couple.

He was glad to see Yadir, even though he wished he could have simply settled into his own bed undiscovered. Yadir would insist on conversation about Oken's travels and Mabruke's travails, even in the darkness of this predawn hour. Oken knew that the old couple must have suffered great anxiety over Mabruke's disappearance. The news had not reached Oken on his journey, so he had been spared the many hours of worry they had surely experienced. He made himself smile as the old man peered out at him.

Yadir showed him a weary, relieved smile in return. The news of his grandson's rescue must have arrived ahead of Oken. "There you are!" Yadir said amiably, putting a gnarled hand on Oken's sleeve to draw him into the apartment foyer. "You've been gone a long time, haven't you? You've been away? Rusland, that's where you've been. Out chasing secrets, weren't you," Yadir went on as he helped Oken out of his jacket. "Weren't you, now?"

He noted the bloodstains with a disapproving cluck of the tongue. "That wasn't my Mik's blood, was it?" There was a fierce look in the old, yellowed eyes. "That wasn't my Mik there been bleeding on your coat?"

Oken put his arms around the old man's shrunken frame and hugged him tightly. "Mik is fine. He was tired and dried out, but when I left him with Sakhmet, he was sleeping fine, and getting what he needs. He'll be back here in just a day or two, for certain."

Yadir patted Oken's shoulder, nodding and clucking to himself.

"Of course he's fine. I knew he was fine, but the old woman, she frets. You know how she frets, don't you?" He folded the jacket carefully, then draped it over the railing of the narrow stairway leading up to Oken's private rooms. Oken could see how the old man's hands trembled. "She's been fretting something fierce, now, hasn't she."

Yadir peered at Oken, searching his face, then touched his cheek at the line of scar. "What's that you've got there? A new scar, that's what you got there, is it? You got yourself a new scar, didn't you."

Oken smiled. "Mik noticed that right off, too. I didn't know it showed so plainly."

"Mik noticed that right off, did he? Did he notice that, too? That's Mik, isn't it. Isn't that just like Mik!" He tapped Oken's cheek again with one long, bony finger. "Of course Mik saw that right off. Of course he did! He's sharp, our Mik. He's sharp, he is."

"He is, sir. He most certainly is."

CHAPTER THREE

OKEN AWOKE to the soft glow of dawn through bedroom windows that looked out, at last, over a familiar view. Waking in his own bed gave the past months a shimmering ambiance of dream: unfamiliar bedrooms and exotic mornings. A childhood prayer his mother taught him, to be spoken after waking from a nightmare, came unbidden to his mind. "I thank ye, Rae, for waking me and giving me another day. I am the Horus of my day, and to Sutekh I do say, 'My Shadow stands behind me!' "

The silence of the apartment brought back the nightmare sheen of the battle at Ibis Gate. Mabruke always woke before him, always had coffee brewing and incense lit in the rooms below Oken's suite. Apparently, the elderly couple, having sat for days in vigil, were sleeping in.

Oken spent the long morning and afternoon in Mabruke's spacious office, writing his report to Pharaoh Djoser—George, detailing what he had learned of Bismarck's network in Novgorod. Bright sunlight shining through crystal prism shapes in the windows scattered rainbows around the room, keeping track of the Sun. The walls, the ceiling, and the rug were Nile blue, as though the room were underwater.

The lovely Natyra had not been Oken's only contact. Blestyak was not his only revelation of Bismarck's determination to unite the Turkish kingdoms with Albert and Victoria's Oesterreich Militia in a civil war against the Egyptian Empire. The details took up many pages in Oken's fine, even handwriting. He was not willing to risk working with a secretary. The fewer eyes that saw this information, the better for Egypt. The late-afternoon sunlight shining through the large windows found him copying the report over for Mabruke's office. He worried, just a little, that no word had come from Mik.

Then a courier from the sakhmetical station arrived with a handwritten note.

Oken took the note card eagerly, telling the courier to wait for a reply.

The simple message heartened Oken considerably:

> *We have been summoned to the Queen's apartment. Meet*
> *me at the Palace Promenade at 8. Send my uniform over.*
> *~ M.*

Oken felt a rush of gratitude for Egyptian sakhmetical wisdom. Clearly, Prince Mabruke had recovered himself.

"Thank you, Sakhmet and Thoth. Thank you, Isis," he whispered reverently. "You did well."

The "uniform" that Oken selected from his friend's extensive walk-in closet was, to the average viewer, the traditional for royalty: a linen kilt and waistcoat over a silk tunic, with a white top hat and white ostrich plume. No proper gentleman's suit, however, would have allowed so many pockets hidden in the lining, nor so many useful things distributed everywhere, hidden behind strategic seams, braid, embroidery, and jewels. Oken added a pair of newly cleaned sandals, and appropriate wristbands and collars, careful to pick out ones he knew Mabruke favored. He had to hunt about in drawers and trunks for a few minutes to find a traveling makeup case. Once that was found, he packed everything carefully into a valise and a hatbox, and sent these off with the courier.

Oken settled back to finishing the copied report, noting, with some regret, the warm colors of the sunset over the Temple of Ptah Sokar. He lit incense on Mabruke's altar, whispering a prayer for the fallen Mathias.

OKEN'S OWN suit was eccentric for his social status. He had no problem with other men wearing kilts. There had just been too many awkward childhood moments during public ceremonies wearing the woolen versions of the native Britannic formal suits for him to be comfortable in one himself. Being the youngest of the four Oken brothers, he'd endured an endless run of pranks, mishaps, and embarrassing fraternal exchanges. The only advantage he found in the Egyptian version was the linen fabric. He was allergic to wool, which produced a rash that gave his brothers no end of delight at his expense. Oken's personal alternatives in clothing styles were further limited by his social status and the conventions of royalty. The simple cuts of cotton trousers and shirts he could wear in private were unacceptable in public, or so his mother, the formidable Spate Archet Eileen MacDur, had made clear. While on his first assignment with Mabruke, Oken had adopted the Parisian standard for gentlemen, not just because Paris was the capital of Europe. He felt that he truly cut a fine figure in the tailored, three-piece silk suit with waistcoat and tails. The European suit, however, had too many layers to be comfortable in the climate of Egypt. His Memphis wardrobe was based on an Oriental model: a high-collared long-coat of embroidered silk, open at the throat, worn with tightly fitted silk trousers. Sandals were the accepted norm; instead, Oken wore heeled boots, most often of ostrich leather. He had never learned to live with sand between his toes as "true" Egyptians could. His jewelry was simple, forgoing the usual array of enameled gold collars and jeweled neckbands. He wore only his silver Horus-torque, a silver ring with the family crest, a single snake-link chain of silver with the family crest as an amulet, and a pair of moon-stone wristbands, also set in silver. He had inherited the moon-stones from his sister, Brenda, born between himself and the eldest brothers. Brenda had died unexpectedly in childbirth at the age of twenty-four, while Oken was away in school. Oken had never met her young man, and had only learned of her death in a letter, hand-written by the indomitable Eileen. The child had died with Brenda; all that remained to Oken of those tender members of his Mercia family was a matched set of polished moonstones that glowed a pale and ghostly blue white in their silver links.

Being European and a Britannic nobleman, Oken did *not* shave his head. He had tried it, briefly, when he first came to Memphis. He found it terribly distracting. Letting someone scrape his skull with a blade made him feel naked and compromised. Creams that dissolved stubble away in a swish gave him a worse rash than wool. Then he discovered that women were fascinated by his rich Celtic curls. The white jacket showed the bronze color of his tanned skin to best advantage. His long black lashes emphasized the startling, storm cloud gray of his eyes. He was long-jawed and long-boned, with strong hands and wrists. Strangers often thought he must be a musician. Many who emigrated from the Britannic Isles were mu-sicians. Oken could not play an instrument, and had no interest in singing, except during temple services, when his voice was lost in the crowd.

Oken checked himself one last time in the array of mirrors in his dressing room; then he picked up the slim briefcase containing Pharaoh's copy of his written report and set out to meet Mabruke at the Royal Palace.

THE MAGNIFICENT façade of the Royal Palace stood three stories tall, with ornamented pylons and cedarwood doors inlaid with eb-ony and gold. Classic Egyptian portraits of Caesar and Cleopatra filled the pylons, each holding their left hands up in gestures of blessings bestowed upon their descendants. Their right hands clasped the combined staffs of the power, inheritance, and authority by which their descendants ruled the empire.

Vividly painted lotus and papyrus columns alternated with sphinxes as big as real lions along the promenade, from the pylon gate to the broad staircase and viewing stand at the public entrance to the palace. Banners of golden brocade were draped on either side of the staircase, with the formal Five Names of the ruling family embroidered in high hieroglyphics, in Trade, and in a dozen other forms of writing, each representing a kingdom that was part of Caesar's Pharoman Empire.

Public gardens on either side were carefully groomed mazes of shrubs, sycamores, cypresses, flowering fruit trees, date palms, and garden beds. Mossy pathways wound around fountain-fed pools, shady alcoves, and glorious little meadows set with benches and hanging lanterns. Music from cithara and harp drifted among the trees. These gardens were a favored spot for courting couples. People strolled along the paths in the twilight. Soft laughter was heard now and then.

Oken reached the curb just as a vehicle bearing the official seal of Thoth's Manor pulled up. Mabruke stepped out, settling his top hat on his newly shaven head as he straightened up. Oken noticed that, although restored to his usual gracefulness, the man moved slowly, a little too carefully. Mabruke was extraordinarily slender, but his carefully tailored clothes and fitted gold collar were loose.

As he hugged Mabruke, Oken thought the man seemed fragile. "Have you eaten?"

"Only everything I could get my hands on."

Oken stepped back to examine his friend. "Perhaps the Queen will set a table?"

"If not, we're going to the Blue Ostrich after this for a decent meal."

"I think the food at Dolphin Street is better."

"Yes, but the service is just too slow."

"The Blue Ostrich it is, then. Even if she does feed us."

They strolled down the promenade, casually ignoring stares from tourists admiring the glorious royal domicile. Guards at the top of the entrance stairway recognized Mabruke and opened an inner, private panel of the huge doors to the main entrance of the palace— the Grand Atrium.

During working hours, officials, tourists, and citizens on royal business hurried back and forth through the nine-sided atrium, to side corridors lined with palace offices and waiting rooms. At this hour, the atrium was hushed. The musicians had packed up their instruments, leaving the golden music stands in place on the stage. Household staff were cleaning for the next day. Palace guards nodded politely to Mabruke and Oken as they walked past. Lights had been dimmed, and the twilight sky was visible through the glass ceiling that curved high overhead, ribbed with steel bands. At their feet, the Nile River ran the length of the atrium, in a rug woven of vivid hues and time-honored designs. They walked the Nile from the public entrance to the cedar doors directly across. Four royal guardsmen stood in front, purple plumes in their helmets and polished armor with the seal of the Royal House of Caesar embossed in gold.

In front of these guards, waiting with charming impatience, was a beautiful young girl of eighteen or so, dressed in a white sheath in the current style, with bare shoulders and long fringes in a slash hem falling from just below her hip on the left to her knee on the right. She wore full makeup that enhanced the golden hazel of her eyes and a wig of chestnut curls, with lapis lazuli and gold beads. Her jewelry and collar were of djed and ankh amulets interwoven with the royal seal. Diamonds glittered on her sandals. She was tall, despite her youth, with a line of curve at her waist that, together with the width of her shoulders, suggested that womanhood promised much for her.

At that thought, Oken finally recognized her as Princess Astrid Janeen, youngest child of the Pharaoh and his Queen. He had not seen her since she left for School. Womanhood had lengthened her bones and glorified her features. She had been a graceful child, quiet, with eyes only for the Pharaoh, her father. Oken himself had been younger then, too.

She hurried forward, catching Mabruke's hands in hers and beaming up at his face. "Prince Mabruke!" She was clearly pleased. "Mum has been so worried about you. She will be delighted to find you looking so well after your ordeal."

"Thank you, My Lady. It is a pleasure to see you returned to the palace."

Mabruke turned to Oken. "I am sure My Lady remembers Lord Scott Oken?"

"You are quite as dashing as I remembered you." She put her hand out to him as he bowed to her. "You danced with me at my tenth nativity gala." She wore heavy armbands in gold and triple rings on each finger. He gently kissed the royal seal on the largest ring while a cloud of lotus and ginger perfume enfolded him.

"I remember you well, My Lady," Oken managed to say. "You are . . . taller and even more lovely." Oken's recollection of a shy, wide-eyed child was difficult to connect with this radiant creature before him. "We spoke of your summer trip to Paris, as I recall. You thought it more exciting than Memphis."

She laughed merrily, her fingers resting in his. "I am sure you do, Lord Oken. Mother says you are quite the best memoryman in the academy's history."

Oken remained caught in her eyes. "I am sure Madam must have meant the best looking."

"I am sure she did, Lord Oken."

"Have you since returned to Paris, My Lady?" Mabruke said.

"No, but I am open to invitations."

"I shall keep that thought happily in mind, My Lady," Oken said.

"Meanwhile, the Queen awaits us," Mabruke said. Amusement on his face was clear, and he smiled fondly at the princess.

She waved a signal to the guards, then slipped a hand around Mabruke's arm. The guards bowed to the princess, saluted Mabruke and Oken. The palace doors silently swung inward.

No one crossed the Queen's Bridge without family as escort. That had always been the rule. Oken was delighted that this time their escort was not the Duchess Neith Susanna, the Queen's aunt. He had no objection to the duchess, only to her continual comments on why he should marry one of her many daughters.

They descended the steps down to the foyer of the private quarters of the royal family, with Princess Astrid Janeen between the two men, her arms looped casually around theirs. The guards standing in front of the main entrance to the royal family's private quarters had already opened the doors. The princess trilled a familiar "Hoy!" to them as she passed by.

The entryway was a wide balcony, overlooking the central courtyard of the royal family's private quarters. The balcony floor was marble tile in red and black, the walls in Imhotep-blue faience. Obsidian columns supported scalloped archways above a railing of openwork designs. Honeysuckle and night-blooming jasmine wound around the columns and peeked through the railing, filling the air with heavy, sweet perfume.

The garden below was ancient, groomed to complete and casual perfection. At its heart was a pool. Lotus blossoms had closed for the evening, blue and white flame-points shining in dark water. Nightingales were singing, and lanterns marked the pathways.

High overhead was the glass-paneled dome that was visible from the outside as a shiny egg resting within the marble nest of the Pharaoh's Palace. Seen from inside, the dome was a curving, crystalline sky. The struts that supported it were fused into its substance, a radial web of shiny steel streaks. They gleamed in the light of the newly risen Moon.

The left-hand side of the balcony had a broad staircase curving downward to the children's quarters, with brass handrails, each a crowned serpent exquisitely undulating into the children's world. On the right-hand side of the balcony, Pharaoh's stair curved down to the garden.

There was no staircase to the Queen's entrance. In front of them was the Queen's Bridge, a narrow span of marble, arching over the garden. The Queen's private apartments were on the other side. The slender bridge looked as fragile as glass, the thin handrails like mere silken ropes, yet once they set foot on the bridge, both felt as solid as steel. It was only wide enough for two, side by side. Oken followed behind the princess and Mabruke, marveling at both the view and the garden.

The Queen's private secretary, Lady Khamanny, was waiting for them at the other side of the bridge. She bowed to the princess, then nodded gravely to Mabruke and Oken. "Madam is waiting for you, gentlemen. Thank you for being on time."

"I'm to go ahead and get the tea service ready." Princess Astrid Janeen raised herself up on tiptoes to give Mabruke a childlike kiss on the cheek. "I really am glad that you're safe, Mikel." She flashed a quick, brilliant smile at Oken, then dashed away.

"There, you see, Mik," Oken said. "We get tea."

The two men followed Lady Khamanny through golden doors set with hieroglyphs and royal seals. The foyer to the Queen's apartment was low ceilinged and luxurious, continuing the motif of red and black with gold and Imhotep blue. Tall papyruses in golden planters filled the corners, each with little sun-globes glowing softly amongst the leaves. Chairs stood between low tables and spinglass lamps in the shape of Isis and Nephthys back to back, with light shining from their upraised palms.

"If the gentlemen would wait here," Lady Khamanny said to them, "I will inform Her Majesty that you have arrived."

Oken spoke up then. "I believe I can safely leave this with you?" He held out the briefcase.

"Of course, Lord Oken," Lady Khamanny said smoothly, taking the case from him without further comment.

Mabruke settled down on the edge of a couch, resting his hands across his lap.

Oken stood beside him, looking at him in concern. Mabruke seemed unusually winded from the walk. "*Are* you safe?"

Mabruke looked up at him. "No one is ever truly safe. Not even in Memphis."

"At least your sense of humor hasn't changed."

"Her Majesty awaits you." Lady Khamanny spoke to them from inside the entry to the Queen's apartments.

Mabruke and Oken each bowed as they entered, then waited quietly to be formally announced.

The secretary announced them with their full names, which was the Queen's way of letting them know that this visit, despite its informal nature, was a matter of royal business.

"Captain-Prince Mikel Kim Julian Khonsu Mabruke, thirteenth son of Michael Nobolo Kim Surat Mabruke, King of Nubia, born of Lady Curren Elizabeth. Prince Mabruke is accompanied by Lord Scott Jaimes Robert Lesley Oken, fourth son of Lord Julian Lesley Robert Scott Oken, born of Princess Isis Eileen Marguerite Rowena MacDur, Arch and Archet of the Mercia Spate in the Britannic Kingdom."

Two cats at the foot of the bed jumped down, hurrying over to Mabruke to rub against his ankles, purring loudly.

Queen Sashetah Irene reclined on a divan, comfortably nested among large pillows. Her cats were sleeping around her, over her, and tangled up with each other. She did not rise. She smiled up at Mabruke and Oken and waved them in, marking her place in the book she had been reading with an eagle feather of solid gold. She put the book on the table beside the couch, faceup.

The Queen was a beautiful woman in her own right. The majesty of her royal rank suited her temperament. She wore it well. Her skin was tawny and smooth, her dark eyes large and round, her features strong, with high cheekbones, and a broad and intelligent brow. Her slender fingers and narrow palms curved back gracefully as she gestured for them to be seated.

Her purple silk robe had pleated sleeves, and she did not wear a wig, but rather wore a closely fitted gauze headpiece of gold and purple stripes. Her gold earrings were a spray of stars dangling from a Watch It Eye.

Oken gave her his most dazzling smile as he bowed, touching his forehead to the hand she held up to him. "Your secretary left out the part about being special agents to the fairest queen in both worlds—of course, we won't mention that beyond these lovely walls, will we, madam?"

She shushed him gently with a slight smile. "Sit down, gentlemen."

Oken then picked up the cat who had rolled over to paw at him, and cuddled her in his arms, making cooing noises while they rubbed noses. He sat down on the edge of the couch at the Queen's feet. Two more cats stood up to rub against his shoulders.

Lady Khamanny stepped forward silently, carrying a low-backed chair carved with leopards and gazelles. She placed this beside Mabruke, bowed to the Queen, and withdrew.

Mabruke sat down, placing his feet neatly in front of him and brushing flat a wrinkle in his starched linen kilt. He folded his hands in his lap. "Pharaoh is well, madam?" he said politely.

Sashetah Irene sighed. "Poor old Dozey. Bored to tears with this business in Rusland. We just can't get the wood anywhere else, it would seem."

There was a soft ring of chimes, signaling that Khamanny had gone into her office outside the Queen's quarters. Mabruke relaxed, leaning back in the chair and folding his arms over his chest. Oken sensed a strange reluctance to speak touching Mabruke's expression.

Oken spoke up. "Khamanny seems put out with me, madam."

"Khamanny's daughters are put out with you. You went touring with princesses in Europe."

"And found not one to match the beauty of women in Egypt, madam. Khamanny's daughters have nothing to fear."

"All seven send you their regards."

"Thank you, madam." Oken smiled. "Seven daughters, you say?" He leaned forward, whispering into the cat's ear. "Maybe one or two of them are getting lonely, what do you think?"

"Careful, Scott," the Queen said. She was smiling. "The three youngest already adore you, and the two eldest have begun serious husband-hunting. You are far too eligible to be safe from them."

Oken pretended to count on his fingers, to the amusement of the cat, who batted at his hands. "That leaves two lonely lovelies!" he whispered to the cat.

Oken and Sashetah Irene often jested with each other about Khamanny's many daughters. The Queen clucked at him fondly, then turned back to Mabruke. "We were greatly concerned for you, Mikel. We are quite relieved to see you looking so well, although you seem to have lost some weight."

"I appreciate the efforts made in my behalf, madam."

"You have had quite an adventure, we believe, and you with only the one man at your side!"

"Had I but known, madam, as the romancers say, I would have attended that party with a full regiment."

"We will not underestimate the Red Hand after this."

"With any luck, madam, this will severely loosen their hold."

"What did happen, Mik?" Oken broke in. "I've been out of the country, remember?"

"Yes, please," Sashetah Irene said. "We would like to hear how you survived. How did you get there to begin with? The Red Hand isn't really your jurisdiction."

Mabruke sat farther back into his chair, as though withdrawing from the memory. He reached up and flicked the plume in his hat, then flashed an embarrassed smile. "I was at a party, actually. In the Wild East sector."

The Wild East was a broad section of rock and desert on the eastern outskirts of Memphis, a suburb of public housing for the steady flow of immigrant workers passing through northern Egypt. They gathered briefly at crew agencies to get training or to find assignments on road crews and engineering projects throughout the Mediterranean, Africa, and Europe, even Central Asia. The Wild East was a place of youthful spirits and restless energy. Dreams collided with great cultural waves splashing around. People there were educated and skilled for the most part, but they were rootless, unattached to families and past. Relationships shifted, merging and breaking up like bubbles in a wild stream.

Oken himself adored the place.

"I had a bodyguard with me," Mabruke said. "I did not go there alone."

"Your bodyguard was nearly killed," the Queen said in mild rebuke.

"Not *at* the party, madam." Mabruke was emphatic. "The dinner party at the Star Osiron went quite well. The trouble came afterwards. The nightclub owner offered us each a complimentary aperitif while we were waiting for our carriage. It was drugged. We passed out right there in the cloakroom. I cannot fathom why I didn't recognize it. I am supposed to be an alkhemist!"

"Never mind," Sashetah Irene said. "Even that is useful information. It's a warning."

"Thank you, madam. I suspect the vanilla shavings must have been strong enough to cover the scent of the drug. I thought it was just an unfortunate garnish. There was also a hint of anise, which might have been a factor as well."

"Mikel," the Queen said, gently interrupting him. "The owner of the Star Osiron and the entire staff have been arrested, and you may question them at your leisure. You were telling us of your terrible ordeal with the Red Hand?"

"Of course, madam." Mabruke reached up and flicked the white plume. "My apologies. As I was saying, when Wast and I woke up, we were in an unlit cell somewhere underground. They had stripped us of everything but our kilts."

"They were keeping you alive for the slave market, weren't they?" Oken said.

"They let us keep our kilts because they were custom-made. Proof to slave traders that we were high-class property." Mabruke sat, head bowed as though unable to look up from his hands resting across his knees.

"We were tied up with silk scarves." He shook his head sadly. "I will have to add this to the training program, madam. Knots of almost any other kind we could have untied, even in the dark, but silk! The knots were as solid as if the fabric had fused to itself, and slippery. We had to chew through them, finally, which seemed to take hours. In the silence and dark, though, I don't really know how long we were at it."

The cat in Oken's lap swatted him to express her displeasure. His grip had tightened around her as he listened, picturing his friend in that dark place. He let her go, crossing his arms over his chest instead.

"Their accents were Daad." Mabruke ignored the cat and went on speaking, his voice steady despite the strain showing in his eyes. "They came to fetch us before we were quite through the bonds. From what I picked up of their patois, the trade ship had docked and we were to be carried onboard for transport to market in Sumatra. They were dragging the first of the captives out when the strands of the silk finally broke and we got free. The others were still unconscious. There was nothing we could do but escape and bring help."

"Help was sent," the Queen said once Mabruke had sat silent for too long, staring helplessly at his hands. "Wast gave the name of the slavers' ship as soon as he was conscious. The Marine Guard was sent after them at once."

"Thank you, madam." Mabruke looked up to meet her eyes.

"You did escape."

"I could tell we were deep underground," Mabruke went on. "I could smell the river, so we did at least have one direction for orientation. We were discovered twice, but Wast is a good bodyguard. He was injured the second time, however, which slowed our progress. We just kept walking, for days, it seemed. There were three, or perhaps four times when we heard men ahead of us. Once they had passed, we took the opposite direction, thinking we could trace back the way they had come by following their stink. Finally, we stumbled onto a staircase going up. I could smell fresh air ahead. We got careless, I suppose. We had been so long in the dark. They heard us. Wast was wounded again, and at that point we stumbled out into the Ibis Road."

Mabruke fell silent, regarding Oken with a puzzled frown. "How you happened to be there, just at the moment we escaped those tunnels, is quite a striking mystery."

Oken shrugged, feeling that peculiar tug of destiny's web. "How it was that you happened to escape at just that spot, just as Mathias and I were passing by." He felt a different, less pleasant twinge. "Osiris Mathias, I am afraid."

Oken fell silent, remembering, then said, "I just felt the need to walk. I needed to feel Egypt under my feet, to breathe Egyptian air."

"You and I are longtime friends," Mabruke said. "Osiris spoke to you. He whispers his instructions through emotions, with need, with impulse. I've known you since you were a child."

The two men regarded each other solemnly. The Queen was silent, intently observing this exchange.

"Mathias is the mystery, I suppose," Mabruke said. "I never met the man."

"Perhaps not such a mystery," the Queen broke in. "The high priests of Thoth can pray some mighty fine and powerful prayers. We personally instructed them to petition every protection the eternal powers could provide. The priests were asked to keep praying until we found you, or had discovered your final fate. We prayed privately to Sutekh to guard you, and to Sakhmet to keep you alive. We prayed to them in every free moment."

"Madam is very kind," Mabruke said. "Sutekh is the guardian of our guild for a reason, it is true, but we can't rely on him. To rely on him is to expect him. To expect him is to mistake his form, and an insult to his nature."

He was staring down at his hands. The damaged nails had been manicured and repaired. His hands seemed shrunken, older.

"Once Wast has recovered more fully, madam"—Mabruke pulled himself up to a more formal posture—"he will draw a map of our meanderings. Wast is a good memoryman. His map should be accurate enough for us to send troops in, after some planning. The Red Hand have been using this underground network to expand their territory for some time. That much is clear from the extent of their reach."

"Finding them so close to Thoth's Manor was shock enough. That's Caesar's Ground, the most sacred in Memphis."

"We will never let them onto the Campus, madam. I may be retired, but I keep my eyes open!"

Queen Sashetah Irene sat up, pulling herself out from under the layer of cats. "On the subject of your retirement from field duty." She leaned forward to tap the book on her nightstand: Heinrich Brugsch's *My Travels with Carl Richard Lepsius Through the Andean Wilderness and Reports of the Natives There*. "Have you read this yet?"

"I have," Mabruke said.

She held the book out to Oken.

Oken took it, focusing on the details. Then he opened to the first page and flipped through the rest with practiced concentration. He lingered over the photographs, complex drawings, and maps, as well as the Queen's personal notes. He took about five minutes to do this, for it was a large volume, with many illustrations.

Queen Sashetah Irene and Mabruke waited, watching Oken as he scanned.

He closed the book at last and returned it to the Queen. "Thank you, madam. I look forward to reading it later."

"We think you will find it most interesting." The Queen stroked the cat curled up at her side, looking down at her and not at the men. She was silent, as if reviewing her intention; then she stood up, slipping her feet into the jeweled sandals waiting on their stand.

Both men rose at once. The lush purring of the cat was loud in the still room.

"First, we must go for a stroll in the moonlight, gentlemen. Come with us." Her purple robe swirled out around her, revealing a flash of a slender ankle and jeweled sandal strap as she strode across the apartment toward the doors at the far side. "Our garden is at its most perfect during the full Moon."

The only entrance to the Queen's private garden in the palace was through her apartment. The garden was on a gentle rise of ground five hundred cubits across, skillfully landscaped with bonsai versions of imported trees and plants, creating in miniature a map of the world. Egypt was at the very top of the rise, with the rest of the world arranged around. Bodies of water were represented by solid masses of lush green moss. The continents and nations were marked by their native trees and plants. An oak from Oken's Spate of Mercia represented the Greater Britannic Isles. There were ginkgo trees and bamboo from Zhongguo; baobab, jacaranda, and cinnabar from southern Africa; tamarind from Andalusia; ash from Helvetia. There was even a stand of little sugar maples from the Confederation of the Turtle, and Persian oranges. A path of white stones, mapping out the course of the Nile, led to the top of the gently sloping mound.

The dome overhead was closer here and more transparent. The central point of the radial web was just above them. In the full light of the Moon, the garden seemed a place out of time, otherworldly.

Sashetah Irene picked up the cat that had followed them into the garden. "This garden is almost nine hundred years old," she said with some pride. "The royal families have kept it unchanged. Queen Hathor Boadicea had this place built in 991, to commemorate the first millennium of the Pharoman Empire. The queen spent the rest of her life perfecting it. Egypt has spent the centuries since perfecting the empire around us. I think we have reached a time of something greater than just good gardening."

"I have great faith in the future of the empire," Mabruke said softly, with genuine feeling.

Oken was silently impressed with his friend. After such traumatic experiences, a lesser man might have lost that faith.

The Queen led them up the white pathway of the Nile. The feathery tops of shoulder-high palms were sprinkled with starlight lamps. At the top were chairs and couches with leather cushions arranged for comfortable conversation. Each piece was supported on a base of spinglass amber frogs, lit from within.

Oken noted with disappointment that Princess Astrid was not there. He wanted to hear her laugh once more. She had directed the tea service, arranged on low tables among the chairs. Individual teakwood-and-silver teapots steamed lazily amid cups, saucers, spoons, and platters piled high with pastries and fruit. He could smell her perfume lingering over the tea set.

The Queen spoke as she took her seat. "I felt it would be more appropriate to discuss this here, in the Garden of the Moon. It is more secure here. I can drop that 'royal we' formality without incurring Lady Khamanny's disapproval."

The two men settled onto the glowing furniture on either side of her.

"I will be celebrating my fiftieth nativity next year," the Queen went on. "I hope the two of you will be back from this new assignment well before the party. I can hardly imagine entertaining without you to deal with the ladies."

"Fiftieth, madam, truly?" Mabruke said as the Queen poured out a cup of tea for him.

"The Queen of the world is ageless, madam, now and forever." Oken was thinking of another woman of an age with the Queen.

"I like the perspective of this half century," the Queen said thoughtfully as she filled Oken's cup. "I can see life as though from a higher tier on the Pyramid, a broader view. Relationships are more interesting than I could have understood at twenty-five or even thirty. From here, I see the dark shape of the unknown continent of the New World and its peoples. I see not an ominous darkness, rather an intriguing mystery. Our side of the world has been linked so thoroughly by Caesar's highways. The world, wide as it is, has limits. We meet ourselves on the other side as we go around it. We cannot afford to go on defining that part of the world as the Dark Continent. The Moon may be our way into that dark."

"The Moon, madam?" There was a note of genuine surprise in Mabruke's voice. He looked at her more closely over the rim of his cup as he sipped.

"Yes. I see the Moon from here more clearly, strange as that sounds. I know why they are reaching up to him."

"Reaching up to him?" Oken sat up straighter. "Who is reaching up to the Moon?"

"I'm afraid I'm taking you out of retirement, Mikel."

"Madam, no! Please, you can't."

"Something extraordinary has come up. The throne needs you."

"Madam!"

Oken was more curious than ever about the royal summons that had returned him to Memphis. Mabruke had retired from field service more than a year before, preferring to use his considerable talents at analyzing field data while teaching the next generation of Pharaoh's Special Investigators. Mabruke wanted to let his cover as a professor of skin-alkhemy become his real life. Oken suspected that the Queen was unaware of the secret pain that had driven Mabruke to change his role in the PSI Guild so drastically.

"Your work at the guild is invaluable," the Queen said. "This assignment, however, cannot be trusted to anyone else. Now is the time, *especially* now. There was so much publicity over your rescue. The death and wounding of so many trained hounds was just too big a story. It was on the front page of every newspaper in Egypt, as well as every international page in the empire. I have invoked royal privilege so far as I could. You and Scott appear in their accounts of that night only as 'foreign noblemen who were attacked by agents of the Red Hand.' The Britannic and Nubian Embassies have been asked to keep you out of this in their records. I implied to the ambassadors that the Red Hand will want revenge on both of you. Your lives might be in danger."

She put her hand out and rested it across Mabruke's. "You *are* in danger. Your cover is at risk of being exposed. We cannot afford to lose you from the guild!"

Mabruke was silent, his face too calm, as if he were debating inwardly. "Of course, madam, thank you."

"You have read Brugsch's account?"

Mabruke raised an eyebrow at her change of topic. "Not the edition you have, madam. I read the original reports, as they were sent to the Pharaoh."

"It is a pity that Lepsius did not survive the adventure. There is a great deal here that makes that Dark Continent seem a most fascinating place."

"Deadly, as well."

"I suppose. Do you know the extent of their use of aeroships for logging along the Orinoco River, or the volume of traffic through the Zotzlotl Aerodrome in central Mexicalli?"

"I learned considerably more than is in the book as released to the public, madam. The Pharaoh insisted that information about the aeroship industry was too important to international defense to be made public."

"Yes—Dozey is afraid that if the Quetzals catch on, then the roads will deteriorate." She regarded this thought with a slight frown.

"I have reassured him often, madam, that such a shift in economics is not likely in his lifetime." Mabruke could be very reassuring, simply with tone of voice. "After all, they have already been in Africa and Europe for a century and more, yet the roads endure."

The Queen glanced up at him. "Have you ever thought about traveling to Tawantinsuyu or Maya Land?"

"That is quite a change in topic, madam. Is Pharaoh planning to invade?"

"Invade? I hardly think so." Sashetah Irene was amused. "I have received disturbing reports about something going on in Tawantinsuyu, the Empire of the Four Quarters, high up in the Andes Mountains. They have made a secret alliance with Maya Land, in pursuit of an astonishing goal."

"Any kind of alliance between those two would be astonishing," Mabruke said calmly.

"The alliance appears to be directed by the temples and not by the palace. Somehow that alarms me more. I want you to find out what's going on."

"What kind of alliance, madam?" Oken said.

"They plan to send a man to the Moon." Queen Sashetah Irene poured herself a cup of tea, while Oken and Mabruke looked at her in astonishment.

"A man to the Moon, madam? Indeed?" Mabruke set his cup

back down on the table, staring at it as though expecting a signal from it.

Oken was, almost involuntarily, seeing flashes of the maps and diagrams he had just memorized. He shrugged. "They do know a lot about flying."

"It is time for us to get involved," the Queen said. "This comes under the heading of 'so impossible, it just might work.'"

"To the Moon, madam?"

"You could learn a lot along the way." Oken had not yet consciously assimilated the mass of material he had scanned. He spoke from an unconscious instinct in response to the imagery. The idea appealed to him.

"We could." The Queen sipped at her tea, gathering her thoughts before she spoke again. "The alkhemist who created radiance technology, a thousand years ago, discovered the material for the suncatchers because he was looking for a sacred Grail that could absorb light, then reflect it back in the dark, just as the Moon reflects back the light of day. We know that he began with a silly notion, but examine the results of that silly notion."

She gestured to the dome overhead. "The panels in that dome are made from the first generation of suncatchers, and to this day they produce the power for everything in the palace. Our spinglass technology was first developed in the ninth century by an Andalusian mystic who had a vision that he could dissolve light in water and store it there, if he could only create the correctly shaped glass vessel. Today, we light our homes and streets with spinglass lamps. We can see, close up, the stony face of the Moon and the raging face of the Sun because of the farscope technology that grew from these fantastic visions. Who knows what technology they will create while they are trying to fly to the Moon? We cannot afford to be left behind in this."

"Am I going as an ambassador or as a spy, madam?" Mabruke's

face was impassive. Oken heard the trace of excitement in his tone of voice.

"First, as a spy." She sipped her tea again. "I need to know if this idea has a real chance, or if it is just a spiritual vision that we should encourage, even if only out of politeness."

"If there really is something to it, then I become an ambassador, is that the idea?"

The Queen nodded. "We keep our radiance technology as secret as humanly possible—they keep their aeroship technology secret. We sell them spinglass lamps and radiance products. We just don't tell them how we manufacture them. We can build our own aerodromes and mooring towers, but we cannot buy Quetzals from them. We can only lease them. Building and repairing them, and the crew to fly them, are a New World exclusive as well."

"I see," Mabruke said. "If this Moon venture is genuine, then we are going to negotiate a treaty to be involved, in return for agreeing to help them with our technology. Is that it?"

"As usual, you think these things through quickly. I am counting on you to gather the details. You went to school with the ambassadors, the LeBrun brothers. They should prove invaluable once you are there."

"I have considerable work to do here, madam," Mabruke said in mild protest. "Exploring the Red Hand network and directing the analysis of the tunnel infrastructure alone will take months."

"You were the only one capable of rooting out the secret of those tunnels, even if only by accident. The follow-up can be done by lesser minds than yours, perhaps not so brilliantly, nor so swiftly, yet well enough to serve. There is no one else in our employ whom Dozey and I can trust for this mission. You are the only mind and eye whom we would dare to send into that dark place. You are the only one who will recognize what you are seeing. You will know what is harmless mysticism, and what is genuine science."

She leaned forward slightly, clasping her hands in her lap in a formal gesture that told both men this was not a matter for debate.

"There are fewer than ten thousand Egyptian citizens in the New World at any given time. What has become clear is that royalty and one's rank in the nobility are vital issues in Tawantinsuyu. You will find that your position in the Nubian Royal Court opens doors for you, and silences protest at your requests. You also happen to be most suited to this, at this particular moment, precisely *because* of the curious coincidence of your rather public adventures with the Red Hand. The headmaster of your college has been sent a letter from your personal sakhmetician. In this letter, it is suggested that Professor Mabruke, although fully recovered and sound of body, nonetheless should be encouraged to take a lengthy rest leave. His nerves have been seriously stressed by the events of his ordeal."

"I see, madam. Not so far from the truth of it, actually."

Sashetah Irene continued, reciting from memory. "Professor-Prince Mikel Mabruke, the eminent skin-alckemist and Head of the Department of Perfumes, Salves, and Unguents at the College of Alkhemy, will be taking a leave of rest from his classes, traveling to far corners of Andalusia in search of new perfumes, oils, and spices for his research. He hopes to return with many exotic samples to share with his students."

She let that sink in. "That is what the official notice in the *Campus News* will say. It will *not* say that you will be heading west, across the Atlantic Ocean to the New World."

Sashetah Irene turned her focus on Scott Oken, touching his wrist with that same fond touch. "You are going with him, my child. You are going along because you are the only one whom I can trust to keep Mikel alive on this journey, to keep him safe in that dark kingdom. A boatful of Dozey's soldiers could not protect him as well as you."

* * *

AS THEY walked back down the many steps to the promenade level, Oken said to his friend, "The Queen said I have to take good care of you, Mik. Let's start by getting a meal into you."

"The Blue Ostrich," Mabruke said absently. It was clear his thoughts were thousands of leagues away. Then he glanced over at Oken, as if startled to see him. "I could eat the whole bird." He reached up to flick the white plume in his top hat.

"It was nice tea, though," Oken said with amusement. "You've got to admit that. A royal tea, you might say."

"I could still eat the whole bird."

CHAPTER FOUR

A SNARLY little wind came up, raising chaotic gusts filled with dusty sand that obscured the road surface and billowed upward to hide the stars. Mabruke sat hunched over the control panel of the little vehicle rented for the journey to Marrakech. He was focused intently on the line of glowing light that marked out the middle of the dark highway rolling out in front of them. Oken was relaxing in the passenger seat with his arms folded, half dozing as he watched the landscape surge past. The Shoulders of Atlas were vast, dark shapes against the dark horizon on their right, and the broad Sahara was an immense presence of emptiness in the night.

The exit to the Marrakech Road had dropped them to the south and west, taking a route around the Atlas mountain range rather than through them. The Grand Sahara Highway was behind them, soaring over the desert sands on ancient aqueduct structures, a straight line of stonework arches from Memphis to the Atlas Hills. Oken and Mabruke were at ground level for the first time on the trip. The drive west from Memphis had been peaceful, high above the desert sands spread out to the horizon in a gesture of infinity. The Exit Inns along the highway served a satisfying variety of cuisines from all over Africa, and the views from their suites were breathtaking.

The highway also had windscreens to keep back the endless sands. At ground level, the winds were free to have their way with them. The low-slung vehicle was designed to slip among the winds, and to grip the road through sand. At times, however, the wind-blown dust reduced visibility, forcing Mabruke to reduce speed.

The line of lighting in the road vanished. Mabruke let the vehicle roll to a stop. Oken sat up, waking abruptly from his half doze.

"There's something ahead of us," Mabruke said. "I think there are some animals crossing the road or else sand has covered the lights."

"Where are we?" Oken said in a sleepy voice.

"Marrakech Exit, east of the Atlas."

"Do you want to know what the Horus Scope is for today?" Oken spoke somewhat testily. He did not like riding in this little vehicle, through a barely visible world. He had wanted to stop at the last Exit Inn up on the highway. Mabruke, however, had insisted that they continue on.

"You've told me already, twice, in fact." Mabruke peered through the swirling gusts of sand to see the road lights.

"Don't go out after dark." Oken was needling the man and he knew it. "That's what it says."

"So you said before." Mabruke was clearly amused. "But we've traveled west from Memphis. Are you really sure what day it is?"

Oken looked out at the darkness ahead. "Is it safe to stop if it's blowing like this?"

"I was considering that." Mabruke inched the vehicle forward, then braked abruptly as a gray and white goose flew out of the night, just missing their windshield, flapping frantically away.

"Anything about geese in the Horus Scope?"

"Not until next week. What's that bird doing out this time of night?"

The wind vanished with the abruptness of the goose's flight, leaving them sitting in the clear night. They were surrounded, however, by several dozen men on camels. The camels were black, and the men were covered head to toe in black desert robes. Man and beast were nearly invisible in the night, a solid mass blocking them in on all sides.

"Camels." Oken turned to Mabruke with a puzzled look. "Tall ones, too."

"Indeed. Tall camels."

Before they could reach any conclusion to that thought, they saw the camels drop to their knees and the men closest to the vehicle slide down from their saddles. The vehicle doors were simultaneously wrenched open. With dismaying swiftness and strength, the men grabbed Oken and Mabruke, fixing masks over their faces even as they dragged them out of their seats. The masks cut off sight and muffled their voices.

Oken tried to struggle. The men were implacable, almost casual, in their strength and the way they held him. He could not see. He felt his wrists being bound in front of him. He was handed up to one of the camel riders and roughly settled onto the saddle in front of him.

The camel lurched to its feet, turned, and ran over the sand at top camel speed. Oken could hear the wind, the unhappy grunts of the animal, and the padded thud as it ran. He could not hear anything that sounded like Captain-Prince Mabruke.

OKEN WAS annoyed when he awoke, annoyed to realize that he could fall asleep in the midst of such dire circumstances. Somewhere during the long, monotonous ride through the Saharan night he had fallen asleep, slumped against the chest of the rider who held him in place. Mabruke often told his espionage cadets that maintaining inner reserves was crucial when in the field. Hunger, fatigue, and, worst of all, dehydration could weaken reflexes and blunt thinking. Grabbing a nap, a drink, or a meal in a moment of relative safety could make the difference in response time when danger struck. Nonetheless, Oken was disappointed in himself.

He tried to sit forward, only to find himself gripped with that same iron strength. They were at an angle, as though the beasts were running uphill. Faint light filtered through the mask, and the chill of night was giving way to the warmth of the African Sun. Even as he noted this, the ride was over.

The camel dropped to its knees. Oken was half carried, half dragged to someplace inside. He could not determine what kind of inside. The whispery, wide-open sounds vanished, replaced by a sudden hush and the cool of a large interior scented with coffee, incense, sweat, cheese, and hashish. Low voices in quiet conversation murmured somewhere to his right.

Oken was stood up on his feet. The mask and wrist-binding were removed in the same gesture.

He found himself in a large, luxurious tent with magnificent rugs covering every surface, and brassware fittings for the supports and fans. Elaborate glass lamps shed a warm, amber-colored glow. Men in layered burnooses and brimless hats sat on cushions, talking quietly, or stood around the perimeter on casual guard. Everyone was armed with swords and knives carried in embroidered sheaths hung across their backs.

Oken stood taking in his surroundings while rubbing his wrists to restore circulation. The men who had brought him made no further move to hold him. They simply walked away to side tables, where carafes of water and trays of bread and cheese waited.

A group of people near the center of the tent parted, revealing Mikel Mabruke sitting back comfortably on a heap of leather cushions in front of a low table spread with an array of dishes, stacks of flatbreads, and wheels of cheese. Tall urns of engraved silver stood on heating stands, with cups hanging on hooks around the rim.

Mabruke looked up and their eyes met. "There you are!" Mabruke called to Oken, gesturing to the pile of cushions beside him. "Come! Sit! Have a bite to eat. You must be famished."

Oken made a careful review of his friend and the men with him.

Nothing in Mabruke's gesture or face suggested anything but a man relaxing among friends. Oken strode over, rubbing his wrists and watchful of Mabruke's expression.

The man seated across from Mabruke gestured toward Oken's feet with his knife tip. He was an old man with a stern, dark-brown face, thick brows, and carefully braided beard and side-locks. Silver rings covered his fingers, rings with finely cut black stones and shining pearls, matched by thick wristbands. A single earring dangled, a silver ram's horn spiral. The scar marring the narrow ridge of his nose ran from the corner of his right eye to the rim of the left nostril. A second scar lifted the corner of his mouth into a permanent smile. The look in his black eyes was guarded and the knife tip pointed with unwavering aim.

Mabruke pointed to his own bare feet. "The rugs are much more comfortable on bare feet, you know." Then he patted the pile of cushions again. "Sit!"

Oken took off his boots and dropped them to the rug, then slowly lowered himself onto the cushions.

Mabruke leaned forward, gesturing with his silver cup. "Master Zaydane, allow me to present Lord Scott Oken, top graduate of the academy, and memoryman on this assignment."

He turned to grin at Oken's sullen look. "Master Moulay Zaydane—he was dean of the academy when I was but a raw young recruit, stumbling over my own feet." He leaned back again, sipping at his coffee. "We became good friends, as things went by."

Zaydane reached up to stroke his beard, repressing a smile. "Once you had learned to keep your great long legs out of everyone else's way."

"He calls me his giraffe calf." Mabruke smiled across at the older man.

Oken recognized the name Moulay Zaydane at once. Zaydane's Trade, though flawless, was accented with a strong flavor of the Atlas Mountains. "Your reputation at the academy survives, Master

Zaydane," he said. "It's an honor to meet you in person, although I don't know that being kidnapped was quite the introduction I had in mind."

Zaydane dismissed this with a wave of his hand, rings flashing. "Have some coffee, Lord Oken. You have had a long and dusty ride."

"I smell like a camel, as well." Oken wondered why he was not in on the joke that these two shared.

"That can be dealt with later." Zaydane took a silver cup from the urn nearest him, held it to the spout, and filled the cup with steaming, aromatic brew, then handed it to Oken.

"He takes honey." Mabruke selected a honey dish from his table and held it out.

Oken took the dipper and swirled the golden brown honey into the cup, all the while eyeing the two men and waiting for them to break into laughter. "If I'd known I was being invited to a coffee klatch, I would have worn my other suit. The one with the fancy cuffs and buttons."

Both Mabruke and Zaydane laughed. A little too heartily, Oken thought. "Then, of course, that suit's in my luggage, isn't it, in the vehicle we left behind?"

"Safely on its way to Marrakech," Zaydane said.

"That's where I thought I was."

"You will be, soon enough." Zaydane's scarred face was unreadable.

"We've been rescued," Mabruke said amiably. "Relax and enjoy it."

"Rescued?" Oken tried to determine whether or not his friend was merely playing along with their captors. Mabruke's look was perhaps too genuine. "Just how would that be?"

"There were riders waiting for you at the exit," Zaydane said. "We were watching for your arrival, as instructed, then men were seen riding out of the shadows at the base of the highway when your vehicle appeared. Our original plan was to ride in escort until you reached camp. We kept just out of their sight, to see what they would do. When that windstorm blew up, we decided to pull you out of harm's way and put our men in your place, as decoy."

"Really? You couldn't just ask? I'm not much for camel riding, but I can be reasonable about it."

Zaydane shrugged eloquently beneath his black robe, turning his palm up in a dismissive gesture. "We knew that the sandstorm would clear as quickly as it came. The moment was perfect, there and then. I made the decision to get you out of the vehicle as quickly as possible, before the men following you rounded the bend and saw us. My men replaced you, and drove on. Explaining, asking, doing anything other than we did might have revealed us to your followers. By whisking you out of there, we avoided bloodshed, and we got away without detection. We fooled them. Those men following your vehicle are being led on a wild goose chase through the Atlas Hills."

"How *did* you manage the goose?" Oken said.

A warm light touched his eyes. "Old Dozey? He scents the winds better than a hound." The thought clearly pleased him.

"Still." Oken began a further protest, then stopped at a look from Mabruke.

"If the people following us had seen Zaydane's men," Mabruke said to him, "they would report only that we had been kidnapped by raiders. Either way, they would not know where we are now."

Oken sipped at his coffee to cover his momentary confusion. He reminded himself that he was a youth compared to these two men, that his indignation at their methods would seem childish. The hot, rich brew and the tang of the honey were distracting, a wilder, more intense flavor than anything he had ever had in Memphis or in Europe. He let that be the focus of his attention. "Excellent coffee." He pointed to the table. "Which cheese would you recommend I try first?"

* * *

AN HOUR or two was spent eating great quantities of fine cheeses, sweet and hearty breads of every kind, olives, mushrooms, and dried dates soaked in honey. Mabruke and Zaydane kept up a steady round of small talk about the food, about horse breeds, and the cost of camels and their bad tempers. Oken listened without much participation, instead taking note of the men coming and going through the large tent. He made sure that he got a look at their faces, so that he would recognize them in the future. If these people truly were on Mabruke's team, Oken wanted to be certain he knew them. If this were an elaborate ruse, Oken wanted to know the faces of his enemies. Until he had a chance to speak with Mabruke in private, he would withhold judgment on either side. He found himself hoping they were not the enemy. They looked to be a tough and formidable group. Oken remembered the hard strength with which he had been captured and held during the night. Better to have such men on his side.

Apparently, only the night riders wore black, and only the older wore braided beards like Zaydane's. The rest were clean shaven, with their hair kept neatly out of sight under the straight-sided, gaily patterned headgear. Most wore burnooses in a variety of colored stripes, with red, bronze, and yellow dominating, although a combination of green and bronze was also popular. A few wore blue and purple striped robes with bright red and blue hats. After a time Oken placed a pattern, in that those in blue and purple sat cross-legged before low writing desks set with quill stands and inkwells, writing steadily in a variety of small notebooks, while checking data back and forth with each other. Oken thought at first that these were younger men; finally he noticed that these scribes were actually women. They dressed just as the men did; their makeup and jewelry were the same. Their dusky faces and almond-shaped eyes had smoother lines. Their scarlet mouths were full. He found himself gazing more often in their direction, wondering how he might strike up a conversation, particularly with a tall, lean woman nearby whose elegantly shaped cheekbones; high, smooth brow; and pointed chin grew more attractive every time he glanced at her. Perhaps if he were to ask if he might borrow a quill?

He was just considering this move when Mabruke gently nudged his knee, at the same moment that Zaydane clapped his hands casually and stood up. "At twilight," Zaydane called out in a clear voice. He turned to Mabruke and said more quietly, "Now you must rest."

Zaydane gestured to the same woman whom Oken had been eyeing. "Sera will guide you. Aziel has brought water for you to bathe, and fresh clothes." Zaydane smiled fondly at the woman, then turned to Mabruke and Oken. "My granddaughter Sera is in command of camp supplies. She knows best what to provide you for the day."

"Will you be riding with us," Oken said to Zaydane, "when we leave tonight?"

"I am waiting for the report on the men who were following you. If they are Red Hand, then I will send troops to dispatch them, and I will ride with you to Marrakech. If they are Black Orchid, then I will personally follow them. I have been trying to locate their base here in the Atlas for months."

"Black Orchid?" Oken looked over at Mabruke, his brow furrowed, feeling once again the sense of being the boy left out of the men's business.

Mabruke flicked his fingers in a subtle hand gesture that told Oken not to press the topic.

Zaydane seemed not to notice, but only waved them on to follow Sera.

That part, at least, Oken did not mind. He wondered if the lovely Sera would linger once the bathwater arrived.

* * *

OUTSIDE THE huge tent, the sunlight struck with a brassy blow. Oken could almost smell the light that stung against his skin and prickled inside his silk suit. The sky seemed very close. The lamps had partly prepared his eyes for the intense brightness; even so, for the first few steps Oken could only follow the dark lines of Mabruke's "giraffe calf" legs striding ahead of him. Once his eyes had adjusted, he looked around.

The main tent sat at the head of a narrow ravine between rugged cliffs of weathered rock. Bony-looking goats grazed on the slopes, guarded by teams of hounds. The fleet of black camels had disappeared. At first Oken thought the ravine was filled with house-sized boulders tossed randomly along either side of a swiftly running creek. Then a flap opened in one of the boulders as someone came out to meet them. Oken realized that these "boulders" were, in fact, tents painted in careful camouflage.

He looked behind at the main tent. It had disappeared into the cliff wall against which it perched. He focused on it sharply, trying to see the tent through the paint. He could, finally, but only because he knew it was there.

He hurried after Mabruke, impressed to realize that his mentor had learned from a man who could hide an entire village of tents in plain sight.

Sera was standing at the open flap. She waved them in with a slight, bemused smile.

This tent was much smaller, but equally cool and luxurious. Lamps showed lush rugs and fittings in a good-sized interior for two, with cushions piled against the wall and a scattering of low tables. A coffee urn bubbled to the side, with trays of fruit and cheese. The most welcome sight was a pair of large tubs filled with steamy hot water, set atop heating bricks. Warming racks with towels and robes stood beside. The bathwater was scented with roses and citrus, giving Oken a momentary remembrance of Natyra and her perfumed skin.

"I hope you enjoy your bath," Sera said. "Master Zaydane wants you to be ready to ride by nightfall, so if you wish to sleep, you have the afternoon." Her voice was rich, like fine, dark honey.

Oken wished she would stay and talk with them longer, just to hear her speak. "Thank you, my lady."

She gave him that same bemused smile, humor touching her dark eyes; then she slipped out. The tent flap fell closed behind her. Oken noticed, as she turned away, that she was wearing a gold earring in the form of the seven-rayed flower and crossed horns of Sashetah, symbol of the holy librarian and keeper of the archives. She was too busy to play.

Oken sighed and addressed his attention to the waiting comfort of the hot water in the tub.

"BLACK ORCHID." Oken sponged water over the back of his neck. "You were going to tell me about that?"

Mabruke did not reply at once, feigning serious interest in the awkward gestures of scrubbing his heels in a tub too small for his long limbs.

"If it's private, I'll stay out of it," Oken said after a moment of watching from the corner of his eye. "I know you and Zaydane are old friends." He waited, and got no response. "It just didn't sound private, the way he said it."

"It isn't." Mabruke continued scrubbing. "I could tell when you arrived at the tent this morning that you had not had a pleasant time on the ride here."

Oken dropped the sponge into the water and draped his wrists over the edges of the tub, giving Mabruke a sour look. "What has that got to do with black orchids?"

"Nothing. It's just that I rode with Zaydane, so we got a chance to talk, quite a lot. I had a pleasant night. I'm sorry yours left you believing we're in trouble."

"We aren't?"

"No—in fact, I had intended that we should meet up with Zaydane, and make a stopover at this camp. I didn't tell you, because I know how you feel about sleeping in tents. I just didn't know things would come out quite this way."

Oken realized then that Mabruke was embarrassed. He suddenly felt a great deal better about the long and difficult night. "I'll get over it. What about this Black Orchid thing?"

"The Black Orchid Society. Zaydane's people just recently found the connection, and lives were lost uncovering that code phrase. Apparently, Victoria and Albert are more organized in their conspiracy plans than we had previously believed. They've revived some obscure, ancient Roman cult, and are initiating their fellow conspirators into it. Their secret code name now is Black Orchid Society."

"A Roman cult?" Oken was surprised by that.

"Victoria's people are determined to undo Caesar's empire, so they reached back into Caesar's time. Apparently, they discovered the writings of cults that were in rebellion against Rome, more specifically in rebellion against Caesar. They've set themselves up as the inheritors of that rebellion."

Oken reviewed what he had been taught about the early days of his most famous ancestors, the man and woman who had started the empire. "Which cult? There were a lot of them in those days."

"They've mixed together elements of this one and that one, as suits their story. Their goal is not spiritual. It's political. They promise their followers spiritual primacy, which gives them political rights over Caesar's Heirs."

Since Oken was himself an Heir of Caesar, he took that somewhat personally. "You don't say. They're calling this new cult Black Orchid? Why orchid?"

"They chose the flower because of its Latin name. They chose the color because it's actually a myth."

"I've seen a lot of orchids lately," Oken said thoughtfully.

Flowers in incredible array had filled the rich homes and royal estates where he had been hosted as part of his tour of Europe, flowers seen most often as colorful backdrops to the beautiful young women who were paraded before him. The youngest son of the throne of Mercia was eminently eligible, a major catch even for a princess. He was royalty born of royalty, with the blood of both Caesar and Cleopatra in his veins, making him kin to every royal court in Europe and most of Africa. His sons could become kings. His daughters could become wife of the Pharaoh himself. His travels might reach only the society column rather than the front page. He was, nonetheless, a welcome houseguest.

"I've seen quite a lot of flowers." Oken focused on a flashing review of the arrangements and selections of bouquets and garden displays, garlands and vases. Usually each court and household had its own special themes and blossoms. A particular image leaped out among those memories. The same arrangements had been repeated. Unusual. "Not everyone used orchids, but the ones who did used the same arrangements. Perhaps a statement?"

"Zaydane predicted that flowers might be used that way. Indeed, he said I should ask you about it."

"I'll make a list."

"They're getting braver." Mabruke did not sound pleased. "To do something like that out in the open."

Oken shrugged. "The world is full of garden societies. A great many of them are run by princesses."

Mabruke reached for the soap vial beside the tub. He poured the rose-scented liquid onto the sponge, sniffed carefully at the perfume. "Ah, I thought so! This is one I designed." He scrubbed vigorously, raising a wealth of foam. "Good stuff, too."

"What has this got to do with orchids?"

"Some lovely perfumes from orchids," Mabruke said mysteriously. The foam covered his face and head, and he ducked under the water to rinse, surfacing with exaggerated huffing and blowing.

"Is that to cover up the smell of their conspiracy?" Oken reached for the same soap vial.

"Nothing can do that. It stinks to high heaven. Victoria is telling her followers that she has 'the one true faith.' She's claiming to be the only true defender of that faith." He looked over at Oken, eyebrows raised, to see the effect of this statement.

Oken looked back at him sideways. "So? All faiths are true."

"Not according to Victoria and Albert. The Black Orchid Society claims their cult is the only—get that—the *only* true faith. That's what entitles them to rule the world instead of Caesar's Blood."

Oken tried to wrap his mind around such an unholy thought. "Sounds unnatural to me."

"Add that little caveat into the lure of a secret society, and a lot of politically restless people are being drawn in."

"*All* faiths are true," Oken repeated stubbornly. "Why should theirs give them any political edge?"

"They call themselves the only, I repeat, the *only* true one. They preach that only *their* image of Paut Nayture is entitled to appoint the Pharaoh or to assign thrones. Apparently, the rest of us are just fooling ourselves."

Oken sat, absently scrubbing himself with the foaming rosewater soap, puzzling over this. "Bit of a paradox in that, isn't it? I mean, if all faiths are true, then this Black Orchid thing is true. But if *it's* true, then every other is false, which means they're *all* false, so this Orchid thing is false. It just doesn't add up."

Mabruke sighed. "Alas, you have grasped the mayat of it. They are fueling a rebellion on a paradox that they claim only they can unravel."

"True may be true for the moment. That doesn't make it mayat," Oken said, brow furrowed. "People are buying into this?"

"If it will buy them a throne that they believe they deserved, but didn't get? What do you think?"

Oken himself stood close enough to a throne that he had a hint, a taste of the frustration and lure of such a belief. Memphis, however, had become the ruler of his heart. His education there ruled his mind. He was happy to have not just one but three brothers standing between himself and the rigors of leadership in Mercia. Power over his own heart, over the mayat, the eternal reality of his own eternal soul was the only throne Oken desired. No one could empower him to that throne but he himself. If he believed that someone else could provide it? What would he do for that?

He felt a shiver despite the steamy warmth of the bath, and scrubbed his chest and shoulders as though he might wash away the discomfort and confusion of these thoughts. "If the people following us on the Marrakech Road were from the Black Orchid Society"—Oken directed himself back to the problem of the moment—"it's likely my fault."

"Why?" Mabruke said, soapy sponge in hand. His face was serious.

"I doubt your cover has been blown, but Blestyak knows that I'm in the guild."

Mabruke sat thoughtfully rubbing his knees. "Perhaps. If it's the Red Hand, they're after both of us. The results, however, will be the same. Zaydane and his people will put a stop to them. They'd be dead already if he were certain who sent them."

"Do these Black Orchid people jeopardize our mission to Tawantinsuyu?"

Mabruke considered this. "Perhaps not."

"Perhaps not? Can we risk going on with it on a perhaps?"

"I have to think on it. I doubt it threatens *my* cover. You're the one who just got yourself in trouble in Europe. It actually makes sense that you would then choose to travel far from there. Taking a job as companion to a mild-mannered and obscure professor on a rest-journey to the wild mountains of Andalusia might seem like an attempt to keep your cover intact."

"Might seem? Perhaps? Mik, these people are dangerous." Oken frowned. "I'd hardly describe you as 'mild-mannered'!"

"I suppose my pupils wouldn't, either."

"It's true, though, that you have worked at maintaining obscurity."

"Except for that Red Hand business."

"There is that. So, I'm supposedly on the run from agents of the Black Orchid Society," Oken said. "Both of us are on the run from agents of the Red Hand." He stood up from the bath with a gentle splash, stepping out and leaving wet footprints on the rug. He dried himself with an oversized towel from the rack.

Mabruke sat in his tub watching Oken, a thoughtful look on his dark face. "That puts the odds on it being the Red Hand who were waiting at the Marrakech Exit."

"I'd put my coin on it."

Oken opened the shaving kit set out for him. The handles were of carved ebony; the brush had camel's-hair bristles. The razor was carefully and lovingly etched with sacred letters, and he read Zaydane's name there.

"Look at this." He picked it up and flipped open the blade. The name of the most famous Egyptian sword maker was stamped on it. There was no doubt of its edge. "He's letting me use his own kit?" He held it up for Mabruke to see.

"I gave that to him. Let me use it, when you're finished. They don't use beard-ex here. They shave."

The shaving foam was also a formula of Mabruke's. His seal was stamped on the bottom of the glass bottle in raised hieroglyphs. Oken tilted the mirror on the stand. When he had satisfied himself as to the smoothness of his face, Oken dried his hair, then handed the kit to Mabruke, still in the tub. Mabruke dipped the brush and lathered his head, starting at the crown.

Oken paced about slowly as he dried himself, then slipped on a plain cotton undershirt with long sleeves and a turtleneck also waiting on the towel rack. A pair of black robes were also provided, the kind the night riders had worn. He put one on, settling the tailored shoulders with a gentle shake before fastening the front with the embroidered silk-knotted pieces.

He then immediately unbuttoned it and shrugged it off, holding it away at arm's length. "Wool! What do I do now?"

"Goat's wool, not lamb," Mabruke said from inside the foam covering his entire head and face. He picked up the razor.

"It's not the animal. It's the wool—and my suit stinks of camel!"

"I'll have Zaydane chase down something else for you."

"If he has to chase it, then it's got wool and I can't wear it."

Oken went over to a bedroll set against the tent wall, relieved to see layers of quilted, padded cotton. "Thank goodness cotton is easier to clean," he muttered as he spread the bedroll out on the carpeted tent floor.

He stretched out flat on his back, staring up at the gently stirring fan and the amber-colored lamp. "Red Hands, Black Orchids, and woolen clothes—this is not starting out well, not at all."

THE MIDNIGHT lights of Marrakech made a soft glow in the landscape below as they rode along narrow passes down from the hidden camp of Zaydane's Atlas Academy. The speckled ponies were sure-footed and hardy, yet on the small side. Oken had to ride with his feet dragging low in the stirrups; nevertheless, he felt considerably more comfortable riding in control of a horse, however small, than lashed to the top of a camel. The thickly woven, multilayered cotton robe they had found for him to wear was not as warm as the wool everyone else was wearing; Oken could only resign himself to the icy fingers of the night air creeping in at wrist and ankle. His handsome collection of gloves was packed up with his luggage in the rented vehicle. The leather pair they had found for him was stiff and scratchy.

Zaydane and Mabruke rode at the head of the column. The men following Oken and Mabruke's vehicle had proved to be agents of the Red Hand, seeking revenge for the loss of their underground kingdom in Memphis. As soon as Oken and Mabruke were out of town, Pharaoh's security forces had gone through the network of tunnels and chambers, wreaking havoc on the entire organization, as well as freeing hundreds of victims who otherwise would have been on their way into slavery in the Indonesian Islands or in deepest Arabia.

Mabruke, although pleased with the results of the report, expressed considerable regret at having missed such a monumental assault on that criminal organization.

Zaydane had only laughed and clapped him heartily on the back, assuring Mabruke that maintaining his secret identity was more important than momentary revenge. "They thought they were chasing a simple professor and an overbred secretary. My men made certain that they reported nothing else to those who sent them after you. Be happy—it has ended with the best possible results."

Oken was happy simply that Mabruke was alive and unharmed, however disgruntled the man might be. Oken still had nightmare flashes from that road battle. He had already in childhood reconciled himself to the permanent nature of his memories. He had yet to reconcile himself, however, to the residue of some of those permanent memories. Once his talent was discovered, his remembrance trainers had prepared him for that drawback. They had warned that sometimes he must simply look away, not turn that corner to see what had happened. Not to know was a kind of security. They also warned that there would be scenes from which he could never walk away. He had been trained in meditation techniques to dissolve the chemistry of emotions that accompany memory. These techniques left him with a cool indifference. Twice in his life, however, they had failed him. The memory of his mother's shaky handwriting, describing the death of her only daughter and only grandchild, always seared through Oken as though each word were carved into his skin with a needle. Every memory of his beloved sister now bore an unbearable beauty, a holy presence in his mind as though he could reach through the veil of time and touch her. The sound of her laughter would never leave him. He comforted himself with the knowledge that she awaited him in eternity. The memory of Mabruke's greenish face and limp form in the sakhmetical station would never leave him, nor would he ever lose the peculiar sense of destiny leading him down that dark Ibis Road.

That same sense of destiny made him wonder about the dark road ahead of them, on this peculiar assignment, halfway around the world to the darkest place on Earth, in a quest for the Moon.

ZAYDANE AND Mabruke led the group out of the mountainside brush and onto a caravan road at some early morning hour. Oken did not like to think he might have dozed. The night passed quickly. Eventually the rhythmic clatter of the ponies' iron-shod hooves became the percussion of a long and lovely dream of riding in the royal coach on a high festival day. His sister was there, smiling down sadly at a small, pale child seated beside her. Oken awoke hoping that child had been himself. He knew otherwise.

They stopped for a couple of hours in an off-road patch of scrub with a rocky spring at its center. Goatskin water bags were refilled while letting the horses drink.

Oken found the icy cold splash on his hands and face to be effectively bracing. So were the incredibly spicy cheese-breads handed around out of saddlebags, along with pleasant smoke from a small, portable hookah. Leather-wrapped jars of hot coffee were also brought out. Oken had learned that their mountain brew was so wildly different from the domestic he was accustomed to, that his usual honey was not necessary. The weariness of hours riding on an undersized animal was washed away.

The men sat cross-legged on the moss or leaned against rocky outcrops, passing the hookah and eating while the ponies grazed among the scrubby bushes. Each had been offered oats from a leather bag. The aromatic leaves around them were apparently more tempting.

Zaydane sat with Mabruke apart from the rest of the men. They leaned close and talked together in low voices, making occasional gestures over their heads, as though signaling sacred beings or birds. Oken left them alone. The women in their purple and blue robes had remained behind in the invisible camp in the cliffs high above them. Oken kept his restless attention on eyes, ear shapes, and the subtle patterns of beards. He would know these men if he ever met them again, even if he was not entirely sure why he should.

Mabruke caught Oken's eye and waved him over. Oken went to sit with them on the outcrop of rock they had chosen.

"Zaydane would prefer you give your list of orchid displays to his memoryman, Aziel, rather than committing it to paper."

"Certainly," Oken said. "I have it on the tip of my tongue."

Zaydane gave a low whistle, and one of the young men rose from the group at once and strolled over, a slender, loose-limbed young man with sensitive features and black hair braided to his waist.

"Aziel," Zaydane said to him quietly, "Lord Oken has a list of royal families in Europe which I need. If you would take a moment with him?"

The young man sat down at Oken's feet and smiled up at him. Oken recited, matching Zaydane's quiet level. The lad's dark, liquid eyes kept straying to Mabruke as he listened. When Oken had finished, Aziel's gaze turned inward for a minute or two as he reviewed and fixed the list in his memory. Then he stood up, his eye lingering on Mabruke.

"Thank you, Aziel," Oken said.

Aziel saluted and strolled away.

Camp was disbanded and the journey resumed by the simple gesture of Zaydane standing up and going to his mount. Their quickly set up rest spot was as quickly erased, and the journey continued, Zaydane and Mabruke in the lead as before. Oken was amused when he realized that their conversation was not to be interrupted by men, animals, or terrain. Mabruke trusted Zaydane completely. Oken registered this realization in his *ib*-heart, his inner world and understanding.

The ride down from the hills after that was a pleasant and relaxing exercise. The day warmed on their backs, drawing a fragrant sweat from the horses. Stretches of road weaved back and forth along the hilly terrain, sometimes leaving them only the sky as guide. The horses kept steadily on.

THE ATLAS Hills were an obstacle to the Great Sahara Highway, not an obstacle of geography or engineering, but rather of tradition. The Atlas were home to the families who lived upon the sacred mountaintops. They had farmed the sacred valleys since the Ur Time, since Creation. Or at least long enough ago that their revered ancestors had been able to work out solid, written contracts with Caesar himself, along the lines of: *You won't let anyone kill my people, and I won't let anyone kill your people. By the way, can I interest you in some handmade woolen rugs or maybe some cheese?*

The cheese was very good, and the rugs of remarkable quality. The contracts held and became the permanent way of things. The only people who wanted to live on those rugged and rocky slopes were the folks who already lived there anyway.

Cleopatra II was so impressed with the cheese that she built a temple in Marrakech, the capital of the mountain kingdom, a beautiful temple of marble and greywacke, merging with the hillside, a stone flower perched among the rocks. The temple was dedicated to Egypt's Nayture Khnoumos, the sacred ram. The ram was the major divinity of these hardy and hardheaded mountain folk, and their even hardier and more hardheaded goats. The Egyptian Embassy was housed on the temple grounds. Tourist hotels, markets, theaters, and clubs sprang up over the centuries alongside the temple, echoing its remarkable architecture, a stone garden of Egyptian cultivation in the rocky wilderness.

Coast roads leading inland to Marrakech were broad and finely paved, encouraging travelers and trade. The roads down from the mountains used by the Atlas men were older, narrower, and vigilantly guarded. Zaydane and his riders had been identified and marked as worthy. No one was going to attack them on this side of Marrakech. Oken fell back to dozing.

He awoke to the white walls of Marrakech glowing a pale flame color in the long rays of the afternoon Sun. A mazelike array of shrines and altars was squeezed together along the base of the city walls, on either side of the arched city gates. Alabaster shrines to Hathor and Neith stood shoulder to shoulder with carved oaken altars of Frigg and Danu, with statues in ivory and gold, ebony and pearl, flint, obsidian, and oak. Marrakech was a very holy city. Tourists and mystics alike flocked to her sacred location. The mystics brought the tourists, and the tourists brought business, so Marrakech was a friendly place. Expensive, but friendly.

Some shrines were simple—hand-molded, sunbaked altars set between woven-reed walls; some were translucent alabaster or glowing marble, splendidly carved. The oldest shrines were the largest, with columns, and marble steps leading up to the altar. Each shrine was a frame for sacred artwork, images of divine Nayture in action, a garden of jeweled colors showing sacred faces, eternal moments, stories of this or that great name. The sky itself was gathered up close against these walls.

Whole families crowded shrine steps and pathways, singing and praying with ten thousand voices. The city seemed to float on its own music, a chaotic chorus of the divine presence. Incense burned on every corner, at each crosswalk, from every altar and niche. The gathered smoke was a fabulous mixture of myriad scents and alkhemies. It was said that nowhere else in the world was there an odor of sanctity like to that in Marrakech.

Individual market stalls were wedged into cracks and alleys, into any space available amid the altars and shrines. The stalls were shaded by fabulous rugs strung across poles, alive with dangling fringes. A steady, restless crowd streamed along beneath the shade.

The first whiffs in the breeze as they rode closer struck Oken as a heady, fantastic perfume, familiar scents mingled into something uniquely unfamiliar and new. The music of the city grew louder, rising and falling in an unfathomable melody, the multiple voices of faith merged into a single song.

The Horse Road into Marrakech, being one of the oldest routes into the city, was at ground level and led past the shrines along the wall. Late-afternoon light tinted every image with mystery. The scented smoke grew thicker, backed by the hypnotic impact of myriad voices, the musical rhythms of sistrum rattles, stringed cithara, and tambour drums.

Oken drank in the scene with solemn, focused attention, lingering on details, while the horses carried them along the road at a gentle walking pace. He made careful note of the faces and the artwork, some ancient, some brightly restored, all original and unique to this sacred city. Here was his private reward for his professional skill at remembrance, a sudden burst of imagery. People, movement, sounds, and smells would always be there inside him, his preview moment of eternity. He could return here in memory and walk among the thronging crowd of the faithful in that sacred lane before the shrines. He could visit the Naytures in their shrines one by one.

His attention was caught by a sudden chorus of children laughing and calling out "Silly rider! Silly rider!"

Children ran alongside Mabruke as he rode, a giggling, smiling mass of children, each dressed in the same cut of a simple green street-tunic and boots. Their heads were shaved Egyptian style, with only the single long forelock, braided with polished beads. They were laughing at Mabruke, who was riding perched atop his small mountain horse in an awkward compromise between the length of his legs and the shortness of the horse's legs. His knees were all akimbo.

To further amuse the throng of children, Mabruke draped the reins around the saddle horn, then stood up in his stirrups, balancing as nonchalantly as though he were on the ground. The stolid little horse reacted to neither the throng of noisy children nor to the unusual pose of his rider. Mabruke beamed around at the children as he passed by. His brilliant white smile in his dark face further delighted them.

Zaydane, riding ahead of Mabruke, halted his mount and turned in the saddle, frowning at the impromptu performance going on behind his back.

The teacher who had been leading the group of children also frowned at the display. She clapped her hands sharply, calling to the group to behave. The children fell quiet, responding to the command. They drew away with giggles, each touching the pointed toe of the Silly Rider's boots before hurrying after the teacher.

Mabruke smiled after them, then resettled into his awkward riding pose. Zaydane was frowning as he nudged his horse forward.

Oken felt better about woolen clothes and camel rides.

ZAYDANE TOOK his leave at the entrance to the embassy grounds. One of his men had gone ahead to have Mabruke's little red rental vehicle waiting for them in front of the hotel entrance. Zaydane had also made reservations for them, a royal suite.

Oken was delighted to see civilization blossoming in this stony, hard place. He was particularly delighted to see his luggage again— gloves and not a single item of wool.

"It has been good to see you," Zaydane said to Mabruke. The two men stood gazing into each other's eyes. Their farewell hug was tender.

"We will see you again upon our return." Mabruke glanced at Oken as if to get his consent.

"I doubt we will see *you* coming, sir." Oken smiled at Zaydane as he spoke.

"I will make certain of that." Zaydane patted Oken on the shoulder in farewell.

Mabruke hurried into the lobby, without waiting to watch Zaydane and his men ride off.

CHAPTER FIVE

OKEN DIRECTED himself at once to their vehicle, parked at the curb in front of the embassy hotel. Four of Zaydane's men stood guard. Private vehicles were rare. People in the crowds passing by on the sidewalks wanted to touch it. Before Oken had the storage compartment fully open, a half dozen uniformed bellhops, doormen, and liverymen swooped upon him, ushering him and the luggage inside to the lobby. Oken was fluent in the language of the kindly lord to servants, concierges, maids, footmen, and head waiters. He learned a great deal from their chatter as the luggage was whisked away. Apparently, he and Mabruke had arrived on the eve of a major social event, with ladies and gentlemen from around the empire in attendance. The lobby was busy with guests and their entourages.

The hotel interior was marble and gilt, similar to the embassy in Novgorod. The ever-present potted palms were especially splendid specimens here, with golden lights sparkling among the sharp spines of the towering trunks. Gentle guitar chords drifted over them from the lounge in the balcony above the lobby.

Oken joined Mabruke at the front desk. He was at last on familiar ground.

* * *

"WE'RE GOING to a party? Already?"

"Well, I packed all these clothes," Mabruke said matter-of-factly. "I have to wear them somewhere."

"We've been at this hotel for less than an hour—how did you manage to get invited to a party?"

"I ran into someone I know in the lobby. There's a world-famous opera house here, you know. All manner of wealthy nomads gather for that."

"You always run into people you know, no matter where you go. You must have more friends than the Pharaoh!"

Even as he said it, Oken realized he was blundering into the older man's private self. The look of gentle bantering between friends vanished from Mabruke's face, replaced for a flicker with a thoughtful, pained inward glance, gone swiftly, leaving only an outward calm that Oken knew was restraint covering a powerful emotional surge.

"People just love that professor fella." Mabruke picked up one of his valises to search through it.

Oken watched him. "If it bothers you so much to be spying on your friends, why did you take another field assignment? You said you were happy just teaching the art. Why did you let the Queen talk you into this?"

Mabruke turned to him with a look of genuine surprise. "She is the Queen of the world! One does not refuse her!"

"*You* could."

"That's why I never would."

"Maybe once we're on the other side of the Atlantic, among the tropical folk, you won't feel so much like you're spying on your friends?" Oken said this on impulse, then realized it was true.

Mabruke thought about that while taking items out of his valise. "Until they get to be friends. People do just love that professor fella, don't they?" He spoke with grim sadness.

Mabruke suffered from overly powerful charismatic charm, the

kind of *ka*, to use the sacred word, that functioned like a natural
force, personal magnetism that was neither trained nor acquired,
an attractiveness almost independent of the person within its field,
yet irrefutable. People thus afflicted (as Mabruke was wont to say
to Oken, describing himself in the third person) could be brutes
and utterly selfish, yet be steadfastly loved, surrounded by un-
shakable loyalty. Mabruke, however, was also a man of singular
compassion. He suffered from a terrible empathy with everyone he
encountered. He had been set on the path of espionage at a very
young age, a destination determined by his father's royal court, not
truly by his own intention. Mabruke's combination of attraction
and understanding made him so good at espionage that eventually he fell in love with his work, even though it troubled him
deeply. The very nature of his work kept him removed from the
humanity whose attention fascinated and sustained him. The tension of this inner discord made him an excellent teacher in the
subject. It also made fieldwork a fiendish strain on his nerves and
on his conscience.

Oken turned to his own set of valises. "What do you want me to
wear?"

AT THE entrance to the embassy's private ballroom, Oken saw
something that struck him cold, frozen in place for an instant: the
opera house posters displayed beside the entrance. The artwork spot-
lighted the lead figures, clinging to each other atop a windy cliff. Her
hair blew across her face, revealing only her green eyes. Her long,
long legs were unmistakable, unique. No other such pair of legs existed in the world. Oken felt sure of that.

DESERT VOICES was printed in bold letters of gilt-edged crimson
at the top of the poster, followed by the tagline: THE WORLD PRE-
MIERE OF GIUSEPPE VERDI'S ANASAZI OPERA, BASED ON THE MAGI-
CAL LOVE STORY OF LONG WALKER AND HIS BELOVED CORN MAIDEN,
PLAYED OUT AGAINST THE LANDSCAPE OF THE INCAN-EGYPTIAN

RESCUE OF THE ANASAZI FROM THE COLLAPSE OF THEIR KINGDOM SIX CENTURIES AGO!

The premiere performance was tomorrow night.

Oken stepped closer and saw the palm-sized, oval publicity photographs of the performers, their names printed in silver glitter beneath. She smiled out from the poster with the imperious lift to her chin he had appreciated the first moment he saw her.

Oken strolled into the main ballroom, alert to every face and gesture, but he did not see her. Mabruke was talking with a group of well-dressed men at the side of the musicians' stage. They were flirting and laughing with the musicians, one of whom Oken recognized as young Aziel, transformed from the simple goatherd to a court entertainer, resplendent in elaborate makeup. Golden jewelry spilled across his bare chest and covered his arms from shoulder to elbow. A diamond gleamed in one ear.

Mabruke flicked the feather in his top hat in a way that said he did not want to be interrupted.

To Oken's surprise, he also recognized a youngish woman of noble lineage whom he had sometimes seen at School. She wore a dress similar in style to that of Princess Astrid Janeen, in crimson silk. She was of Caesar's line, born of one Caesar's favorite household servants, thus she had been studying to be a lady-in-waiting to those from the line born of Cleopatra or her sisters. Oken's acquaintance with her had been casual. He remembered her because he remembered everyone. He wondered if she might remember him.

She did, drifting his way as soon as he made eye contact.

He bowed. "Mademoiselle Marietta—I travel in the wilderness and find a lovely compass rose."

She gently brushed the back of his hand with her fingertips. "Lord Oken, how delightful to find you here in the wilderness. I heard you were in pursuit of princesses in Oesterreich."

"Yet I remain unattached, mademoiselle, having safely escaped the numerous wiles of Europe."

"Could it be that you are here for the occasion of the new opera, Lord Oken?"

He let a smile cover his flicker of alarm. "Why else, mademoiselle?"

"I find it difficult to picture you seated at an opera."

"I have become an ardent admirer of every aspect of the stage."

Mademoiselle Marietta's laugh was practiced, easy. "Oh, of course you have."

"I promise!" Oken said with mock dismay. "Mademoiselle, you mistrust me!"

"You are traveling with a prince, I hear?"

Oken gestured toward his friend across the room, using the wineglass in his hand. "Professor-Prince Mikel Mabruke."

"I thought I recognized him." Mademoiselle Marietta's attention was directed across the ballroom. "He was our professor for makeup and perfume."

"He was also our professor for wine tasting."

"He was. I never liked those classes. He was always so distracting." She turned her smile on Oken, a curious look in her eyes. "You are accompanying him as companion, or in his employ?"

"He needed a memoryman for his new line of research in Andalusia."

"You became a memoryman? Intriguing. So you will remember me?"

"Always."

"Then you will introduce me, so that I may ask him to dance?"

"Happily, mademoiselle. You will find Prince Mabruke to be an excellent escort, a superb conversationalist, a magnificent dancer, and a gentleman, first to last."

Her lovely brow drew in as she considered his words, then smoothed, and a slight smile touched her lips as she comprehended his meaning. She tilted her face up to meet Oken's eyes, the question in her mind clear in her expression.

"I am his greatest love because I am completely unattainable."

There was no jest in Oken's voice. "I am a man with full respect for love, and I am hopelessly in love with every woman I have ever met." He leaned more closely toward her, tentatively touching the circle of her personal space, the invisible barrier she kept between herself and the world.

She tilted her face away, raising her hand to place her fingertips on the golden rectangle of the Neith pendant resting between her breasts. She drew back slightly, a gesture showing the grace of gentle disappointment. "That is a charming speech, Lord Oken, but women do not wish to be loved as a group."

Her gaze lingered on Prince Mabruke, then moved back to Oken. "A pity. I *will* dance with him, though."

"Certainly you will, my dear."

Oken also drew back, more amused than disappointed. He was well accustomed to the power of his friend's charisma to draw the attention of sensitive souls. Animals and children responded to him the same way. Oken was also accustomed to being the lesser light in his friend's presence. He had learned not to feel threatened. He knew the price Mabruke paid, the constant internal struggle to maintain the balance of power between himself and that *ka*-image. Too often people did not want *him* so much as they wanted to stand in his light. Oken gently took her hand to rest it across his arm. "Allow me to introduce you."

She let her hip brush across his thigh once as they walked together, a silent thank you. Oken smiled down at her. Her attention was fully on the tall, dark man across the room.

"Mademoiselle Marietta is an acquaintance from School," he said as they met up with him. "You may recall her from our classes on fragrance and tasting."

Mabruke bowed, smoothly covering any dismay at being interrupted. "Indeed, and your lovely mother, Mademoiselle Marcella. I trust she is well? Your essays were always far more entertaining. Please, do not tell her I said so."

Mademoiselle Marietta smiled up at him. "Thank you, sir."

"She has turned me down, in order to request the honor of a dance with you."

"Indeed, mademoiselle," Mabruke said, meeting her smile. "I applaud your taste and discrimination. I am certainly a finer dancer than Scott."

She nodded once in acknowledgment of the compliment, putting her hand out to rest on Mabruke's sleeve. Her expression was thoughtful and self-confident. She was a tall woman, yet she had to tilt her head back to look into his face. He took her hand, smiling at her with a solemn and penetrating gaze as he rested his other hand on the bare skin of the small of her back.

Oken stepped aside as they swirled away to join the dancers in the center of the room. Other dancers did not interest him, just the one. She made no appearance at this gala event. Oken continued to drift through the crowd, acknowledging respectful greetings from those who recognized the symbols of rank on his silver torque, slipping in and out of conversations as protocol demanded.

A woman who had come to the party with Mademoiselle Marietta caught Oken up, boldly introducing herself as Marques Glorianna from the Andalusia Spate. Her gown and jewels were a match to Marietta's, in a sunny yellow that offset her olive skin and dark hair. Oken was delighted to meet her. Glorianna chattered at him happily about her travels with her friend Marietta, and their traveling companion, Simone.

In a quick whisper behind her fan she said, "Please, Lord Oken, he must see me speaking with someone whom Marietta knows."

Oken did not inquire. Her large dark eyes had flashed with fear.

He learned from her that the opera company was at dress rehearsal this evening. "Isn't it a shame that dress rehearsal is not open to the public?"

"Truly," Oken said.

"The opera is new, Lord Oken, not yet performed in public. The world premiere is tomorrow night—but, of course, you know that. Wasn't that your reason for coming to far Marrakech?"

Oken allowed that that must certainly be the truth.

Mabruke, across the ballroom, was standing close to Aziel. Their unheard conversation looked breathy and bold. Aziel was only slightly shorter than Mabruke, tanned an amber bronze against Mabruke's plum-dark skin. The two whispered face-to-face, flirting with subtle gestures of shoulders and eyes.

Oken watched until they disappeared into the moonlit shadows of the garden terrace beyond the ballroom's glass doors; then he turned back to the warm glow of the party and asked the marques to dance.

She was astonished into silence, and danced with exhilarated grace. He enjoyed it. As they spiraled around the dance floor, he reviewed in his mind the security of the embassy grounds. The terrace was the only public entrance. The garden itself was walled in for privacy. Guards watched at strategic sites along the outer wall. Mabruke had gone there with the young man because he knew it was safe.

After several more dances, Glorianna thanked him with a breathless and excited smile, and excused herself. She hurried over to Mademoiselle Marietta, who sat with a pair of elegantly dressed older women. They wore matching orchids. He made note of the flower arrangement as he drifted toward the terrace entrance.

Oken sought out one of the servants in the crowd and asked for a glass of wine. He continued to enjoy the delights of the party without letting his attention waver from that garden entrance, keeping faithful watch on his friend's back.

Aziel returned first, looking flushed and happy as he stepped up onto the stage. The rest of the musicians had begun playing without him. One of them leaned forward to whisper to him, something teasing, making him blush deeply.

Five minutes passed, leaving Oken momentarily concerned; then

Mabruke reappeared, slipping back into the crowd with practiced ease. His clothes and jewelry were perfectly arranged, his makeup untouched, with only the slight and tender smile he flashed to Oken.

Oken raised his glass to him in salute.

ON THEIR return to their suite at the top level of the embassy hotel, Oken braced himself inwardly for the inevitable melancholy that overtook Mabruke after an evening of such apparent frivolity. Oken knew why Mabruke so often cocooned himself behind the walls of Thoth's Manor, why he wanted loved ones close by.

Mabruke sat down at the dressing table, removing his jewelry and packing it into the case with mechanical gestures. He stared into his own eyes in the mirror and absently ran a hand across the evening stubble on his cheek.

Oken strode across the suite to his own room and changed into a silver-embroidered silk robe and slippers. He returned to the bar in the sitting room, poured two glasses of brandy, and went back to Mabruke's room. He put a glass on the dressing table and settled into a leather chair close by to sip at his drink, waiting.

Once Mabruke finished removing his makeup, Oken said, as casually as he could, "Nice-looking lad. All I got was a tango."

"Aziel, you mean?" Mabruke said. "Zaydane sent him here in case we need to send for help."

"Are we in trouble?"

"Not yet."

"Tell Aziel to steer clear of ladies with orchids in their hair," Oken said.

"You saw them, too?"

"Four of them. One from Andalusia."

"The *Campus News* reported that we were headed that way."

Oken stared into the golden liquid in his glass and thought about Glorianna's frightened look, and timid voice.

"Ladies with orchids in their hair." He sat forward, his face serious. "Marques Glorianna was afraid of someone. She mentioned Marietta's traveling companion, Simone. Perhaps Aziel can find out why she had to be seen with someone Mademoiselle Marietta knew?"

"You didn't ask?"

"A gentleman never asks."

"He just makes discreet inquiries elsewhere."

"He also pays handsomely for it."

"Aziel should not be working in public," Mabruke said, much too evenly, as though he expected no one to hear. "He should still be in training." He at last noticed the brandy glass and picked it up, making an elaborate show of swirling, viewing, sniffing, and tasting. Then he drained the glass in a single swallow. He held it out to Oken without looking at him and went back to staring at himself in the mirror. The expression on his dark face was unreadable. Oken had seen it before. He went back to the side bar, and refilled the glass.

Mabruke followed him and sprawled across the daybed, drawing his silk lounging coat tightly around him. Oken handed him the glass and sat down on the chair beside. He observed his friend's face carefully as they both sipped the brandy. Mabruke drank his more slowly this time.

"Nearly four hundred students go through my classes each year, Scott. Every day I look at their faces and I ask myself, who among them will be killed in their first year of service to the Pharaoh?"

Oken knew how many of his schoolmates were gone, simply missing in action or returned home in a jar with no explanation. "I'm still here." He knew at once it was the wrong thing to say, yet he refused to regret the impulse to say it. Mabruke's stricken look was a clear mixture of guilty relief and profound sadness.

"So far, so good, anyway," Oken added with a shrug, looking away. "It is a proper alternative to war—isn't that your first lecture?

We do what Egyptians do. We share information. We answer questions. We are the talk-to-me nation."

"Knowledge is power," Mabruke quoted in his professorial voice. "Always has been."

"Always will be. What power does that give me—the knowledge that forty of my students will die because of something I failed to teach them?"

"The rest survive because of what you *did* teach them." Oken gestured to Mabruke with his glass. "Other professors lose more of us. You're the best the academy has. Do you have to be perfect?"

Mabruke drained his glass. "Forty families wish I were perfect."

"You're tired—you need another drink."

"I'll take your word on that."

MABRUKE WAS always up hours before Oken. Oken had found his way to the coffee and the bath by the time Mabruke returned.

"We're going to the opera tonight," Mabruke said in grand announcement as he strolled in. "The manager himself, Signore Alberto Burrococcio, will lend us his private viewing box for the occasion."

Oken had decided, the night before, not to speak to Mabruke about the photograph and the name on the opera poster until both of them had a good night's sleep. He told Mabruke to sit down.

Mabruke sat down to listen, resting both hands across the knob of his walking stick. When Oken finished, Mabruke looked at him, calculation in his eyes. "You're certain she's Natyra, *your* Natyra?"

"They even spelled her name correctly." Oken recalled the sensation as she had spelled her name on his bare skin with her fingertip, from his shoulder to his thigh. She knew he would remember. Natyra found his "talent" amusing, and played memory games to tease him. "This opera suits her style," he said.

"Verdi is a superb artist," Mabruke said, "at the peak of his style by now, I should say. I wonder why he would cast a dancer in the lead."

Oken shrugged. "I assume he's in love with her. All artists are in love with her."

Mabruke leaned back and crossed his legs. He sipped his coffee, his attention turned inward.

Oken continued with his morning routine.

A PERFUMED note from Mademoiselle arrived with Oken's breakfast tray. There was a single yellow orchid in a crystal vase beside the covered dishes. The blossom was a match to the ones she had worn in her hair, and the vase was engraved with her family crest.

Mabruke selected a pastry from the tray and said, "She is inviting us to share her private viewing booth for the premiere tonight."

Oken glanced up at his friend, then back to Glorianna's trim handwriting. "And dinner before, if we would care to join her. She will bring Marietta with her, for my entertainment."

"Mademoiselle Marietta is a lovely dancer." Mabruke put a pastry on his plate and cut it into quarters.

Oken pointed to the flower vase on his tray. "Orchids? Focus."

Mabruke smiled at Oken with half-closed eyes as he recited: "'Lord Oken and Professor-Prince Mabruke regret that they will be engaged on embassy business until well after the dinner hour. We send our fond hopes that we will see the ladies Glorianna and Marietta in the lobby of the opera during intermission.' The note was accompanied by a bouquet of tulips."

"You had a busy morning, old man."

"I also got the name of the garden shop that provided your breakfast orchid."

"We have a lead?"

"With time to see the opera."

Oken checked his face in the mirror, noting again the new scar on his cheek.

"Shall I inquire?" Mabruke was also looking at Oken's face in the mirror.

Oken considered. A woman like Natyra rarely traveled alone, if for no other reason than needing an army of porters for her wardrobe and guards for her jewelry—she wore nets of pearls the way other women wore lace.

"Only about that Blestyak bloke," he said.

"What do you plan for today?"

"You said we would be at the embassy. I think I will have a look at their library."

"I suppose I should have another chat with Aziel. Warn him about the orchid ladies."

"Warn him about Blestyak, too." Oken smiled at Mabruke in the mirror and stood up to finish dressing.

OKEN'S SOJOURN in the library was informative. Under the guise of a bored nobleman perusing various newspapers in the comfort of the private reading lounge, he used the society columns to trace the Marques Glorianna's travels over the last six months from social event to social event around Europe and in Oesterreich in particular. Mademoiselle Marietta was mentioned alongside Glorianna, as well as their mysterious companion, "Simone."

Even knowing how to read between the lines of the familiar code of society-column writing, Oken found that Simone was little more than a famous name. Always referred to as "Simone," never in the third person, Simone's gender was obscure. The single photograph in the *London Discriminator* showed a tall figure in tight trousers and a well-cut jacket, with a hat brim tipped across the eyes. It was taken with Marietta and Glorianna in front of the Paris Majestic Theater.

Oken wondered if the photographer had caught the grace of Simone as effectively as the one who created the poster for Verdi's new opera, *Desert Voices*. Those long legs.

He remained in that comfortable chair in the library, watching afternoon light color Marrakech blue and golden, while he worked out in his mind Simone's travel itinerary as sketched out in the society news. Marietta and Glorianna traveled without Simone during the winter months, preferring the sunnier climate of Andalusia. Simone apparently dropped out of the social circuit from time to time, appearing nowhere in the columns except in the occasional remark on Simone's mysterious absence.

OKEN AND Mabruke dined in the privacy of their suite, taking time between courses to dress for the opera.

Mabruke hummed to himself, enthusiastic about the anticipated performance.

"You had a good day," Oken said as he spread honey on another piece of spiced bread.

"I did. I have the locations of four orchid farms in Tawantinsuyu that have ties to the families you listed for Zaydane. I also wrote a long missive to Yadir, telling him of our travels. He enjoys reading about the meals others have eaten."

"Did Aziel find anything on Blestyak?"

"The lady of the opera has her own bodyguard. Everyone is afraid of him, including her personal maid."

"That sounds like Blestyak."

"Aziel will report this to Zaydane. He will set someone to watch them."

"*Is* this a coincidence?"

Mabruke shrugged without meeting Oken's eyes. "Burrococcio allowed as how the cast for this opera were hired more than a year ago. They have been rehearsing in secret, in various places around Europe."

Oken raised an eyebrow at that. "Perhaps she is wondering if it is a coincidence that *we* are here—is it?"

"Zaydane did say something about the opera, that we might

enjoy seeing it, since we are on our way to the heart of that civilization."

Oken frowned. "You never mentioned that."

"He said nothing about the cast. Only that it was a new Verdi. He and I attended the premiere of *Aida* in Memphis a few years ago. He knows I enjoy Verdi's work. If he had mentioned Natyra, I would have told you instantly."

"We're back to coincidence."

"I have never believed in coincidence."

Their eyes met, both men remembering that desperate night in Memphis. Mabruke turned away abruptly, taking up the condiments stand to spoon spicy red sauce over the slice of roast on his plate.

CHAPTER SIX

AT THE entry to the opera hall lobby, they were given copies of the souvenir program, elegantly bound in stretched ostrich hide, with gilded letters in Sacred and in Trade: DESERT VOICES, BY MASTER GIUSEPPE VERDI. Under the title was a quote from the opera, also in gilt letters: BEAUTY BEFORE ME. BEAUTY BEHIND ME. BEAUTY TO THE RIGHT OF ME. BEAUTY TO THE LEFT OF ME. BEAUTY ABOVE ME. BEAUTY BELOW ME. I WALK THE POLLEN PATH, AND BEAUTY IS ALL AROUND ME.

These souvenir programs were handed out by young lads in the costume of the Anasazi, loose-fitting white tunic and trousers, with woven leather belts and sandals. Their braids were adorned with feathers and thick silver bands. Aziel was among them, looking most natural in this different costume. He and Mabruke exchanged quick glances, otherwise ignoring each other so gracefully that only Oken noticed.

Oken flipped through his program, noting with pleasure that there was a copy of the poster that caught his attention the day before, as well as photographs of Natyra, two of them, and one was a full page, standing in costume for the opera, unmistakably her. A souvenir of more than Marrakech.

Mabruke tapped the cover of his program book to get Oken's

attention. "You will enjoy the opera better if you do not read the translation until *after* you have seen and heard the opera performed."

"Translation?" Oken opened to a page and focused on it more closely. Blocks of text were arranged on the gilt-edged pages with the native language and Trade side by side. The native was intricate, with odd vowel combinations scattered in lacy patterns amid guttural consonants.

"The performance will be in the Trade tongue of the Plainsmen of the Confederation of the Turtle," Mabruke went on. "Not much different from watching a performance in Frankish or Latin. Opera expresses the emotions of a story."

Oken lingered on the central page, then tucked the program under his arm, taking Mabruke's advice about when to read it.

Signore Burrococcio, manager of the Grand Opera Hall of Marrakech, was visibly thrilled to be hosting Professor-Prince Mabruke and his guest, Lord Oken.

Oken was relieved to see that the private booth was just that, private. There was seating for only two, comfortable enough to accommodate more than just watching the opera. He smiled as he stood to the side, slowly removing his gloves while Mabruke dealt with the manager's stuttering excitement.

Conveniently placed shelves held silver trays with crystal pitchers of ice water and crystal goblets. There were also dark brown bottles of the local wine, spicy and fragrant. Oken settled into a chair and poured himself a glass of water.

Mabruke stood leaning in the doorway, smiling down at the manager's eager face. "I will, indeed, mention you to the Queen, Signore Burrococcio, be assured."

With the door to the booth closed and firmly locked, Mabruke sank down beside Oken. "Lovely man. Lovelier if he could listen more while he talks."

He picked up the bottle of wine, read the label carefully, nodded approval, and held it out to Oken. "Open this for me, would you?"

Oken took out his pocketknife. The handle was carved elk horn. His father had given it to him when he was a small boy. His father had also hunted down and killed the elk that provided the horn. Oken liked it anyway. It was useful, and brought his father vividly to mind, more than just a memory of an event, rather a sense of the man himself.

They had arrived early, in order to observe the patrons as they came in. The opera hall was grand, more than three stories tall at the apex of its domed ceiling. The dome was twilight blue glass, sprinkled with constellations in gold. The horizon around the base of the blue-glass sky was a wide band of gold, with the names of the people who had designed and built it engraved in sacred letters, tall and proud.

The proscenium was Egyptian haeka glass, in the shape of classic Egyptian temple pylons, to show that the stage behind it was sacred ground. At the moment, it was mirrored, reflecting the audience. The coliseum-style seating rose in tiers to the level just below the private viewing booths.

The orchestra was stationed in high balconies on either side of the stage. The musicians had come in, and were sitting or standing, depending on the instrument, tuning while reviewing the musical score on the scroll-reader stands in front of them. The orchestra in the balcony on stage right was the usual European grouping of strings, woodwinds, brass, and percussion, tailcoats and silk shirts. On the left were musicians from Tawantinsuyu, in native dress, feathers, paint, and jade, with gaily decorated drums and rows of tall bamboo pipes.

Mabruke reviewed the audience through a pair of gilded opera-eyes. There was a second pair on a stand at Oken's side. He did not need the farscope view. "Simone" would not be in the audience. He was waiting for the velvet curtains to pull back.

A few minutes later, they were interrupted by a gentle knock at the door. Oken set down his glass and went to open it. Signore Burrococcio stood there, beaming.

"Lord Oken, the Mademoiselle Marietta begs the honor of having you put your signature to her program, on the center page?" He held the program out to Oken, smiling broadly.

Oken took it with a smile. "Extend to the Mademoiselle Marietta my gratitude. I shall return this to her during intermission."

The manager bowed his way out, nearly losing his top hat, reminding Oken of a similar moment in faraway Novgorod.

Oken went back to his seat. "Curious." He turned the program over in his hands.

"Indeed," Mabruke said. "Women have curious ways. Does Marietta want to dance with *you*?"

Oken opened the pages slowly. On the full-page illustration in the center, he found the message, marked with drops of green wax as a private seal: *You do not know me. We have never met. You have no interest in me.* It was written in demotic.

He held it out for Mabruke to see.

Mabruke read it in a glance. He reached out to touch the wax with the tip of his finger, testing its surface. "Your dancer from Novgorod?"

"Yes."

Mabruke regarded the wax droplet solemnly, analyzing its color and shine. Then he lifted the page to his nose and sniffed, very gently. He looked up at Oken, an eyebrow lifted in query. "Is this—?"

"Yes," Oken said quickly.

Mabruke nodded. "She was sure you would get this."

"Yes." Oken's voice was tenser this time, the syllable clipped.

Mabruke looked amused.

Oken tried to decide if he were angry or pleased, or perhaps both at once. The scents were hers, the green wax. The handwriting itself was the detail that troubled him, not the message. He had never seen Natyra's handwriting. He had not seen Blestyak's hand, either. Would she have told Blestyak the private meaning of green wax between her and Oken?

"This could have been sent by Blestyak," he said reluctantly.

"You will know for certain if she storms up to your rooms tomorrow, scolding you for ignoring her after the performance."

Oken could only agree. He put the program on the arm of the chair and took his pen from his pocket, considering his words. Then he opened his own program to the center page, and wrote:

> *A beautiful compass rose in the wilderness, my dear*
> *Mademoiselle Marietta—may you guide me once again*
> *to such pleasures as those encompassed in this volume,*
> *as our paths will surely meet again someday.*

He signed it with all Five Names and used the seal on the top of the pen to mark his family crest as well.

Oken looked over at Mabruke. "You may dance better than I do, but she asked for my signature as a remembrance, as you may take note."

Mabruke took the tease in good spirits. "She has asked if she could introduce me to her dear cousin Humberto, when we are next in her spate." He tilted his head slightly to one side as he smiled at Oken. "Humberto has, according to Mademoiselle Marietta, a garden of orchids to rival the Inca himself."

Oken laughed. "The world seems awash in orchids, Mik. We appear to have arrived on the eve of the orchid revolution!"

He had meant it as a joke. The solemn look his friend turned to him bespoke a seriousness to these events as nothing else yet had been able to do. Oken put the copy with Natyra's note on the table beside the wine bottle. He put the one he had signed inside his jacket, so that there was no chance he would get them confused at the last moment.

Mabruke had nearly finished the bottle of wine by the time the houselights dimmed and the audience fell quiet.

The curtains drew back to show a single figure on the stage, kneeling and bent over, back to the audience and covered by folded wings. The colors were uncertain, sand and stone. There were hints of reflected sunlight. The backdrop showed the figure on a cliff overlooking a vast canyon, bathed in sunlight. The audience's viewing angle in the magical backdrop was several cubits above the kneeling figure. The red Sun was sinking to the horizon. Music swelled, reedy, low, and mournful. The Sun's red beams made the kneeling figure glow on fire. The sky around was also on fire, fading to deep blue that merged with the twilight-blue ceiling of the opera house.

The figure stood, spreading arms wide to reveal green-feathered wings that made him larger than life. Outlined by the setting sun, he began to dance, slowly and gracefully, an interweaving of wings and limbs. Hypnotic drumbeats drove him, always so close to the edge of the cliff that the tension mounted along with the quickening beat of the orchestra and his dance. The glass projection shifted subtly until the audience was level with the figure.

The sun descended and stars came out, some just sparkles, some five-pointed Duat stars. Each Duat star's appearance was marked with a different five-note theme that then joined the music. When the last of the sun disappeared, the horizon faded to dark blue and each star opened to reveal a glowing, golden face. These faces sang a chorus, all vowels and emotion, mournful and haunting. Clearly, this was not just sunset. This was the ending of a world. This chorus of doom mounted as darkness filled the hall. On the final crescendo, stage lights blazed on and the background changed instantly.

The scene was now perched precariously on a ledge halfway up a cliff face that met in a sharp line with a fiercely blue sky. Homes had been built on this ledge. Ladders went up and down the cliff. Figures climbing down seemed to descend from the sky. The orchestra was deep-voiced, with breathy pipes and a pattering of drums. Strings droned a somber background in cello and basso profundo. The voices were intricately interwoven, mostly women, with men chanting a mournful staccato in the background.

The villain of the story was Thunder, a powerful warlord who controlled the only valley with enough water left to grow maize. Thunder was the human villain. The true enemy was the dramatic change in weather that had been starving the Anasazi peoples for more than a decade. Thunder demanded Corn Maiden, the beloved of Long Walker, as payment for his grain, sustenance for the dwindling peoples of the cliffs. Long Walker and his beloved had been destined for each other, but the sacred powers of sky and earth, water and grain, had cast a demon in the path of their destiny. Love must be tested by another as powerful, lest it be undervalued.

MABRUKE REACHED for his top hat. Oken debated remaining in the booth during intermission, but that was rude. House staff would be in to replace the glasses and replenish the wine. As expected, Mabruke slipped away to speak to Aziel, who was carrying a tray of wineglasses for the guests in the lobby. Zaydane needed to be told about Natyra's note as soon as possible.

Oken drifted through the crowd, nodding at the people around him, slowly making his way over to Mademoiselle Marietta and the Marques Glorianna. They interrupted their conversation with quick, guilty glances at one another when he presented himself, holding out the program. "My ladies, I thank you for the honor. I hope you are enjoying the performance."

Their nervous laughter and overly enthusiastic praise for the performance suggested that he had been the topic of their conversation. He smiled and said nothing more, letting them carry on.

Signore Burrococcio came to his rescue, with Mabruke in tow.

"There are other royalty here, my lords, and I would be remiss if I did not take this opportunity to introduce you. This is permitted, yes?"

It was. Oken nodded farewell to the ladies, and followed the men across the lobby to a group of people at the row of seats against the wall. The wall behind was mirrored and Oken watched himself as he approached them.

"Prince Mabruke, Lord Oken, I have the honor of introducing you to the inheritors of Chief Long Walker—Princess Martha Ravenwind and her brother, Prince Horus Greenspire."

Oken had noticed the princess's exotic face and intense gaze at the party the evening before. She and her brother were part of a group of people who had ignored him, laughing and talking together in the window seats overlooking the temple grounds. As a descendant of Long Walker, first of the living dynasty of the Cliff Dwellers kingdom, she was of an equivalent royal rank in her world as Oken was in Britannia's.

Her high cheekbones were elegantly curved, her nose, also. Her hair was the rich black of the raven that had named her, carefully woven into braids on either side of her face and flowing over her bare shoulders to her waist, ornamented with silver beads. She wore a close-fitting, ankle-length gown in blue velvet that matched her wide and intelligent blue eyes. Her piercing gaze fixed Oken as surely as an arrow as she greeted him.

Prince Greenspire was her twin, although taller by a head. He wore his hair in the same braided style, with gold clasps. His suit was classic black Parisian silk, although the jacket was longer than the standard, almost to his knees, with a distinctive cut to the front. Oken had a suspicion that the design would be all the rage in Paris in another season. The prince's voice was deep and melodious, with a lazy, relaxed manner.

Oken commented that the two seemed to speak with the distinctive accent of the southern part of his family's kingdom, Kent or perhaps the melting-pot cultures of London Town?

"Princess Ravenwind is a gossip for the *London Discriminator*," Signore Burrococcio broke in hurriedly, in a tone that suggested warning, perhaps even disapproval.

"Excellent photography in the *Discriminator*." Oken bowed to her.

"I will make a point of relaying that to the lad, with your kind permission, Lord Oken. He lives for his work."

"You employ only the one photographer at the *Discriminator*?"

"No. You are referring to the photograph of Simone with Marietta and that squirrel Glorianna."

Oken was amused, not just because the attribution of "squirrel" to the Marques Glorianna was so apt. Princess Ravenwind's deep blue eyes sparkled so beautifully when she said it. Despite her exotic appearance, she spoke with the familiar accent of his homeland. Her mouth shaped words so exquisitely when she spoke that Oken was in danger of losing track of what she was saying, and he almost ignored the slight surge of alarm that she had connected him with Simone.

He could, however, feel Mabruke watching him. Oken shook himself mentally and smoothly stepped back, putting a slight distance between himself and the princess.

Princess Ravenwind followed, keeping him within her personal space, smiling up at him as she spoke. "I am here for my grandfather, to write a review of the opera's premiere. He collaborated with Signore Verdi. He wrote the native verses. Perhaps you would tell me what you thought of it? Having your name in the review would thrill my editor, and please the old man." She grasped his hand firmly. Her hands were warm, almost hot. A cold disk, however, was pressed between their palms. He closed his fingers smoothly around it as she withdrew her hand. Her eyes never left his, and the sparkle flashed more brightly.

He put his hand in his pocket as he bowed to her, dropping the disk into it.

It had felt like a key, in that brief, hot instant between palms and pocket, a metal disk with a patterned edge. The weight of it suggested gold.

The embassy hotel keys were disks of solid gold. Oken smiled, meeting Princess Ravenwind's bold blue eyes. He nodded. "I'd be delighted," he said.

STORIES WERE sung on the desert winds about the legendary Wind Walkers who made powerful alliances with wizards of the upper air. Long Walker agreed to seek these great men, to bring them to help his people and save his beloved from the lust of Thunder. He set out on foot, running the length of the Anasazi roads.

The farewell duet between the lovers proved that Natyra was a better dancer than singer. Long Walker's vocal, however, was clearly meant to overwhelm the maiden's grief with his confidence and resolve. Oken noted that, other than in that duet, Natyra sang only as part of the maidens' chorus, dancing in front of them so magnificently that their voices became *her* backdrop and rhythm.

The scenes of Long Walker's journey showed the magic of Egyptian haeka glass and haeka Thothmen and artists. Long Walker ran at the center of the stage, leaping, flinging himself forward in the eagerness of his quest. The stage moved beneath him so that he remained in place while the scenery flashed around him—fabulous vistas of the extreme landscapes of the Cliff Dwellers and Plainsmen of the Confederation of the Turtle: deserts with stone formations as bizarre as dreamworlds; raging rivers that made the Nile seem tame and small. Towering trees in vast groves went on league upon league, more trees in a minute than grew in the entire land of Egypt. Grasslands swelled to the far horizon on every side, grazed by extraordinary bison in untold numbers.

Duat stars in the sky sang the chorus accompanying Long Walker on this journey. Sung in both native and Trade simultaneously, it presented dazzling counterpoint to the lone figure on the stage.

Long Walker ran all the way to the royal court of Mexicalli, and to the Egyptian Embassy there. The Egyptian ambassador took up his cause, convincing the ambassador of Tawantinsuyu to send a fleet of Quetzals to bring the Cliff Dwellers to Mexicalli, where they lived in peace until the climate changed again, and they could return to their cliffside homes.

IT WAS a magnificent production, a stirring rendition of a moment in history. The final scene was a wild display of lightning, accompanied by thunderous orchestration, while the hero rescued his beloved, holding her closely as he clung to the rope ladder of the last Quetzal lifting off from their village. Wolves and wildmen howled at their heels.

The high emotion of the scene, however, was lost on Oken. His focus was on those long, beautiful legs.

The purple curtains came down, the houselights flared up into a pinkish tinge of intimate lighting, and the audience rose to their feet as one with wild applause.

Once they had quieted, Mabruke leaned over to Oken and said, "Was she as vibrant in your bed?"

Oken thought about the question. "She is an artist," he said at last. "I was her audience."

"Then you do understand," Mabruke said with professorial approval. "Do not mistrust that understanding."

The cast came out to take their bows, and Oken thought Natyra seemed to be scanning the audience with more than her usual breathless appreciation of applause. Was she looking for him?

THEY WAITED in the private viewing box for a time, letting the house empty out, in the hope of slipping away unnoticed. Conversation drifting up sounded satisfied and upbeat. Oken had a moment of pleasure enjoying Natyra's success. He knew what applause meant to her.

Their escape, however, was intercepted once again by Signore Burrococcio, who swished through the crowd in the lobby and presented himself in front of Oken and Mabruke. "Please, my lords," he said, "would you royal and most noble gentlemen do me the supreme honor of allowing me to present to you the genius who created tonight's magnificent work, the composer himself, Signore Giuseppe Verdi? To have such royalty present for the premiere of his great work is quite an honor to him, is it not?"

Oken was curious about the man, and found he had no objection. The opera was a remarkable work, giving him a sense of the unknown world toward which they were bound. Mabruke accepted with his usual grace, although Oken could tell by his tone that the man had other plans. Nonetheless, they followed as Burrococcio eagerly guided them toward the cluster of people gathered around Verdi.

The maestro's high, broad forehead and deep-set eyes showed the piercing gaze of genius who would not waste time with fools. He was master of this event. He wore an embroidered black tailcoat, with the Order of Hathor in gold and rubies pinned to his cravat. He was not a tall man, yet his presence gave the sense of scope and horizon, so that Mabruke did not loom over him despite his greater height.

Oken was impressed.

Burrococcio insisted on using their full names and titles as introduction to Signore Verdi. Oken thought Verdi looked a trifle impatient by the end, although he put his hand out with graceful ease and thanked them for coming to the premiere.

"I found it most enthralling," Oken said with genuine enthusiasm.

Mabruke's Italian was flawless as he spoke of his admiration for the work.

Verdi beamed up at Mabruke and, with an exaggerated expression of pleasure, asked in Italian if the prince had ever performed onstage, with such a voice.

Verdi then turned to Oken, switching smoothly into Trade. "I am telling him how he has such a beautiful voice. Do you agree? He should be on stage, yes? What do you think, my Lord Oken?"

"Having been a pupil of Professor-Prince Mabruke for a number of years, I can assure you that his voice is most effectively employed in the service of the Pharaoh."

Verdi bowed smartly in acknowledgment of this. His smile was radiant. This was his night, and his new opera was exceptional, a masterpiece from a mature and illuminated composer.

"This is my son, Icilio." Verdi drew the man standing next to him close, with an arm around his waist. Icilio seemed pleasantly relaxed in the presence of his illustrious father, basking in the reflected glow of his triumph. "Icilio, he travels beside me as my advisor and guide." Verdi beamed around at them with paternal pride. "He keeps the ministers, and the magistrates and the costume designers from my path, so that I need think only of music, music, music!"

Icilio bowed to them politely, his bemused smile shielded behind a large brindle mustache. His face, though as handsome as his father's, was marked by scars of a childhood disease. The cut of his elegant silk suit was designed to make graceful a left shoulder with no arm attached. "My father is honored by your presence at this premiere, Your Lordships," he said to them. "You have our gratitude if you found any of it enjoyable."

Princess Ravenwind had joined the cluster of people around the master. She caught Verdi's eye and said, in her clear, pleasant voice, "May I ask, Signore Verdi, for my readers, why did you choose Marrakech for the premiere of this piece?"

Verdi beamed, clearly delighted to be asked this very question. He waved grandly at the ceiling with both hands as though drawing heaven down to him. "This magnificent stage is the closest opera house to the Manco Capac Aerodrome at Casablanca, because, as most certainly you know, my dear princess, in Casablanca, this is where the people from across the Atlantic first landed upon our shores."

Oken recalled the name Manco Capac from the book. The landing tower at Casablanca was the oldest one on this side of the Atlantic.

Mabruke then confirmed Oken's sudden guess that this was why he had taken this particular route. "We have also come here because of Casablanca's historic aerodrome," he was saying to Verdi. "My flight to Madrid will begin at the beginning!"

PRINCESS RAVENWIND'S suite was as spacious and luxuriously fitted as theirs, yet the warm scent of a woman's presence made it grander, a more welcoming place. The canopy drapes around her bed were pulled aside. Flickering candles in wall sconces cast warm shadows and light on her tawny skin as she smiled up at him. Her long braids had been loosed and waves of midnight tresses spilled down over her bare shoulders and arms.

She drew the coverlet back, showing herself to be slender and high-breasted, with a long torso and small feet and hands. Her skin was the color of a wildcat, golden and inviting.

"You shall admire me while I watch you disrobe, Lord Oken. You are a beautiful man. I wish to remember the look of you."

"Talk to me, my lady," Oken said as he loosened the belt of his silk robe and slipped it off. "When you speak, your mouth is profoundly erotic."

She laughed, a soft, easy sound that melted his spine and stiffened his manhood. He lay himself down on the bed beside her, resting on one elbow so that they were face-to-face.

She touched him with cool fingertips in a way that promised lightning. "I have been anticipating this moment since I saw you in the lobby yesterday, Lord Oken. I see you will not disappoint my anticipation."

He reached out to stroke her hair. "I am called Scott by my intimates."

Her eyes were as blue as ocean water, with depths as mysterious and as alive. "Scott." She put her lips close to his ear and whispered, "They call me the Raving Wind."

CHAPTER SEVEN

FROM A distance, the Quetzals flying over Casablanca were an astonishing sight: magnificent, giant birds with brilliant plumage, beautiful despite their peculiar shape. Oken knew their design in detail from the book that Sashetah Irene had shown him. The reality there in the sky was deliriously different from lines on the page. He had seen Quetzals in flight over Paris while en route to Novgorod, savage shapes against serene skies. He had paid them little heed, beyond noting the momentary wonder of flying machines that looked alive. He had never traveled by air, preferring the Egyptian sensibility of road travel along the grand aqueduct lanes that soared over mountains and valleys with equal disdain. That was as far above the landscape as Oken cared to be. Quetzals had been flying various routes over Europe between major city centers for more than a century. Oken felt it meant only that the technology was fairly new.

The Quetzal was a fat, oval ring of laminated bamboo more than five hundred cubits long. This provided the structure for giant tubes of a stretchy material, *caoutchouc*, inflated with a lighter-than-air gas, *Tlalocene*, and lashed to the bamboo ring with netting. The engineers of Tawantinsuyu apparently had great faith in nets, in laminated layers, and in a whole plethora of plant resins, glues, and lacquers. Fanfold sails around the oval were controlled by lines of hemp rigging and painted in tropical colors, red and blue and green. These "wing-sails" spread both above and below the bamboo ring.

Suspended in a net in the center of the winged oval was a fish-shaped sky-ship, twice as large as a royal barge. Round windows at the front looked out like eyes arrogantly surveying the landscape below. These windows gleamed in the morning sunlight, enhancing the image that the flying-fish thing was alive.

Seen for real in the light of day, they seemed impossible to Oken. Orders were orders, but he would have preferred a long, leisurely voyage across the Atlantic by ship. The idea that he would be suspended high over ocean waters in such an unlikely vessel became increasingly uncomfortable as he watched the Quetzals hovering over Casablanca.

Sashetah Irene's book had noted that the safety record of the Quetzal was reassuring. In addition, the sky-ship could float on the water if the flying ring failed, and they carried their own little flocks of messenger pigeons to summon help. Oken wished he felt more comforted by words in a book. The Quetzals looked like giant, fragile butterflies. The vast Atlantic stretching out to the horizon was bigger than the whole world. He said nothing.

Mabruke, meanwhile, was as excited as a child about the opportunity to travel by air. Oken was amused by the enthusiasm that rippled around him as they drove toward the aerodrome.

Mabruke pointed westward, out to the wide blue sky over the wide blue Atlantic, and said cheerfully, "That will be us in a few days!"

Oken shaded his eyes with a gloved hand and saw a distant shape in the blazing sky. He could make out the silhouette of a Quetzal far away, poised against the western horizon like some magnificent falcon of the giants. As they watched, it dwindled away to a moving speck, eventually vanishing in the blue.

Oken made himself smile at his friend. Behind the smile he reviewed relevant pages in his memory, reassuring himself in detail
of the safety record of the Quetzal flying machines of the New World.
As they drove toward the Quetzal station, he paid particular attention to emergency procedures, exits, and loos. On every page in his
memory, the corridors seemed very narrow.

THE STATION was built of the finest marble, gleaming in the afternoon sun. Columns on either side were shaped neither like papyrus nor lotus, but rather an exotic tree shape much like palms in
Memphis. On the lintel were carved foreign hieroglyphics that
Oken recognized from the book on Quetzals. He scanned his memory to find the translation: "We walk the sky with you."

Oken considered that he would rather not; nevertheless, he followed his friend up the many marble steps into the aerodrome
station's interior.

There were few people in the lobby. A dozen or so travelers
lounged in comfortable chairs or stood before the world map
covering one wall. Oken and Mabruke were greeted by a cinnamon-
skinned woman flamboyantly dressed in brilliant feathers and geo-
metrically patterned beadwork. Her bare breasts were painted as
flowers. Her perfume was also of flowers—hot, vivid, and exciting. She bowed to them, fingertips together and touching her forehead. Her face was pleasingly broad and flat with high cheekbones
and sloe eyes. Black hair hung in long braids on either side of her
face. A forehead band of gold was set with letters carved of jade.
Oken consulted his recall of Brugsch's book once more, seeing there
that the letters were her name, Jaia. Her title was station hostess.

"Welcome to the Casablanca Aerodrome, gentlemen." Her voice
was lilting and her accent strange.

"Thank you, Mademoiselle Jaia," Oken said. "I wish I could say
I was happy to be here."

The woman was startled to hear her name spoken by an apparent stranger. She searched their faces with narrowed eyes.

Mabruke stepped in, smiling his dazzling smile. "Pay him no mind, Mademoiselle Jaia," he said. "He's never been up in the air before, and I think it makes him nervous."

Puzzlement flickered across her face. "And you have, sir?"

"Never once, but I think it will be fun."

She smiled.

"Our luggage is in our vehicle," Mabruke said. "If that's not a problem. We also need the vehicle returned to the transport agency."

These duties Mademoiselle Jaia could manage. She bowed again and led them to a counter across the open space of the lobby.

The woman seated there was as beautiful as Jaia, and even more colorfully dressed. Her petal-painted breasts were in flaming jungle colors. Oken read her name as Jaianne. Looking back and forth between their faces, Oken saw that they were as alike as their names, more than sisters, perhaps twins. Jaia spoke to Jaianne in a language Oken had never heard before; he had a feeling he would hear it again and often in the days and weeks ahead. He hoped the women who spoke it would also be as beautiful as these two.

Mademoiselle Jaianne was delighted to see to the transfer their luggage and the return of their vehicle. She smiled with her teeth as she told them that it was easily done. She was even more pleased to report that they had time for dinner before they had to go on board. Mademoiselle Jaia recommended the café on the roof of the station.

The air outside was brisk, even with the Casablanca sunlight warm on their backs as they climbed the staircase on the outside wall to the roof. The café terrace was dotted with umbrellas in peppery hues of yellow, red, and green over round tables. Everything was made of bamboo in one form or another; indeed, bamboo dominated the design—airy and lightweight. Brilliant feathers of tropical birds were arranged on the tables in jade vases, with flowers of the same colors. There were no orchids.

They were served an exotic meal, mostly of bright red and hot yellow, with flavors as fiery as the colors. The view of Casablanca from the café apparently charmed Mabruke. Oken was too aware of the expanded view of the Atlantic that they must cross. The geometric designs of the stucco buildings and the dark green of the palm trees beneath the blue sky did not have their usual calming effect on his soul.

After their first bottle of wine, a magnificent Andalusian rosé, Mabruke finally asked Oken why he seemed so distracted.

"There are monsters in that deep," Oken said after a moment's consideration. "Fear is the least among them."

"I've never known you to be afraid of the water. That's not like you."

"Well, it's not the water," Oken said. "It's the distance we fall before we reach it."

Mabruke laughed, but he avoided Oken's eyes. "I would never let you fall. Anyway, you're a better swimmer than I am. You'd probably end up saving me."

"I do not swim better than you—I just don't care as much about what happens to my suit." Oken made himself smile.

Mabruke raised his glass in salute.

Oken did as well. "May your suit stay as dry as your humor."

A flash of hot color caught Oken's eye. He glanced over and saw one of the lovely cinnamon twins emerging from the stairwell. The highlights in her dark hair were pinpoints of blue diamond framing her face. She folded her hands one atop the other in front of her in the Gesture of the Attendant, her eyes downcast for the privacy of her clients. Her flower-petal breasts looked rounder in the dazzling sunlight, with the blue sky behind her. Her flower petals were clearly paint, not tattoos, a paint that concealed and revealed in the same gesture. Oken found himself wondering how that paint might taste.

"She has a layer of a soporific coating over the color," Mabruke said, breaking into Oken's contemplation. "At least, the breast on this side does. The other might be something different. I can't tell from this angle."

Oken turned an annoyed look to his friend—at the same time just as amused that Mabruke could read him so easily. "How can you tell that?" He tried to sound stern. Laughter sparkled at the edge of his words.

"That specific formula is from my earliest days of training," Mabruke said with a dismissive wave of his hand, nonetheless with a tone of casual pride. "I've seen it used in a variety of ways. Hers is lovely, if unoriginal."

Oken turned back to the colorful if soporific view, noting with a pulse of pleasure that she was approaching their table. "Every breast is an original," he said with arch reverence.

"Indeed?" Mabruke crossed his arms over his chest, tilting his head to smile at Oken's profile. "Her left breast is slightly higher than her right."

Oken returned to her. "As one looks at it, sir?"

"*Her* left," Mabruke repeated.

Oken kept his smile. It was Mademoiselle Jaianne, the twin from behind the marble counter.

"The nipple, however," Mabruke said very softly, "is poison. At the tip."

"The left or the right?"

"Both."

"Ah." Oken's smile, as she walked up, was slightly more forced. His eyebrow tilted in a line of regret.

She stopped beside their table and bowed with the same formal touch of hands to forehead. "The gentlemen are enjoying the view up here?"

"We are, mademoiselle," Oken said generously. As she straightened up, he tried to determine whether Mabruke was correct about

the attitude of her breasts. He was. "What can we do for you, my
dear?"

"The gentlemen would come with me, at such time as your re-
past is complete?"

Mabruke touched his napkin to the corners of his mouth, then
laid it upon the table and stood. Mademoiselle Jaianna was suddenly gazing at the buttons of his jacket. Oken admired the view
from his seated position, then stood as well. "Lead on, my dear."

She bowed and turned on her heel, revealing that the gracefully
contoured lines of her bare shoulder blades were painted in the
tawny gold and black markings of a jungle cat. She led them down
the steps, but at the bottom she turned, not to the left toward the
lobby entrance but rather to the right, toward the rear of the station.
Oken could see the corner of a small railed balcony that extended
around to the back of the building, overlooking the shore of the
Atlantic beyond.

He was not too keen on that view. The obvious distraction of
the lovely but poisonous Mademoiselle Jaianna got on his nerves.
He was reminded of a pair of white breasts glistening with droplets
of water, glowing in a pool in faraway Novgorod. An ambush had
been waiting for him that night.

Mabruke put a finger on Oken's wrist, gently, with clear meaning. Oken did not look at him. He nodded in a gesture indicating
the woman in front of them.

Mabruke shrugged.

When they turned the corner, the balcony was not empty.

Oken and Mabruke each took a step sideways to increase the
distance between them.

There were four men dressed in long white robes, turbans, and
boots, and wearing the formed and lacquered silk masks of desert
people, each painted with the stylized face and enigmatic smile of
Leonardo's Lady. They gestured simultaneously with drawn scimitars, directing Mabruke and Oken down a narrow set of steps in

the middle of the balcony that led to a cobbled path to the nearest wharf.

They walked along the cobbles with an honor guard before, at each side, and after.

"Are these more of your friends, Mik?"

"I have never seen those masks in my life."

Oken contemplated the specific wording of this while walking along the cobbled path threading through hillocks of beach grass. Mabruke had acknowledged only that the mask was unknown, suggesting that the faces behind the masks might be known, or not.

"I do wish you would just tell me whether we are hostage to friends or to enemies."

"If I did, how would you learn?"

Oken glared at him.

Mabruke shrugged, evading Oken's direct gaze. "I won't always be here to pick out the dangerous ones. You have to find out for yourself what the cues are."

"So be it, Professor."

"Like your life depended on it."

Oken focused on the men walking with them, trying not to look directly into the glare off the surging Atlantic.

The clue finally got his attention: the scimitars were ceremonial. The grip and the angle at which they were carried was formal and stylized—the gesture of an honor blade, not that of a weapon. Oken slipped his hands into his pockets and marched grimly on.

From the corner of his eye, he could see Mabruke trying to suppress a smile.

THE ACCUSTOMED view from the deck of a ship made Oken more comfortable with the promise of the journey ahead. The Atlantic was only as big as the horizon from here, with the water itself touching the hull. He found himself hoping that this was the real journey, that the preparations for traveling by aeroship had been made so openly for the very reason that he and Mabruke would not actually be on board. He did not bother to ask Mabruke. Oken did not fancy having to unravel another riddle just then.

Mabruke was riding in the fore of the ship like an eager dog, sniffing the ocean winds that blew across his face and made his coat flutter around him, mad wings striving to take flight. Oken was amused by Mabruke's sheer delight in the journey itself, traveling for the sake of traveling. The puzzle was that Mabruke had nevertheless opted for a teaching career that might have kept him in one place for generations of student lives. Oken had yet made only a few journeys out of Memphis in search of the secrets of the Pharaoh's enemies. He had enjoyed every such affair. He enjoyed returning to Memphis even more. He knew the older man would explain it to him someday, when his professorial muse was ready. Oken wondered if, perhaps, the professor himself did not yet know his own heart in this matter.

A cloud-enshrouded mountaintop resolved itself on the horizon ahead of them. Oken felt a brief disorientation. Surely they had not yet crossed the thousand leagues of the wide Atlantic to be this close to the New World continent so swiftly? Then he saw Mabruke grip the fore-rail to keep his balance in the winds and turn, gesturing for Oken to join him.

Oken did not want to leave the relative comfort of the windbreak where he sat, but he stood reluctantly and went over. The craft rode with amazing smoothness, considering the speed at which the water jets were pushing her. Oken felt the decks quiver beneath his feet, as though he trod on a living beast and not on a wooden deck and laminated hull.

Mabruke turned his face back into the winds, pointing to the misty mountaintop growing taller out of the horizon. "Madeira!" He had to shout to be heard above the wind rushing past their faces. "That's our next stop. We will be boarding a Quetzal there."

Oken nodded, but he sighed inwardly. Too good to be true. A

flight above deep waters was yet ahead of him. Still nodding, he went back to the bench and sat down, arms folded tightly across his chest. He closed his eyes and spent the remainder of the boat ride walking through his memories of the Avenue of the Sacred Places, gathered closely against the walls of Marrakech.

CHAPTER EIGHT

THE ATTENDANTS referred to their aircraft in the masculine, the opposite of sailors, who saw the feminine nature of their watercraft. It made sense to Oken. Women and ships were far more accommodating in their interiors. The corridors of the Quetzal were even narrower in real life than they had seemed as lines on a page. Both men had to duck, then bend their heads sideways to get through the entryways. Mabruke could stand in the middle of their cabin and touch both sides with his fingertips, and he had to bend his head respectfully so as not to scrape the top of his head if he did. Everything was bamboo, the ubiquitous building material of the Quetzals—carved, bent, formed, layered, and laminated with colored resins, sometimes embedded with flakes of mica so that corners glittered.

Sunlight shone in from a single round window. The pane of glass was crystal clear and just big enough to permit a view of the ocean far below.

The beds, at that time of day folded up flat against the walls, were ornate frames with intricately woven leather straps as a mattress. The cup and basin set out in front of a shaving mirror were hollowed-out bamboo sections, polished smooth and lacquered a pale rosy color that emphasized the grain. To Oken, the images of the two pieces as they reflected in the mirror looked as though they were slowly oozing lines of blood from a hundred cuts.

No matter. He was thirsty after the long trek across the island and the even longer climb up the stairway to the top of the Quetzal station, then the nerve-racking walk up the ramp into the Quetzal himself. The only water Oken was interested in just then was the drinking water in the pitcher, set in a niche above the basin. He ignored the bloody-looking image of the cup and filled it from the pitcher. The water was icy cold, and especially thirst quenching because of the bubbles dancing through it. He poured a second cupful and drank that. Then he filled it a third time and passed it over to his friend.

"Good of you to test it for me," Mabruke said with a tease in his voice.

Oken teased back. "Shouldn't you wait a bit first to see if there was anything slow-acting in it?"

Mabruke took this with a totally serious look. He frowned at the cup, then bent his head and sniffed at the water carefully, several times. He closed his eyes, searching memory, and sniffed once again.

He opened his eyes, looked at Oken, and smiled. "Just a nice bit of bubbles! You shouldn't be so suspicious."

"If I weren't," Oken said in retort, "how would I learn?"

Mabruke emptied the cup in a single draft, then held it out for more.

WHEN THEY were later seated in the crowded dining compartment, the Quetzal lifted up and away from his mooring atop the station, so gently that the two men almost failed to notice. Oken, however, glanced out the nearest porthole, and felt a delicious thrill through his flesh when he realized that the station building was falling slowly away. Not an altogether unpleasant thrill. He had felt the same thrill when he once stepped up close to the grand windows in Natyra's apartment, in order to lean his forehead against the cool glass. Novgorod, far below, was quilted with a layer of white velvet and diamonds, gleaming in the soft light of the full Moon. He had had too much champagne, at Natyra's insistence. He felt, just for an instant, that he was falling downward, spiraling toward that moonlit quilt. He had taken himself then to the silken quilts of Natyra's bed and recovered. That instant of thrill remained.

This was the same, the thrill of surrender.

"Fear is not the least among them," Mabruke said, quoting Oken's words.

Oken met his friend's intense gaze. "How can I serve Egypt if I am so transparent?"

"You are too well trained as royalty to be transparent about anything." Mabruke lifted his glass of wine to see its color in the light. "I am curious to hear if you had a quote from the Horus Scope about why we should not be flying today."

Oken did. "Do not sail on any wind this day."

Mabruke saluted him with the glass, then sipped at the wine, rolling it in his mouth carefully before swallowing it with a show of pleasure. "I thought you might say that. No winds here. Not even a breeze to ruffle your hair."

"Never mind my hair—look at your glass."

Mabruke was holding his wineglass level, with a steady hand, yet the wine was slightly askew, pooling as though creeping up one side to escape. Startled, Mabruke released the glass in midair, snatching his hand back as if the glass were suddenly too hot to hold, or too dangerous.

Oken reached out swiftly and caught the glass by its stem just before it hit the table. Droplets of wine splashed over the rim onto his hand, and onto the cuff of his white silk jacket.

"That's too fine a vintage to waste on sleight of hand," Mabruke said, much too evenly.

The edge in his voice struck Oken's ear. He put his hand up to his mouth, and quickly licked the drops from his skin. "Not the least bit underhanded." He drank the wine in a long, slow draft, then set the empty glass in front of Mabruke.

Mabruke carefully laid one dark, long-fingered hand on the table, placing the other hand as deliberately across it.

"They use uneven flotation on first launching," Oken said as explanation. "The sails get better purchase on the winds closer to the ground that way. The passenger section rotates to adjust. Our flight should level out shortly."

"It said that in the book, did it?"

"You read it, too, long before I did."

"Not as permanently. You must remind me, from time to time."

"THERE IS clearly nothing holding this ship up in the sky—at any instant, everyone will realize it, and we will plummet into the sea!" Mabruke spoke wearily, despite his effort to make a jest.

Oken had wondered why Mabruke insisted on taking his meals in their cabin, and kept the curtains drawn. Oken was surprised and dismayed by this explanation, however, accustomed as he was to Mabruke's childlike pleasure in traveling for traveling's sake. "The physics of it is in the book."

Mabruke shook his head, then reached up to rub his forehead. "Pay no attention," he said. "I am not myself yet, I suppose. Having gone from captivity underground to captivity in the sky is not the journey I had anticipated. Please, do not take this amiss. I need sleep, and our travels so far have provided me with very little. The quiet here is peaceful."

Mabruke sighed and his countenance grew still, introspective. Oken waited for him to continue.

"Just let me sleep. I will return to my usual self before we arrive."

"I'll go back to prowling around the ship, then, shall I?"

"Prowl on! Take your key, and lock the door behind you."

Oken assessed the contents of his pockets and selected a pair of gloves. "Pleasant dreams," he said cheerfully as he went out, making certain that the lock clicked clearly as he pulled the door shut.

A NARROW catwalk was woven into the netting that bound the Quetzal's top tubes together. Despite the seeming frailty of the materials, the bamboo treads between the curved walls of the gap were as surprisingly stable as the Queen's Bridge. Oken could easily place a hand on the bamboo railing on either side. Even filtered by the net, the view was overwhelming.

The aeroship moved with serene calm. The only sign of their speed was the brisk wind that tossed his thick curls about. The sky above and the ocean below were unchanging, eternal, calm, and endless, the sublime expanse of the Atlantic. As the pilots said, up here they were "one with the sky." Oken felt his spirit shift and expand to encompass the vastness of the world seen from the Quetzal's vantage. There was no place within that vastness for fear. The voice of the wind was a wordless cry of triumph.

The ship's staff were from the Andes in Tawantinsuyu, the Empire of the Four Quarters. They wore beaded and embroidered cotton vests and trousers and feathered armbands, and walked silently through the ship barefoot. Each had the same traditionally braided black hair and golden skin of the cinnamon twins, Jaia and poisonous Jaianna, in Casablanca. There were, however, no native women. Oken had wondered about that since noting it in the crew manifest.

Most passengers thought the crewmen looked alike and addressed them simply as "lad." When Oken introduced himself, he pleased them immediately by knowing their individual names and duties, skimmed from the manifest. After that, they had endless fun teaching him the correct pronunciation of their native names, which was returned by his fanciful translations of those names into Trade.

This daily walk around the open ring was his reward for these efforts. The staff were so delighted by his unusual enchantment with the experience of flying that they had given him the freedom of the entire Quetzal. Even the brilliantly colored macaws welcomed him when he appeared on the bridge. Each pilot had his own such bird as assistant, to act as liaison with the albatross outrunners, the true navigators.

The intention to secure the secrets of their Quetzal technology had led to the curious convention of keeping the bridge and engine room completely separate from the passenger section. The only exit from the passenger section of the vessel, suspended in the nets at the center of the winged-rings, was through a hatch at the very tip of the aeroship's tail, the passenger entrance when the aeroship was moored. The wing-sails, sleekly folded down in full flight, created a streamlined covering around the ring, protecting the catwalk. Stepping out to the flotation ring itself took a brief, albeit breathtaking, climb up three bamboo steps, holding on to a hemp lead line. The only entrance to the bridge and engine room of the Quetzal was halfway around the ring at the fore, via a daredevil slide down a double rope with a harness around the waist clipped as a security line. The crew did this barefoot. Oken quickly learned to use the heels of his fancy pointed boots to keep himself in place.

Once through the opened hatch, bamboo ladder rungs led down into the bridge and engine room. Drummers and pipe players sat in a small alcove overlooking the bridge, setting the rhythm of the cyclers as they worked, as well as entertaining the crew.

In a sunken recess across the bridge the engines were situated. Seven young men were riding atop dual-wheeled cycles, pedaling in place to rhythms played out by the drums and pipes. Intricately interlaced gears were set to whirring furiously by the young men. These, in turn, operated complex pumps and bellows painted with giant, grotesque faces that alternately grimaced and grinned as they worked. They made a rhythmic breathing noise, slow and powerful.

Another group of young men lounged on woven mats, resting before their turn at the wheels, laughing and joking among themselves.

Bowls of shredded coca leaves were passed among them, and everyone was chewing them. Some were singing along with the music, in a language startlingly similar to the words in Verdi's opera. The whirring noise of the many gears was a steady, happy hum droning through the music. Seven more slept in hammock-slung rugs around the perimeter of the bridge.

"Tawantinsuyu is a well-organized state," Brugsch had written:

> Lacking the draft animals whose loyalty and strong backs powered the earliest civilizations of the Old World, the civilizations of the New World devised a multitude of ingenious ways of harnessing human power. This practice led to a greatly enhanced appreciation of the individual's contribution to the smooth working of the empire as a whole, an ethic that echoes that of Egypt. This shared sensibility has helped greatly in smoothing the initial contacts between Egypt and these distant peoples.

The Queen had marked that passage with a carefully inked-in line of stars, making it stand out in his emotional response to the material. He saw the living enactment of it here, which pleased him. He would be able to report this observation when he returned to Memphis.

The cyclers waved at Oken in greeting. He saluted them in return. Two of the macaws who were not actively engaged in navigation work fluttered up from their perches and settled, one on each shoulder.

"Hoy, Oken!" The bird on his left shoulder tilted his head to regard Oken with both eyes.

"Hoy, Chocolate Roll." Oken stroked the animal's head with one finger as they greeted each other. Oken reached into his pocket and fished out a cacao bean. Chocolate Roll took the bean and winked at Oken as he spun it around in his beak with a dexterous flip, then quickly chewed up and swallowed the precious cacao. His eyes closed and he demonstrated his name, Chocolate Roll. The pleasure of the bean made him roll his head around, eyes closed, wings akimbo.

The bird on Oken's other shoulder laughed, shaking out his wings like a dancer on display. Chocolate Roll thanked Oken, pressing his brilliantly green head against Oken's cheek before lifting off in a flurry of wings to return to his human partner.

The bird on Oken's left shoulder winked at him, bobbing his head once. "Hoy, pretty-man, Oken!"

"Hoy, pretty-bird, Duster," Oken said, giving the bird a tickle in the rich feathers of his neck.

Duster held out his clawed foot, waiting for his bean. He snapped it up, then fluttered his wing tips swiftly over Oken's face, laughing, his head pointed skyward.

"All yours," Oken said to Duster, leaning his head toward the bird.

Duster nuzzled through Oken's rich, dark curls then carefully, with due deliberation, selected just a single strand and plucked it out. He walked down to Oken's wrist before fluttering off to his perch. The strand of hair was placed in a pullout drawer at the base of his perch. When Duster first asked Oken for hair, the captain had explained that Duster's mate, Chochoc, was nest-building. Oken felt the strands were an excellent contribution, since he suspected that his easy acceptance of the bird's request had marked him as the proper kind of reasonable—trusting him.

Oken strolled over to the helmsmen on their dais, seated before a broad panel of color-coded levers. Oken kept his hands casually in his pockets and did not speak to them. Their concentration was focused on the view through the glass windows that gave the aeroship its lifelike appearance when seen from afar. Just visible ahead was the flock of albatross that flew in careful formation in advance of the Quetzal, guiding the helmsmen. A fine gridline was etched onto the inner surface of the windows, creating reference points for the relationships of bird, sail, and wing. These crewmen were "Wind Walkers." Their counterparts, the albatross, were "Wind Riders." "Cloud Talkers," the macaws, flew back and forth between the pilots and the albatross as messengers, bridging the gap between human and avian minds.

The helmsmen, for their parts, controlled the arrays of fanfold sails placed around the ring with the lever system before them, making constant but slight adjustments back and forth across the board, according to the positions of each albatross in the grid. During most of the flight, the great expanse of sails was folded close. Even though their gazes remained fixed on the birds, the pilots chattered rapidly back and forth in their native tongue.

Watching the teamwork and coordination required to fly the Quetzal was endlessly fascinating for Oken. Here he found one of the rare instances in his life in which a perfect memory was little help to understanding. The subtleties of wing and sail would not unravel into any sense or structure he could grasp. They hardly needed their strict security measures to keep the secrets of the Quetzals. The single concept he was able to unravel with any surety was that each lever controlled a single hemp line. Lifetimes were needed to encompass this incomprehensible performance.

The change in the music announced the shift change. Space in the bridge was limited, so the shift change was done as a lively, ritualized dance. Oken had learned he could only get in the way. The captain helped him into the harness that held him safe as he climbed the rope steps back up to the catwalk. After unbuckling the harness and steadying himself on the railing, he worked his way to the aft and the ladder down the tail of the aeroship. Before descending inside, he stood watching sunset over the distant horizon. Evening and starlight appeared with startling swiftness. The stars were lost as the ship's lights flickered on, outlining the ring, the ship, and the masts with a bright blue glow.

Oken climbed down the bamboo rungs to the passenger section, welcomed by the spicy fragrance of yet another exotic dinner.

"I FIND it curious that the crew allow you such freedom of the ship's works when their entire nation guards those very secrets with laws and treaties."

Oken shrugged. "They think me to be something of a buffoon, playing with the birds and spending my time fascinated by watching the cyclers at their work. I am hardly dangerous. I believe, though, that the truth is in something that the captain said in a casual moment. He commented that the heart of their technology was not gears and wings, but rather the substance of the ship's frame, the alloys of the engines that compress air to run the jets, the fabric of the sails. I have also witnessed the interaction of the helmsmen and their avian navigators. The training of those birds seems considerably advanced upon the teaching of Thoth's beast-men in Memphis."

"That does explain a great deal, I suppose." Mabruke did sound strangely relieved. "Earlier descriptions seemed rather lacking in credibility as being adequate to keep this contraption in the air."

Oken feigned dismay and clasped his hand over his heart. "You wound me! *Viracocha* is hardly a contraption! He's the flagship of the Atlantic fleet."

Mabruke laughed gently at the shared jest. "I think you have discovered the navigation we will use once we reach the mainland of Tawantinsuyu."

"A little bird will tell us?" Oken was smiling.

"I shall be keeping a sharp eye and nose for evidence of their materials technology."

"More fun than sniffing out orchids."

Mabruke nodded, regarding the younger man with gentle regard. "You did well," he said finally. "Even Brugsch had little to say about the configuration of a Quetzal's bridge compared to what you have described. I think Djoser-George and the Queen will be enthralled by your report."

Oken gave a slight bow in return. "This does make their Moon scheme more believable, although getting an albatross to lead them to the Moon . . ." He shrugged. "I want to meet the Cloud Talker who can talk sense to *that* bird!"

CHAPTER NINE

OKEN STOOD close to the main window of the observation dome on the roof of the island aerodrome, watching twilight fall across the brilliant tropical greens of the island below, and the deep blue of the Atlantic around them. The station was built in the style of native temples of the Sun and of the Moon, a pyramid with a broad staircase leading down the middle of each face. The steps ended in the dense green sea of treetops surrounding the station, flowing, uninterrupted, to the stony beach where ocean waves prowled. Just visible overhead, three Quetzals floated serenely at their moorings, glowing blue along the ring and masts.

The lights in the room came on slowly and Oken's reflection emerged on the glass, backed by the sudden night and the stars. He could also see the reflections of their fellow passengers seated in the lounge chairs, sipping hot chocolatl from painted ceramic cups.

The observation lounge was too public for any conversation beyond a polite and neutral exchange. Mabruke was relaxing on a chair facing the windows, immersed in one of the many travel brochures set out appealingly on the side tables. Their eyes met in the reflection, and Oken turned, walking back to him. He stretched out his long legs, sat down, and stared at his boot tips.

"It is the hour for serving wine downstairs," Mabruke said quietly. "Shall we?"

Oken stood up by way of answer.

Mabruke picked up a pair of brochures he had set aside, slipping them into an inner jacket pocket as he stood.

Oken followed Mabruke down the stairway into the interior of the station building and the dining room for the embassy guest quarters. He noted, as they turned the corner of the first landing, that the other passengers were following them. He was amused. During the voyage, curiosity about the professor-prince who refused to leave his stateroom had rippled through the passengers on the swift wings of rumor, disguised by concerned remarks about the gentleman's change in appetite as Oken returned the dinner tray, or offers to lend this or that book, "for the good prince to pass the hours in flight more amiably." None of the books, however, contained messages in green wax. Mabruke was as disappointed as Oken; however, they both read the books. Each was returned with suitable inscriptions regarding the gentlemen's enjoyment of the text, yet without a glimpse of the prince himself.

The aerodrome's dining room was furnished with pieces built of the same rock as the building itself. Paintings in vivid colors covered every surface with mad contortions of human, plant, and animal shapes linked together by crimson flames, beautifully unfurling and writhing around them. Cushions of polished cloth, scattered in comfortable piles for guests to choose from, were of simple, solid colors, in contrast to the intricate art. Egyptian lanterns hanging down in rows from the corbeled ceiling shed a soft yellow glow, warmer than candles.

Plump brown lads filled cups with a hot wine poured from ceramic bottles shaped like crouching monkeys and bats. They passed the cups around with encouraging smiles as the guests settled down on the benches. The other guests were rich businessmen and their wives, exporters on purchasing runs, and embassy officials returning from family visits in Egypt. Their tables were part of the walls, with stone benches covered by beautiful rugs and cushions. The chatter was lively, covering furtive glances at Oken and Mabruke.

Oken himself was a prince of Britannia, fourth from the throne. He had earned the rank of lord in the Egyptian court through acts of gallantry for the Queen. He counted that the more valuable title. As a prince of Nubia, Mabruke outranked almost every European or Egyptian he might encounter on this side of the Atlantic, except perhaps the ambassadors themselves. Nubia, "the Land of Gold," had been Egypt's closest neighbor long before the days of Caesar. Nubian blood coursed through the veins of Caesar's children as hotly as Caesar's own. Oken might sit closer to the throne of his own father's spate in Mercia, but Nubia sat closer to Egypt's heart.

As "Captain-Prince Mabruke," master of the PSI Guild, he outranked even the ambassadors—but only when it was worth risking his cover.

Oken sipped at the hot wine. He was growing accustomed to the peppery burn that sang through the New World cuisine. He thought it struck a particularly eloquent harmony with the wine, although he could not identify a single flavor. The mystery delighted him.

He was about to speak of that, but stopped himself. Mabruke had spread the brochures out on the table between them. "Scott," he said, tapping the one closest to Oken, "I have discovered these to be the most friendly little items. They list the best hotels in the country, the embassies, and the Quetzal stations. It has a map, see?" He was speaking with relaxed calm, a casual remark to a friend. "I feel certain that we can find a destination to suit our fancy."

Oken picked them up one by one, reviewing each as though deeply interested, slowly tilting his head this way and that as he scanned the pages. Red and black line drawings and terse text in Trade hinted at exotic foods, wines, and women in dramatic and bizarre landscapes, unlike anywhere else on Earth. These hints were sparingly phrased, so that much could be read into them. Across the top of each brochure was printed:

> Please do not remove from the Wat'a Mona Aerodrome,
> thank you, courtesy of the management.

They marked out the main attractions and locations that, for his and Mabruke's purposes, were best avoided. Also listed were the names and titles of the most recently appointed Egyptian officials, butlers, protocol officers, and musicians among embassy and hotel staffs. Maps and native hieroglyphs for cities and embassy compounds were printed in red, as though meant to be vague. Trade names in black overwhelmed them.

"Here is a particularly friendly warning," Oken said, smiling at Mabruke. He leaned forward over the table and read aloud: "'The European traveler will quickly discover that their accommodations, wherever they may be, will be situated much like the facilities here at Wat'a Mona Aerodrome. This is to say, quarters, as well as furnishings therein, are constructed of stone of one kind or another, making practical the swift removal of mold or fungal growths, which remain a constant nuisance in this moist and vibrant landscape. It is good practice to report to staff the slightest hint of mold.'"

"Friendly advice, indeed," Mabruke said. He tilted his head, eyes unfocused in thought, and took a long swallow of his wine. He tapped the tip of his nose. "I wonder if an antifungal and -mold formula might do well in the market here?" He looked pleased with the idea. "I might design one." He tapped his nose again.

Oken agreed and went back to scanning the brochure, focusing on the maps. He put them aside when the steward brought in the first course of the evening meal: bowls with orange cubes of fruit heaped atop a thick, creamy custard. Cocoa powders were sprinkled over. This was served along with refills of the hot, spicy wine.

There was a course of small potatoes of different colors served in hot broth and seasoned with chopped green herbs and red peppers. After this came roast fowl covered with a rich chocolate sauce, stuffed with peanuts, peppers, and round, white edible pearls. The birds were small, no bigger than squab, with a wild and tender taste. When one roast was consumed, another was quickly served up in its place. Mabruke ate three, one after the other, with calm deliberation. Oken was more interested in lingering over the sauce.

The pleasant murmur of conversation grew stronger as people relaxed, exclaiming over the dishes, the delicacy of the spices, the novelty of the seasonings. "Better than in-flight meals" was heard going around the group. "Nice to have fresh fruit again."

Oken and Mabruke ate in silence. Oken let his gaze drift around the room, storing up memories of the vivid, enigmatic artwork on the walls.

ONCE THEY had settled into their suite, Mabruke pulled out the brochures and spread them on the bed. "We are currently off the northeast coast of the southern continent," he said, unfolding the map. "Our ultimate destination is Qusqo, so let us find a suitable meander, a leisurely pathway for two carefree gentlemen tasting the sights and sounds of this wild place."

Oken stretched his lean self out on his bed. He folded his hands under his head and closed his eyes, calling up in memory the pages of the brochure Mabruke was reviewing. " 'Qusqo, the center of the Cosmos and the source of all creation,' " he recited from it, then interrupted himself. "I always thought that was Memphis."

"It is," Mabruke said absently, examining the fine lines of the map.

"Ah, of course. All faiths are true."

"We are on the far side of the world. Tawantinsuyu and Egypt are civilizations growing up behind each other's back. Qusqo may well be the center here."

"Then we shall treat it as such," Oken said agreeably.

"Tomorrow, you and I will board an Egyptian-owned ship, *Moss Rose*," Mabruke said, "for a pleasant sail across the Carib Sea to the northern coast of Tawantinsuyu. From there we shall eventually catch a Quetzal to Qusqo directly."

"Eventually," Oken echoed. "Perhaps by then you will be rested enough to enjoy the flight."

"Oh, I am quite prepared for that. I told you it was lack of sleep."

"Good."

Before they set out from Memphis on this mission, the Queen had shown Oken a second book about their destination, a who's who of the imperial courts of Tawantinsuyu and Maya Land. A great many of the royal descendants, especially in the recent generations, had the same names as their ancestors, separated only by numbers, as in Quyllur Misi III and IV; Wankakanka XII and XXI; Viracocha Inca Yupanqui XII, Inca of Tawantinsuyu; and Satiltzoj II, President of Maya Land.

The two most important names after the aging Emperor Inca Viracocha Yupanqui XII himself were the Inheritor and next in line, Pachacuti Yupanqui IV and his brother, Viracocha XIII, the only surviving adult princes. The only princess, Usqhullu, was very popular. She had been widowed at a young age, and spent her time traveling around her father's empire, indulging in the "decadence" of Egyptian embassies and European trade centers. Usqhullu was older than Oken, but not by much, and he was learning to appreciate women with some experience in life—their conversation made the time pass so pleasantly.

With that happy thought as inspiration, he compared pages in his memory with the active list from the brochures. There was much to be learned.

THE PSS *Moss Rose* was a medium-size cruise ship, with more spacious accommodations than the Quetzal, yet Oken felt strangely constricted. He missed the sky. The crew were mostly Portuguese, and under orders not to talk to the passengers. "This ship is a little piece of Egypt in a strange land," the captain had said as he ushered them on board. "You will find my crew are well disciplined." Oken rather suspected that everyone was showing off for the visiting noblemen. Mabruke took it with his usual grace. He was often to be found at the fore of the ship, leaning on the rail, coattails flapping around him, gazing in solemn contemplation at the new continent appearing before them. Oken preferred the view from the comfort of the observation deck, out of the wind.

Late on the last night before the scheduled docking, Mabruke spoke up a few minutes after Oken had put out the lamp over his bunk. "Your breathing tells me that you are also still awake. A favor, then, would you? Read back to me from the brochure on the embassy at Zulia. Something nags at me, suggesting I have forgotten an important detail."

Oken was also feeling the restlessness of the limited activity on shipboard. He rolled over to face Mabruke in his bunk. The images flashed across his mind's eye clearly enough to be seen in the dark. He resettled the blanket over his shoulders. Once comfortable, he began to recite: " 'Situated at the northernmost tip of the southern continent, the Egyptian Embassy complex in the district of Zulia is the first landing on many travelers' tours of the Empire.' " He stopped himself as a thought struck him. "Mik, does that mean we draw less attention by going there first?"

"That was the plan."

"Was that the missing detail?"

Mabruke considered. "No."

Oken continued, " 'The traveler's first sight upon docking is the imposing stone architecture of the Port Authority building, where officials of the Egyptian Embassy are available to provide guidance for further travels within the Tawantinsuyu Empire and Maya Land. From there, our well-trained staff will transport you and

your luggage along the statue-lined thoroughfare to the Gate of
Isis, and into the lobby of the embassy hotel. Along the way, the
traveler is treated to magnificently ornamented murals on every
surface, relief sculptures of the native builders at work, showing
how they lifted the forty-two columns of the façade into place, as
well as the pair of obelisks facing the ocean. Each workman's image is an actual portrait. The earnings these workers brought to
their families, villages, and temples were the foundation of the
trading port city in the more hospitable region just south of the
embassy—Coro, known to the locals as Sky City.'"

Oken heard the breathy sound of Mabruke's light snoring.

He turned on his side and waited for sleep, walking the Quetzal's catwalk in his mind.

SLEEP WOULD not visit him, however. As the air began to lighten,
he drifted into the half sleep of deep relaxation, and almost missed
the sound of the lock mechanism clicking. The captain did, indeed,
run a tight ship. No one would have dared to enter their cabin without knocking and speaking first. Instinct and training acted for
Oken. He leaped off the bed, springing silently across the cabin to
stand behind the door. The attacker stealthily opened the door and
took one step inside, leaning forward. His arm was raised. In the
light from the corridor, Oken saw the glint of a blade poised to throw.

Oken slammed the door hard against the would-be assassin, hit-
ting him squarely in the face. Oken heard the blade clatter to the
deck as the man staggered back.

"Mik!" Oken called loudly as he yanked open the door.

This was no crewman. He was a native from the deep rain forest, wearing only red ochre paint and a smear of black across his
eyes. He was lunging for the dropped dagger.

Mabruke turned on his lamp and leaped out of bed, shouting
"Steward!" loudly.

With a single well-placed kick to the attacker's head, Oken knocked the painted man unconscious. Then he went back into the cabin, picked up his silk morning coat, and put it on, slowly shaking his head.

The night steward came rushing up, lamp in hand. "What is this? What is this?" he cried, shining the lamp over them.

"Get the captain!" Mabruke snapped.

"We'll need rope to bind him before he comes to," Oken said, returning to the corridor. He put one foot on the neck of the unconscious man, just in case.

The steward hurriedly ran down the corridor, snagged a coil of rope, and ran back. He gave the rope to Oken, then rushed off for the captain, calling loudly as he ran.

While Oken tied the unconscious native's hands behind his back and bound his feet, Mabruke crouched beside him, carefully examining the man's paint and the beadwork knotted into his hair. "Roll him over," he said once Oken had finished the knots. "I want you to see his face."

"You think I should recognize him for some reason?"

"Just in case we should see him again—or perhaps we have seen him before." Mabruke leaned close and sniffed lightly at the paint on his face, then at his lips. "Hmmm . . ." He stood up, gazing down at the man. "It is native ochre, but it has been applied using olive oil. A rather cheap grade of it, too, I should say." He put his hands on his hips and frowned at the man. "There's no scent of brine on him. He did not swim here. He's been drugged. Laudanum and coca."

The steward returned, running ahead of the captain. Two of the night watchmen ran behind them, weapons drawn. The captain stared at the scene before him. "Who is this person?" he said, pointing to the man tied up on the deck. "How did he get on board?"

Oken tied the silk belt of his morning coat, leaning back against the doorframe. "He tried to get in here. He was armed." He nudged the dagger lying on the deck with his toe.

The steward reached out to pick up the dagger, but Mabruke put out his arm to stop him. "There is poison on the blade—touch only the handle."

The man on the floor came to and writhed desperately toward the dagger, making a sudden snatch at it with his teeth. Before they could stop him, he had managed to stab the poisoned tip into his cheek, killing himself before he could close his eyes. His painted, naked body went limp in its rope bonds.

The captain shouted wordlessly in shock.

"So much for learning who sent him," Mabruke said regretfully.

"This is horrendous!" the captain said loudly. "This is not possible! This ship is embassy property, embassy territory!"

"A little piece of Egypt in a strange land." Oken spoke quietly. "Just like home."

"You didn't kill him," Mabruke said to him. "He would have killed us."

"This is an assassin?" the captain cried out in even greater dismay and shock.

"A paid assassin by the look of him," Mabruke said. "I doubt the Red Hand League is capable of pursuing us across the Atlantic, however."

"Red Hand?" the captain said angrily. "What Red Hand? He is red all over!"

"They will want to examine the body at the embassy when we arrive," Mabruke said. "Secure him in the hold until then."

The night watchmen obeyed without even glancing at their captain for confirmation of Mabruke's orders. They were very careful not to touch the dagger as they picked the body up by Oken's knots and carried it away. The night steward followed them out. The captain looked helplessly at Mabruke, stuttering an apology.

Mabruke dismissed this with a casual wave of his hand. "I am quite certain that you and your crew are not involved in this, have no fear, captain. Investigators at the embassy will deal with this well enough."

The captain was very grateful and rushed away, shaking his head and calling to the watchmen to prepare a bird for a message to send ahead.

Oken sat on his bed, staring blankly at the memory of a dead man's eyes. "'Protect the living and honor the dead,'" he said, thinking out loud. "That's what I've been taught all my life."

Mabruke stood before him, arms folded across his chest. "I know that look," he said to him quietly. "You did not kill him—you saved our lives."

Oken blinked, forcing the image away, then nodded, grateful.

"Don't give in to guilt. You protected the living, and you have my gratitude for that."

Oken tried to smile.

Mabruke spoke more emphatically. "Yes, a life was lost. The only guilt is the dead man's—you *saved* our lives."

"I know. Remind me."

"THIS IS a serious and most unfortunate circumstance," Ambassador Mario Castillo said unhappily. He snapped his fan shut and tapped it rapidly on the back of his hand. The ambassador was a short man, and seemed unable or unwilling to look up at the towering noblemen who had arrived at his office. "When His Highness, the prince, hears of this attempt upon your persons, he will be incensed!"

"What prince might this be?" Mabruke said in polite inquiry.

CHAPTER TEN

THE ONLY other human being Oken had ever seen who was quite as big as Prince Viracocha was that golden bear from Novgorod, General Blestyak. Oken would have had to put them side by side to see who was actually the larger. Prince Viracocha was built wide, broad of forehead, broad of face, shoulder, and chest, with thighs like tree trunks. The extraordinary quality and fit of his sky-blue European suit pleasantly emphasized every muscle. Unlike Blestyak, however, this man had a look of intense intelligence about him, with piercing black eyes that missed nothing, an eagle assessing his prey. A royal collar was draped around his shoulders and across his powerful chest. Designs in green, red, and black feathers spelled his name and rank in the sacred glyphs of Tawantinsuyu: "Prince Viracocha XIII, Seventh Son of Emperor Viracocha Yupanqui XII, Favored of Heaven." A golden circlet on his brow bore a stylized puma flashing hot, ruby eyes. The prince's skin was the same cinnamon color as the beautiful ladies Jaia and Jaianna, his long hair as shining black as Princess Ravenwind's.

Oken was inclined to like him.

Prince Mabruke and Prince Viracocha bowed politely to each other in equal measure, royal sons of similar status, sons of thrones.

Oken bowed just slightly lower, and was last to straighten up. Ambassador Castillo, having completed his duty by introducing them with their names and titles in the correct order, stood to the side, nervously fingering the gold filigree on his cuffs.

Mabruke reached up and flicked the white ostrich plume on his top hat. "Your Highness is most kind to have journeyed so far from the palace just to greet strangers."

Prince Viracocha smiled. "Your Highness is most kind not to condemn us for the inhospitality of your greeting, an assassin sent by strangers." His Trade was barely accented, with the deep, throaty tone of controlled power Oken had come to recognize as a trait of the native peoples.

Mabruke also smiled. "Were they, indeed, strangers, Your Highness?"

"Death is no stranger in this world, Prince Mabruke. He prowls as he pleases. He takes whom he will."

"Yet he did not take us."

Viracocha's smile was suddenly genuine. "I thank the Sky for that! I have been eager to share our world with you since I first heard that you would be coming here."

Oken's attention focused on that. Viracocha turned his eagle gaze on Oken. "You are the memoryman?"

Oken met that intense gaze and held it, then nodded. "We came here in a Quetzal named after you, Your Highness. I enjoyed it immensely."

Prince Viracocha looked at Oken, then said, "Actually, that was named for my mother's ancestor. I just happened to be born on the same day of the *k'atun* as he."

"I am also named for my mother's ancestors," Oken said, "but only because my mother is sentimental."

Viracocha laughed, a generous sound. "Your world fascinates me, gentlemen. When I heard that men of your quality would be traveling here, I determined that I should be your guide and companion, sharing with you the beauties of my empire, while you regale me with stories of yours."

Mabruke beamed. "Excellent, Your Highness. Excellent."

"First, however," Viracocha said, "this matter of the assassin." He folded his big arms over his broad chest. "I do not like this. Tawantinsuyu has no quarrel with Egypt."

"Tawantinsuyu is not the whole world, Your Highness," Mabruke said in gentle reply. "There are those who quarrel with Egypt wherever they want."

"I shall put my best lieutenants upon it, Your Highness," Viracocha said. "And only those whom I trust."

"Indeed," Mabruke said, his eyebrows rising. "You think this might have come from the palace?"

"I want to know, no matter the source."

Mabruke's smile relaxed. "Your Highness, we have much to talk about, you and I."

"THIS PERSON is *yunka runa*," Prince Viracocha said. "That is, he is a jungle person from Maya Land." He was pacing slowly around the examination table on which the corpse of their would-be assassin lay. "At least, the clan markings on his face and hair are from the Yanomamo. Something about it does not seem quite right. The Yanomamo are not assassins. They're good salesmen, not killers."

"Do the Yanomamo use olive oil in their body paint?" Oken said.

"Olive oil?" the prince said, puzzled. He looked at Oken for further explanation.

Mabruke spoke up. "The red ochre was mixed with olive oil, a rather poor grade, and almost rancid."

Prince Viracocha turned to the embassy's examiners standing to the side of the table. "Is this true?"

One shrugged; the other shook his head.

"Smell it," Mabruke said to them, gesturing to the corpse.

The younger of the two leaned over the body and sniffed at the paint on the skin. He straightened up, eyebrows raised. "Olive oil," he said, sounding surprised. "And rancid."

"Was there any evidence that he swam to the ship?" the prince said.

Mabruke shook his head. "There was no brine."

The prince folded his arms across his chest, staring down at the dead man's face. "That suggests he stowed on board at the aerodrome on the island. The oil would have gone rancid while he waited in hiding."

Mabruke nodded. "That is suggested."

"We will have the ship searched, Your Highness," the embassy's man said.

"I will send troops to search the island as well," Prince Viracocha said to him. "Find a photographer, and get him up here. I want close-ups of this face, both with and without the paint. Knowing who he is will lead us to who sent him."

"Whoever it is, Your Highness," Oken said to the prince, "you will likely find that there are orchids involved."

"Orchids?" Viracocha drew his brows together. "What have orchids to do with this?"

"A very dangerous, exotic flower, Your Highness," Mabruke said.

"Indeed, Prince Mabruke, we have much to talk about." Viracocha motioned to the captain of his personal guard, who was standing protectively behind him. "We will go on board," Viracocha said to him. "Have Hanaq Pacha prepare for launch."

"*MIXCOMITL* IS the fastest Quetzal in the world, gentlemen." Prince Viracocha waved grandly at the brilliantly blue heavens. "I can sail from the top to the tip of the empire in just seven days."

"He's quite the magnificent beast," Oken said appreciatively. *Mixcomitl* was the largest Quetzal he had ever seen. Giant golden wings dazzled the sky. Instead of being fish-shaped, the aeroship suspended in the nets was a golden condor with half-raised wings and a fierce beak between window-eyes. He seemed an appropriate vessel for the larger-than-life prince.

Mabruke stood gazing silently upward, his expression unreadable.

From the mooring tower atop the embassy headquarters, their view encompassed the Carib Sea on one side, and desert scrubland stretching southward in hard country to a stony distance on the other. Oken felt this was an impressive demonstration of Egyptian foreign policy. Egyptian embassies were required to build on non-arable land, with as little impact as possible upon the countryside. The adobe buildings of the embassy workers' town clustered around the embassy like goslings huddled close to mother goose. The unspoken policy was that the embassy was the golden goose, instilling Egyptian values and sensibilities by providing not only jobs but also education and lifelong careers for the native peoples. Oken wished he had the opportunity to walk among those adobe houses and see the layers of Egyptian and Andean as they were interwoven there. He was young yet, however. It was something to remember for later in life.

Prince Viracocha said grandly, "*Mixcomitl* and everything aboard him are made entirely of chocolate!" He then laughed heartily at the looks of surprise on Oken and Mabruke's faces at this strange declaration. "European humor does so entertain me!" He beamed at them. "This is my favorite—when something is built by the finest craftsmen, no expense spared, we say it is made of chocolate. Do you see?"

They did.

"The sacred bean is the finest coin in the land. Always has been. Always will be." The prince grinned, amused by their amusement.

Mabruke's gaze drifted skyward once more. "Chocolate wrapped in gold foil," he said quietly, almost to himself. "In a land where money grows on trees. What a splendid journey of discovery this promises to be, Your Highness," he added more clearly, turning to smile at Viracocha.

Oken wondered at his friend's overly calm voice. "Sacred beans to buy a sacred cow?" he said, matching Mabruke's smile.

Prince Viracocha tilted his head to look at Oken, eyebrows furrowed in puzzlement, one corner of his lip curled pleasantly. Then a light sparkled in his dark eyes and he nodded, his smile widening. "Indeed, Lord Oken—that big fellow with the beanstalk. We have a similar tale. My ancestors became quite wealthy trading sacred beans from Tawantinsuyu for sacred cows from Egypt. My father's throne controls the largest herd of cattle on the continent."

"And Egypt controls the distribution of cacao in Europe," Mabruke said thoughtfully, looking at the prince with sharper focus.

"It is a happy arrangement, Prince Mabruke."

"Oh, please, call me Mik." Mabruke turned his full attention to Prince Viracocha, so that the two men were locked eye to eye in silent conversation.

Viracocha reached out a giant hand and patted Mabruke affectionately on the shoulder. "Mik, my European companions usually just call me 'Lucky.'"

"So be it," Mabruke said. He touched Oken lightly on the back. "Call this one Scott."

CHAPTER ELEVEN

BOARDING THE *Mixcomitl* was soundly different from boarding in Casablanca, where the boarding ramp reaching up into the sky had seemed insubstantial for the task. Oken rather suspected that was the beginning of Mabruke's discomfort with flying. Disembarking at the island aerodrome at Wat'a Mona had been no better, with wind making the ramp sway. *Mixcomitl,* however, was moored to a wide boulevard of stone arching upward. Statues of pumas crouched atop the walls on either side. Their teeth were gold and they had ruby eyes. Living guards in jade armor were stationed between these, with puma designs painted on their faces and helmets. They saluted Prince Viracocha as he walked past.

Oken was pleased to see how casually Mabruke strolled alongside the prince. His friend was showing the more usual signs of his enjoyment of travel, the pleasure at the journey's anticipation. Oken turned his focus to memorizing the elaborate creature before them, layers of golden wing-sails amid blackened lines, bobbing ever so slightly at his mooring as though eager to return to open flight. As they got closer, Oken could see that every surface was engraved with the same wild and furious designs, coiled and swirling and outlandishly different.

They were preceded by a dozen nude porters, painted as a matched flock of brightly colored birds, carrying their luggage. Oken knew he was going to enjoy this.

He immediately appreciated the interior of the prince's Quetzal, larger and grander in every scale, mostly consisting of the ubiquitous bamboo. Oken was especially pleased that, in addition to greater size, the lounge and bridge were combined. There were two engine pits, one on either side of the bridge dais at the nose, backing the claim about the aeroship's speed.

A brace of tall pipes and painted drums awaited the musicians on a pair of balconies on either side of the bridge windows. Beaded curtains covered the arched entrances to the crew positions. The bird perches were wooden carvings of nude women, painted in macaw colors, kneeling, heads bowed and hands raised up, with palms spread wide for the birds to rest upon. Three of these knelt facing the broad front windows, so the birds could see the same view as the pilots. The carpets strewn across the deck were red and gold on black, woven variations of the imperial puma in fatal embrace with a condor.

"What a delightful change from the standard," Oken said. "A much more comfortable way to fly."

"Yes," Viracocha said happily. "I do so love the music of flying. It is too quiet in the corridors of the standard Quetzal, don't you find?"

Oken agreed. "The music gets into the blood. I discovered that on our flight here."

"*Hara'wi*—the sacred music—this is the heartbeat of the Quetzal. Without *hara'wi*, he is just a machine." Viracocha's voice was strangely gentle. He gazed over at the bridge and the view from the windows with an expression of deep fondness. "You are the first Egyptians I have brought on board. My father disapproves. He fears you will steal the secrets of the Quetzal, and sell them to the world."

"Your secrets are safe with me," Oken said quietly. "I already understand why they cannot be stolen. No one else in the world can do what Tawantinsuyu has done. No one else could build one, nor could anyone else train the pilots and avian navigators as Tawantinsuyu trains them."

"My father would be pleased to hear this," Viracocha said. "I do not think, however, that I will tell him how you came to know it." His dark eyes were slightly hooded as he spoke, looking at Oken.

Oken knew from Viracocha's expression that the prince was not referring to the *Mixcomitl*.

"I have my own agents. Very loyal agents."

Oken bowed slightly in acknowledgment of the prince's meaning. "Loyalty is a most valuable asset. It can make a poor man into a king."

Viracocha nodded. "And a king into a poor man."

Mabruke strolled over to the lounge area and stretched himself out comfortably on the closest divan. Coverlets and pillows were piled about the bamboo furnishings, with the puma-condor design woven in rich fabrics.

As if out of nowhere, a young woman appeared, carrying a bamboo tray with a jug and three brightly painted bamboo cups, carved and lacquered as thin as the finest porcelain, almost translucent. The handles were slender female forms with painted breasts. The woman carrying the tray was painted to match the cups. The silver circlet on her brow bore the white jade profile of a rabbit with bared fangs and a forked tongue. She set the tray on the table at Mabruke's elbow, bowed to him gracefully, turned, and disappeared.

This time Oken was watching from the corner of his eye and saw her slip behind a tapestry of feathers and gold thread. He smiled, remembering another entrance hidden behind a tapestry. "What does your brother think of *Mixcomitl*?" he said casually.

A sneer flickered across Viracocha's face. "The Inheritor is not allowed to fly. Neither is our father, the Inca. It is considered unlucky. The only emperor of Tawantinsuyu ever to board a Quetzal was killed, struck by lightning on his first flight. He crashed into a temple of the wind gods, and the high temple courts made it law."

Oken smiled at Viracocha. "I have also discovered the benefits of being at a remove from my father's throne."

Viracocha did not respond to that. He sat down on a larger, wider seat clearly designed for him, and picked up the choclatl jug. He lifted the lid, caressing the breasts on the handle with his thumb while swirling the jug gently. He closed his eyes to sniff the aromatic steam rising up. "Excellent," he said pleasantly. He filled the three cups carefully, pouring from a height to make the foam rise up to the rim. The warm scent of fine choclatl filled the lounge.

Viracocha raised his cup in salute. The glyphs on his cup matched those on his feathered collar of rank. "Gentlemen, you will find that a good potato vodka added to hot choclatl provides an excellent way to spend an evening!"

Mabruke stared into his cup thoughtfully, as though reading something in the foam. "Have you considered adding a bit of vanilla?"

"Let us try it, Mik. Let us try it." Viracocha clapped his hands sharply.

The same woman appeared, falling gracefully to her knees and bowing her head before the prince, hands folded in her lap.

"Find a bit of vanilla from the galley, little one. The prince here would like some in his choclatl."

She nodded without answering, and disappeared behind the tapestry once more.

"It will take a moment," Viracocha said. "The galley is a distance for Runa's feet." He sipped at his own choclatl, gazing out the huge windows at the nose of the bridge. "Runa. She is the Inheritor's eldest child," he said then, more quietly. "Her mother is a slave at the Queen Mother's estate. Pachacuti pretends he is being kind by putting us in each other's care. Runa spies on me for her father, because she believes that pleases him."

"Does it?" Mabruke said.

"Does it what?"

"Does it please him?"

Viracocha scoffed, bitterness twisting one corner of his mouth. "My brother is pleased that she spies on me. He does not care that she is his daughter. Runa and I have great fun deciding what next she will tell him. She is a quick study."

"Does she enjoy flying?" Oken said. "Being on board, I mean?"

"I do not know," Viracocha said with a shrug. "Yet this is something her father, for all his power, will never experience."

"Are we in flight now?" Mabruke said. He looked at the cup in his hands, not out the windows.

"I have not yet given the order for flight," Viracocha said. He fell silent as Runa reemerged from the tapestry, carrying a small tray.

"Ah, thank you, Mademoiselle Runa," Mabruke said, turning the intensity of his smile on her as he took the tray and set it on the table beside him.

After Runa had been caught in Mabruke's gaze for too many seconds, Viracocha said to her, "Runa, go!"

She scurried away, turning her head to look over her shoulder at Mabruke before ducking out of sight.

Mabruke made a show of sniffing the vanilla, eyes closed. He then took a carefully measured spoonful and stirred it into his hot drink. He sipped slowly, swishing it around his mouth before swallowing, as one tastes a fine wine. "Finest quality vanilla. Finest quality!" he said finally. "The two flavors complement each other handsomely. Would you care to try?"

Viracocha leaned forward in his seat to hold his cup out, as did Oken. Mabruke measured and stirred as carefully for them.

As the coffee served in tents in the Atlas Hills had outshone the best coffees of Europe, the choclatl and the vanilla were markedly superior. Oken spoke agreeably. "I am not as familiar as I would wish to be with the degrees of either choclatl or vanilla, yet seriously doubt I will ever taste finer anywhere else in the world."

"You speak the wisdom of innocence," Mabruke said. He sipped at his again, and held his cup up in brief salute. "I, too, have never had better. Let us send our compliments to the galley crew!"

They drank a toast to this. At that moment, the captain of the *Mixcomitl* emerged from the bridge entrance, announced by the gentle tinkle of the beaded curtain parting.

The captain was similar to other crewmen of the Quetzal, in that he was of slight build, like a jockey primed for riding champion racers. His oversized lungs gave his deep-barreled, hardy look a slight sense of disproportion. He was different, larger than life despite the greater size and rank of the noblemen before him. His skin was polished mahogany, and tattooed on every visible bit with bloodred swirls and flame-colored curls flowing around upside-down faces and eyes. His kneecaps and elbows were condor heads, and a serpent in vivid green inks coiled around his neck and up his cheek, with the serpent's head swallowing the Third Eye on his forehead. The Third Eye was done with such living detail that Oken expected to see it blink. Over these the captain wore only a short kilt of carved jade tiles that made a gentle clicking sound as he moved. He was barefoot and walked with the focused grace of a bird in flight. He bowed before the prince, and Oken fancied for an instant that he heard the sound of folding wings.

"We are ready for flight, then, Hanaq Pacha?"

Captain Hanaq Pacha straightened up, met the prince's eyes, and nodded.

"Excellent!" Viracocha turned to Mabruke. "Ready?"

Mabruke shrugged, leaning back into the divan and stretching his legs out in front of him. "By all means, let us take wing."

Viracocha nodded to the captain, who turned and sprang across the bridge to the captain's seat. On an unheard signal, the bridge crew emerged as one through the beaded curtains, settling themselves into crew positions in unison, including the cyclers leaping up to the saddles of their wheeled steeds. The musicians appeared on the balconies at the same signal, each one going to her instrument with a single flourish. Their nude bodies were painted to match the colors and patterns of the macaws, and their hair was spread across their shoulders like shining capes. When the human crew were all in place, the macaws flew in, emerging from round openings high in the chamber.

Mabruke had set his cup back on the table with a curious gesture, pushing it back so that he could not see the level of the choclatl in it. "What can you tell us of our destination?" Oken said to Viracocha.

"Quillabamba." The prince seemed pleased. "My mother's estate is there. We cannot fly over the temples, not anywhere near the sacred lake or Tiwanaku, so we will go to the queen's mansion first, to get different transportation."

"Indeed?" Mabruke said. Oken could see by the tilt of his head that this fact had struck Mabruke as new and useful information. "Why is that?"

"It is considered to be spying on the gods in the temples and the Inca in his palace."

"Is it, now?" Mabruke said thoughtfully. "I can appreciate that." He glanced at Oken, meeting his eye with a knowing look.

"We will be several days in flight, gentlemen, depending on how often we stop to look at the sights along the way." Viracocha gestured around at the *Mixcomitl* with his cup. "Meanwhile, I think you will find the accommodations and cuisine on board to be far superior to your Quetzal ride over the Atlantic."

"I'm already more comfortable," Oken said, stretching back in his seat to demonstrate. "I think this is going to be a fine vacation."

Flight was smooth and power sang through the aeroship in harmony with the musicians. The musicianship was superior even to the musicians of Verdi's opera. Perhaps it was because Verdi's musicians were hindered by wearing clothes, Oken thought to himself as he admired the women and their inspired performance.

Mabruke stood, casually brushing down the folds of his kilt. "I

think I'll have a nap," he said to Viracocha, barely audible above
the music.

Oken pulled himself to his feet.

Viracocha clapped his hands sharply, and Runa at once popped
out from behind her tapestry. Oken was amused. She had obviously been standing there, listening to them.

Viracocha signaled her silently with an elaborate hand gesture
that suggested these two were accustomed to communicating in
the midst of the symphony. Runa bowed, smiling happily, and sprang
past the lounge tables, waving for them to follow her.

Guest quarters were on a deck above the lounge, up a spiral stair
with bamboo steps and railing. The corridor was narrow, although
wider than expected. Their cabin was spacious, with comfortable-
looking beds at either end. An elegant bar, adorned with black and
white feathers in complex patterns, lined one wall. A selection of
Andean wines and beers with exotically adorned labels was lined
up neatly, reflecting in the mirror behind the bar. The wall beside
the exit to the corridor was also mirrored.

"Gentlemen may share or have private cabins, as you wish," Runa
said. She seemed very pleased.

"This will do, mademoiselle," Mabruke said, turning his smile
to her. "Lord Oken is my bodyguard. I sleep more safely when he is
here."

Her dark eyes got big as she looked back and forth between them.
"You are afraid here, with my lord Viracocha as your protector?"

"No, my dear," Mabruke said kindly. "Sometimes he just has to
guard me from bad dreams."

This she apparently understood at once, for the confusion on
her face cleared. She nodded promptly. "This kind of bodyguard is
good." She beamed at them. "My uncle guards me against such demons." She made it sound important, at least to her. "You are ready
for your luggage, if these quarters are suitable?"

"Please, mademoiselle," Oken said.

She bowed gracefully, then sprang away as if dancing to the music of the engines. When the door closed behind her, the volume of the music dropped, becoming only a soothing murmur in the background.

"Definitely an improvement," Mabruke said as he crossed over to the bed farthest from the entry and stretched out on it. "This does seem a most pleasant turn of events. I think I am going to enjoy this. As you said, a fine vacation, most diverting."

"A working vacation," Oken said. "I hope this is not too diverting."

"Nonsense. This is an *ideal* development—Prince Viracocha will, quite literally, carry us over many of the initial obstacles to this assignment."

"How is that? The Queen said it was a temple conspiracy, not in the government."

"We just learned that flight is not allowed over the very temple complex that is most implicated in the Moon project, the Temple of the Moon in Lake Titikaka—the sacred lake. Do you really think the gods are afraid of spies?"

"None that I know of."

"I have the feeling that Prince Viracocha may well be a most useful contact," Mabruke said thoughtfully, gazing upward, almost speaking to himself. "In more ways than one."

"Agreed," Oken said. "This is, at the very least, a most pleasant way to travel."

"Oh, more than that. I think it is likely this prince travels in the kind of circles where ladies wear orchids in their hair."

"Fair warning," Oken said, nodding approval. "By the way, the vanilla was a nice touch. What made you think of that?"

"The vanilla would have produced a telltale scent if there were anything in the choclatl besides cacao and vodka. I did research on that before we left."

Oken nodded gravely, remembering Mabruke's chagrin that he

had been fooled by the drink in a Wild East bar. "Will you be more comfortable here?"

"Yes."

Oken did not speak.

Then Mabruke raised himself up on one elbow, turning to look fully at Oken. "As I told you, I was sleeping poorly. I am better rested now."

Oken considered this. He could see in Mabruke's face that there was more to be said. "What is it?" he said quietly.

Mabruke looked up, distress clear in his eyes. "I am disappointed in myself. There is no question that—" His words stopped as though his mouth had suddenly gone dry. He licked his lips and closed his eyes, turning his face away from Oken. "I find as a result of my recent captivity that I experience an uncontrollable dismay in confined quarters. I have let my training address this as best I can, but fear rides upon Sobak's crocodile tail. I am the ape upon his back, and out of my depth."

"You discovered this on board the Quetzal?"

"I would never have undertaken this journey if I had known!" He sighed heavily. "And now I face the journey home. I had thought it was the flight itself, which I had originally anticipated with such pleasure. Our stay at Wat'a Mona, however, convinced me that it was the size of the cabin on board the Quetzal."

Oken turned on his heel slowly, taking in the measure of the cabin. "Is this space adequate?"

Mabruke nodded. "Indeed, and I find hope returning that I will, in fact, come to enjoy flight, perhaps even as much as I had originally imagined it." He smiled, leaving Oken aware of the strain.

"*Mixcomitl* is the beast who can best Sobak, my friend," Oken said to him. He stood, looking at Mabruke as he considered a plan. "Take a nap," he said. "I'll wake you for dinner."

Oken went to speak to Viracocha.

* * *

"I GOT used to walking the upper ring of the Quetzal on the flight here," Oken said to the prince. "The best part of the journey, I thought. Just sky and ocean out to the horizon. I miss that."

"I have just the thing," Viracocha said at once. "Follow me."

Viracocha called to the captain, "The viewing platform, Hanaq Pacha! My friend and I are going up to the sky."

Better than expected, Oken thought to himself.

The captain called out brisk orders to the cyclers, the Quechua syllables ringing with pride. Hanaq Pacha seemed to appreciate Oken's enthusiasm for *Mixcomitl.* Viracocha stood, hands on his hips, looking up.

The sound of gears shifting in the complex mechanism of the ship's engines was an eager growl of anticipation. Viracocha turned his head and nodded to Oken, then gestured skyward. A circular section of the hull overhead separated, descending in a gentle and controlled spiral that opened out into a bamboo stair. When it reached the deck, the section of the hull that formed the base of the spiral stair buzzed softly as clawed clamps unfolded, curving themselves downward into rings set in the rug.

Gears sang again as the overhead hatch irised open. The brilliant blue sky became visible at the top of the spiral stair, and the rush of wind was loud.

Oken was delighted. "Mik will want to see this when he wakes up."

"What will I see when I wake up?" Mabruke said, emerging from the arched entry. The beaded curtain swirled around him with a tinkle like laughter.

"I've wanted to show you this since we left Madeira," Oken said.

Mabruke joined them, craning his neck to look at the blue sky in the opening. "I heard the engines change pitch, and wondered if something was wrong."

"Follow me," Viracocha said as he stepped onto the spiral stair. The two men followed, looking at the sky.

The hatchway opened to a circular viewing platform on the forehead of the condor. A waist-high railing of woven bamboo strips was just locking into place, complete with safety lines hanging in coils on the uprights. The hatch irised closed once they were clear.

"You must anchor yourself to the platform," Viracocha said, pointing to the coils of rope fastened to the railing posts around the platform. The rope was braided of fine leather, supple and strong. Viracocha demonstrated by taking the closest one from its hook and looping the belted end around his waist. The line was thicker and more densely woven than the others, the buckle shaped as a puma's paw with claws extended.

Mabruke buckled his in place and tugged at the line, testing it.

The Quetzal had slowed enough that there was only a stiff breeze. The sky was clear blue, with a scattering of white clouds on either hand, dappled with sunlight, like sheep grazing the sky. The horizon ahead of them rose steadily—jagged, raw mountain peaks capped with white. In the purple distance these were majestic, sleeping giants of transparent blue, shadowed in violet and crowned with ice, sacred beings from the beginning of the world.

"*Mixcomitl*," Viracocha said proudly. "It means 'Cloud Vessel.' Here, we are one with the heavens."

The view from this vantage, a third eye above the window-eyes, was far grander in impact than Oken had anticipated. His attention, however, was on his friend. Mabruke had, during the first seconds, clung tightly to the railing with both hands as he gazed around. Oken could see, however, that Mabruke was feeling the same changes within himself that Oken had experienced when he first saw such an expanse from such a height.

Viracocha was also focused on Mabruke. When Mabruke looked away from the sky and smiled happily at him, the prince said, "What do you think, my friend?" He spoke with casual volume, accustomed to shouting against the wind.

Mabruke glanced at Oken before answering, eyes sparkling. "Celestial!" he said.

Viracocha touched controls on one of the posts, and a farscope on a viewing stand unfolded from the hull, cleverly assembled from polished bamboo, rising to a comfortable viewing height.

Oken leaned over to the farscope, examining the mechanism that housed and presented the scope.

"It does improve the view," Viracocha said.

Mixcomitl's speed had settled to a slow drift at a lower altitude, making speech more comfortable and the view more entrancing and detailed. Oken surveyed the landscape passing below, terraced fields and shining lines of irrigation channels reflecting the sky. Cities in the larger valleys were laid out in orderly grid patterns, with cattle herds covering the high plateaus, it seemed, in their millions. Villages spread like spilled toy boxes along the narrow shores of rivers, and temples set on hilltops were sacred Andean glyphs set out for the sky to read. The great Andes Range, from this height, was a sea of stone, waves and swells frozen in place, icy foam on their crests, holding green islands up close to the sky, to Inty, Father Sun. Oken could understand Viracocha's easy confidence. Standing here on the brow of the golden condor, he himself felt like a king or an immortal being, floating over the world.

After a time, Oken turned the farscope over to Mabruke. Oken watched him as he bent over the view piece, then relaxed. Immersion in the sky had overwhelmed the reptilian influence of Sobak. Mabruke was recovered. He was once again the eager traveler, thrilled by the journey itself.

Viracocha knew the name of every piece of the landscape below them, speaking as fondly as a man describing his many children and noble ancestors. He leaned his elbows on the railing, pointing from time to time to direct Oken or Mabruke to aim the farscope here or there, telling them stories of what they were seeing.

The Sun set in fiery splendor, rivaled by the wild display of stars as the sky darkened. The Milky Way grew as clear as diamond dust. The Moon rose, pouring silver light over the land below. Mabruke at last pulled his jacket tighter around himself and said to Viracocha, "I'm ready for dinner. What do you say?"

AS PROMISED, the cuisine onboard *Mixcomitl* was superior even to the meals at Wat'a Mona Aerodrome. Viracocha was relaxed and jovial, and he spoke gently to Runa. She was the only one permitted to come to the table while the prince dined with his guests. The other servants, each painted to match Runa's current design, prepared individual plates from dishes on wheeled carts, bowing to Runa as they held each one out for her to carry over to the table, first to the prince, then to Mabruke and to Oken. The other women, working over the steaming dishes on the carts, stood with their backs to the men. Their hair was worn loose, like the musicians, as a black cape spread over bare shoulders.

The musicians had withdrawn to meals in the crew quarters. *Mixcomitl* floated in serene quiet through the night air, enfolding them in their conversation, the clink of dinnerware, and Runa's laughter as Mabruke teased and complimented her. He spoke with her as she served them, addressing her always as "mademoiselle," which seemed to please her.

Oken noted over the course of the evening that Runa's use of Trade changed subtly, becoming more fluid in use and less awkwardly composed. Her vocabulary expanded to include words used by the men in their conversation. Oken also noted the familiar authority with which she managed the women. They responded to her quick commands with practiced ease.

Near the end of the meal, Oken said to her, "Mademoiselle, do you enjoy being so high up in the sky? Do you enjoy flying?"

Runa nodded contentedly as she placed their emptied cups on her tray. "Yes, sir. I am quite at home here."

Viracocha looked at her thoughtfully. "Are you, my child?"

"Yes, Uncle." Her smile was serene.

"Why is that, mademoiselle?" Mabruke said.

She turned her serene smile to her uncle, then to Mabruke. "I feel so very safe up here, sir." She hurried away then with the tray, put it on one of the carts, and sent the women off to the galley, following behind them.

Mabruke watched her leave, then turned back to the table. "You know," he said to them, "I have to agree with the young woman."

"DO YOU trust our Prince Lucky?"

"How can we know in so short a time?" Mabruke said with a shrug. He sat down on his bed and took off his sandals. "I do intend, however, to make the most of our acquaintance while we can."

"The *Mixcomitl* speaks well of his taste, if nothing else," Oken said.

"I am also impressed by his fondness for his niece."

"Runa's name, however, does not speak well of her father."

"Runa is a lovely name. She's a lovely woman."

"A slave-princess. Her name in Quechua means 'person.' Her father is the Inheritor of an empire, yet his daughter is handed off as a servant."

"This is the other side of the world. Perhaps being acknowledged as a person is more than the daughter of a slave would ordinarily have here."

"Slavery," Oken said quietly, almost under his breath.

"She is a lovely woman," Mabruke repeated firmly. "And she is fortunate to be in the care of her uncle rather than her father. We must leave it at that."

"I shall remind myself of where I am."

"And of who you are," Mabruke said, his voice and eyes serious. "Treat her as the princess she is, but never forget that a slave can work for two masters. Whatever the truth about duplicity to her father, she has his ear. What she tells him could be the death of us."

"Yes. A princess and a lady."

"But shake out your boots if she cleans them for you."

Oken chuckled softly. Mabruke had said that so many times in class, a constant reminder that trust is treacherous in their line of work. "I won't forget."

Before turning out the lights in their cabin, Oken rechecked the lock on the entry door. A bell in their cabin chimed when it was unlocked, from either side, and a comfortably audible click sounded when it locked. Oken did not let himself fall asleep until he heard the gentle, relaxed sound of Mabruke snoring.

Good, Oken thought to himself. He fell asleep walking through sky-pastures, with golden condors and the golden puma of the Sun.

CHAPTER TWELVE

A MACAW soared in through the birds' entrance, announced itself with a loud call, and then fluttered down to Hanaq Pacha, landing neatly on the backrest of the captain's seat.

Hanaq Pacha listened intently to the bird's rapid-fire delivery. *Mixcomitl*'s macaws turned to listen as well. The bird fell silent, bobbing his head, and held one foot out to stretch his claws open. He was holding the handle of a talking-knot as small as a cushion tassel. Hanaq Pacha took the talking-knot, bowed to the messenger, and strode over to Viracocha.

Viracocha sat forward in his seat as the captain approached. Hanaq Pacha bowed, showed him the talking-knot, and then gave him a softly spoken translation of the avian patois. Viracocha read the talking-knot with a serious expression, seemed satisfied with it, and stood up from his lounge chair. Hanaq Pacha sprang back to the bridge. At his signal, the *hara'wi* changed, gradually slowing down. The pilots signaled the macaws, who took wing and soared up and out through their private exits.

The pilots then made a series of rapid changes in the multiple levers controlling the lines to the sails. Oken found the dance of their hands over the control panel entrancing because he could not comprehend the pattern. He had spent nights going over and over a single moment of their workings in memory, yet the pattern eluded him.

Hanaq Pacha spoke briefly to the messenger perched on the backrest as he returned the talking-knot. The messenger was gone in a flash of color.

Cloud wisps passing by the windows showed that *Mixcomitl* was slowing.

Viracocha remained standing. "A Mayan patrol Quetzal has requested my attention, gentlemen."

"Is that something unusual?" Mabruke said.

"They patrol their forests regularly against tree-pirates. I have been of help from time to time. It is good for border relations, and we, too, must protect our trees."

"Especially the ones with money growing on them," Mabruke said.

Viracocha liked that. "Especially those."

Oken settled himself into focused attention, scanning the view outside with slow deliberation, marking the way the pilots so intently watched the birds in flight before them. Seen from high above, the forests were a sea of green to the far horizon, unbroken save by the gleam of wide, sluggish rivers looping through.

"If I could have your indulgence, gentlemen," Viracocha said. "I would prefer that the Mayan crew remain unaware of your presence."

Oken and Mabruke rose from the lounge chairs. "Quite understandable," Mabruke said. "We will withdraw at once."

"If you simply stand to either side of the windows, you can see and hear, yet remain unnoticed. You may find this exchange interesting, perhaps even amusing."

Oken and Mabruke strolled over to the assigned spots. The pilots ignored them, intent on the view outside.

The Mayan Quetzal emerged just below and to their starboard, trailing cloud wisps. He was close to invisible until he had risen fully clear of the cloud bank. Oken immediately thought of Zaydane and his disappearing tents. The Quetzal was painted to look like a bit of cloud himself, difficult to see directly despite his remarkably complex sails, themselves of a mirrored fabric that reflected the sky. The out-flying navigation birds had settled in cubbies along the underside of the aeroship, and Oken could not discern the breed.

The macaws returned, settling onto their perches and craning their necks to see the albatross loop around to return to their own entrances in *Mixcomitl*'s hull.

"Won't their bird tell the Mayans that we're onboard?" Oken said to the prince.

Viracocha replied without turning his gaze from the approaching vessel. "We must take that chance. He had a message, and may not have noticed you. I have many servants on board."

Mabruke flashed Oken a knowing smile.

Mixcomitl drifted slowly toward the cloudlike Quetzal, while it rose steadily to match their altitude. Oken could finally discern that the aeroship in its nets was dolphin-shaped, with lines of nozzles where a dolphin would show teeth in his smile.

Prince Viracocha folded his arms across his chest, standing at ease as he watched the Mayan vessel maneuver until it floated at rest a mere hundred cubits or less away, nose to nose with *Mixcomitl*, as if these two were also engaged in some private, animal form of communication.

"Any closer and we risk tangling lines," Viracocha said quietly. "You should be able to see them well enough, however."

"Yes," Mabruke said.

Oken saw that his friend was devouring the Mayan Quetzal with his eyes, his dark face alight with a child's delight at a brand-new toy. At this close range, the captain and pilots were visible in the bridge windows. They stood looking back at Viracocha with equal intensity. Their outfits were alike enough to be uniforms, although the captain had a headdress of feathers, as well as jade bands on his wrists and forearms. The captain's tattoos were less flamboyant than Hanaq Pacha's.

"What is he named, this one?" Oken said quietly to Viracocha.

"The Quetzal."

"In Trade he is named *Snatcher*."

"How do they stop the tree-pirates when they snatch them?"

"Fire."

They watched in silence as the messenger macaw flew toward them from *Snatcher*. The bird emerged onto the bridge, returning to his perch on the captain's seat. His message to Hanaq Pacha was more involved this time, including a number of sudden head rolls.

Apparently Viracocha also understood the bird's message. He gave clipped orders in Quechua. Hanaq Pacha spoke to the messenger, who then flung himself into the air, soared up to the exit, and was gone. They watched him return to *Snatcher*, emerge onto the bridge, and flutter down to the captain, who listened closely, then looked directly out at Viracocha. He signaled with both fists touching the eye on his forehead; then he returned to his command seat.

Viracocha unfolded his arms and strolled back to the lounge.

Oken watched as *Snatcher* returned to his pirate hunt, melting down into the clouds.

"Most interesting!" Mabruke said. "Most interesting, indeed."

"The captain lost his prey in the cloud cover," Viracocha said. "He wanted to know if we had seen them. We may see them yet. I have told Hanaq Pacha to take us farther from the Mayan borderlands. I do not care to deal with pirates on this trip."

"Do they catch many pirates?" Oken said, settling back into his chair. He picked up his choclatl cup and sipped at it.

"More every year. The market for Mayan wood grows faster than the trees."

"Tawantinsuyu is smart to grow money on its trees instead of selling them as lumber," Mabruke said amiably.

Viracocha saluted Mabruke with his choclatl cup.

* * *

OKEN AWOKE to the surging throb of *Mixcomitl's* engines running at a burst of full speed. He sat up and saw Mabruke sitting on the edge of his bed, robe and slippers on. He was freshly shaved, his makeup in place.

"Good morning," Mabruke said pleasantly. "That was only a change in the engines."

"Actually, it was the music." Oken stretched luxuriously, then reached for his robe and pulled it on. "It got louder. You are up and dressed early."

"I promised myself that today I would watch the Sun as he clears the horizon from this vantage point. I have been awake for some time."

"HOY, GENTLEMEN!" Viracocha was standing behind the captain's seat, arms folded over his chest. His suit was moss green, with a simple geometric embroidered in gold thread. The pattern gleamed in the morning sunshine, emphasizing his superb physique even more than the impeccable fit. He did not change his stance, looking out at the skies ahead as he spoke. "Runa will bring your breakfast if you wish."

Oken went over to stand beside the prince. "Quite a view, isn't it? I never get tired of it myself."

Oken noticed then that a panel in the hull between the nose windows had been pulled aside, revealing what had seemed, at first glance, to be another window. The view, however, was different. The clouds were thicker and something oddly angular moved among them. Oken realized all at once what he was seeing. "Is that *Snatcher* following us?" he said to Viracocha.

"No. The birds say he will not name himself."

"Is that unusual?" Oken said.

"This is *Mixcomitl*. Everyone talks to *Mixcomitl*. We can lie to each other—birds cannot."

"Pirates?"

"Pirates paint themselves to be invisible among the treetops. Border patrols are the only fleet allowed to use sky paint. A patrol ship would have identified himself to *Mixcomitl* at once. A Mayan patrol ship would never follow me this far into Tawantinsuyu territory."

Mabruke had come over to join them. He stood listening, looking more at their faces than at the mirror-view.

The macaw to Hanaq Pacha's left rolled his head around and looked at the captain from this upside-down view, then muttered at him. He straightened with a shake of his feathers, ruffling his neck up and smoothing it down.

Hanaq Pacha turned and spoke in rapid Quechua to the prince.

Viracocha's brow drew down in consternation. "That is curious." He put his hands on his hips, tilting his head as he looked at the mirror. "Senga has just asked why the Quetzal behind us stinks like a swamp-brew."

Mabruke gave a terrible start and put his hand on Viracocha's shoulder, leaning close to his face. The restrained calm as he spoke was more alarming than his words. "Tell the captain to get *Mixcomitl* as far away from that Quetzal as he can—quickly! Quickly! We may already be too late!"

The urgency in Mabruke's command was clear.

Viracocha responded at once, barking out an order. Hanaq Pacha whistled sharply, clapped his hands, and then waved them upward. The macaws disappeared in a flash of color, reappearing outside in swift flight toward the albatross ahead.

The musicians changed the *hara'wi* to a fierce and driving beat, and the cyclers leaned into their task. The whirr of the gears growled and rose in a song of power. The pilots' hands were a near-blur on the controls, resetting the sails.

"Can *Mixcomitl* outrun alkhemy?" Mabruke said. He was nearly shouting. "Our lives are the prize for winning or losing this race!"

"When I inherited him, my great-uncle told me that *Mixcomitl* could outrun anything but lightning and hate—and I have doubled his speed since then."

The macaws returned, fluttering down to their perches. They shifted their feet from side to side, clicking their beaks at the captain. He gave orders to the pilots, and a moment later, they could feel *Mixcomitl* bank to starboard.

Mabruke was watching the rearview mirror as intently as Viracocha. After long minutes had passed and the image continued to fade into the clouds, more difficult to discern, he said, "How far behind would you estimate him to be?"

Viracocha repeated the question to Hanaq Pacha in Quechua. The captain answered with calm certainty.

"A quarter league, and falling behind."

"Then likely we are safe," Mabruke said. "At this range, wind dispersal would make them as vulnerable as we."

Even Hanaq Pacha looked at Mabruke, curious.

"*Kaebshon*," Mabruke said matter-of-factly, expecting this to explain.

"Farts?" Oken translated the Egyptian. "You mean methane?"

Mabruke nodded. "Thank you. Just at that moment I could not recall the Trade term."

Viracocha did not look amused.

"Explaining will take some talking," Mabruke said to the prince. "When it's quieter."

Viracocha shook his head. He gave lengthy instructions to Hanaq Pacha, then gestured for Mabruke and Oken to follow him. He led them to the spiral stair opposite their guest quarters. The entry was covered with a curtain of faceted crystal beads on golden chains. Viracocha held this aside for them, letting them enter ahead of him.

The parlor was big, fitted comfortably for conversation and bright with morning sunshine from a pair of large portholes. "Make yourselves comfortable, gentlemen." Viracocha strode past them to a desk between the windows. He pulled a series of small levers set in the bamboo trim above the desk, and a door of solid bamboo panels slid across the entry, immediately cutting the sound from the bridge.

Oken let Mabruke settle first, on a lounge chair similar to the ones below. Viracocha's chair was larger, more sturdily built, and embossed with the imperial seal of Tawantinsuyu.

Oken chose a seat that let him see both men's faces, Mabruke's and Viracocha's.

"Explain," Viracocha said as he sat down. "How did you recognize that Quetzal, and what is methane?"

"I did not recognize the Quetzal," Mabruke said.

"Then how did you know they were a threat?"

"The bird said he smelled like a swamp-brew. You said the Mayan patrols fight with fire. That could only have been methane, which is produced in vats called 'swamp-brew.'"

Oken heard the professor in Mabruke's voice. He settled back to watch.

Viracocha said nothing, waiting for more.

"Ah," Mabruke said thoughtfully. "Let me retrace my thoughts for you. The patrol fights pirates with fire, is that correct?"

The prince nodded.

"Do Mayans power their Quetzals with methane?"

"No. I don't know. I have never heard of methane. Quetzals fly with *Tlalocene.*"

"Indeed," Mabruke said. He sat forward. "Methane is related to *Tlalocene,* which is named 'hydrogen' in Trade. Methane, however, is far more volatile."

"*Tlalocene* will explode if not treated with proper respect," Viracocha said.

Oken was amused to see these two transform so completely into happy teacher and eager student. He was getting an interesting impression of this foreign prince.

"Indeed, but *Tlalocene* honors your respect more resolutely than methane," Mabruke said.

"You are saying that the patrol uses methane to destroy pirate Quetzals?" the prince said.

"There is only one reason a Quetzal would reek of methane at this altitude. It is the source of their fire-attack."

"A patrol Quetzal would also stink of methane."

"If they were preparing to attack, yes. Methane is too volatile in storage. They would generate it as needed in the same fashion that *Tlalocene* is produced for flotation, but only during the final stage of preparing that fire for attack—swamp-brew."

Viracocha said nothing. His expression made it clear that he understood.

A chime over the door rang. When the door slid open, *Mixcomitl's* song was suddenly loud behind Runa, standing at the threshold. Viracocha signaled her with brisk hand gestures. She bowed and turned away, disappearing down the spiral stair. The door closed again.

"Hanaq Pacha will take us directly to my mother's estates," Viracocha said. "I can be more certain of your security there than if we go to Qusqo as I had planned." He shook his head slowly, with a look of great sadness. "That was a killer Quetzal. There is no other explanation. I did not know I had such enemies."

"You don't," Mabruke said. "You were not the target."

"An attack on *Mixcomitl* is a declaration of war against Tawantinsuyu," Viracocha said matter-of-factly. "To protect themselves in such a situation, Maya Land would have to ally with Tawantinsuyu against Egypt."

The prince sat, looking back at Mabruke's steady gaze. "Let us then be glad we have outrun them."

"Indeed."

Viracocha's face became even more thoughtful. "There is a drinking song of the Mayan Air Patrolman," he said quietly. "I translated it into Trade when I was a boy." He then recited, in a gentle tone:

> The Eagle and the Dragonfly
> Met in the sky one day.
> Said the Eagle to the Dragonfly,
> "How can you fly that way?"
>
> The Dragonfly flew silently,
> Her shining wings a-blur.
> She did not care to speak to things
> With feathers or with fur.
>
> The Eagle followed eagerly.
> He could not comprehend
> The hard and shiny promise
> Of that Dragonfly's rear end.
>
> The Dragonfly flew faster.
> The Eagle followed after—
> Ah! I see by your sad laughter
> That you know how this must end!

When he had finished this recitation, his expression was most serious.

"I see your point," Mabruke said.

"I determined as a child that I would never be the Dragonfly," Viracocha said. "That is why I had *Mixcomitl*'s jets improved."

"I like a man who knows how to plan ahead," Oken said with genuine feeling.

CHAPTER THIRTEEN

MIXCOMITL DRIFTED slowly, as though reluctant, toward the mooring tower at the imperial family's private aerodrome on the Queen Mother's estates in Quillabamba Valley.

"It's called Xochicacahuatl, that is, 'Flowery Cacao,'" Viracocha said to Mabruke. "For the cacao orchards here." He was standing in his usual pose behind the captain, watching the approach. "This is my home," he added, sounding both pleased and troubled.

"My mother is here," he went on, "but I do not think we will see her."

"I hope she is well." Mabruke, standing next to him, leaned closer to be heard.

"She does not approve of my interest in Egypt, in the world beyond Tawantinsuyu."

They were descending into a lush green valley set between rocky mountains, a short distance around the river bend from a city of white stucco walls and red tile roofs in the next valley. A single white tower stood between the river and the rock wall of the mountain behind. The windows were dark and still. Cacao orchards climbed the mountainsides in orderly rows, with stone huts among the trees. Herds of goats and llamas and sacred vicuña grazed on the mountainsides above the river, tended by men wearing ponchos and black hats. Beyond the little city of small, square buildings, greening fields climbed in neatly staggered steps up the slopes. Young women, with brilliantly colored skirts hoisted up around their waists, tended these fields like patient birds, bending and picking. The narrow streets were busy with people coming and going from the open market in the main square.

The estate itself was on a slope out of sight from the city. Within a high stone wall was a compound of buildings, gardens, yards, barns, and stables around an imposing, three-story manor of gray blocks. No block of stone in these walls was the same size or shape as another, yet each was larger than those in temple walls in Memphis, fitted together with a mastery of the masonry art that defied logic. The purpose, however, was quite logical. The irregular shapes withstood the stresses of the earth groaning and shifting far better than buildings built neatly of blocks. Stacking blocks of identical size and shape seemed child's play next to this intricate fabric woven of solid stone.

The mooring tower was a pyramid painted red with designs in green, yellow, and black, set back from the river and to one side of the estate. A paved yard around it also enclosed a ball court and viewing stands. Young men were at practice, with some people watching them. When *Mixcomitl* reached the tower, the game stopped and everyone stood, arms raised in salute.

The birds had informed the staff that the prince was arriving. Apparently, this was an event. Guards stood between the stone pumas on the sides of the boarding ramp. In the center of the ramp was a group of men in the Inca's livery attire, red kilts and black sandals, with black feathers as stiff headdress. Late-afternoon breezes were cooling and the light was turning gold. The captain of the guards, at the head of this group, had red gloves and a single red feather. Each man had the imperial seal tattooed on his forehead in red. They went to one knee, heads bowed, when Viracocha stepped out of the golden Quetzal.

Viracocha greeted the captain of the guard with a salute and a grim smile; then he bade the kneeling men to rise. They stood as one and shouted a welcome to their prince that struck Oken as similar to the chorus in the opera. Verdi had caught the nuance of the native voice.

The passageway between the mooring tower and the manor went down in zigzag staircases through the interior of the pyramid to an underground corridor lit by Egyptian spinglass lamps and carpeted with rugs of the same red, black, and gold of *Mixcomitl*'s lounge. Incense had been lit along the way ahead of them, in censers shaped as various demons and gods of Xibalba, the inner world of the people here. Each little statue held the censer bowl in its hands as if offering it in temple.

A pair of guards stood on either side of the entry and saluted as the prince's party went past. Oken, lagging slightly behind, noted that many of these guards seemed to have pleased expressions behind their soldierly calm. The prince's arrival was genuinely welcome here.

They emerged in a paved courtyard, walled in with the same complex stonework. Arched entries led to side corridors and gardens. Guards stood waiting at each entry. Viracocha went directly to the largest archway across the courtyard, which led to another closed corridor, identical to the first. This led to tall doors that swung inward as the prince strode toward them, and a high-ceilinged entry hall, larger than the entire common room at Oken's family castle. On one long side were glass doors on brass hinges, standing open at that moment, letting in the fresh breezes and the light of the Sun sinking behind the mountains.

Obsidian censers, shaped as warriors holding fire in their fists, stood against the side walls. Furniture of semiprecious minerals and golden fittings lined the wall opposite the open glass doors. Couches and chairs were set on either side of a large receiving throne of porphyry carved as a reed raft, supported by a pair of snarling pumas.

No one sat on the porphyry throne or waited for them in the hall except the guards at the side doors. Viracocha led them past the glass doorway to a smaller side door that opened onto a perfectly groomed terraced garden, with dozens of flowering plants in ceramic pots and little pools, walled in by a solid hedge cut in staggered waves. The pots were of various sizes, shaped and painted as fat frogs seated on toadstools. Living frogs leaped off moss beds and splashed into the pools.

Oken glanced up. *Mixcomitl* floated high above, gleaming with hard, gold light against the blue sky. Stony mountainsides, misted in mauve, enclosed the view on both sides.

The bamboo gate in the hedge opened to the rear door of the manor proper. The door was an ancient carving in deep relief, of masterful design and work. The founder of Tawantinsuyu, Manco Capac, was shown in ecstatic communion with Inty, the divine Sun, rising from the mound of first creation in the sacred lake, Titikaka.

Oken was reminded of a similar image, half a world away, in the Temple of Rae in Memphis, where the Sun rises over the mound of first creation, newly emerged from the waters of Nun, wakened by the cry of Geb, the Great Cackler.

This back door to the manor opened on another long corridor, extending equally to their left and right. These side corridors were not lit. Their depths were revealed only by reflected gleams on golden fittings.

Viracocha took the left, striding more swiftly as though eager for the final destination. Oken and Mabruke lengthened their strides to keep pace with him, as did the retinue following quietly behind.

At a doorway third from the end, Viracocha stopped and the

door swung inward. A fragrance of incense, fresh straw, and flowers poured over them as they followed him inside.

They found themselves at the bottom of a spiral staircase. The steps were jade, carved with a wave pattern. The railing was a serpent beaded with multicolored crystals, held up at every turn of the spiral by a golden serpent-staff, the railing in his mouth and his tail resting on a jade step.

Another double row of servants waited at the top of this stair, kneeling, heads bowed.

"Runa will take care of your luggage," Viracocha said to Mabruke and Oken. He sighed, shaking his head unhappily. "I must speak with the Queen Mother." He sighed again and strode away, down the darkened corridor on the other side of the stairs. The guards and servants rose up and hurried after him.

Runa was waiting for them in the foyer to the guest quarters, standing as calmly as if she had had the entire day to prepare for their arrival. A dozen or more maids were behind her, wearing only small red skirts and paint of the imperial seal on their tawny skin. They were kneeling, heads bowed, their loose black tresses falling in simple waves over bare shoulders.

Runa gestured toward a narrow entry with a curtain of crystal beads. Oken lifted the curtain aside so Mabruke, then Runa and her attendants, could enter their quarters. He followed last, letting the beaded curtain fall back into place with an excited trill of crystal laughter.

Their guest apartments were magnificent. There was no other term. Even Mabruke was gazing around in surprise. Their royal suite at Marrakech was servants' quarters by comparison, and this was just the parlor. The floor and walls were green tile. The ceiling was lapis with golden stars. The furnishings were carved from a pale and luminescent green stone, piled with cushions in shades of yellow. The daybed was a long leaf shape, held up by stone lizards. The side tables and footstools were turtles with flattened shells.

The chairs were seashells resting on the backs of arching fish. The animals had mother-of-pearl eyes that stared at them as they came in.

"You should be comfortable here, sirs," Runa said, gesturing around. She pointed to the right-hand side, and an arched entry with a beaded curtain of blue and purple crystal. "That is your suite, Prince Mabruke."

She pointed to the opposite side. The beaded curtain was in green and blue. "That is for you, Lord Oken. Is this satisfactory? Or do you wish to be together, as you were before?"

Oken looked at Mabruke for instructions. Mabruke shrugged. "I am likely safe enough from the demons of my dreams here on solid ground, mademoiselle. Perhaps Scott will find occasion to enjoy some solitude after such a long journey in my company."

Oken also knew that his friend was giving him the freedom to share his bed with one of these nude lovelies if he wished. Oken considered this as he nodded at Mabruke.

"Your luggage will be here quickly," Runa said. "Do you wish for us to unpack for you?"

"Mademoiselle, I am certain that you have much to attend to yourself," Mabruke said. "Scott and I will fend for ourselves quite well."

"Very well, sirs." Runa seemed reluctant to leave, and stood looking around the room for inspiration. Then she bowed to them and clapped for the girls to follow her. They sprang to their feet and stood behind her.

She clapped again, more loudly, and more maids came hurrying out of the side rooms, slipping so skillfully between the strings of the bead curtains that they made barely a rustle, despite their clear haste.

Once the last patter of bare feet had faded into silence, Mabruke spread his hands wide, gesturing around. "Quite something, isn't it." He sounded pleased.

Oken agreed. He went through the bead curtain to his side, and found himself equally astonished by the beauty and opulence there. The tiles were a soft pearl gray, the furnishings were creamy soapstone, carved as women in elegant repose or curled up provocatively, each lovingly rendered. The bed rested on a pair of oversized beauties stretched out on their sides as if sleeping there, their hands gracefully folded under their heads. Shelves of soapstone, carved as curling waves, lined one wall, with two women kneeling, foreheads resting on their knees, and their hair falling forward over their hands. These proved to be trunks, the tops sliding to one side at a gentle touch. The women's eyes were closed, less intrusive than the staring eyes of the animals in the parlor.

The chandelier was Egyptian spinglass. A woman's torso emerged from the ceiling with a shining globe in her outstretched hands.

Oken was impressed. "Not much like home," he said to the stone ladies. "Not like home at all."

There were no windows as such. Round holes pierced the outer wall in a spiral pattern, letting in afternoon sunshine and breezes. The holes were only a couple of inches across. Oken counted forty-two. Velvet drapes, the color of ivory, were held back by a pair of waist-high ladies. He did not think he would miss having a view. He liked the security of limited access.

The bathroom was similarly designed. Ladies coiled around the rim of the bathing pool and supported the basins. The fittings were of gold. The walls were mirrored, reflecting multitudes of women. Oken smiled at his many selves among the stone beauties, and went out.

Mabruke was not in the parlor. Oken went into his room and found him stretched out comfortably on the bed. The room was similarly fitted to Oken's, different in that the stone was black basalt and obsidian, and the figures were men. The openings in the outer wall spiraled in the opposite direction.

"I could definitely get used to living in this kind of style," Mabruke said.

"If this is just the Queen Mother's estate, I can't imagine what the palace must be like!"

Mabruke raised himself up on one elbow. "Once I have changed clothes, I want to see more of this magnificent place."

CHAPTER FOURTEEN

"YOU BRING alien demons into my house and you expect me to greet them!" The Queen Mother hurled these words at Viracocha as soon as he entered her room.

"They are not demons, Mama," the prince said patiently. "They are sons of kings."

She waved away the maids who were rubbing oil onto her bare skin, sending them scurrying off.

"Demons have kings." She spat the words out, rage clear in her aged face.

The Queen Mother had been beautiful once, an Andean beauty of the first order, with broad hips for childbearing and large, full breasts to nourish the children. Twelve pregnancies and the ravages of time had not been kind to her. Her gray hair was braided with gold thread and coiled to cover the thinning spots. The lines and folds of her face exaggerated her every expression, turning her into a final caricature of herself. Thick gold bands covered her neck, forearms, and ankles, with skin bulging out around them.

Viracocha loved her with proper devotion, even now. Her disapproval hurt him. It did not, however, alter his belief that Tawantin-suyu was *of* the world, neither apart from nor above it. His birthright was the freedom to explore and to learn. He knew, also, that she had seen too many of her children slain in the name of the civilization that had made her an empress. Clinging to the glorious past was the only solace she had.

"My friends are not demons, Mama. They are good men. We will not disturb you."

"They are *here*," she said, her anger hot. The Queen Mother was known to maintain a rage for days and days without relenting. "*That* disturbs me."

"I had to bring them here, Mama. They are here under the protection of Tawantinsuyu, and twice now attempts have been made on their lives."

Through hooded eyes, she glared at him.

"They will be safe here," Viracocha continued, despite the churning he felt inside at the rage radiating from his mother. "When I find who is behind this, I will come back and take them away from here."

"Hurry," she said sharply.

"The second attempt would have destroyed *Mixcomitl* and me along with them, Mama!" He fought the urge to shout at her. "Would you have me dead just to be rid of strangers?"

She had no answer, but turned her heated gaze from him. "Do what you must. They will be safe here in my house."

"Thank you, Mama." He bent and kissed her forehead, then turned and marched himself out. He wanted to smash something, but he just walked fast and hard through the echoing stone corridors to his private office. He thrust the beaded curtain aside so violently that it smashed against the doorframe with an outraged noise of breaking crystals.

CHAPTER FIFTEEN

OKEN AND Mabruke were just emerging from their rooms when Viracocha returned. His manner was intense, and dismay made his lips tight. "I will have to leave you here for a few days, my friends. I hope that is not inconvenient."

Oken looked over at Mabruke. Mabruke shrugged. "We should be quite comfortable here. What is the problem?"

"I have to find out who was in that Quetzal, and why they were preparing to fire on us. I have to find out who sent that assassin to Zulia. I have to go to the palace to do this, so I cannot take you with me. You will be safer here, anyway. The security that guards the Queen Mother will protect you well. Runa will stay close and see that you are cared for."

"I am sure Mademoiselle Runa will be a most charming hostess in your absence," Mabruke said, his voice serious. "You are on an important mission, but watch your back, my friend. These people have proved that they will kill *you* as well if you get in their way."

"Then they have taken on one enemy too many," Viracocha said. "When I find them, they will learn that."

He turned and strode away, his private guard hurrying to keep up.

"Sirs, if you would care to come with me?" A soft voice behind them made both men start and turn around.

An elderly Andean stood there, having appeared as if from the air. He was graying at the temples, and slightly stooped. The imperial seal tattooed on his forehead had begun to run at the edges, and his face was lined. He stood with simple dignity, clad only in the household kilt and sandals. "I am Qusmi, Madam's household manager. I am instructed to make you as comfortable as possible." The lines of his face showed that he had smiled often in his life, and that he laughed easily.

"A pleasure, Mr. Qusmi," Mabruke said. "Just being here is comfortable. We put ourselves happily in your charge."

Qusmi bowed. "It is easy to become lost here. There are many doors and many rooms. May I show you the way to the dining hall?"

"Indeed, Mr. Qusmi!" Mabruke said. "You have quite read my mind!"

"That is my job, sir," Qusmi said. "I am very good at my job, sir, if I may be permitted to say so."

"Indeed, sir. Indeed," Mabruke said. "Lead on, my good man. Lead on!"

Qusmi bowed, and turned to lead them down the corridor.

"*Qusmi* means 'smoke,'" Oken said quietly to Mabruke.

"I should have been able to guess that one."

OKEN PUSHED his chair back from the desk and turned in his seat to survey the library. The windows looked out at blue mountains kissing the blue sky. His glance through the open window caught Runa entering the courtyard garden, heading toward the kitchens. Her paint was different today, a spray of Incan Venus-hieroglyphs over bare skin.

Her concession to leaving the privacy of the prince's aeroship was a simple wraparound skirt of purple, belted with a chain of reddish gold links. Tiny bells announced her every move with a pleasing sound. It was a lovely ornament, yet Oken felt a twinge of annoyance. It was gold. It was also a chain around her. She was a

princess, belled like a prowling cat, controlled, restrained—chained.
It rankled his Egyptian sensibilities. It was more than the immo-
rality of slavery. He had been raised in a world where women
were sacred, valued as more than just vessels of pleasure and of
life.

Oken stood, returning his pen to his jacket pocket. He left his
letter to Yadir on the table. The ever-efficient Mr. Qusmi would see
to its delivery to the embassy. Oken went over to the window and
rested one hip on the ledge. He leaned out and called, "Mademoiselle! A lovely new flower blooms in the library garden."

Runa gave him the same startled look she always did when he
broke her concentration. She went about the estate with an expression of deep thought concerning her destination.

Oken thought it charming. "Where might you be headed, mademoiselle?"

"I must tell Mama Kusay that the Queen Mother has changed
her mind yet again about her sunset meal."

"May I accompany you? I could do with a nosh."

She smiled and bowed slightly to him. Oken noted, with some
pleasure, that she no longer bowed quite so deeply before him as
she had when they first met. He hoped perhaps that meant she was
relaxing around him.

Trusting him.

She said, "I would be glad of your company, sir. This is the third
time today the Queen Mother has changed her mind. Mama Kusay
will not be happy."

Oken swung his legs around and leaped off the window ledge,
neatly clearing the stone-lined ditch around the base of the building. Regularly spaced holes in the bottom let the rain seep through
to underground cisterns. Snails crawled along the inner edges, clearing algae as they made their slow way. Oken stepped carefully over
the border of ancient moss and joined her on the path, bowing to
her.

"I shall be your steadfast defender against Mama Kusay and all her minions, my lady—especially if there is a bit of a nosh in it!"

Runa laughed merrily, and continued on. "Yes, sir. I will surely find you a bit of a nosh."

They walked through a gate into a busy servants' garden between the kitchens and the stables. Several dozen children of various ages were playing in groups in a side yard, with the littlest ones tended by older girls. The pavement was strewn with straw padding, and leather hoops stuck out along the walls. The children were bronzed and fit looking, laughing and tumbling about in happy abandon, tossing balls of woven grass at the hoops and at each other. Their voices were a chorus of Quechua birdsong.

Oken stopped at the gate to watch the ball game. The professional version of the sport, *Tlachtli*, was terribly popular throughout this hemisphere, and played a major role in maintaining peace between Tawantinsuyu and Maya Land. National pride and national aggression were ritually activated and appeased by the violence on the field. European enthusiasts were creating their own variations, with their own rituals. Oken was not a student of the sport, preferring games that involved cards and dice and pleasant drawing rooms. Mabruke had shown interest, however, so Oken made a mental note to mention the children's games to him. Seeing innocents at play while learning the rules themselves, he thought, would help to put the spiritual metaphor into perspective. Their gods played the game with the heads of heroes as their toys. This substitute of woven grass that the children thrashed about in their play had a story of its own.

"That one is mine," Runa said, pointing to a slender, handsome boy of about six, perhaps a little older, playing close by the gate. He was taller than his playmates, and had a sharp, intelligent look to him, alert. Oken told her he was a fine-looking lad. "You must be proud of him."

Runa shrugged. "His father is the Inheritor."

The boy saw his mother, and left the ball game to come over to her. The others played on without him.

They bowed to each other politely. "*Rimaykullayki,* Mama," the boy said. His speech was clear and confident.

"*Rimaykullayki,* Wawa." Runa gestured to Oken and said to the boy, "Warmi Irqi, this is my friend, Lord Oken. He is a friend of Uncle."

"*Rimaykullayki,*" the boy said, bowing to Oken as he had to his mother.

She smiled at Oken. "Lord Oken, this is Warmi Irqi, my firstborn."

"A pleasure to meet you, Warmi Irqi, firstborn of Lady Runa." Oken bowed to the boy. "Your mother has been of great help to us in our travels here."

The boy bowed to him again. Oken could see he was trying to hide his smile.

"*Ripuy,* Wawa!" Runa said to him sternly. The boy turned away and ran back to his companions.

She looked up at Oken, her face serene once more. "He has been instructed not to use foreign languages in the presence of others."

She continued walking toward the kitchen.

Just as Oken was considering the safest way to phrase the question, Runa answered, speaking softly enough that only he could hear her. "The Queen Mother has many spies, even among the children. She does not approve of alien languages."

"She seems to tolerate *you* well enough."

"Father needs a spy who can understand Trade Speak."

Mabruke had once said something very similar, on the other side of the world and years ago, about his own childhood and the course his father decided for him.

"Does the Queen Mother speak often with Warmi Irqi?"

Runa stopped to look up at his face, perhaps to determine if he jested in kindness or in ignorance. She blinked solemnly, then said, "Why would she? He has never misbehaved."

"I am sure he is most well behaved. He is the son of a prince and a princess. I merely wondered if his grandmother were fond of him." He saw something raw and unhappy flash for an instant in her eyes, then she turned and continued walking.

When he had caught up with her again, she said, "The Queen Mother does not know, sir. Father wishes it."

Oken reviewed his lexicon of Quechua, coming up with the dismaying realization that Warmi Irqi meant simply "Boy Child." He kept his dark thoughts to himself, but could not help doing the math. Runa was perhaps nineteen. Oken knew he was not going to like the Inheritor if he ever met him. He walked in silence for a time, letting the beauty of the gardens calm him; then he said to Runa, as casually as he could, "Will Warmi Irqi join you on *Mixcomitl* someday?"

"It is my hope."

"What does your uncle say about that?"

"It is my father's choice to make."

Oken saw her shoulders tense, ever so slightly, in defiance. "Any father would be proud of such a fine son," he said to her quietly.

Runa continued walking.

"He must miss you when you are away flying with your uncle."

"He misses me, but he knows I am safe there."

"Then he is a son to be proud of."

Oken refrained from asking Runa if she missed her son. He could see that in the set of her shoulders as she walked.

The estate kitchens were separate from the main house, with a long, covered walkway between the kitchen and the serving hall. It was built of the same interlocking stonework as the main house, with broader windows and more chimneys. The windows were open. Rows of ovens heated the kitchens during the cool evening, and in daytime steady breezes cooled them. Mama Kusay was in charge of more than just the Queen Mother's fickle appetite. The entire estate was fed from her domain.

Women with woven baskets balanced on their heads were tossing handfuls of kernels to a noisy flock of black and brown chick-
ens, turkeys, and small, fat geese. Workmen unloaded baskets from
patient donkeys. The men had handsome mustaches, and hair tied
back by red bands of cloth embroidered with the imperial seal,
which matched their loose clothes. They called and joked to one another merrily, elaborating their stories with flourishes of hands and
feet. Younger boys scurried back and forth, holding bins open and
leading the donkeys away.

Once Runa and Lord Oken were sighted approaching, the men
fell quiet and hurried about their work. Runa did not look at them
as she walked past. Oken nodded and smiled at them.

Runa did not lead him into the kitchens. She stopped outside
one of the waist-high thresholds of the windows. She stopped to
shoo away the many brown and white guinea pigs wheeking and
hopping about. They were scrambling after the food scraps tossed
out the window by a large, impressive woman working at a cutting
table. She scraped and diced vegetables with alarming speed, chanting as she worked, chopped syllables barked out in time to her
blade. She had a gold hoop dangling from her left ear and the imperial seal tattooed in red on her forehead and woven into her apron.

"Mama Kusay!" Runa put one hand on the window frame and
leaned in so that she could be heard. "Mama Kusay!"

The woman stopped her work and her chanting long enough to
glare at Runa; then she went back to chopping with renewed vigor.

"Mama Kusay!"

Oken waded through the little animals hopping and leaping
about his feet, to the other corner of the window, and pulled himself up onto the window ledge. Mama Kusay stopped her blade and
glared at him. He smiled at her, then put his hands together before
his forehead and bowed to her as he had seen embassy servants do
when requesting attention. She stared at him with calm astonishment, then at Runa, expecting her to explain.

Runa covered her laughter by putting her hand to her mouth; then she leaned forward into the window, whispering to Mama Kusay. Mama Kusay, in turn, laid down her blade and came around the table to lean closer to Runa in the window.

Oken made himself look away, pretending to turn his attention to the furry little guinea pigs, who were overcoming their fear of him and returning to root about for the expected dinner scraps. He folded his arms across his chest and closed his eyes, focusing his full attention on what he could hear. Runa and Mama Kusay continued their whispered exchange.

The endless song of the ovens was the backdrop. Voices of the many servants, assistant cooks, fire-stokers, and sculleries rippled through the flames. The breezes tantalized with the mingled scents of roasting meats and peppers, and the ancient essence of fresh bread baking. After a few minutes, the conversation between Runa and Mama Kusay had become the rapid back-and-forth of intimate exchange. Oken raised one eyelid enough to see the kitchen rooms behind Mama Kusay.

Cooks wearing only grease-stained aprons with scorched hems hurried back and forth over the straw-covered floor. Boys of twelve or so brought baskets of vegetables, leafy herbs and fruit, and stacks of bowls and plates on trays, and carried out covered dishes. A far corner was cordoned off with a waist-high net, where four infants slept peacefully on piled straw. A little brown hound slept with them, puppies in a tangle around her.

The scene brought to mind Oken's many happy childhood hours spent in the castle kitchens, sitting on a side shelf out of the way and chatting with the cooks and scullery maids and porters as they worked, all the while being handed an endless round of delightful snacks and tastes of this and that. He had learned a great deal about his father's kingdom and the world in general while sitting on that shelf. Of course, Oken reminded himself, those women did not work in the nude. That might have enhanced the experience.

"Lord Oken?"

Runa's voice interrupted his reverie. He opened his eyes and smiled at her. "Yes?"

"Mama Kusay asks what kind of nosh you would like?"

"Just a cup of broth, please. Puts the heart in me without weighing me down."

Mama Kusay seemed surprised by this simple request. She went to one of the cauldrons herself and filled a large cup with a dipper. She handed it to him and watched intently as he took his first sip.

"Wonderful, Mama Kusay!" He could not identify any of the flavors other than pepper, which made it a delightful discovery. Under her watchful eye, he sipped at it until it had cooled enough to drink. He drank slowly, perusing his mental lexicon until he found the word he wanted. He finished it to the last drop, returned the cup to her with a smile, and thanked her, saying, *"Misk'i!"* It was Quechua for "delicious." *"Misk'i!"*

Mama Kusay took the cup automatically, staring at him, astonished.

Runa spoke to her, laughter bubbling in her words. Mama Kusay nodded, bobbed her head to Oken in a brief bow, and went back to her blade. She picked it up as though momentarily confused by its existence; then she went back to chopping the vegetables. She and Runa exchanged a few more sentences. Runa bowed to her and left the window ledge.

Oken jumped down, careful of the little animals.

"Lovely woman," Oken said as cheerfully as he could. "I will enjoy my meals twice as much now that I have met her. You must tell her I said so."

"I will, sir. You are the first European Mama Kusay has ever seen. Uncle's guests have never come down here before. She will be most attentive to your meals, sir, especially having seen your pleasure at the cup of broth."

"Ah, Runa," Oken said, "that was no mere cup of broth. That

was warrior's brew! Armies could march for days with such fortifi-
cation in their veins!"

"It is named demon's piss," Runa said matter-of-factly.

"I could not have chosen a better name myself!"

"Mama Kusay decided to prepare it because the fire gods are
fighting with demons over the mountain there again." Runa pointed
to the stony hills across the river. "Their battle has been lighting
the night sky with fire these past few days, terrible fire."

"Heavens!" Oken said pleasantly. "Does that happen often?"

Runa nodded. "Every few months or so, but sometimes not for a
year or more. They fight only when Uncle is away, so he does not
believe the stories, but I saw the fires of their battles when I was
younger. I used to sneak away at night to watch them."

"I wouldn't mind seeing such a thing," Oken said.

"No one is allowed on the slopes of that mountain anymore, sir.
My father's soldiers guard it now. They are as mean as demons."
She said the last as though it were a matter of fact.

"What a pity," Oken said. "I've never seen a demon before. It
must be quite a sight, wouldn't you think?"

"Mama Kusay says that the sight of a demon would burn your
eyes out."

"Would it really?" Oken said amiably. "I have no experience of
demons. Thanks for the warning."

"Don't they have demons in Egypt, sir?"

"Of course. We humans find demons wherever we go."

"What do people in Egypt do about demons, sir, if I may ask?"

"We hire them," Oken said. "We train them, and put them to
work."

"No!"

"You would be amazed at the work it saves when demons are
under control."

Runa tilted her face to look at him sideways. "You are teasing
me."

"No, not at all, mademoiselle!"

She did not look convinced. "What kind of work?"

"Well, let's see!" Oken said. "There's old Sobak, the crocodile de-mon. He's every kind of fear wrapped up in a thick, scaly hide. We hire him to give extra strength to courage when we need it. He warns us, too, when we're in danger and don't know it. Quite use-ful, actually. Then there's Apophis, the granddaddy of them all, a giant serpent—he's the towrope of the Sun, keeps the day on course."

Runa at last looked impressed. "You must have powerful priests!"

Oken nodded. "Perhaps that's why I travel so much."

He caught Runa's eye, noting that she was looking at him as if deciding something. He wondered if he would ever find out what it was.

Mabruke, dressed in his usual white suit and hat, was seated in the library garden, writing notes in the latest of his small black bound notebooks. From the looks of it, he had just started a new one. The academy had an entire alcove in the archives with shelves of Mabruke's little black books. Mabruke most often wrote notes in private. Seeing him here gave Oken an idea.

"Mik," he called casually. "How's your appetite?"

Mabruke looked up from the page with an easy smile. "Same as always."

"Good! I've just the thing." Oken turned to Runa. "Do you sup-pose Mama Kusay would be willing to spare my friend here a taste of her fabulous brew?"

Runa nodded. "I think she would be honored."

"You are in for a treat," Oken said, "and it's more than the broth—just taking a breath outside her kitchen is a meal in itself!"

Runa giggled.

Mabruke tucked the notebook and pen away in his inner jacket pocket. He flicked the plume on his hat and stood up to join them.

Oken and Runa retraced their steps toward Mama Kusay's win-dow, with Mabruke in tow.

"By the way, Mik," Oken said as they entered the herb garden, "the word you'll be looking for is *misk'i.*"

"Misk'i," Mabruke echoed, then repeated it again to test the pronunciation. *"Misk'i."*

Runa turned her serene smile to Oken.

The little pigs squealed and wheeked as the three of them approached the kitchen window. Oken pulled himself up to the same spot on the ledge. Mabruke, mindful of his white suit, stood just outside, smiling at Mama Kusay's look of concern.

Runa explained hastily, and Mama Kusay burst into smiles herself, nodding, and laid down her blade. She wiped her hands on her apron as she hurried across the kitchen to the cauldron. She poured broth into a cup and returned to present it to Mabruke with a bow.

Mabruke was at his professorial best. First he bowed to her, then took the cup in both hands. He closed his eyes and let the steam from the cup fill his nose, inhaling with the proper show. Then he sipped carefully, letting the hot liquid roll about in his mouth before swallowing. He took another deep breath, then opened his eyes, and gave Mama Kusay a big smile. *"Misk'i!"* he exclaimed with the proper enthusiasm. He bowed his head to her, said, *"Misk'i!"* again, and sipped, slowly and luxuriously. He stood so still that the little pigs got over their fear and crowded around his sandaled feet, snapping at fat, clumsy flies.

Runa and Mama Kusay were staring in fascination. The other cooks looked on with amazement.

Oken settled back to watch the magic happen.

He was not disappointed. When Mabruke had finished the last drop, he touched the rim of the cup to his forehead and bowed to her. He held the cup out to her, smiling his best.

Mama Kusay put her hands around it, unable to look away from his smile.

Mabruke said to Runa, "Runa, if would be so kind as to translate for me?"

"Certainly, sir." Runa was clearly holding back giggles.

"Please tell Mama Kusay this: The professor craves knowledge of the names of these wonderful smells and flavors in your realm. In Egypt he is considered a man of much knowledge about smells and flavors. He teaches the young how to know the world by scent. You put his knowledge to shame. He would learn from you, if you would so honor him."

Runa put her hand to her mouth, her eyes wide. "You want me to say *that* to Mama Kusay?"

"If you would be so kind." Mabruke was smiling at Mama Kusay as he spoke.

"Sir, you are a prince," Runa said hesitantly. "Should I not introduce you as Prince Mabruke?"

Mabruke shook his head. "I am not here as royalty, only a humble scholar seeking knowledge."

Runa's face became serious as she translated this to herself; then she turned to Mama Kusay. The words tumbled out, faster and faster. Mama Kusay listened, frozen.

Mabruke continued to smile encouragingly at her.

When Runa had finished, Mama Kusay nodded slowly, then gestured to the front entrance to her kitchen realm, her eyes still caught by Mabruke's glowing smile.

Oken leaped off the window ledge, careful of the guinea pigs who bobbed up and down and ran away. He and Mabruke followed Runa around the big kitchen building to the door standing open to the herb garden within the compound walls.

The men unloading the donkeys were peering around the other corner of the building, watching with solemn eyes.

Oken stopped in the entry to the kitchen, folded his arms, and leaned back against the doorframe to watch. Mabruke would be counting on him to fill in the details.

Mabruke had taken out his notebook and pen, and stood smiling down expectantly at Mama Kusay. She, for all her girth, was only slightly taller than his waist. She whispered something nervously to Runa, then curtsied to Mabruke as though she had run out of ideas.

"Perhaps we might begin with the demon's piss?" Mabruke said, anticipating Mama Kusay's question. He gestured toward the cauldron of broth with a wave of his dark, elegant hand.

Mama Kusay's round face lit up, and she went over to the cauldron, motioning for Runa to follow. Mama Kusay was already bubbling over with words. She filled another cup with the broth and held it out to Mabruke, speaking to Runa in Quechua as she did so.

Mabruke bowed respectfully before taking the cup, holding it reverently in both hands.

Mama Kusay waited for Runa to translate.

"Mama Kusay's secret to this broth," Runa began.

Mabruke interrupted her. "I do not ask for her secrets, Runa. I have not yet earned the honor of that." He continued to hold Mama Kusay's gaze as he spoke. "I wish only to learn the names of her ingredients, as a humble student. Beyond that, if she would honor me with the names of the master farmers from whom I might purchase my own supplies, I would devote myself to their study when I return to Egypt."

For nearly an hour this continued, while the other cooks and sculleries tried to complete their work. Mabruke wrote many pages of notes in his minuscule, elegant hand, and both women relaxed, chatting comfortably as they decided how best to answer Mabruke's endless questions.

Oken focused on their voices, so that he could help Mabruke later with pronunciations. Runa clearly enjoyed being the translator for this magic show. Oken spent as much energy remembering her delight as Mama Kusay's carefully pronounced names for spices, herbs, vegetables, and fruits. Long before they were done, Oken had become impressed by the many uses for maize and roots, as well as the many different kinds of *papa* there were, or "potatoes."

Under Mabruke's respectful gaze, Mama Kusay grew more confident, walking over the straw-covered floor of her realm as though she walked on the magnificent rugs in the manor.

Once they completed the round of cauldrons, ovens, cutting tables, and bins, Mabruke put away his notebook. Mama Kusay stopped in midsentence, blinking at him as if dazed. Mabruke strolled over to the corner where the infants were napping. The little mother hound was sitting up amid her sleeping pups, giving Mabruke a breathy canine smile, tongue flashing. Mabruke knelt beside the net barrier and reached over it to put his hand out to her.

The hound came over, shedding puppies, to lick his fingers, her tail wagging. The puppies rolled about yawning and stretching, then scrambled up to follow her, yipping. Their eyes were not fully opened, yet they were nearly half their mother's size.

The voices of the pups woke the infants, who also yawned and stretched, showing red tongues in toothless mouths. Their opened eyes tracked the familiar reaches of the kitchen, then fixed on Mabruke, kneeling before the little family of hounds. Tiny fingers waved at him, and the infants laughed.

At a word from Mama Kusay, the parents of the infants put down their work and went over to the netting. This was lifted aside, letting the eager hounds crowd around Mabruke, kneeling on the straw. The pups jumped and pawed at him, and his dark hands moved among them, petting their heads and tugging their ears, letting the mother sniff his hand and wrist and sleeve with savage intensity. She sat back abruptly, putting her chin up so he could tickle the soft triangle under her jaw.

The infants made cooing, happy gurgles. One by one, their parents knelt before Mabruke, holding their children up for him. He asked Runa to tell him their names; then he greeted them, repeating what she said to him. He touched each infant's forehead with his fingertip, and the babies smiled at him.

With this ceremony completed, the children were returned to their beds, the netting was put back in place, and the parents hurried back to their work, casting glances at Mabruke as they could.

"These are the children of Mama Kusay's people," Runa said to Mabruke. "Mama Kusay is the daughter of the headman of her village. Those who work for the Queen Mother bring their children here for her to bless them, in the presence of her hearth fires."

Mabruke thought about this, then said to Runa, "Tell Mama Kusay that Professor Mabruke begs her to add his blessings to those who come to her hearth. Her wisdom exceeds his. Her knowledge has brought awe to him, and he begs her to consider him her humble servant, now and always."

"That is more than I can tell her, sir!" Runa put her hands to her face in alarm.

Mabruke looked at her with the serious consideration of a teacher challenging a favorite student. "Is that a matter of her language skills or yours?" His voice was kinder than his words. "I ask this only to know how to rephrase my question."

"She is property of the imperial family, sir!" Runa dropped her voice almost to a whisper. "No one has *ever* spoken to her as you have. I do not know what to tell her." She clasped her hands under her chin. "I do not know how to ask your question!"

"Then just ask it," Mabruke said gently. "Let Mama Kusay decide."

The entire kitchen staff hung on Runa's words as she translated this to Mama Kusay. Some of the women gasped.

Mama Kusay took a deep breath, then breathed out a sigh of contentment. She stood to her full height before Mabruke, looking up at him as he gazed down at her. He bent over to her, and she raised her hands and patted his cheeks as one might a small child, even though she had to rise up on her toes to do so. She stepped back and put her hands to her own cheeks, smiling up at him. The two bowed to each other.

Mabruke said to Runa, "We must let Mama Kusay return to her important work. If you would extend our thanks?" He gestured then to Oken, and strode out of Mama Kusay's kitchen kingdom. Oken bowed to Mama Kusay and followed him.

CHAPTER SIXTEEN

VIRACOCHA HELD out the talking-knot for his father the Inca to see. "Papa, I have found proof that Pachacuti sent an assassin to kill a royal prince of Egypt."

The Inca flicked impatient fingers at the slaves waiting patiently at his feet. "Go!" His hands looked old, and he no longer filled the golden chair.

The many girls gathered around him leaped up, scattering the cushions, and vanished into the several doorways of the sunroom.

Once they were alone, Viracocha tried again, almost speaking calmly. "Pachacuti tried to blow up *Mixcomitl*, Papa. He would have killed me as well."

"Quetzals are death," the Inca said to him. "You spend too much time in the sky."

Viracocha held the talking-knot closer to the old man's eyes. "These assassins work for my brother, Papa. This is the record of the payments he has given them—look! It has the Inheritor's seal on the handle!"

"Your brother has no quarrel with this prince of Egypt," the Inca said with sharp dismissal. He clutched his robe closer to his chest. "Why would he do such a thing?"

Viracocha looked around helplessly at the familiar opulence of his father's private sunroom—red marble and redder gold, looking out over the imperial gardens. Lush ferns softened the window ledges, and cooling mist drifted from a fountain in the center of an exquisite little pool. This place had once been the heart of family warmth, bathed in light, while his father's favorite women sang the ancient stories of heroes who battled demons and gods in the dark dimension of the Afterworld. In Viracocha's imagination, his father had played the hero who made the Sun rise—and his fierce, demented brother Pachacuti was every vicious monster in the dark.

He had never understood Pachacuti's mind when he was a child, and time had only increased the distance between their hearts. Viracocha struggled to find words large and simple enough to make his father understand. "Papa, if we ask him, he will lie." He tried to speak forcefully. Despite his manly bulk, he never felt full-grown in the presence of this man.

The Inca shrugged thin, bony shoulders, age pressing against him. "I know he lies," he said with resignation. "He has lied to me his entire life. I know." He put his hand out to Viracocha, meeting his eyes with a kindlier expression. "Your brother is the Inheritor, and he must make himself ready to take the throne of our world. But you are my Best Boy, Viracocha. My *Best Boy*! He cannot take that from you—do not try to take his throne."

Viracocha flinched ever so slightly, then caught himself. "I do not want his throne, Papa. Not if he gave it to me."

"*Liar!*"

Pachacuti stepped through a doorway from the shadows where he had stood, listening. Behind him, in the half light of the corridor, a pool of blood was slowly spreading, and there were no guards. The Inheritor was narrow to his brother's width, wiry rather than strong or agile. He bore the puma face of the imperial family tattooed on his high, narrow brow. His hazel eyes were narrow under the thin lines of his eyebrows, matching the thin line of his sneer.

"*Liar!*"

He flung the word at his brother with an icy friendliness that made Viracocha cold. Pachacuti's voice had knives in it.

Pachacuti strolled up to his father and rested a hand on his shoulder. "My brothers have all wanted my throne, Papa. You and I know that."

Yupanqui Inca looked up at his firstborn, smiling the sad, involuntary smile of a parent uncertain of what success he could expect from the next generation. "Your brother is *moxie*," he said to him. "You are my Inheritor, Pachacuti. He will not have your throne."

"Viracocha—a traitor who consorts with foreign demons—" Pachacuti's grip on his father's shoulder tightened to a claw, pinning the old man to the golden chair. The Inca whimpered. Pachacuti leaned close to his ear, and whispered, "The things I have done for you, Papa? The things I have done in your name—yet Viracocha is your Best Boy? Your *Best Boy!*"

In the bright light of the room, his pupils were pinpoints, and a searing rage Viracocha had never seen looked out. "*Both* of you think to take my throne! I see now, Papa. *You* led these conspiracies against me—*you* from the beginning!"

"No!" Viracocha stumbled back a pace, appalled to see his mother's mindless fury reflected in his brother's face.

"You are my Inheritor!" The Inca gently caressed Pachacuti's hand, gripping his shoulder. "You are firstborn of my flesh—nothing can change that. You are the energy of my youth, and my throne will be yours when I die!"

"You are Papa's *Best Boy.*" Pachacuti hurled the words at Viracocha, his breathing loud in his throat. "You are his blade. *You* are the knife in my back!"

He sneered, his glare focusing on his brother. "You think you and your Egyptian spies fooled me?"

"They are not spies." Viracocha could barely force the words out. Memories from a childhood chained by constant fear of his elder brother, of "Slasher," surged through him, locking his bones in place.

"My empire is greater than Egypt," the Inca said, irritation at his sons sharp in his voice. "And you are my Inheritor." He tried to pry Pachacuti's fingers loose.

"Egypt will learn to fear Tawantinsuyu," Pachacuti cried out. "I will rain down *fire* upon them, fire from the Moon."

"No!" the old man groaned, reaching up to his son to protest.

Pachacuti leaned forward, seeming to stroke his father's throat with a loving caress. Blood welled out through his fingers. Pachacuti released the Inca with a moan of triumph, leaping away so swiftly that the gore barely touched his silken robe. He threw away the dagger, giggling hysterically.

Viracocha sprang to his father as the old man slumped out of his seat. Blood spilled across the sleeves of the prince's jacket, across his feathered collar. "Papa!" he cried. He put his hand over the flowing wound, trying to stanch the blood with his fingers. "Papa!"

The old man peered up at Viracocha, struggling to speak past the gurgle in his throat. His eyes stilled.

Viracocha held him tenderly to his chest as he knelt there. Then he looked at Pachacuti, suddenly cold, eagle-sharp. "What have you done?"

The mask of Pachacuti's face was white, with spots of hot blood mottling his skin, and he drew himself up to his full height. "Little brother, you think you are a god up there in the sky, with your golden demon wings? Pachacuti—*me*—I am the god! I am the Inca, son of the Sun! Life and death are *mine* to give—and to take!"

He slid his bloodied hands into the wide cuffs of his silk robe to hide them. "Guards!" His eyes were locked with Viracocha's, the light of triumph harsh in them. "Guards! Assassin! Assassin!"

Viracocha looked down at the face of his father, flecked with blood, staring into eternity. He closed those eyes, to conceal the dismay and remorse frozen there. He rested his cheek against his father's brow, keening a prayer for the dead he had sung too many times.

He barely heard the loud command as his brother ordered the guards to arrest him, to take him to the Tower for the assassination of the Inca. A half dozen guards were needed, and more than one was injured, before they could safely wrest the old man's body from Viracocha's grasp and drag the weeping prince away.

CHAPTER SEVENTEEN

"I INQUIRED of Mr. Qusmi why we were assigned to this particular suite in the guest wing of the manor." Oken sank down into the cushions of the parlor chair and put his feet up.

Mabruke tilted his head to one side, smiling indulgently at the younger man. "I am sure that his report was most informative."

"It would seem that this is a suite designed for husband and wife, hence the differences in the bedroom décor."

Mabruke broke out into a hearty laugh, genuine amusement bubbling through and shining in his eyes. "Well, tell me. Were you the newly married guest, which room would you choose for making love to your bride?"

Oken had to smile. "Any place my lady pleases. Ever and always."

"Spoken like an Egyptian."

"To the core."

"Have you noticed that the women here seem particularly vulnerable to the simplest of gentlemanly behaviors?"

Oken felt a stab of wordless guilt. He put his feet down on the floor and sat forward to reach for the ceramic jug shaped like a puma coiled to strike. The vodka it held was carefully distilled and quite powerful. He poured a considerable portion into Mabruke's choclatl mug and then added a smaller portion to his own.

Mabruke took the mug and sipped from it, held it up as a salute to Oken, and then took a long drink.

Oken picked up his mug and leaned back into his chair. The light from the spinglass chandelier was as warm as candlelight. Night breezes blowing into the spirals wafted through the rooms with the exquisite perfumes of Quillabamba's many gardens.

"I have noticed. You know that I have. I keep reviewing my own moral soundings, to keep my feet under me."

"Women as suppressed as these Andean lovelies are surely the weak point of their civilization."

"Women and the Moon have a long association."

"Well, I do have to defer to your superior knowledge of the sex. You will have to be my navigator in these foreign waters."

Oken had already determined that. It eased his conscience to know that Mabruke was also aware.

Oken recalled Runa's warning that the Queen Mother had spies everywhere. He signaled Mabruke by cupping his hand behind his ear. "Care for a walk?"

"Indeed." Mabruke stood, brushing down the hem of his kilt. "Let me get my sandals. I do feel inclined to take an evening stroll."

"Good," Oken said, standing as well. "Let me get my gloves."

Mr. Qusmi met them at the bottom of the spiral staircase. He carried a silver tray with a choclatl pitcher wrapped in a red towel. He showed his weary smile. "I was just bringing you a refresher for your drinks, sirs."

"Help yourself to it, Mr. Qusmi," Mabruke said lightly. "Scott and I are going out for a stroll, to take in the night air."

At the suggestion that he might drink the hot choclatl intended for noblemen, Qusmi blanched and almost let go of the tray. "Sir! I would never!"

"Oh, please, be my guest," Mabruke said. "If you fear someone may see, then you may go up and sit in our parlor."

The old man turned pleading eyes to him. "I would not dare. The Queen Mother would have me flayed alive!"

"Seriously?" Oken said. "It is very good choclatl, but I doubt they would kill you over it."

Mr. Qusmi could only nod, his eyes big.

"We can't have that," Mabruke said. "Why don't you just set it on the stair, then. We'll have it when we return."

"Thank you, sir. That is most kind of you." Qusmi set the tray on the step with trembling hands. He bowed to them. "The best view for evening walks would be this way, sirs. If you would follow me?"

He led them to the wide receiving hall. The glass doors were closed for the night. A side door let them out into the open air and a long driveway down to the river. Paved with crushed seashells, it gleamed in the lights from the manor. The air was sweet and fresh.

"Guards along the walls will protect you," Qusmi said. "The doors will be left open for your return." He bowed and went inside.

They strolled for a few minutes over the crunching shells. Oken was glad of the gloves and long sleeves of his silk jacket. The evening breezes had grown cool under the brilliant stars.

Mabruke pointed skyward. "The Milky Way has astonishing clarity at this altitude."

Oken looked at the long turn of diamond dust in the night. "The river of fire in the sky."

"What's that?" Mabruke said.

"The Milky Way is their Nile. They cross it to the Next Life. The other side of the world."

"They think they can fly over the Milky Way to get to the Moon? Is that what we are here to find out?"

The two men were silent, taking in the dazzle of the sky. The mountains enfolding Quillabamba and the imperial estate were dark shapes, the shoulders and arms of gods enfolding the human community in their protecting circle, holding them close to heaven.

The song of the river was as constant as breathing, the sighing of the night and the sky.

"Mik, something tells me that your natural attraction has worked its usual magic. We are in the place we need to be."

"Your instincts are good."

"I do my best."

"Even the Queen could ask no more."

"She will not like this story," Oken said. "I can assure you of that."

"She did not send us here to change the ways of their civilization. Just to find a way to join in their endeavor."

"Speaking of stories, Runa told me a story today that should interest you."

"Indeed?"

"Evidently their gods battle with demons on the other side of the mountain across the river. The fire from their battles lights the sky, she tells me."

"Indeed?"

"She saw the fires herself."

"The Queen did say that this research project has existed for some years."

Oken nodded. "According to Runa, these demons battle only when Prince Viracocha is away."

"Perhaps we really are in the right place."

They stood for a time in silence, struck by the beauty and strangeness of the place, transformed by the blanket of darkness and the closeness of the sky. Even the Duat stars in Verdi's opera had not evoked the simple awe of this celestial display. The sighing of the river was a swift song in the night.

After a half hour or so, there was a low rumble that seemed to come from the ground and grow to a roar. A long, black arrow shape, like some monstrous fireworks rocket, leaped up from the dark horizon, balanced precariously on a tail of white-hot fire.

It did not climb far, however. The tail of fire split into two and sputtered. Smoke trailed behind as it spiraled upward crazily, exploding finally with a series of booms that rang through the night and echoed off the stony mountainsides. The glowing pieces sprayed around with sizzling sounds.

The echoes of the explosion faded, and the night's breathing was quiet again.

Oken shook his head. "What those people need are some albatross for navigation!"

Mabruke spoke quietly. "Indeed, we are in the right place. The Queen will definitely be interested in this."

"Listen!" Oken said, reacting to a sense of alarm. There was a growing noise of voices from guardhouses along the river. "We are definitely not in the right place just this minute."

They turned at once and went back toward the stone and glass entry to the Queen Mother's manor house, the white shells crunching under their heels sounding loud in the darkness. The yellow glow of lamps in the courtyards and corridors made the façade look like a warm place, ancient and complex, shining in the dark.

The mountains around them had become black shapes blocking the stars.

The voices behind were louder, calls and sharp commands.

The doorway, despite Mr. Qusmi's assurance, was locked. Oken gestured for Mabruke to follow, and headed to the side of the manor. The bamboo gate was locked, but that was only the work of kicking the cross latch, snapping it in half. They went through, and Mabruke closed the gate behind them.

Mabruke let Oken lead. The library window was closed. Oken jumped lightly over the stone ditch, catching himself on the ledge. Mabruke crossed the ditch simply by taking a long step over it, catching the ledge as Oken had. Oken demonstrated silently that they were to push inward at the same time.

The heavy pane swung inward on its silent hinges, lifted by a counterbalance system. Oken had experimented with it earlier in the afternoon, attempting to puzzle out the unusual mechanism. He had also placed a carefully folded wad of paper blocking the lock.

Oken liked being a man who knew how to plan ahead.

He and Mabruke leaped up onto the window ledge and inside. Oken closed the window, careful to retrieve the paper and pocket it. "This way," he said softly. He threaded through the tables and chairs by memory in the dark. He opened the library door, and the two men slipped out.

The hallway outside the library was lit, but empty. Oken reviewed his internal map of the manor and smiled at Mabruke. "Two gentlemen out on an evening's stroll who got lost in the manor."

Mabruke set off down the hallway, taking the first door on the right. Mr. Qusmi was standing just on the other side, smiling his weary smile. "Good evening, sirs," he said. "I hope you enjoyed your stroll?"

"The night sky was quite dramatic," Mabruke said. "The air is very clear up here."

"Good for the blood, sirs. Would you care for an evening refreshment?"

"I think we'll just finish up the choclatl you set out for us, Mr. Qusmi. That should conclude our evening quite successfully."

"Thank you, sir. You are most kind. If you would follow me? I will show you the way."

"There were some loud noises in the night earlier, Mr. Qusmi." Oken decided to risk the question. "Is there anything wrong?"

"I do not know, sir. My hearing is not what it once was."

Oken had his doubts about that, but he said nothing more.

"SO, WHERE are these delicious foreigners my brother has brought home for me?"

Oken and Mabruke were seated in the library garden, discussing the events of the previous evening. They both turned at the voice, a melodious, bold woman's voice, with a lazy kind of accent that Oken found instantly appealing.

When he saw the speaker, that conclusion was enhanced. She was clearly a princess, despite her European riding habit and dusty boots. She did not need a crown. Royalty spoke in everything about her as she strode up to them with swift confidence. She was smiling and the effect was breathtaking. Her black, Andean tresses were curled European style, piled in glorious masses around her exquisite face and pinned with golden ornaments. She wore Egyptian makeup, and an emerald choker of outstanding quality.

She put her hand out to Mabruke at once. "Usqhullu," she said to him by way of introduction. "It means 'Wildcat.'"

"Indeed, my lady," Mabruke said as he took her hand and bowed over it. "I am Mik Mabruke, and this is my good friend, Scott Oken."

Princess Usqhullu put her hand out to Oken. He took it in both of his, bowing as Mabruke had, marveling at the beauty of her skin and the immediacy of her presence. "It is a pleasure to make your acquaintance, my lady," he said with sincerity. "We are quite fond of your brother, and I will always be in his debt for this moment."

"Ooh, aren't you the fancy one!" The princess's laughter was as bold and forthright as everything else about her. "Do you dance?"

"Only when I am not standing still, my lady."

She laughed again, turning her brilliant smile to Mabruke. "Mama is simply livid that Lucky left you on her doorstep. I hope she hasn't been making trouble for you?"

"No, my lady. We have had a most enjoyable stay here," Oken said. "Mr. Qusmi has been our faithful support."

"Dear old Smoky," she said with a fond smile. "If Mama knew what he was really up to around here, she'd have him skinned alive!"

Mabruke said, "We have endeavored to keep his hide intact during our visit."

The princess smiled at Mabruke as one might look at a marvelous painting. "Aren't you something," she said with astonished delight. "Meanwhile, however, where is that rascal, Lucky? I expected to find him here with you."

Mabruke and Oken exchanged quick glances. Oken decided to let Mabruke field this one. "We have had some unfortunate adventures during our journey," he said gently. "Your brother has gone to investigate at the palace. He felt we would be safer here."

"Ooh, this sounds exciting!" the princess said. "I must hear all about it."

"We shall make every effort to entertain, my lady," Mabruke said.

"I think you will," she said. "First, however, I really have to get out of these clothes. I have been riding since daybreak, and I stink like a horse."

"I am actually rather fond of the way horses smell, my lady," Mabruke said to her. "It reminds me of my childhood."

The princess looked at him with surprise, then laughed. "Ooh, you two are going to be so much fun!"

She winked at Oken then. "I'll be back in a half an hour or so."

"Delightful, my lady," Oken said.

"Just you wait," she said to him. "I haven't started yet."

She strode off with the same energy, disappearing into the library.

"Quite a family," Mabruke observed. "I was not expecting such a surprising creature."

"A wildcat, indeed," Oken said with appreciation. "An imperial wildcat."

"A little plump, don't you think?" Mabruke said.

When Oken turned to comment, he saw Mabruke's mischievous expression. "Voluptuous," Oken said. "Not a bit plump."

"I think I will leave her to you. I am going to take a nap before dinner."

"She's quite a handful of woman," Oken said, suppressing a smile. "I may need your help."

"I doubt that." Mabruke strolled off.

Oken sat down again to await Princess Usqhullu's return.

HE FOUND the time was not wasted. Princess Usqhullu, when she returned, was transformed. She still wore the fabulous emerald necklace, with a pair of bracelets and earrings. Her silk dress was a matching green, tight at the waist and bodice, with a long, full skirt and green slippers. The décolleté was low and the sleeves a short frill.

He stood up to greet her. She strode over to him quickly, motioning to him to sit, seating herself beside him. "Where's your tall, dark friend?"

"He usually naps before dinner. He will join us later."

Usqhullu shrugged. "So. Tell me about your adventure."

Oken had been thinking about that while waiting for her. He reasoned that there was no need to conceal anything from her, other than their true purpose for being in Tawantinsuyu. He told her about the assassin in Zulia, and the mysterious Quetzal that had been preparing to fire on *Mixcomitl*. She listened without interruption, clearly fascinated. Oken found himself warming to the telling. He liked the way her eyes grew wide, and the way she leaned close to him as he talked. The scent of horse had been replaced by an alluring perfume of gardenias and spice.

When he got to the end of his narrative, she shook her head in disbelief. "That makes very little sense to me. I'm sure Lucky thinks that scrawny rat Pachacuti is behind it."

Oken raised an eyebrow in surprise. "The Inheritor?"

She shrugged, a graceful gesture. "He and Lucky have been at each other's throats since they first grew hair on their balls. Papa's old now, and I think Kuchillu has been making plans."

"Kuchillu?"

She shrugged again, and made a face. "It means 'Slasher.' He was always making holes in his clothes when he was a boy, trying to carry around concealed knives—heaven knows why. Mama threatened to make him wear patched-up clothes if he didn't stop. Never mind, it's an old story. Did Lucky say when he would be back?"

"Alas, no, my lady. He was in considerable haste."

"He's always in a haste, as you say. Always going someplace else. I was hoping he would fly us to Qusqo, but we can always ride."

"Your brother did suggest that it was not safe for us outside of your mother's estate."

"Nonsense. I'll watch out for you. Don't worry. I have my own private guard."

"I am sure they are most devoted, my lady."

She laughed again and put her hand on his knee. "The finest corps of fighting ladies in the land. I think, though, I might have to protect them from you instead."

"My lady, in your presence, no man would notice another woman was in the room."

"Ooh," Usqhullu said, patting his knee expressively. "I am going to keep you around for a while. Shall we go in? Smoky is in the window waving at us, which means he has dinner waiting."

Oken rose, putting his arm out for her. She stood and took his arm in both hands, pulling herself close to him. Oken decided that, except for the occasional assassin, this was a lovely country.

In the corridor outside the dining hall, Runa came running toward them. She was smiling broadly. Usqhullu released Oken, striding off to sweep Runa up in her arms and swing her around. They were both laughing. When Runa's feet touched the ground again, she threw her arms around Usqhullu, hugging her tightly.

Oken was well pleased to see this, and he knew Mabruke would be equally pleased.

Usqhullu stepped back. "Have you been behaving yourself, Petal?"

"No."

"Oh, good. I was worried about you."

"I was with Uncle. I was safe."

"Is Mama being horrible?"

"Just the usual."

"You poor thing. I didn't know you were back until Ambrose told me yesterday evening. I set off at first light, but it took me all day to get here."

"Did Uncle tell you to come here?"

"No. I came looking for him." Usqhullu turned her smile to Oken. "Actually, I came here to meet the princes Lucky brought home for me." She winked at him. "I see, however, that you have been keeping them to yourself!"

Runa looked down at her feet modestly.

"I'm sorry, Petal," Usqhullu said gently. "I am only teasing you. They have not been unkind to you, have they?"

Runa looked up at her, smiling, and shook her head. "They have been most kind, Hulla. As kind as Uncle!"

Usqhullu hugged her quickly. "Good." She tilted her head to one side and regarded her niece with a serious expression. "Your Trade Speak has gotten better. You've been practicing."

Runa smiled at Oken. "They have been most kind."

Mr. Qusmi appeared suddenly at Oken's elbow. He bowed to Princess Usqhullu.

She went to him and hugged him gently. "Everyone is singing your praises, Smoky," she said. "Even Mama said she was grateful."

"You are quite generous, my lady," Qusmi said. His smile was less weary as he looked at her.

Usqhullu took Oken's arm. "Lead on, Smoky. I am hungry enough to eat the horse I rode in on!"

The table was a wide oval of picture agate, a mineralized landscape of purple hills, crystal meadows, and frothy forests under a layered sky. They were seated on benches of moss agate, comfortably curved. Mr. Qusmi was silent server on the gentlemen's side of the dining table. Runa served Princess Usqhullu, trailed by her own retinue of maids carrying silver trays and covered dishes.

Over the course of the dinner, Oken and Mabruke, in response to the princess's many questions, talked in detail about life in fabled Memphis, about the beauty of Queen Sashetah Irene, about the numbers of Quetzals flying the skies above Europe. They learned little about her in return, beyond the striking elegance with which she played her role as hostess.

They did not ask her about gods and demons fighting in the mountains.

CHAPTER EIGHTEEN

"PLEASE, WAKE up!"

Oken threw the coverlet aside and was on his feet, adjusting his newly wakened eyes to the midnight hour. His ears told him he had wakened to Runa's voice, even as he recognized her slight form standing in front of the beaded curtain to his bedroom.

He sat back down on the bed and yawned, wondering how gracefully he could say no.

"Quickly, sir!" she said urgently, without coming closer. "Put on your strongest shoes and warmest clothes—and quickly!"

Oken sprang up, grabbing items from the shelf, sliding the lady-trunk open with a nudge of his bare toe. He sat back down on the edge of the bed to dress, then spoke as quietly as he could. "Why?"

"I have to get you and the prince out of here before my father's warriors reach this side of the manor!" Her voice was a fierce whisper.

Oken double-timed his dressing and dashed to Mabruke's room as soon as he had pulled on his boots. Mabruke was struggling into a pair of black pants. Oken pulled on his jacket, then held up the gloves for Mabruke to see, reminding him he might want a pair as well.

Runa led them out into the parlor, then motioned for them to wait while she leaned silently through the beaded entry curtain, looked both ways, and then resettled it with barely a click. She dashed back across the room to the wall, braced herself against it with one hand, and reached up to her full height to press a spot hidden in the stone. The control had been invisible. A slight rumble could be felt in the floor; then a section of the wall pulled backwards and slid to the side, revealing a narrow hallway lit by sconces of Egyptian crystal. She motioned them inside, pressed the control again, and then leaped in beside them just before the wall closed behind her. She held her finger to her lips, indicating silence, then hurried down the hall ahead of them.

Oken noticed in the brighter light here that Runa was wearing more clothes than he had ever seen on her—a belted black tunic and pants with soft leather boots up to her thigh. Her hair was bound in a simple, long braid down her back. The climate here was mild. These looked like hiking clothes. He was suddenly glad of the sturdy pair of boots he had chosen for himself.

This short hall led to a stairway going downward at a sharp angle. The light below was dim. Runa ran down these, taking two steps at a time despite her diminutive height. Oken and Mabruke exchanged troubled glances and followed her as silently as they could.

This staircase led to another short corridor, cut through the solid rock of the mountain's roots. The air was stale and the light dimmer. Oken felt momentary concern that Mabruke's newly found fear of confinement would slow him here. Mabruke, however, was smiling ever so slightly. Oken realized that excitement was a cure for many ills.

He returned his concerns to the more immediate moment.

The door at the end of this corridor was also of stone, a single huge slab so finely balanced that little Runa could push it open with no effort. They stepped out into the herb garden between the stables and the kitchen. Light from the kitchen windows spilled into the yard, providing wedges of illumination.

Runa pushed the door closed, and it became simply another piece fitted into the outer wall of the manor. She motioned for them to wait, then dashed across the yard to Mama Kusay's window.

Mama Kusay was at work, kneading a huge mass of dough with the same intensity with which she wielded her blade. She did not stop in her work as Runa spoke to her. Whatever Runa asked drew a frown on her broad face, but she was nodding.

Shouts were heard from the upper floor of the manor, hard, angry words in Quechua command. Mama Kusay froze, then looked at Runa with sudden fright. She nodded quickly and gestured them into the kitchen.

Runa climbed up onto the window ledge, motioning for them to join her, and she jumped down into the kitchen. Oken and Mabruke sprinted over, leaping up onto the ledge together and into the kitchen.

The shouts from the manor sounded again, louder and more angry.

The night was rent then by a horrific wail of agony and pure rage. It went on and on, human grief expanded beyond human measure. The silence when it stopped was harsh.

Work in the kitchen stopped.

Runa stood with her hands clasped to her face. "That was the Queen Mother!" she whispered urgently. Then she repeated this in Quechua to Mama Kusay, clearly asking if she had also recognized that distorted, anguished howl.

Mama Kusay nodded curtly, her face gone cold and hard.

"What did my father do to her?" Runa's voice was barely audible, and she turned wide, frightened eyes to Mabruke in the dark.

"Would he come here, to the queen's manor?" Mabruke said to her calmly.

"No. He never comes here. Oh! I don't know!"

Mama Kusay became a blur of action that quite belied her bulk. She hurried over to the cauldron of demon's piss and hastily filled a cup and held it out to Mabruke. He took it at once, and handed it to Runa. Mama Kusay filled two more, gesturing that they should finish it quickly. She then hurried around the kitchen, snapping orders to the staff and grabbing items from the tables. One of the sculleries gave her a backpack, which she filled with flat loaves of bread and fruit. A second pack appeared, then a third, and her staff began grabbing things to put into them.

Mama Kusay snapped a quick order to Runa, who responded by refilling their cups. Oken was glad of that, but he wondered if his offhand comment about the power of demon's piss were about to become prophetic.

Once Mama Kusay was satisfied with the contents of the backpacks, she lashed them closed herself. Runa hugged Mama Kusay when she took hers. Oken and Mabruke bowed to Mama Kusay. She actually giggled, then hustled them out. She stood in the doorway of the kitchen, backlit by the ovens, watching, her hands clasped anxiously before her, as they hurried away.

Runa led them to the back wall of the compound, performed the same miracle of moving stones by standing on her toes, and then motioned them into a corridor almost identical to the one that had led to the kitchen, but inclined upward so that walking was more strenuous.

Runa tried to resettle her backpack, and Oken helped her, readjusting the straps and lacings.

"Thank you, sir," she said quietly.

"Can you tell us anything?" Oken also spoke quietly.

She shrugged, showing sudden fear and dismay. "Uncle has been arrested. My . . . the Inheritor claims Uncle killed the Inca." She looked back and forth at their serious faces, her eyes pleading. "You do not believe that!"

Mabruke shook his head solemnly. "Lucky is a good man, Runa. A good man, a good prince, a good son. He would not kill his father."

Her eyes were wide, rimmed with tears. "*My* father would."

Both men regarded her silently; then Mabruke said gently, "His sins are not yours, little one. You are a princess, through and through. I have known that since I first met you."

"Thank you," she whispered.

"Is Usqhullu safe?" Oken said.

Runa nodded. "Father's warriors did not come here for her."

Oken finally understood. "They came here for us."

She nodded as tears spilled down her cheeks.

"Then, my lady, we owe you our lives, and I pledge to you that we will not let you come to harm for it."

She wiped tears from her face with the back of her hand. "We have to hurry."

"Lead on, my lady, lead on," Mabruke said.

Oken noted with gratitude that Mabruke had marked the change in address. Runa was no longer mademoiselle, no longer a slave of the empire. She was an outlaw, and their equal in this situation. Oken watched her walking ahead of them, and wondered if she and her son might not end up as the lone survivors of this crazy imperial family.

The corridor was long, slanting steadily upward. Runa finally called a halt. "Wait here," she said, and hurried off.

She disappeared around the bend, leaving them with their own dark thoughts.

"I do not think an imperial assassination was what the Queen had in mind," Mabruke said. "I don't think we are responsible for this turn of events."

Oken exhaled sharply, shaking his head in dismay. "I'm just glad you're the one who has to file this report."

Mabruke squared his shoulders manfully. "I shall endeavor to face the Queen's wrath, and protect your delicate hide, to the best of my ability. It is my duty."

The two men grinned at each other.

Runa reappeared, signaling them to come ahead.

They found themselves in a large building with a high ceiling. The scent of raw cacao was heady in the darkness. Oken could just make out long tables in rows, piled high with filled sacks. Runa whistled, a sound exactly like the night birds in the gardens. An answering chirp came from the far end. She ran forward, the men at her heels.

Warmi Irqi stepped forward, and the two hugged each other quickly. She gestured to the men. "You may trust them, my child," she said quietly. "They may hear your words."

The boy bowed crisply to them. He was dressed in black, much like his mother, and also carried a backpack. "I am honored to meet the prince who makes such excitement in our household." His diction was clear, his child's voice an echo of Runa's.

Mabruke bowed in return. "It is an honor to meet the firstborn of Lady Runa, young man."

Runa hastened them forward, out into the cool night air.

They were on the mountainside above and to the side of the Queen Mother's manor, with the stand of trees between them. The rocky riverbanks were a few hundred cubits downhill. Runa started to lead them toward the river; then the shouts of men from the manor docks made her freeze.

Oken motioned for them to stay under the cover of the trees while he risked a look.

Warriors in black garb were boarding a small riverboat from the docks in front of the manor. Apparently, having failed to find the foreigners they sought, they were leaving. Oken thought that strange. Why were they not searching the grounds? He wondered what Usqhullu had told them that sent them away. What had made the Queen Mother scream so horribly? Was their Princess Wildcat safe from Pachacuti?

Oken went back to where Runa and the boy were waiting under the trees with Mabruke. "They're leaving," he whispered. "Nine men."

Mabruke also thought that strange. "They're not searching for us?"

Oken shrugged. "They got in a boat, headed to town by the looks of it. If we wait here, they will be out of sight in a few minutes."

"Was my father with them?" Runa's question was barely audible in the night.

"No—they were just soldiers."

Shouts of command from men on the river sounded fainter already. Mabruke made them wait, until Runa was vibrating in place with anxiety. After ten minutes or more, he relented, and they went down the slope as quickly as possible without sliding on the steep ground, until they reached the riverbank, where hard, red stone met the rushing water.

Runa led them away, upriver from the manor, with her son close at her heels. Oken kept glancing over his shoulder, expecting pursuit. The voice of the river was clear in the night. The manor house behind them was lit brightly, as though some sort of commotion were taking place. Oken frowned and hissed at Mabruke, gesturing behind them. Mabruke threw a quick glance over his shoulder. He shook his head then with an unhappy look, and kept running.

Runa halted abruptly. She and Warmi Irqi dashed off the path into a stand of trees. They returned quickly, dragging a boat built from bundled reeds. It was small, yet adequate to carry the four of them. A head with a puma face, carved from a large squash, was lashed to the prow. In the starlight, the head looked startlingly real.

Oken and Mabruke helped her and the boy drag it down to the river. Once it was on the shore, Runa took out the oars and gave one to each of the men. She lifted the boy and climbed in, seating herself behind him so that she could hold him close to her. Mabruke took the fore. Oken pushed the boat down the shore the last few inches, then leaped into it.

Out in the open water, Mabruke turned his head and said quietly to Oken, "To the opposite shore. We have some demons to visit."

"No!" Runa said in a fierce whisper. "Usqhullu said I must take you to Ricardo, in Quillabamba!"

Oken agreed, and the men paddled as quietly as they could, pushing up around the bend to the opposite shore. In a few minutes, the boat was scraping against a spit of sand across the river. Mabruke leaped out, and pulled the boat onto the stony shore. Oken leaped out to join him. They gave the oars to Runa.

Her face showed terror and dismay, and she pleaded silently.

Mabruke leaned close to her to look her in the eyes directly. The starlight was bright there, so close to the river. "Please, Runa," he whispered to her gently. "You and your son are not safe with us. Find Usqhullu. She will protect you. She loves you. Scott and I have to find a way to get your uncle out of this. I promise you, my lady, we will do everything we can in his behalf!"

Runa nodded. Tears ran down her cheeks, shining in the starlight. She settled herself in the boat, hugged the boy, and whispered something to him; then she took the oars. The two men pushed the boat off into the water. She skimmed away, oars dipping silently.

They watched until Runa and the boy disappeared around the curve of rock that stuck out into the river. Then Mabruke looked up the mountain, tilting his head from side to side as he considered.

"There," Oken said quietly, pointing to a cleft where vegetation had a hold in the rock, visible in the starlight as a dark, ragged line against the lighter stone running up the stony face.

Mabruke agreed and the two men climbed. The stone was rough and the brush scratchy. They climbed together, one on either side of the cleft. The incline was relatively sharp, but after ten or fifteen minutes, they stepped out onto a dirt walking path that gleamed in the starlight, hard-packed by the passage of many feet over time.

Oken looked across the river to the manor, now below them. He could see into the central courtyard and the gardens, made sharply visible in the night because the three floors were alight, every window of the manor. Shadows of people moving within suggested dramatic events. Mama Kusay's kitchen kingdom cast wedges of firelight onto the servants' yards.

Mabruke pointed to the left, and the two men set off at a jog. The path zigzagged back and forth, switchbacks snaking sharply up the stony slope in silvered lines. The river sang below, and the stars sang above. The unreal nature of the night's events grew to terrible proportions in the predawn dark, with only the stars as witness.

THEY REACHED the top of the stony ridge with dawn glowing ahead of them, drawing a fine mist that flowed across the treetops and hard stone like a caress from the sky. Every breath tasted of rain. They looked down into a blanket of silver fog, to another small vale perhaps a half league across.

The river sound was only a faint whisper behind them. There was the buzz of insects flitting around in search of skin, the scrabble of gravel disturbed by their passing. The ground was reddish orange and crumbly. The slopes held clumps of scrubby pine, with scatterings of smaller trees and spiky grasses. The stone huts among them looked deserted, the thatch decaying. There was no temple compound, no building big enough for rockets. Sections of trees and scrub had been burned and rocks blackened. Pieces of burnt and twisted metal were flung across the scene, speared into the stumps of blackened trees. Fog covered them in a translucent shroud.

"They must be farther into the hills," Mabruke said finally.

"Good thing I wore my hiking boots," Oken said, taking out his pocket farscope. He methodically scanned the scene before them. No one moved among the trees or around the buildings. He put away the farscope and the two men descended into the little vale along an ancient path at the western end. A cold stream ran down the center. They stopped there to drink, finding the icy water bracing. The air was still. They startled wild conies from time to time, who ran out from the brush and dashed away from the men's feet. There were not many birds. Fire falling from the sky had perhaps chased them away.

The day was warming as they climbed the next slope, a half league or so from the manor, Oken guessed. A path zigzagged up this slope as well. Oken noted the faint marks of heavily shod boots on the path, with a familiar pattern from the hard heels of European-style boots. He wondered about that, and pointed them out to Mabruke.

Mabruke examined the heel marks carefully, then looked around at the quiet landscape. "Let us rest here a bit. The air is thinner here than in Memphis, and I do not want to tire us out too quickly."

They picked a site under the thickest stand of nearby pines and settled on the stone beneath the roots, which was swept clean of fallen needles by the winds. Mabruke pulled off his backpack, and Oken did the same. Inside they found leather flasks, capped with gold and still warm, containing another hardy serving of demon's piss. "Excellent," Mabruke said as he tasted his. "What was this called again?"

He was pleased when Oken told him. "Fortifying, indeed."

Oken sat, knees drawn up, surveying the options of the land-scape around them. The fog was thinning as the Sun rose. The sky was turning blue above the wisps. The innocence of the place seemed to float along with the mist, as though nothing could happen here that was not accepted by the gods of the land.

The corpses of the gods' demonic enemies lay scattered over this valley. What were the priests telling the people about these burnt-metal bones on the sacred battleground? Oken felt a moment of cultural superiority, accompanied by a pang of guilty pride. No Egyptian child could behold such a scene without wanting to understand the reality behind it. No Egyptian adult would tolerate such intentional obfuscation of the facts.

Mabruke was surveying the vale's silent story with a look of scholarly dismay. "They have been doing this for years. What keeps all those people silent? Surely they saw what we saw? Heard what we heard?"

Oken shrugged. "Whatever the priests are doing, it's working." He picked up his backpack and slipped it on. "Let's go ask some questions."

At the top of the next ridge, they found it in the little vale below. The Sun had dried the mist, leaving the temperate air comfortably fresh under a clear blue sky. A long slope led down to their goal—high stone walls around a compound that could easily be the site from which the errant rocket had taken off, ending its flight so abruptly.

Oken and Mabruke stretched themselves out flat on the sharp ridge of reddish rock to survey the landscape before them. Oken took out the farscope and adjusted it to see the inner courtyard of the compound. Mabruke waited patiently beside him, chin on hands, seeing what he could with the naked eye.

The compound was quiet. There was no movement, no sign of guards. A central courtyard was surrounded on three sides by low buildings attached to the compound wall. The fourth wall was a fortified entrance with heavy steel barricades. Everything within the compound, and on the perimeter for many cubits, was coated with soot, so that the bright sunshine was dimmed, a pall hanging in the air.

At the center of this was a square block, a giant altar with a blackened gantry atop it, much like the railing around *Mixcomitl*'s viewing platform, but thicker and more complex. A stone-covered access corridor led from the middle building to the outer edge of the blackened altar. A noise teased the morning air, almost beyond the edge of hearing, a snarling, unhappy sound of metal on metal.

Oken memorized the layout of the buildings ahead of them, then handed the farscope to Mabruke.

He took it without comment and scanned the scene before them, then returned it to Oken.

Oken put it away and looked over at Mabruke, an eyebrow raised in query.

Mabruke nodded. The two men slipped over the crest of the ridge and slid down the face of the rock to the single path leading to the compound. They ran quickly down this path, then dashed into the stand of pines at the bottom of the slope. Mabruke motioned for Oken to stop.

"What's the plan?" Mabruke said.

Oken almost laughed. "You're leading this charge!" he whispered.

"I am just consulting your expertise."

"We can use the trees as cover," Oken said. "That will get us close enough to work out the next step."

They turned off the path and slipped deeper into the shadows under the trees. As they made their way toward the compound, the grinding snarl grew clearer, accompanied by muffled bangs, which made them bolder. Their approach might be seen, but no one would hear them. They paced through the trees, scanning the walls as they went past. The walls were high—seven or eight cubits, Oken estimated—and of the same enigmatic stonework, so closely fitted that no fingerholds could be found.

The sound of hounds barking caught them up sharply.

CHAPTER NINETEEN

MABRUKE POINTED in a direction, and they took off through the trees as quietly as they could.

The next sounds were even more ominous. A steel barricade was raised with a hard clang. Oken and Mabruke ran, more concerned with distance than quiet. The barking of the hounds stayed relentlessly behind them.

Oken had a sudden idea, and called a halt. "How are you at tree climbing?"

"I grew up in the desert. I can ride anything on four legs, but I've never ridden a tree."

Oken quickly slipped off his backpack and unlaced it just enough to reach inside and find, by touch, the leaf-wrapped dried fish. He shredded the fish quickly, scattering the pieces into the brush beside the path. He then motioned for Mabruke to run in the opposite direction, to a stand of wind-twisted pines. In the center of the stand, Oken hissed at Mabruke, then pointed upward. "Like this," he mouthed, then leaped up to grab a low-hanging branch with both hands and swing himself up. As he climbed from branch to branch, he kept looking down at Mabruke, watching his progress. They reached a section of dense needles, where the branches from several trees pushed together, and Oken signaled a halt.

Mabruke drew the hieroglyph for Nubia in the air with his fingertip. Oken nodded.

Tense minutes passed while the barks and whines of the hounds weaved around the confused trail Oken had set out. Much too quickly, the baying of the hounds came closer, bringing with them the tramp of booted feet.

Oken kept a tense watch on the ground at the base of their perch.

A trio of black and gray Alsatian hounds appeared, circling the base of the tree while sniffing eagerly at the trunk. They wore leather collars banded with steel spikes, as well as protective leather guards around their ankles. They raised their heads, and their eyes lit with triumph. They whined, and pawed at the tree as though they might climb up after their quarry.

A man called the hounds with a voice immediately commanding and pompous, *"Stumm, kinder! Sitzen zie!"*

The dogs sat, with eager whines in their throats.

The man stepped into view and leaned his head back to look up at Oken, meeting his eyes.

Oken's first impression was a man made of iron—shiny, gray, and hard. He was not young. Long years of experience and pressure had shaped his face into strict lines behind the sharply trimmed thatch of his mustache. Oken did not need the immaculate cut of his gray military uniform, cuffed gauntlets, and thigh-high boots to recognize this man. Oken had seen photographs and portraits of that face since his first classes in the PSI Academy. This was Graf Otto von Bismarck himself, Minister of War for Victoria, Queen of Oesterreich. The only person more determined to destroy Egypt than Bismarck was Victoria herself.

"Meinen herrn?" Bismarck said crisply.

Oken smiled amiably. "Hoy!" He made his voice slip into the brogue of his childhood bodyguard, the happy Gaelic soldier. "Fine hounds, those be. A fine afternoon for a run with them, eh?"

"*Namen?*" Bismarck said in sharp demand. His iron-colored eyes did not leave Oken's face. His expression did not change.

"Hoy, names you be wanting!" Oken gestured at Mabruke, not daring to look away from Bismarck's fierce gaze. "This be Professor Mabruke, from Nubia. Not a word of Trade. He's stubborn that way, just like his mum. Me? Scott Oken, along as his interpreter. And yourself, sir?"

"Bismarck. Graf von Bismarck." An expression in his eyes, a brief flash quickly submerged, told Oken that the right note had been struck.

Mabruke nodded gravely, greeting Bismarck in High Nubian. He smiled down at him as might Osiris or Rae, drawing mere humans into his golden gaze, then flashed a look at Oken, in a gesture of one accustomed to waiting for a translator's exchange. He returned his powerful beam to the man looking up at him.

"The professor, here, he says that you have some beautiful hounds," Oken said. "He wonders if you might introduce him?" Oken smiled as one might while indulging a child or a favorite nephew—or a less than brilliant employer. "He's quite fond of animals, ain't he, now, the professor. Quite fond of animals, he is. They are fond of him the same, ain't they now."

Bismarck continued to stare at Oken, brows drawn down.

"You speak Trade, sir?"

Bismarck nodded, inclining his neck in its high, stiff collar without releasing Oken from his gaze.

"Hoy, that be fine, then. The professor and me been weeks in these mountains, looking for new plants and such for his perfumes and skin-oils. He heard tell of some fabulous black orchids growing in this magical valley here, the Land of Endless Summer." He glanced over at Mabruke with an indulgent smile. "Ain't had no luck on that end, though." He turned his smile to Bismarck. "You maybe heard rumors of black orchids in these parts, sir? If you been here long enough?"

At the code name "Black Orchid," Bismarck's eyes narrowed,

and he drew up straighter, his hand straying to the hilt of the military sword at his side. *"Nein,"* he said, with less bluster.

"Can he meet your hounds, then?" Oken smiled down at Bismarck. "He's keen on hounds. You have a handsome brace of them, there, don't you, sir. A handsome brace!"

Breathless seconds passed while Bismarck stared up at him, the calculation in his gaze as powerful as Mabruke's fierce attraction. Then Bismarck barked a command to the hounds, and they backed away from the tree. Oken told Mabruke in a patois of Swahili and Nubian that they were invited down to meet this gentleman and his beautiful hounds, and he waited until Mabruke began an awkward descent. Once Mabruke safely reached the ground, Oken made himself turn his back on Bismarck and climb down as well. He swung down from the last branch, getting a swift glance at the men behind Bismarck.

There were six of them, six of Oesterreich's special guard, in neatly tailored uniforms, leather, wool, and brass. Oken smiled casually around once he had landed on his feet, showing his gloved hands with a rueful smile. "Another fine pair of gloves ruined by pitch—but then he will insist on climbing!"

The hounds came forward and sniffed enthusiastically at their boots. Bismarck let them.

Mabruke went down on one knee, his face alight, a genuine smile gleaming in his dark face. He held his hands out to the hounds, palms up, his long fingers relaxed, and crooned at them soft and low. He had used the same sound and tune when introducing Oken to the security hounds of Ibis Road in Memphis, on the other side of the world. Oken had been just a youth, having only just gotten "hair on his balls," as Usqhullu said. On such a connection, those hounds had died for him.

Oken stood unmoving, smiling down with fake indulgence, insincere innocence, deliberately ignoring Bismarck and his men with the same confidence as Mabruke.

The hounds whined in the back of their throats, straining against training and instinct. Instinct won. They crowded close to Mabruke, tails wagging, clipped ears forward, and tongues showing in open canine smiles.

Bismarck watched with clear fascination.

Mabruke held his hands out to each animal, speaking to them with skillfully modulated tones. They licked his palms, his wrists, his face, and then each other in their growing delight. He rubbed their handsome heads, tugged at their ears, roughly combed the dense fur along their throats with his fingertips. They raised their heads in delight as his fingers moved down their necks. Hind feet began to thump. Tail wagging made their entire bodies sway.

Mabruke, with perfect timing, looked up at Bismarck, and poured out a question in Nubian.

When Bismarck turned to Oken with the automatic expectation of a translation, Oken felt a dangerous thrill. "The professor here, he wonders if you would introduce him to these fine beasts?" His easy expression said that this was not an unusual request from his employer.

Oken was surprised by how surprised he was that Bismarck, the most dangerous man in the world, went down on one knee among his hounds and introduced them, beginning with the female in the middle.

"Brunhilda," Bismarck said with pride. "She is the mother-bitch of my best trackers." When he touched her, she turned her head to grin at him, tongue lolling.

Bismarck tugged at the ear of the hound to Brunhilda's left. "This one, he is her firstborn dog, Schwarzkopf." He patted the third hound. "This is her youngest bitch, Gutrune."

Gutrune spun around, licking Bismarck's face with puppylike happiness, then turned back to Mabruke.

Mabruke snapped his fingers in front of Brunhilda's chest, tilting his head as he met her eyes. She put her paw up, and he took it in his hand as he would a new friend's. "Brunhilda," he said soothingly. She keened in the back of her throat and licked his fingers.

He released her, and Schwarzkopf immediately offered his paw. Mabruke repeated the greeting, then again with Gutrune.

Bismarck stood up, briskly brushing dirt from his knee. Oken and Mabruke also stood casually, waiting for Bismarck to speak.

"It is good my hounds have found you," Bismarck said. The downturned lines of his eyebrows said otherwise. "These hills are dangerous, especially at night. You would do well to join me. I have quarters close by. You will join me for dinner."

"Splendid!" Oken said enthusiastically. "It would be a pleasure!" He turned to Mabruke and repeated the offer in High Nubian.

Mabruke smiled broadly at Bismarck.

Bismarck signaled his men. They turned with clean precision and stood aside in two rows of three to let Bismarck and his guests pass between them. The hounds leaped up and ran ahead, their tails wagging happily.

Bismarck gestured for Oken and Mabruke to precede him. They did so without hesitation. Bismarck stepped in behind Mabruke; then Bismarck's men lined up behind him. Once they returned to the wider path, Bismarck caught up with Oken and walked beside him. "Where does your professor teach?" he said.

"He does a few classes in Memphis—perfumes and makeup for royals. He prefers Barcelona—have you ever been there? The most fascinating young architect was discovered there recently, Antoni Gaudí. Do you know the name?"

Bismarck regretted that he did not.

"My professor, he's on a rest leave—at least, that's what he tells me!" Oken made a scoffing noise. "I've done more walking up and down mountainsides and tree climbing in the last few weeks than in my whole life!"

Bismarck was listening closely, his head tilted toward Oken. He smiled at those words. Oken was sure he saw a look cross Bismarck's face, for just an instant, suggesting Oken had been dismissed as a useless dandy, perhaps even assumed harmless by the evaluation.

"Has he been ill, your professor?" Bismarck said.

"He was brutally attacked by a criminal gang—almost sold into slavery, he was!"

"I see." Bismarck frowned at Mabruke walking ahead of him. "*Schrecklich.*"

Oken shook his head in apparent dismay. "He'd have done just as well in Andalusia, if you ask me. This is a strange land, full of strange people!" He held out his gloved hands. "How do I find a new pair of these in such a place!" He made an unhappy "Tsk, tsk" as he peeled them off and folded them away in a pocket.

Bismarck was brushing the left wing of his waxed-down mustache with a serious gesture. Oken wondered if translating from Trade was awkward for him. After that, Oken just walked, smiling with the giddy disbelief of one who has momentarily escaped the gallows.

A quick glance at Mabruke saw a similar expression. Mabruke met his inquiring gaze and winked lazily, just enough to let Oken know that this was going well.

The march back to the compound was a casual affair. Oken kept his hands in his pants pockets and grinned with idiotic delight at the scenery around, listening harder than he ever had before in his life.

The hounds were led away by one of Bismarck's lieutenants when they reached the towering outer wall of the compound. The steel barricade was opened for them, and once they were inside, it clanged shut behind them with a disturbingly final sound. The courtyard reeked of burnt smells, denser than exploding powder. Mabruke wrinkled his nose as if displeased. Oken could see, however, a look of intense excitement in his eyes. This was the kind of fieldwork dearest to Mabruke's mind and heart.

Oken would have preferred a slightly different outcome—but at least they were still alive.

Bismarck did not speak as he led them along the inner wall of the compound to the door of the first building. The raised path had been cleaned, yet clouds of black puffed up at every step. A soldier stood at attention, holding the door open for them. They entered a small foyer room, with stone benches around the walls, and hooks and shelves for coats and hats. A washstand next to one bench held a pile of clean towels and a pitcher and basin. A corporal stood at attention beside this.

"Gentlemen." Bismarck indicated the washstand. "Soot in the courtyard is insidious. Hintermann will clean your boots for you while we have tea."

Corporal Hintermann saluted smartly, then held out a basket with colorfully embroidered silk slippers. Oken and Mabruke slipped off their backpacks and piled them on one of the shelves, then sat down to remove their boots. Bismarck also sat down, and the corporal sprang over to wipe his boots. Bismarck did not take them off.

Oken's and Mabruke's hands were blackened by the time they had their boots off. They put on the slippers and washed their hands in the basin. The water turned gray.

The interior of the building was spacious, more "a little piece of Egypt in a strange land" than the *Moss Rose* had been. Egyptian spinglass sconces provided light, despite the lack of windows. Lush rugs covered the floor. Ebony chairs upholstered with dark leather were grouped around a wall map of the world at one end of the chamber, and a curiously shaped control panel was at the other. Oken was reminded at once of the control panel on *Mixcomitl*. He did not look at it, but strolled over to one of the chairs before the map and sat down with an exaggerated sigh of relief. "Much kinder to the arse, sir," he said. "Much kinder."

Bismarck served them Jägermeister in pewter mugs with hunting scenes in deep relief, stags with mighty antler spreads. He was generous in the servings, pouring it himself despite the aide standing at his shoulder. After a few rounds, more aides brought in bowls of hot soup, dark and aromatic, with fat dollops of sour cream, as well as platters of roast goose and venison, with crackling glazes and thick gravies. Loaves of black bread, still warm, with white butter and sliced radishes were brought out, as well as boiled white asparagus, onions, and wedges of yellow cheese. Glass bottles of dark brown beer were generously handed around. Oken wondered who the Mama Kusay of Bismarck's kitchens might be.

Bismarck asked about the search for orchids and perfumes, although the questions seemed automatic, as though he did not care about the answers. He looked hard at Mabruke's face as he talked, tapping the rim of his pewter mug on his mustache.

All he would say about his own presence in the Andes was that he was doing research.

"I do not understand why these plagued mountains attract people with research, Herr Graf, if you will forgive my saying!"

"Not at all, not at all. What led you and your professor up here?"

"We were having a lovely stay in Qusqo. Beautiful city, just beautiful. Gold everywhere you look. The professor here, he meets up with some fancy horticulturists."

Oken interrupted himself to sip the Jägermeister. "Some beautiful women in those horticultural societies, Herr Graf, some very beautiful women!" The two men raised their mugs in salute to beautiful women.

Mabruke looked up from his plate, tilting his head as though curious about this. Oken repeated himself in Swahili. Mabruke nodded, lifted his mug, and sipped. Then he went back to his food.

Oken continued with this fantasy. "Next thing I know, I find myself riding on a sorry nag into the *dreariest* country. We started out with a native guide, fella by the name of Qusmi." Oken leaned forward on his elbow, giving Bismarck the classic look of sharing an inebriated confidence. "Everyone says, Qusmi, this lad's the best guide in Tawantinsuyu, they tell us. If anybody can find whatever weird botanicals my professor wants, this is our man. His name, Qusmi, it means 'smoke,' Herr Graf, did you know that? That's the way he disappeared, in a puff of smoke!"

He made a gesture with his hands to back the word, and Mabruke, with a grin, echoed the gesture and went back to eating.

Oken laughed and picked up the story again. "Just the other night, don't you know! Scared off by fireworks from some festival or something. Left us high and dry in the hills. Took those scrawny horses with him, too." Oken gestured to Mabruke, who was busily spreading sweet white butter on his eighth slice of black bread. "This one, he says to me—we don't need a guide, my lad! We just follow our noses!"

Oken shook his head, warming to his imaginary tale. "I should have up and followed the smoke! He ran so fast, ain't even asked for his pay. I knew trouble was coming."

"These people are unreliable in many ways," Bismarck said with a slight sneer. The alcohol had brought out his accent, although his gaze was as intense. "I do not know how they created such an empire in this difficult place."

"You be wise to have your own lads about you, Herr Graf," Oken said, raising his own mug in salute. "I will sleep soundly for the first night in too many, under your protection!"

Mabruke smiled amiably when the men raised their glasses to each other in salute, and picked up his own to join them.

Oken told him in swift Swahili slang to phrase a credible question about the conversation.

Mabruke asked in Nubian if the mention of Qusmi's name meant that Herr Graf knew of him.

"My professor, he wonders if you might know of this Qusmi fella?"

Bismarck shook his head. "I do not like these people, these

Andeans." His accent was thicker than before. "I am here only to be away from interference." A curiously sly look touched his gray face. "My wife does not approve of my research. Here, no one complains of the noise."

Oken raised his mug again to Bismarck. "Here's to freedom from the complaints of women!"

Bismarck's laughter was drunken yet genuine. Oken tapped the pewter mug once against his forehead before drinking to his own toast.

CHAPTER TWENTY

"AMBROSE! WHAT am I going to do? They've all gone insane!"

Princess Usqhullu flung herself against the tall, solid frame of Steven Ambrose LeBrun. LeBrun put his arms around her in an automatic gesture. Dawn pierced the windows of his bedroom with a soft, urgent light.

"What have they done now, my little princess?" he said kindly. The fragrance of her hair, mingled with the sharp intoxication of sun-dried sweat and lingering perfume, woke him more keenly to the moment.

"Kuchillu has killed Father, and put Lucky in the Tower for it!" Usqhullu quivered with rage and disbelief, then threw her head back and looked up into LeBrun's face. "You know Lucky. You watched him grow up! You know he would never do that!"

The adrenaline of shock woke LeBrun with a cold wash of reality. "The Inca has been killed?" He held tightly to the princess. "How is that possible!"

It was Usqhullu's turn to draw back and look at him in surprise. "You do not know?"

LeBrun released her and stood back a pace, his hands on her shoulders, looking seriously into her tearstained face. "Usqhullu, what has happened?"

Usqhullu was struck dumb with surprise, and the two of them gawked at each other. LeBrun recovered himself quickly and drew her against his chest once again. "Come. Sit down, my dear. You have clearly had a terrible shock. Calm yourself, then you can tell me what has happened."

He guided her gently to his bed and sat down beside her. He took both her hands in one of his, and with the other brushed aside dark curls clinging to the tears on her face. "Let me get you a drink," he whispered. "It will calm you."

She shook her head, taking his hand and pressing it to her cheek. She inhaled deeply, drawing strength from his Egyptian calm, then smiled weakly at him. "Ambrose, you are the top Egyptian ambassador in this entire bloody madhouse of an empire! If *you* have not been told, then—could it be that it is not true?"

"What is not true?"

"That Pachacuti killed father, and blamed it on Lucky!"

"The Inca is dead?"

"Oh, I don't know what to believe!" Usqhullu flung his hand away and stood with a swift, feral motion, pacing around the room with feline edginess. She began to wring her hands, then stopped with a deliberate shake, only to run her fingers anxiously through the masses of curls fallen loosely about her face.

"Talk to me. Tell me slowly," LeBrun said to her evenly, patting the bed beside him. "Come sit here, and talk to me."

Usqhullu stared at him from across the bedroom, her hands caught in her curls, astonishment making her dark eyes wide and round. "Ambrose! I was two days on horseback getting here. The Inca of Tawantinsuyu was *assassinated* three days ago, and *you* don't know about it!"

Hysteria brought a cold and sudden stillness to her. "You don't know about it." Her voice had sunk to a whisper. She made the sign of the Holy Mother Tree, then sat beside him on the bed. Her beautiful hands lay helplessly in her lap.

He took her hands in his and pressed her fingers to his cheek. "Your hands are like ice, my dear Wildcat," he said. "I know how hot your blood runs. Only the truth could chill you so terribly."

He put his arms around her, drew her close to rock her back and forth, ever so gently, as he had when she was a little girl crying over her brother's cruelty. "Talk to me, my princess," he whispered.

The story tumbled out of her in frantic sentences, words piling up and interrupting themselves. She stopped herself, took a deep breath, and said, in one fast, steady rush, "Then two nights ago Pachacuti's private guard stormed the manor, searching for the two Egyptian princes. Qusmi and I stalled the guardsmen as long as we could, while Runa got them safely off the grounds." Tears spilled again as she went on. "When Mama was told why the troops were there, she screamed!"

Usqhullu squeezed her eyes shut and put her hands over her ears, as though to shut out the memory. "Oh, Ambrose. It was so horrible. Mama screamed and screamed, until her heart burst, her soul just flew out of her—and she dropped dead right there! His guardsmen took her body away. I could not make them tell me where they were taking her."

LeBrun ran his hand once through his own thick, graying hair, shaking his head in disbelief. "Mikel Mabruke?"

She opened her eyes and lowered her hands. "He is such a beautiful man, Ambrose. The most wonderfully dark skin I ever saw on a human being." She let her head drop back to his shoulder.

"I was told Prince Mabruke would be traveling in Tawantinsuyu on rest leave." LeBrun realized that the news brought to him by the princess had to be true. Pachacuti, the Inheritor, had apparently grown impatient waiting for his father to die of old age. Evaluations circulating secretly among the embassies recently had projected this as a possible scenario.

The involvement of Prince Mabruke and Lord Oken, however, had never been part of *any* scenario regarding Tawantinsuyu's future course. "If Mikel Mabruke has had to get himself involved in this, then I am afraid we must believe that the Inca and the Queen Mother are dead. I have to stop a civil war."

"No, Ambrose! Scott and Mik had nothing to do with it! Kuchillu killed Papa—I know it! You know it, too!"

LeBrun nodded solemnly, his face serious. "Of *that* I have no doubt, my princess. And he has had *three days* already to put his forces into place. I have to get birds into the air—quickly!"

AMBASSADOR LEBRUN finished signing the last of the memos, rolled it up tightly, and pressed the wax sealer onto it, holding the silver handle long enough for the wax to cool. He handed it to the secretary waiting patiently beside the desk with a stack of little memo scrolls on a silver tray.

"That should get things started, Clarence," LeBrun said. "Once you have delivered these to the aviary, go directly to the hotel and request that the gentleman in the Etruscan Suite come to my office at his earliest convenience. Do this in person, Clarence. Speak to no one else of your purpose there. Take Cornelius with you, and have him remain there, so that he can accompany the gentleman and his men to my office. When you return to the embassy, report to me at once. I have a much longer report to dictate for Her Majesty."

Clarence bowed and strode out. His rust-colored eyebrows were drawn down sharply in concern. The ambassador had rousted him out of breakfast with his wife, and nothing but a matter of the utmost gravity would have permitted such a discourtesy.

While hurrying through the halls of the embassy office building, Clarence reviewed LeBrun's curt explanation for the unusual intrusion into the morning sunlight on their private balcony. Most disturbing of all, Clarence realized, was that the ambassador had dressed in haste. He wore no tie and no makeup, and his hair was mussed.

Clarence ran his fingers through his own tousled red curls and debated stopping at his quarters to make himself more presentable.

The urgency of LeBrun's words quelled that thought quickly. "The coup has struck, Clarence," he had said, "the most severe scenario, beyond projections. Mabruke and Oken have been implicated. We have to get birds in the air."

Most alarming, however, was the number of multiple avian messengers requested for contacting the embassy network, as well as the request for an escort of trained eagles. Birds of prey in this country were a constant threat, so copies were a regular part of quick messaging. The numbers today, as well as the escort request, implied the deliberate threat of trained predators, directed intentionally at the Egyptian birds.

When Clarence reached the aviary, he tapped gently with the knocker, a silver pigeon with half-opened wings. He waited, impatient despite knowing that entrance to the aviary required preparation. The birdmen insisted that their charges see no other humans in their territory, only their handlers.

When the door opened, he stepped briskly inside and bowed to the attendant, then broke precedent by speaking. "This is a crisis. Your birds may be deliberately hunted." He gestured with the tray and its pile of message tubes. "You see by the numbers. They will need eagles with them as guard."

The attendant was a young man, Charles-Anton, in apprenticeship. He had already achieved the detached, birdlike stillness that marked the birdmen guild. Clarence recalled him as a lively lad when he first arrived from the academy in Paris. At this news, a bit of that youthful energy emerged. He nodded, wide-eyed, and took the tray to the bin, sorting the little scrolls rapidly into the proper puff-tubes.

Clarence let himself out and hurried on to the entrance to the staff quarters to collect Cornelius. He realized that he would be repeating LeBrun's interruption of the breakfast meal on Cornelius and Cornelia's sunny balcony.

"That is what assistants are for," he said to himself with a sigh.

CHAPTER TWENTY-ONE

OKEN PROWLED the perimeter of their generously sized guest quarters, doing his best to look like a bored idiot pacing his room. This was not presented as house arrest, yet every instinct in Oken told him that it was.

His suspicions had awakened that morning when Bismarck did not join them to share their breakfast meal of fried sausages and onions, sauerkraut and freshly baked rolls with sweet butter and honey. Corporal Hintermann would say only that Herr Graf was dealing with a supplies issue, and looked forward to a hunting expedition with his guests when he returned.

"Hunting," Oken had said in surprise. "What is there to hunt about here besides orchids?"

"Birds, mostly, *mein herr,*" Hintermann said. "Closer to the Urubamba River, there are several breeds that are quite tolerable eating."

"What kind of gear?" Oken looked at Hintermann as if eager for details of equipage. "I'm pretty good with a bow and a throwing stick."

"Herr Graf will bring what is required." Hintermann poured tea with unnecessary concentration. "You might prefer, *mein herr,*" he said finally, "to be dressed for hiking, when the *graf* returns."

"Good, good." Oken picked up the cup of tea and inhaled the aromatic steam with a show of contentment. Mabruke echoed the gesture with his own cup, then nodded just enough to declare silently that he smelled nothing treacherous in Hintermann's brew.

"I think I'll take a walk while we wait for the *graf* to return," Oken said then. He said that again in Nubian, and Mabruke nodded.

"I do think Herr Graf would prefer that you remain within the compound," Hintermann said before withdrawing.

Oken had begun then to understand Mabruke's dismay at being underground.

Mabruke was on the bunk, stretched out on his back, hands folded behind his head, pretending to meditate. Oken frowned at him as he paced by. Perhaps he really was meditating. Or napping. Guild rules: Water when you've got it. Nap when you're safe.

There is no safety, Oken reminded himself. There was certainly no safety here. There was, however, an extraordinary bit of information: Graf Otto von Bismarck was shooting off rockets in the Andes Mountains. Big rockets. Ones that exploded. The map in the common room had an ominous red circle drawn around Memphis, which was a rather large, weighty bit of information. Oken paced to keep from staggering beneath it.

His contemplation of their situation was interrupted by a brisk knock.

Mabruke sat up at once. His eyes were not the least bit sleepy.

Oken strode up to the door, then made himself stand calmly for two seconds. Never show haste to servants. When he opened the door, Bismarck's aide was standing at parade rest.

"Hintermann, good afternoon!" Oken said amiably.

Hintermann bowed curtly, clicking his heels. "Herr Graf wishes to speak with you, gentlemen, regarding some black orchids. If you would care to join him in the workshop?"

Mabruke sat still, smiling, looking back and forth between them, waiting for Oken to translate.

Oken repeated this in Nubian, making his voice sound pleased.

Mabruke put on his jacket as he stood up, fastening it as he joined Oken at the door.

The entry to the workroom turned out to be one of the many locked doors along the corridor. Hintermann opened it with an iron key. There were many keys hanging from a chain on his belt. He stood back at attention, waiting for them to enter.

They went in, finding themselves on a landing before a brief staircase cut into the stone of the mountain. Oken was immediately reminded of the tunnel through which Runa had led them in their escape. This was clearly the same superb workmanship, the same furnishings and lamps. The golden braces that held the spinglass lamps looked as though they had been converted from torch holders, the stone behind each blackened with centuries of soot.

The door closed behind them and Oken turned, expecting further instructions from the corporal.

They were standing alone. Mabruke knelt, looking around carefully for signs of wires or lenses. He stood, and they descended the stairs. At the bottom, the corridor went in both directions, but only one was lit. They walked down this side by side. Mabruke pointed to the sculpture holding an empty censer dish. The little werecat infant was crouching in fear of the smoke he held in his fist.

There was only one door, at the end of the corridor. A pair of guards stood at attention on either side. Oken felt sorry for them. The air in here was muggy, and their uniforms were leather and wool. Beads of sweat decorated their foreheads and dripped from their chins. The soldiers opened the door, standing aside to let them enter, closing it behind them with echoing finality.

They were in a large, round underground workroom. Long stone tables were set in a cross pattern in the center, cut from the same stone as the floor. These were bare, and looked recently cleaned.

Engineering toolboxes of brushed stainless steel lined one section of wall, rows of flat drawers with security locks. Despite the austerity, the scent of the courtyard's burnt metal hung in the air. The only sound was the background whirr of ventilation fans.

The wall directly opposite had a glass panel covering the top third, showing a haeka-glass view of the platform in the courtyard. Bismarck stood before this view, hands clasped behind his back.

"Come in, gentlemen," he said quietly, without turning around. "Stand with me."

They did not dare look at each other. Haeka glass meant they could see, and be seen. "You've got yourself a peaceful place to work, Herr Graf," Oken said, looking with interest at the haeka-glass view. "Isn't that the way we came in?"

Bismarck nodded.

Mabruke let Oken lead. He also let Oken stand between himself and Bismarck. He folded his arms across his chest, tilting his head to smile at the glass. He tilted his head the other way, leaning toward Oken to ask pleasantly in Nubian, "What is he waiting to see?"

Oken turned to Bismarck with a smile. "The professor wants to know what we're waiting to see?"

Bismarck did not move. "Wait."

"How intriguing," Oken said, working his smile despite the alarms set off by Bismarck's tone of voice.

The three stood in silence for only a minute, no more. Bismarck's soldiers came into view, marching in single file. They lined up on the right side of the barricade, standing at arms. Oken noted that they were in fancy dress uniform, embossed brass buttons, shoulder braid, and helmets with a spike on top.

The barricade rose.

Oken tensed, trying to see who stood outside the walls. The afternoon sunlight was harsh on the foreground of the soot-blackened courtyard.

Imperial Tawantinsuyu troops marched through the barricade, turning sharply to the raised walkway on the left and out of sight into the common room. Their armor was black, with red sacred letters. Black feathers adorned their helmets. Each had puma-painted faces, and black gauntlets with claws at the fingertips. One guardsman, taller and more elaborately armored, strode in behind them. The puma-paint on his face was red, and he carried a long sword in a sheath on his belt. His vicuña boots had puma faces. Three more rows of puma warriors marched in behind him, then more. Oken counted eighteen.

"Holy Hathor!" he heard himself exclaim out loud, with clear excitement. "You do have some fancy guests here, Herr Graf!"

Bismarck made a noncommittal noise.

Mabruke said in the patois of Yadir's village that this was surprisingly similar to his father's own Nubian guard.

For the first time, Bismarck inclined his head to look at Oken, clearly awaiting translation. Oken met those cold eyes with an easy smile. "Reminds him of his father, out on a big day."

Bismarck held Oken's eyes for what seemed endless hours. Then Bismarck made a deprecating smirk and turned back to the haeka glass.

Mabruke flicked Oken a look that told him to continue.

Before Oken could pull his nerves back from the chill in that iron-hard gaze, Bismarck said, "General Hukuchasatil will join us in a minute. You will kneel when he enters the room."

"Dancing to the tune, Herr Graf!" Oken said pleasantly. He repeated that in Swahili to Mabruke. He would have smiled at the look on Mabruke's face, were it not for the depth of the sinking sensation that assaulted his middle regions.

Guardsmen surrounded Hukuchasatil as he entered the workroom, then lined up around the perimeter. Two warriors stood directly in front of the door, blocking it.

Oken and Mabruke dropped to one knee as soon as the general

crossed the threshold, resting their left arms across the upraised knee and bowing their heads. Both wondered if they would still have their heads attached when they left this room.

"These are your guests?" Hukuchasatil said as he stalked toward them.

Bismarck had not kneeled. "Scott Oken and Mikel Mabruke."

"They wish to find black orchids here in our mountains?"

"So they claim," Bismarck said.

Oken could not see Bismarck's face, but the sneer in his voice was audible.

Hukuchasatil strode up in front of them. Oken found himself staring back at puma eyes snarling from his boot tips. "What is it you wish to know about black orchids?" The general's Trade was stilted, almost halting. The arrogant hatred, however, was vividly clear in every syllable.

Mabruke muttered under his breath in Nubian, "Hold your cover." Then he straightened his back, raising his head, and looked straight at General Hukuchasatil. "'Black orchid' is the code word for those loyal to Madam, and to Her Sacred Destiny." He spoke in clear Trade.

Oken made himself look up at Mabruke in feigned astonishment, as though he had never heard his professor speak in Trade.

"You *did* come here to spy on me!" Bismarck said angrily, taking a step toward the kneeling men. "She sent you here to spy on me!"

Mabruke turned his head only enough to look at Bismarck. "You have had too many failures, Herr Graf. Victoria does not approve of failure."

Oken had a flare of admiration for Mabruke's nerve, a brief hope that they might carry this off. That was abruptly dashed when Hukuchasatil slapped Mabruke across the face, hard enough to throw him to the ground.

"You are spies for the Pharaoh. This fool believed you. The Glorious One, Pachacuti Inca, is no fool."

Every ounce of his control was needed to keep Oken from jumping Hukuchasatil. Suicide, however, was banned by his contract with the guild. Mabruke did not get up. He signaled Oken to remain still.

"He may be telling the truth," Bismarck said coldly. "Madam can be devious."

"*All* women are devious," Hukuchasatil said with an iciness that made even Bismarck step back. "You are a fool to take orders from a woman, Herr Graf, even a queen. The Glorious One, Pachacuti Inca, tolerates you because you wish to make an end of Egypt. If you cannot, the Glorious One may cease to tolerate you."

Hukuchasatil ordered his guards in sharp Quechua to arrest the spies. Oken did not need to know the language to understand the intention.

Then Hukuchasatil spoke again, in clear, hard words directed to the men at his feet. "Pachacuti Inca, the Glorious One, will personally cut out your beating hearts, as offering to the ancestors you have offended."

CHAPTER TWENTY-TWO

THERE IS a first time for everything—the first breath, the first step, the first kiss, the first passion, the first heartbreak. The first arrest was so far down on Oken's list that he had not even bothered to review his training for it since graduating from the academy.

He reviewed it during that long afternoon and evening, while Hukuchasatil's puma warriors force-marched them over mountainous terrain.

Rule Number One: Do not antagonize your jailors. Civilized behavior earns civilized treatment. Oken was going to petition for an addendum to Rule Number One. He and Mabruke had been roughly seized and searched, and everything but their clothes and boots was taken away. Mabruke had managed to stash a considerable number of small and very useful items in his jacket pockets. He surrendered them with a pained silence. Oken winced at the crackle of lenses in the farscope breaking when the warrior tossed it onto the worktable.

They were bound, not with cuffs or shackles, but with their elbows behind them, lashed to a hard wooden rod across their backs. An iron chain linked Oken's rod to the warrior behind him. An iron collar around his neck had a chain linking him to the warrior in front of him.

The warriors set the pace, and used blows from metal-tipped lashes to move them along. Oken's clothes were too heavy for such a march, but he did not care, because they offered some protection from the whips. Oken recognized stretches of the same hard-packed walking paths over which he and Mabruke had climbed before. Once he even glimpsed his own boot print. The leagues they had covered before were now an endless run through black visions. Oken could not see Mabruke. Talking had been discouraged by a blow across his face that Oken suspected might cost him some teeth. The taste of the blood drying on his lips was a steady reminder of what else there was to lose.

They were given no water. When they slid or fell, the warriors used the chains to pull them back up to their feet. During one of these interruptions, Oken caught a glimpse of Mabruke. Deep slashes made bloody streaks across his face. His eyes, however, had a calm, even look that reassured Oken considerably.

Mabruke was, after all, a man who knew how to plan ahead.

ONCE THEY reached the outskirts of Quillabamba, walking became easier. Oken had withdrawn, reaching a level of meditation that kept him moving automatically as needed, yet did not let their change in fortunes dominate his thinking. Quillabamba was in a flat valley between flanks of stone. Adobe houses crowded closely to one another along the river and pushed up against the mountainsides. The narrow streets were empty. No lights showed in the windows as they were marched through the town. Starlight, and the last sliver of Moon, glittered on the polished stones and statues. Fear hung in the air, a stain on the lingering scents of incense, evening meals, and fireplaces. The silence made the stamp of their feet hard and loud, their breathing harsh. Cobbled streets were easier, but the warriors double-timed them. In the thinner air, Oken felt his blood pounding and his lungs making painful demands. His hands had gone numb hours ago, and ached with chill.

Oken had to consider that Mabruke was older, and that this was the second such assault on his endurance.

Dark streets amid dark houses and shops wound finally to a district on the eastern shore of Quillabamba's center. Statues of Incan kings stood on either side of a wide boulevard within gold-covered walls. Towering buildings made angular shapes against the star-spangled sky. As soon as they stepped out onto the boulevard, tall doors at the far end opened, spilling lurid red light into the darkness. Armored figures with tall pikes stood just inside, and the golden walls shed bloody shadows. Oken could not see beyond them as he marched dully forward.

The red-lit interior was a maze of narrow corridors and low ceilings, constant right- and left-hand turns with no pattern. They were forced to halt by yanks on the chain before a bewildering series of wooden doors and gates of barred steel. Oken clung to the task of simply moving forward.

The purpose of that tour through the mysterious building was inscrutable as well. They emerged onto stone docks built into the Urubamba River, and from there they were loaded into reed boats, similar to the one Runa had used, but larger and sleeker looking. Instead of a pumpkin head at the fore, a wooden puma snarled down at the water, with lamps in his eyes.

They were untied, a moment of exquisite pain that pushed Oken's reserve more than he liked, adding to his determination not to let these silent, cold men see weakness in him. He shook his hands vigorously to bring life to them, but they were numb, and barely responsive.

Mabruke managed to signal Oken as he was marched past by folding his hands before his face as though praying. Mabruke touched both thumbs to the Third Eye spot on his forehead, which meant, "Both hands know what the other is doing." Applying it in this context was less than heartening. They might know what the other was doing, but did anyone know where he and Mabruke were?

A new round of warriors loaded him and Mabruke into separate boats, handling them as impersonally as cargo. Once on the boat, they tied his hands to a bar in front of him, holding him firmly in place. Oken had to pray for the skill of the boatmen. If the vessel overturned, they were doomed.

He tried to see the men in the boat, but in the dark they were just shapes, part man, part beast, hunched over their oars. The rush of water filled the night as big as all the waters of the world. Once again, even in the miasma of discomfort, and pain, and the awkward position, Oken fell into a long dream of water demons that looked like Alsatian hounds swimming after him, snarling, their eyes glowing as red as rubies on fire.

THE FIRST light of dawn found them sailing up to a wharf in a bend of the Urubamba at the base of a cliff. Oken could see only a dark gray wall rising above them. Once untied from the boats, they were finally given water, a long drink of the coldest, most refreshing elixir Oken had ever experienced. He almost thanked the guard for giving it to him, but they were immediately hustled across a courtyard, under an arch into deep shadow.

Before his eyes could adjust, Oken was roughly seized and lifted up into the back of a horse-drawn wagon, covered on the top and sides with fabric. Oken could not see the horses, but he smelled them, and heard the soft whinny. Mabruke was hauled up onto the plank-seat across from Oken, and two guards in leather armor leaped inside with them. Their hands and feet were tied, this time to brass rings in the wagon bed.

Orders were shouted from somewhere outside, there was the slap of reins, and the wagon set off with a lurch, emerging into morning sunshine. Oken could finally see Mabruke sitting across from him, their knees almost touching. He was leaning his head back against the fabric cover, eyes closed. The scratches across his face had swollen, distorting one eye. Oken doubted he himself looked much better. The sight of Mabruke, however, was reassuring. Oken could tell he was not asleep. The gentle rhythm of his fingers, drumming almost imperceptibly within the bonds, showed that he was meditating, a trained withdrawal meant to conserve physical and emotional energy.

Oken knew he should be doing the same. The bright sunlight, and the sight of the blue sky, held him with a memory of freedom, high in the sky on the Quetzal, that perhaps served him just as well. For the next long run of countless hours, they were treated to the irony of riding on an Egyptian highway, built on stone arches that hugged the mountainsides, crossing flat valleys and wild rivers with equal disdain. Oken had just enough view out the front, over the driver's shoulder, to see that the roadway was Egyptian-engineered, yet clearly built by Tawantinsuyu, in their style of architectural fabric woven of solid stone, irregularly shaped, huge, and so cleverly merged with the natural rock that mountain and road seemed to be one entity. Mountains like giant steles, with words graven into them by immortal hands, overlooked flat valleys and terraced slopes, spilling over with green in orderly rows and climbing up the hard, upright stone.

CHAPTER TWENTY-THREE

THE LONG climb up the winding stairs was endless, forcing leaden feet and numbed legs to keep pace with the tug of the iron chain held by the guard ahead of Oken, and the iron prod of the guard at his back. His hands were once more bound behind him, which made the climb more precarious, forcing him to lean, from time to time, on the cold stone walls. The staircase was narrow, barely wide enough for one man. Water dripped down the walls, and Oken ached for it, almost prepared to die if he could have just one drop for his parched self. A blackness had begun to crowd at the corners of his vision, and he could no longer feel himself moving.

He kept climbing.

Abruptly, the march was over. They were stopped in front of yet another dark door. As it was opened, their bonds were undone, and the collars unlocked. Mabruke was pushed up beside him, and before Oken could react, the guards opened the doors and shoved them both through.

The solid thud of the door closing cut the last string that had held them up. Both men crumpled downward to their knees, then collapsed.

Oken was next aware of large, strong hands lifting his head, and of broth being dribbled into his mouth. He welcomed the broth, drinking greedily despite his dry lips and aching throat. Strength seemed to flow into him, slowly and steadily. The broth was not hot, and it was not demon's piss; still, it served well enough for the moment. He was able to open his eyes finally, and found himself looking up at Prince Viracocha's face, marked with fading bruises. His hair was loose and tangled.

The prince helped him sit up, propping him against the base of a stone table. Oken looked around. Mabruke sat beside him, leaning back on the same table and rubbing his hands together slowly. His one eye was swollen shut, and the scratches looked raw and inflamed. Stubble covered his skull and cheeks. He was scowling.

The pain of sensation returning to his numbed hands and shoulders got Oken's attention, and he rubbed his own hands, wincing at the touch.

Prince Viracocha stood, moving slowly as though he, too, were in pain. He walked around the table and out of sight, returning momentarily with the cup refilled. He knelt, holding it out to Mabruke, saying to Oken as he did so, "I apologize that I have only the one cup. If you drink it too quickly, however, it will not stay down. You have had a hard journey here."

Mabruke held the cup with both hands and had a long drink; then he held the cup out to Oken. "We are in Ollantaytambo?" He said to Viracocha, his voice a husky whisper.

Viracocha nodded. "The Tower of Shadows." His voice was hollow, sorrow in every syllable.

Oken struggled to steady his hands enough to hold the cup. He had to sip, not wanting to risk spilling a single drop of the precious fluid.

Oken finished the broth and held the cup out to Viracocha. His fingers could barely grasp it. Viracocha put it on the floor and sat down, carefully favoring his left side. Oken recognized at once the gesture of aching ribs. The prince settled himself so that he was facing them, leaning back against the door, his legs out straight. He was barefoot. His collar of rank was gone, and his silk suit had once been bright yellow; blood stained the sleeves and the front, and dirt stained the rest. Seams were ripped, and the pants were torn at the knees. He stank, too, even more than Oken and Mabruke, of dried blood and sweat. Clearly, his journey had also been hard.

While shaking his hands against the stinging and ache, Oken gazed around. The cell was of the same wonderful stonework, imposing and raw, perhaps five or six cubits square. The only light came through slits high in the wall opposite the door. Sleeping surfaces were just stone niches along the walls, piled with straw, and straw covered the floor in uneven layers.

"What is this place?" he said to Viracocha. Talking made him cough, and Mabruke looked at him with concern.

Oken smiled, then suppressed a wince. The bruises on his face had stiffened.

"Welcome to the palace." Viracocha sighed, letting his head fall back, and closed his eyes. "Let's see." His voice had gentled. "The river and the gardens of Ollantaytambo are that way." He gestured weakly to the wall with the slits. "At this time of day, blossoms have just begun to close for the evening, and breezes bring the scent of twilight down from the mountain slopes. The bell of the last hour of requirement rang a short time ago. Wives are preparing evening meals, and the flavors rise with the smoke from their cooking fires. Not far from here is a stone bridge that crosses the river between the palace gardens and the workers' village. Workers from the palace, and from the gardens and the fields, are walking home across that bridge. They sing as they walk. They laugh, and talk about their lives."

He shifted his weight uncomfortably. "Over this shines the Qurikancha, the Temple of the Sun, in the last rays of evening and the first rays of dawn. The bells of the hours are rung, and in the courtyard, the Aklya Kono dance for their Inty, for the Sun. Their brown limbs move in the light like sparkles on the water."

Viracocha's brow furrowed as though he struggled to remember something; then he sighed and continued. "In the workers' village, today is a festival, so children have strung little lanterns among the trees and along courtyard walls. When twilight comes and the music of the festival begins, these lanterns make the village glow. When the ceremonies and the speeches are done, the people—the men and the women and the children, the very old and the very young—they parade through the streets and admire the lanterns, and they thank the children for being the Bringers of Light in Darkness. They sing for the entire night, singing for the dawn, all of them together, one great voice, like the mountain himself singing. Echoes reach as far as the palace. We will hear them."

"The palace—interesting," Mabruke said. His voice was stronger, and he had pulled himself up straighter.

"I prayed that you were safe," Viracocha said. His eyes opened, the pain on his face clear. "I am most ashamed that I have failed you, that I left you to this fate."

Oken found he could flex his fingers at last. "Did you know Bismarck was working with your brother?"

Viracocha looked at him blankly. "Bismarck?"

Oken nodded. "There is a large compound in the mountains northeast of the manor. What is that for?"

This time Viracocha turned his puzzled look to Mabruke. "That was a prison once, a long time ago. It has been abandoned for a century." He sighed with deep sadness. "Kuchillu and Urco and I played there as children."

"That explains a few things," Mabruke said to Oken.

Oken agreed. Strength was returning, although he was still shaky.

"Explain to me," Viracocha said. He shifted uncomfortably again. "I have heard nothing since they put me in here."

"You were present when your brother killed the Inca," Mabruke said. It was not a question.

Viracocha leaned his head forward and put a hand across his eyes. A half sob escaped his lips. "I could not stop him," he whispered. "I could do nothing."

"Runa knows you are innocent," Mabruke said kindly. "Runa and your sister believe in you."

Viracocha pulled himself up to his feet with a surge of restless energy. He picked up the cup and went around the table, returning with it full. He knelt before them and held the cup out to Mabruke. When Mabruke had drunk half, he gave the cup to Oken.

"My brother sent the assassins," Viracocha said. He stood up, hands in his pockets, digging at the straw with his toes like a boy. The sadness and grief in his voice were too big for a boy, too big even for lesser men, larger than life. "He said you were spies for the Pharaoh."

"We are," Mabruke said simply.

Confusion showed in the prince's face; then those eagle-eyes narrowed. "What does that mean?"

"It means that Scott and I were sent here to investigate your father's plans to send a man to the Moon."

"My father's what?" Viracocha's voice was suddenly hard, and too quiet.

Oken shrugged elaborately. "We were supposed to ask if we could help, actually, when you get down to it. The Queen thought it sounded like a fine idea."

Mabruke held Viracocha's hard eyes. "Your father had a noble idea, and Egypt wanted to join and support him in that noble endeavor. The Queen sent us only to find out if your father and his priests were involved in a viable project. We were sent secretly, so as not to embarrass him if it were an unrealistic endeavor. As it turns out, Pachacuti was working with Graf von Bismarck behind your father's back, using that research instead to create rockets to drop bombs on Memphis."

The prince's face paled, and he took a deep, shuddering breath, his gaze at once turned inward as he wrapped himself around this fact.

Oken knew the feeling. He let Viracocha work out his own reactions. "This is madness," Viracocha said finally. "Bismarck—who is he?"

"Queen Victoria's top military advisor," Mabruke said.

"My brother's favorite kind of playmate. What has he to do with the Moon?"

"Egypt is closer to Tawantinsuyu than the Moon."

"Pachacuti thinks this Bismarck will help him to destroy Egypt." Viracocha slumped back against the door. "That is what he meant about raining fire down on Egypt from the Moon. I thought it was only a part of his madness."

He looked up at them sharply. "He is mad, you know. Mama and Papa poisoned his mind with their hatred and fear his whole life, and now he sees only demons. In our words, we say that such a man has swallowed his own shadow. That is my brother, Pachacuti—Kuchillu. It means 'Slasher.' He can no longer see the light, only darkness. Killing Urco put the darkness into his mind. Since then, black guilt has eaten him away. Killing Papa was an act of that blackness."

"He killed your brother?"

"It was called a duel. The real reason was madness, just madness. Kuchillu accused Urco of plotting to force Papa to make him the Inheritor. Urco's friends and servants were beheaded, then Pachacuti insisted he had to defend Papa himself. He made sure that Urco could not win the duel. Mama swore she would never forgive him, but she did. Kuchillu is her favorite, her firstborn, the son who made her an empress."

"The official report was that Urco and his entire hunting party were killed in a landslide," Mabruke said thoughtfully. "The embassy was able to determine only that the palace was concealing the facts of his death."

"Then the truth will die with me," Viracocha said with great sadness. "Usqhullu was in Qusqo when it happened. I never told her the truth, for fear that he would kill her for knowing."

"I hear your brother plans to cut our beating hearts out himself," Oken said. "Same thing for you?"

Viracocha nodded. "Our dying screams of agony will delight the ancestors."

"Yours, as well?"

"Especially mine. My ancestors will watch us die through Pachacuti's eyes. They will hear our screams through his ears. Through him they will taste our blood, to feed the hungry ghosts."

"Do you believe that?" Mabruke said.

Viracocha shrugged. "What does it matter? Kuchillu *does* believe it. He has always believed."

"All faiths are valid," Oken said.

Viracocha sighed wearily. "You have much faith in that belief."

"Egypt has much faith in that belief," Mabruke said.

"Then Kuchillu is right, and our blood will feed the hungry ghosts."

"Only *his* hungry ghosts," Oken said.

"Or my faith is valid, and Egypt will rescue us." Mabruke spoke as a professor.

"Both hands know what the other is doing."

"I dare to hope he will leave Usqhullu in peace," Viracocha said.

"I dare to believe that Princess Usqhullu can take care of herself," Oken said, hoping to sound cheerful. "If you ask me, I think she could take him."

Viracocha smiled. "You have met her?"

"We have had that pleasure, my friend." Oken tried stretching a few more muscles, grimacing at the results. "She smelled like horse when she arrived at the manor, and on her, horse smells good. Made me want to ride."

Viracocha sighed. "Our Princess Wildcat."

"She mentioned Ambrose," Mabruke said. "Would that be Ambassador LeBrun?"

Viracocha nodded. "We have known Ambrose since we were children, and there are many friends in the embassies. Perhaps they will be able to keep her safe."

"I have hopes for more than that," Mabruke said.

"Your faith?" Viracocha said. "Egypt is very far from here, my friend."

Mabruke smiled, a curiously confident smile. "Egypt is in my heart. She goes with me wherever I am."

"Then I will endeavor to have faith in your faith, my friend," the prince said to Mabruke. "My sad fate must not be yours as well."

"How long before they get to the cutting-out-our-hearts bit?" Oken said.

Viracocha shrugged. "My brother knows that those loyal to me will not simply lay down their arms and transfer their allegiance, not until I am dead. Even then, there are lieutenants of mine he will have to arrest and detain, or else his throne will never be safe. If it becomes known that he has . . ." He broke off, a troubled look crossing his bruised face.

"That he has a son?" Mabruke finished the sentence for him.

Viracocha was startled enough to draw his hands out of his pockets as if to protest. "You know this, too?"

"He is a fine lad, smart and most grown-up for his tender years."

"Although I do not think much of the name his father gave him," Mabruke put in.

"No," Viracocha said. "Runa wanted to name him after me, but

I told her that she must not, or else rumors would arise that I am his father."

"She knows who his father is."

"Who will take a woman's word for that?" Viracocha said offhandedly, then was surprised by the shocked look on their faces. "In Egypt this is otherwise?"

"Who could know better than the woman herself?"

Oken almost laughed at the look on Viracocha's face. "It's the other side of the world," he said. "Let it go at that."

Viracocha could only nod.

Mabruke said, "Does Ambrose know?"

Viracocha shook his head.

"'Rumors run swifter than shadows,'" Oken quoted. "'For good or ill.'"

Mabruke sighed. "They will become targets of both assassins and seducers," he said sadly. "They will need your protection."

Viracocha agreed. "They will always have my love. For good or ill. I determined when she was born that I would free Runa, and give her the honor of her title, as Firstborn of the Firstborn, if I ever had the power."

"Keep a good thought," Oken said.

There was little else any of them could say after that, and the weariness of their arduous journey was stronger than further need for conversation. Viracocha stood when Mabruke pushed himself up to his feet. Oken stood when he heard water being poured into the cup. Viracocha showed him the covered jugs of broth and water, as well as the other meager comforts of the cell. A hole in the floor in the corner was the closest they had to plumbing.

The men felt their way to the beds, making what bedding they could of straw to lie down on. Oken was amazed at how comfortable cold stone and loose straw could be. Music and singing from the festival reached them in the darkness, distant angels singing them to sleep, filling Oken's dreams with happy children and glowing pumpkin lanterns dancing through midnight streets.

THE BLARE of sound and light that woke him was woven within the fabric of sleep for long seconds before Oken realized he was no longer dreaming nor asleep. Guards pushed and shoved the sleeping men roughly, shouting for them to stand. The light was from flaming torches, held by guards standing to the side.

Oken was almost proud of how many guards they needed for just three weary men.

They were cuffed and chained as before, with Viracocha placed between Oken and Mabruke. They put Mabruke in the lead and marched them out. The light from the dancing torches was only enough to orient up from down. Oken focused on keeping his feet under him.

At ground level, they were loaded into another wagon. Oken knew they were outside only when the cool breeze touched his face with dark perfumes. The voices of the villagers singing were loud, a clear, pure song filling the night.

The clatter of hooves, and the rush of the river's voice, marked the bridge. After that, the song grew distant, and they smelled the wild perfumes of the imperial garden. Oken could hear Mabruke sniffing eagerly, like a dog on an outing. He focused on making that sound the theme of the ride.

THE STAIRCASE they were led or prodded up this time was not a spiral to the top, but rather a series of long, straight climbs, zigzagging like switchbacks on the mountain slopes, shorter at each level. They were inside a place that sounded hard, and heavy and tall, and smelled old. Dim light from crystal lamps showed whitewashed walls and stone steps. They had to wait on every landing for an iron gate to be unlocked. Oken was able to catch his breath a little at each.

The stairway led to an open area, the rooftop of a building of pink stone, and there was a brief moment standing in the clear night air beneath a midnight sky alive with stars. The Milky Way was a clear pathway of light. A tall structure in the center of the roof stood in the starlight, carved with an open grillwork of fabulous animals and figures. Oken recognized it as the top element of the primary temple design of Tawantinsuyu. A section of the grillwork opened inward, showing the chamber inside the structure—the Attic of the Sun.

Even in the dark, it was clear that their new accommodations were an improvement over the last. The air was cleaner, and night breezes floated through. Stars glittered in the many openings in the walls.

Viracocha asked a question of the guard in Quechua, and got a noncommittal grunt in reply. They were untied and released as before, left with no explanations or instructions. The wall swung shut behind them, and they heard the grinding sound of the stair mechanism, the resounding thud as the stairway was closed.

The song of the mountain was fainter. Oken stood still, waiting for his eyes to adjust to the dim light. Viracocha and Mabruke groped their way to the sleeping platforms against the walls, stretched out, and went back to sleep almost at once. Oken paced slowly, peering into the corners and through the open shapes in the wall that let in the chill night breezes. Through one section, he could see the spangled garment of Noot, as innocent as if shining over Memphis, rich with diamonds spilled in the void.

Oken made himself lie down finally, listening to the mountain singing.

DAWN FILLED the chamber with an exquisite light. The stone walls were translucent, glowing with a rosy hue, and bright beams, shaped by the carved openings, painted sun-colored animals and swirls on the floor. Oken allowed himself a few first seconds of being charmed by the light before waking fully to the moment.

He sat up, stiff and sore in every part of himself, and plagued most strongly by a powerful thirst. The sound of water pouring into the cup woke Mabruke, and he sat up slowly, wincing. The swelling on his face was worse, his eye closed. Oken drained the cup in a single gulp, then refilled it, and took it over to Mabruke, who also drank it in one gulp. He was blinking sleepily, and yawned. Oken brought him another cup of water. After drinking that, Mabruke lay back down and rolled over, to return to sleep.

Oken wondered if he should do the same. *Water when you've got it. Nap when you can.* He drank another cup of water while admiring the delicate shades of light. They were in a long, tall, narrow chamber, the color of a Britannic baby's bottom. There was no table, just narrow shelves of the same pink stone. Straw was piled up in the corners. The center of the floor was a sunken fire pit, perhaps two cubits across, cold, blackened, clean of ashes.

Elaborately carved openings in the walls let in the light and air. Oken knelt at the largest of the openings. He could see the flanks of the Qurikancha, and the ball court at its base, ringed by terraces and plazas. Statues of deities and kings stood in fabulous poses, guarding the entrances between levels. Morning mists hung heavily, cloaking the scene with innocence. The gardens beyond the temple walls were illusive, mazes of color in the mist.

A bell rang out from high above, on the ridge overlooking Ollantaytambo, a bell with a voice big enough to ring through the valley and echo from the mountainsides, accompanied by a rush of wings on the other side of the glowing wall, hundreds of birds taking off at once. From his peephole, Oken saw a flash of colorful feathers.

A yearning for the open sky filled him with a sudden weariness. He lay down on the straw-covered shelf and fell immediately to sleep.

ROSY CLOUDS floated past on the breeze of Viracocha's voice, a strong, gentle, yet weary voice, drifting in and out of the swirls and streamers of mist. "... the river in the sky from which the rain falls. That one is the llama, with the baby llama at her heel. Behind runs the fox, and here are the turtle, the quail, and the bird. These lines are lightning, the plumed serpent who is Quetzalcoatl." As each one was named, it formed itself in the rosy light and dashed away. Then the mountains rang a double stroke like a great bell. The clouds were blown clear by the sound, revealing a cold, grim landscape toward which Oken fell, headlong and helpless.

He sat up abruptly. The rosy light was real, the Sun shining through the translucent walls. The bells still echoed, signifying the midhour of the morning.

"Welcome back," Mabruke said. He and Viracocha were sitting cross-legged before the front wall, deep in discussion about the artwork of the carvings.

"Hoy," Oken said thickly. He pulled himself up, wincing at the aches and stings, and the stink of his own sweat, thick in his clothes. Viracocha pointed to the fire pit, guessing at Oken's first question. There was a drain hole in the center. Oken relieved himself, drank more water, and then lay back down, falling into a dark, restful sleep without dreams.

He awoke several hours later, according to the changed positions of the sunny beasts on the floor. Mabruke and Viracocha were still talking philosophy. Mabruke was stretched out on the shelf, lying on his back with his hands folded across his stomach. Viracocha sat cross-legged on the floor beside him, and had just begun speaking as Oken tuned in. "How do you mean, we are shaped by the land, Mik? We are masters of the land."

There was no point in interrupting them. Oken settled back, letting himself enjoy the luxury of being rested, more or less.

Mabruke was quiet for a time, considering his words. "In Egypt, human beings overwhelm the landscape. What we build is made by our hands, by our minds, by our souls. The Pyramids transcend space and time. Even our gardens and growing fields are sustained only by our work. Without us, the land is only sand and mud. In your world, the land shapes the humans. Earth decides what you build, what you make. We have the vastness of sky, and the solitude of the desert, the magic of a single river. You are overwhelmed by Earth's life here. Life in the sky, in the treetops, in the soil, in the waters. The Earth is so dominant that you are creatures of the forest, and of the mountain, as surely as the puma, the llama, the eagle. The skull-sized egg of Africa's ostrich gave us our metaphor of creation. You have that metaphor around you in every instant, life and death entwined in a dance as relentless as lightning, and as ancient as the hills. Your gods are the size of mountains, and as powerful as the winds. Ours are small enough to fit within the human skull."

"Ah, the skull-sized egg!" the prince said. He was leaning forward, arms resting on his knees, listening to Mabruke with his head cocked to one side like a child in school. "The secret of life locked up in the seed of death."

Oken was roused by the annoyed shriek of birds somewhere close by.

Mabruke teased him as he stood drinking his second cup of water. "No comments from the Horus Scope for such a day?"

Oken shook his head. "We are too far away from the horizon of Memphis. I think the rules of a different calendar are at play here."

"That would explain a great deal, I suppose."

There was a single hard thump on the wall, jolting everyone into tense silence. Mabruke sat up, and Viracocha rose to his feet, less awkwardly than the day before. Oken stayed where he was, finishing the water in the cup quickly, just in case.

The stone panel of the door swung into the chamber. A pair of guards stood in the doorway, one armed with a spear held to the ready and aimed, the other holding a large platter piled high with fruit. The spearman covered him while he stepped into the chamber only far enough to clear the door.

"Pomakanchy," Viracocha said amiably, addressing the man with the tray by name. The prince did not stir from where he stood, directing a rapid question in Quechua to the man.

The two guards exchanged troubled glances, and the spear was lowered an inch or two. Pomakanchy set the platter onto the floor. He straightened, staring at the fruit, then raised his gaze to meet Viracocha's eyes. His answer was terse, almost muttered. The two men then hurried out, and the door swung shut behind them so hard that they could feel it reverberating in the floor of the chamber.

Viracocha picked up the tray of fruit and carried it over to them, setting it on the shelf beside Mabruke. "Try this," he said, selecting a fist-sized orange and red fruit. The scent of roast fowl caught their attention at once, and Viracocha pushed the top layer of fruit aside.

A brace of beautifully roasted birds, in a honey glaze, had been hidden among the fruit. Viracocha laughed. "I see that I have not lost all my friends. Those to be sacrificed must be pure, no flesh, no drink."

"Then I would say these birds are flavored with the exquisite spice of hope," Mabruke said. He took a large leaf from under the fruit and used it to pick up one of the birds.

They followed Viracocha's lead and tossed the bones through the openings in the stone wall. Each bone was met by a squawking of birds on the other side as they fought over it.

"What did you ask him?" Oken said to Viracocha finally.

"What his orders were, what is next for us." Viracocha tilted his head to one side as he thought more on the guard's words. His expression was not happy, his eyes hooded. "We are being prepared for the *Tlachtli*, the sacred ball game."

Oken had a unbidden flash of memory of vividly painted murals of the severed heads of captives being used as the ball in *Tlachtli*. "I take it they will not be playing with a ball of grass?" The innocence of the children playing the sacred game in the Queen Mother's gardens seemed part of another world, just a scene in a play.

Viracocha turned his hooded gaze to Oken, then caught the meaning, and scoffed mirthlessly. "No, they will not be playing with our heads. That is not what he plans. Our hearts will be the victory meal at the end of the games, shared by Kuchillu and the champions of the court."

This was met with a chilled silence.

"They will come for us when the game has been won," Viracocha went on. "We will know they are coming when the bell of victory rings. The people sing the anthem of the winning team, while the losing players carry the winners on their shoulders around the ball court. They cheer and scream as the captain is carried up the steps to the altar, passed from hand to hand. A wonderful moment. The excitement used to thrill me."

Viracocha sighed. "Everyone chants the captain's name louder and louder as they climb, then they put him on the altar." Mabruke and Oken both frowned, and Viracocha shook his head. "The priests switch the captain with a deer for the actual sacrifice. The people see the spray of blood on the first cut, and the blood poured down the steps from the ceremonial bowl. The deer's meat is served at the team's victory dinner, and the winning captain takes home the skull."

"Why would the captain of the winning team have accepted being the sacrifice as his reward?" Mabruke said. "That seems a cruel punishment for victory."

"They once believed that such a death would deliver them directly to the court of Inty," Viracocha said, "directly to the eternal court of the Living Sun in the high heavens. To die in this way saved them from the terrible journey through the blackness of Xibalba. They go to heaven without fighting demons and angels, as ordinary people do."

"The players no longer believe?"

Viracocha shrugged. "To each his own. Kuchillu believes."

Mabruke seemed ready to debate this. "But if he believes, doesn't he risk sending *us* to the court of Inty in the high heavens if he sacrifices us this way?"

Viracocha's laugh at this was a short, bitter sound. "You try to put logic before madness, my friend. He believes whatever suits his purpose of the moment, and his purposes are dark, terrible things."

Mabruke mused, "He must be a lonely man."

Viracocha was surprised by this. "You pity him?"

"Loneliness is the root of evil," Mabruke said. "It can lead a person into their own blackest depths."

"It was his own evil heart that drove everyone away from him," Viracocha said in protest. "His evil *made* him lonely!"

"Only his *ba,* his own experience of his life, can know which came first," Mabruke said. "Only in his inner world is that time line registered."

Oken could not pull himself away from a fascination with the bloody mural shining against the stone. "How long before the games?"

"Two days." Viracocha shook his head in dismay. "My brother is afraid."

WHEN THEY peered through the openings in the wall, they could see workmen hauling potted trees to various places on the lower plaza, as well as long trays filled with blooming plants to line the walkways and entries. Viewing platforms and bandstands were being assembled. Young men, wearing only blue and yellow kilts, were washing down the brilliantly painted walls of the *Tlachtli* court, immense murals of kings playing against monstrous gods and demons of the underworld. The brilliant bloodreds shone as if freshly flowing, and the eyes of the demons were round white seashells that gleamed with life.

On the top plaza, just below them, an altar was being dragged out of the temple building, an elegant, nobly carved warrior, lying on his back, head and knees raised, meeting his fate with calm face and open eyes.

Viracocha quietly called it to Oken's attention. "Another sign of Kuchillu's insanity—that altar is a relic from the days when Tawantinsuyu and the Aztec nation were separate. The Aztec used it to sacrifice prisoners, in horrendous numbers, to feed their bloody-minded Sun."

"How did it get here?"

"A gift, a symbol of the union of our two nations. It sat in the foyer of the main chapel for four hundred years," Viracocha said. "My brothers and I used to dare each other to climb it and plant a kiss on his forehead." His face was grim. "When we were small."

"The Aztec were a separate nation once?" Oken said. The history of this Dark Continent had many pages he had never read.

"These days they are mostly members of the Inca's guard," Viracocha said. "They say dying for the ruler of an empire is better than dying for a king."

"Dying seems a popular theme," Mabruke said. "Aztec poetry I've read doesn't get far from it."

Viracocha nodded. "A romantic lot, I must say. My own guardsmen tell me the truth is that women of the empire were so beautiful that dying for them was romantic." He spoke fondly. "Hopeless romantics."

"The priests must be very afraid if they let him move that altar."

"Why is everyone so afraid of him?" Oken said. "I mean, other than the being insane part?"

Viracocha laughed, a short and bitter sound. "He is the Inheritor. He has been named. The old Inca is dead, and Pachacuti is the Firstborn of the Inca, so he owns Tawantinsuyu. He owns us all."

"Even if he's insane?"

"Is it otherwise in Egypt?"

Oken shrugged, gazing down at that grim and ancient altar. "No. Egypt had an insane leader once, three thousand years ago. He ruled for twenty years, and nearly destroyed Egypt. His daughter even tried to put a Hittite prince on the throne. That pharaoh is still called the Heretic. He is the only madman in our history, though. Insanity comes in many forms, even in Egypt. We do try these days to spot it in leaders *before* they become omnipotent, though."

"You can do that?"

Oken nodded. "You knew your brother had lost his mind a long time ago, didn't you?"

"I have always known. I watched it happen."

"In Egypt, your opinion of him would have been taken into account."

Mabruke sat up, surprising Oken because he was sure the man had been soundly asleep. "Aren't these games held in Qusqo?"

"The national games, yes," Viracocha said. "This ball court is for games played before the Inca. The national teams practice here, for the Inca's amusement. Kuchillu cannot sacrifice us in Qusqo—that would start a civil war. He will hide this the way he hid Urco's murder."

"Egypt can be very persistent about uncovering the murder of royal princes," Mabruke said. "You can be certain about that."

"It will mean war," Viracocha said sadly.

Mabruke shook his head. "Egypt does not believe in war. Battles, yes. Espionage and subterfuge, yes. But not war."

"I make a good living on that belief," Oken said.

Viracocha frowned, with a puzzled expression. "What do your gods demand of you, your Naytures of Egypt?"

Oken thought about that, deciding where to start. "That I learn to be a decent, civilized human being."

"That is all?"

Oken smiled, shaking his head. "That's quite a lot. I'm still learning."

"Your faith is strong?"

Oken did not know how to answer that at first. He had simply never thought about it that way. His faith was unquestioned, as natural as breathing. "I'm still learning," he repeated finally. "All I can say is that it has never let me down."

Mabruke spoke up. "What is that sunken courtyard?"

"The people's ceremonial viewing court. The Qurikancha is a model of reality, of the cosmos. That courtyard enclosure is Pachamama, the here and now, the place in time where we stand together. The upper rim is the horizon, the dividing line between time and eternity. When they are here for the great ceremonies, the people stand on Pachamama, and they see the Temple of the Sun high above them in the levels of heaven, so that they witness ceremonies in the dimension of Hanaq Pacha, the upper seas of heaven encircling them, high above their horizon, above the moment now, outside of time."

"Most effective," Mabruke said. "The temples of Egypt serve a similar function—however, what you accomplish by building upwards, we accomplish by building inwards, interiors inside of interiors."

"The skull-sized gods?" Viracocha said. "Is that the secret of Egypt's power—that you carry your gods around with you in your minds?"

"What do your gods expect of you, Lucky?" Mabruke said, echoing Viracocha's earlier question to Oken.

"Our blood," Viracocha answered promptly. "Our blood feeds the ceremonies. The duty of the Inca and of the Inca's family is to keep the ceremonies moving through the cycles of the year, to guide the people in their daily lives."

"How literally is that taken?" Mabruke said.

Viracocha pushed up his left sleeve, revealing scars on the underside of his forearm. Color rubbed into the cuts had made the scars into slashed tattoos. "However, cutting out hearts is no longer the common practice, if that's what you mean. My brother revived that one on his own."

CHAPTER TWENTY-FOUR

THE IMPERIAL Palace was in a small valley jutting off from the larger valley of Ollantaytambo, the fabled "Resort Palace of Ollantay," the imperial residence for the last four centuries. Steep mountainsides provided natural protection for the family's private quarters. A single gap between these was the only way into the palace grounds, and this gap was sealed off by the imposing multistory Qurikancha, Temple of the Sun, on a raised plaza. The first level was painted red, and shone like freshly flowing blood. The second level, set within its own plaza of white marble, was painted the green of newly grown plants, and the third was the blue of the sky. Wide staircases led up the front, each step covered with sacred hieroglyphs that told the story of creation, from the bottom level to the top, where a splendid pink stone chapel stood. The peaked roof was openwork art, a phantasm of sacred animals and sacred designs, representing the Milky Way.

The imperial family entered and exited from the palace through the Qurikancha for public ceremonies, so that the Inca, the emperor, appeared from the temple as though he had descended from the sky and would return there. The palace stood on sacred ground, guarded by Inty, and by the mountain gods enfolding it. Ordinary mortals like priests and servants used a side tunnel, cut through the solid rock of the mountain wall that backed the temple. The tunnel was lit by Egyptian crystals set in glowing patterns in the walls. Statues of the werecat infant held censers that burned the sacred copal day and night. Ihhuipapalotl hurried through, his insides tightening every time he thought about the dangers of having to deliver this particular message—and the number of lives that hung on Pachacuti's response to it.

"Glorious One, the rumor has surfaced that the Inca is dead." Ihhuipapalotl spoke calmly, despite his racing heart.

"My father is dead," Pachacuti said in a too-calm voice. "My brother killed him. He cut his throat."

"Yes, Glorious One, true. However—" High Priest Ihhuipapalotl drew back slightly, taking a calming breath. "—we must keep secret the death of your parents . . . and the arrest—until after the games, or else Viracocha's men—"

Pachacuti cut him off with a glare. "Viracocha's men will have their hearts cut out," he said. "And soon."

"Of course, soon, Glorious One," Ihhuipapalotl said. "This will not be popular."

"My brother's popularity is irrelevant, Priest. The old Inca is dead. I am Inca. I am the son of the Sun."

"True, Glorious One, true." Somewhere inside, beneath his official layers of jade and feathers, beneath the anxiety and uncertainty, Ihhuipapalotl knew a terrible sadness waited. His Inca was dead, murdered.

A group of servants emerged from the Doorway of the Wives, balancing large bundles on their heads. From the rooms behind them came the sound of women crying.

Pachacuti whirled on his heel and shouted for them to shut the door. He took a step toward them, drawing breath to shout again. The high priest put a hand out on his arm, and said soothingly, "Your father's women will be moved out of here by evening, Glorious One, I promise you. Our business would be better done—"

"Our business is done, Priest," Pachacuti said, shaking Ihhuipa-palotl's hand from his sleeve with a fierce gesture. He strode away to stand in front of the window looking down on the Garden of the Maidens.

"Make certain my bed is brought in time for my afternoon meditations, Priest," Pachacuti called loudly.

Ihhuipapalotl stopped in his tracks, took a deep breath, and then said, "Workers have been busy at that since you gave the instructions this morning, Glorious One. It must be moved slowly to preserve the stonework. You would not wish to damage such a precious thing, Glorious One."

"No, it must not be damaged."

"As you say, Glorious One." Ihhuipapalotl looked over at Pachacuti, outlined by the light from the window—tall, straight, rigid.

Ihhuipapalotl shook himself, and hurried away. The situation was slipping out of his hands. If he did not hear from his agents soon . . . he had to think!

"NO, I am sorry, Exalted One." The secretary was twisting his hands together nervously as he scanned the people rushing back and forth through the tunnel. They stood between gilded werecats, veiled in plumes of incense. "There have been no birds since this morning."

"Go and sit outside the aviary. Do not waste a minute sending my bird with the message when it comes!"

"At once, Exalted One, at once." The secretary bowed his way out and ran down the tunnel.

"What do I do now!" Ihhuipapalotl chanted under his breath as he dashed away in the opposite direction, frantic plans chasing themselves unhappily through his unhappy brain.

"HOW DID the Glorious One take the news about Bismarck?"

Ihhuipapalotl glared at his secretary Taripay, then passed a hand in front of his eyes, rubbing his forehead wearily. His fingertips

brushed the jade rim of his headdress, focusing his scattered attention. He sighed, sinking down cross-legged on the cushion in front
of his desk. "The Glorious One does not care about Bismarck. We
can save that news until after the games. Let Victoria deal with
Bismarck. Let Egypt deal with Bismarck!" He sighed heavily. "I have
to deal with the lightning," he muttered to himself. "Let Egypt deal
with the thunder!"

The entry chime to his office rang, announcing the temple re-
ceptionist. Ihhuipapalotl waved for Taripay to deal with this.

"There are gentlemen here to see you about the *Tlachtli* games at
the Qurikancha," Taripay announced. He sounded impressed.
"Foreigners."

The men came in, a pair of Europeans, one tall and dark, the
other a larger, wider man sporting a considerable blond mustache.
Both men had very solemn faces, but Ihhuipapalotl felt his dark
mood vanish in a blaze of hope.

"Oh, please—come in! Come in!" Ihhuipapalotl sprang up as he
spoke. "Taripay!" he called to his secretary. "Have choclatl brought
for these guests—and chairs!

"I am Ihhuipapalotl," he said to the men. "You are an answer to
my prayers!"

Taripay hurriedly dragged a pair of chairs over to the high priest's
viewing platform and arranged them in front of it; then he ran out,
making certain that the door closed silently behind him.

HIGH PRIEST Ihhuipapalotl released the pigeon, watching as it
flew swiftly up to the ridge above the temple walls and disappeared
in the brilliant blue sky. Then he leaned one hip against the stone
railing of his balcony and unrolled the little scroll the bird had
brought him. He read it, then took a lens from a pocket and held it
so that it focused a sharp beam of sunlight onto the paper. He waited
patiently until smoke spiraled up from the paper, and a flame flickered into life; then he held the paper by one corner as it burned

until flames licked at his fingers. He dropped the ember to the floor and let the last bit burn; then he smeared the ashes with his foot, until nothing but a gray smudge was left.

He went through his quarters to his office, to wait for the courier whose arrival had been announced by the message.

He did not wait long. The woman was slight of build, as most embassy couriers were, and covered with dust and sweat, smelling strongly of horse. Her four-league ride from Urubamba had been hard run. She showed him the ring she wore, signet of the one who sent her, then gave him the file case. She bowed, and stood waiting patiently for further instructions.

Ihhuipapalotl pressed his fingertip against the lock, waiting for the metal surface to register his fingerprint. The lock clicked open, and he pulled out the folder, returning the case to the courier as he read the note atop the file.

"You may refresh yourself, mademoiselle," he said to her without looking up from the page. "A memo by bird will suffice as answer to this. Return at your own convenience."

She bowed and thanked him, then left, humming quietly to herself the tune of hooves beating time against the road.

WHEN HE had seen the material in the file, he told Taripay that he was going to report to the palace.

Ihhuipapalotl did not hurry as he walked, reviewing the matter presented by the file he carried, and considering various methods of presentation. The death of the Inca had left the Inheritor in a moody, violent state of mind, and his responses to the usual manipulations were no longer predictable. Preparations for his coronation and ascension to the throne of Tawantinsuyu were consuming Pachacuti's attention, yet he was obviously troubled by something deeper. Ihhuipapalotl was keenly aware of the Glorious One's secret guilt, and he was shaken to the core by the situation in which this knowledge placed him. He had to make the best of it that he could.

In the bright sunlight of the courtyard before the palace entry, Ihhuipapalotl was met by General Hukuchasatil, head of the Inheritor's elite private guard. He was coming down the steps of the palace, his face clouded with thought. They greeted one another, then the general stopped, and put his hand out on Ihhuipapalotl's shoulder. "Bring only good news, Priest. For your own safety."

Ihhuipapalotl nodded, giving the general a quick smile, and watched as the man hurried down the steps. The priest's manner was brisk as he went inside. The guards at the entrance to the palace saluted him as he walked past, but he hardly noticed.

"GLORIOUS ONE, I have excellent news. A very famous European dancer has arrived to honor the throne of Tawantinsuyu, and your good relations with Queen Victoria. She is the choreographer for the Black Orchid Dancers, Glorious One. I am told that she is splendid, just the thing for your *Tlachtli* games."

Ihhuipapalotl held out a large, gilt-edged program book, opened to the central page. The woman in the photographs was startlingly beautiful. Seeing the spark of interest in Pachacuti's eyes, he continued. "The Ruslander who is her personal bodyguard has been loyal to Victoria his entire life, Glorious One."

Pachacuti continued to stare at the photograph. "And this woman? Where does her loyalty lie?"

Ihhuipapalotl spoke solemnly. "To herself, Glorious One. She spends more than she is worth."

At this casual insult to the woman, Pachacuti turned that sharp gaze to the priest's face. "Why are they so conveniently available?"

"*Tlachtli* is popular in Europe," Ihhuipapalotl said smoothly. "The woman in question is a tourist, Glorious One. Apparently, a great artist is creating an opera on the sacred story of Manco Capac, and this woman came here to study our dances. She asks the honor of dancing for the Inca at the *Tlachtli*."

Pachacuti's eyes narrowed. "Do my priests allow this?"

"Much of Europe remains ignorant of the might of your empire, Glorious One," Ihhuipapalotl said. "Such a performance would make better known the sacred nature of your throne."

When Pachacuti did not immediately challenge this, Ihhuipapalotl was heartened, and he added, "This artist recently had great success with the opera about that Anasazi matter. Tawantinsuyu was actually depicted as the hero, rescuing the peoples of the pueblos."

Pachacuti had regarded the priest's face with sleepy eyes while listening. He looked back to the photograph. "Who brought this to you, who in the embassy?"

"Cornelius, Glorious One—an assistant to an assistant of the ambassador."

A sneer curled the corner of Pachacuti's thin mouth. "Let her dance."

CHAPTER TWENTY-FIVE

A TRILL of drums sounded from the plaza below.

Mabruke did not stir. He was asleep with his face to the wall. Prince Viracocha sat cross-legged, meditating in a patch of sunlight. Oken stopped pacing and knelt at the nearest opening in the wall to look.

Guards stood at various posts on the plaza below. Musicians were filing in through the western door from the Hallway of the Musicians, and the Aklya Kono dancers were coming in with them, leaping and twirling to the drumbeats. The Mama Kunas stood in somber line against the wall, watching their charges, the Virgins of the Sun.

The women leaped forward with vivid, lithe displays of their native dance, beautiful, wild things, like mountain birds moving through ritual patterns a million years old. The dancers wore only sheer tunics with flowing sleeves, and as they danced, their brown limbs did, as Viracocha said, "sparkle like Sun on the water." They were entrancing.

Then Oken saw an impossible pair of legs that stopped his heart for an instant, and the entire world shifted around that beautiful view. She was nearly twice as tall as the native dancers. Natyra paced alongside the Aklya Konos, her gaze fixed upon each little dancer as a hawk upon its prey. She mimicked their steps with studied, graceful precision.

Oken thrilled at the intensity of her focus, at the impossible presence of her, there in the courtyard below. The compass of his inner world swung eagerly to true south. There could be only one explanation for her inexplicable presence down there with the Virgins of the Sun. She had come to rescue him.

Oken called eagerly to Mabruke, "Mik! Natyra! Natyra is here!"

Mabruke awoke with a start and looked around in confusion.

"Natyra!" Oken said again, more urgently. "She's here!"

Prince Viracocha broke from his meditation and twisted around to peer through the grille. "You know this woman?" He could not take his eyes from her. Then he turned to Oken, distress clear in his face. "She is *your* woman?"

Oken shook his head. "She is *no one's* woman, and she never will be. She is her own self, completely. I claim only the honor of her acquaintance."

"I hope to earn such an honor," Viracocha whispered, face transformed. He went back to gazing at her.

Oken joined him. "Soon as we get out of here, I'll introduce you."

"Do you fancy Natyra came all this way to rescue you?" Mabruke had raised himself on one elbow and was looking at Oken with the intense expression of a professor testing his best pupil. "That would be something quite striking, wouldn't it, like finding Bismarck in the Andes."

Oken wanted to protest. He glanced at Viracocha, who was kneeling before the opening in the wall, enraptured by the vision in the courtyard below. Oken said, finally, "Women are the eternal mystery—now and forever."

"We will discover her reasons when we meet her," Mabruke said, and he lay down again, turning his face to the wall.

Oken slowly scanned the other people in the ball court, the guards standing along the rim, the Mama Kuna and her matrons in their formal rows, guarding their maidens. The doors to the dancers' entry from the Hallway of the Musicians stood open, a wedge of sunlight stealing in. A man stood there. He was more out of place than Natyra. His black suit belonged in Paris or London, not Ollantaytambo. He was on the far side of the court, but the width, bulk, and blond mustache of the one standing boldly in the light were unforgettable—General Vladimir Modestovich Blestyak.

On that revelation, Oken's confidence wavered. Blestyak's secret alliance with Victoria, together with Bismarck's presence in Tawantinsuyu, erased the golden apparition of Natyra. Unbidden and unwanted, the opera program with her handwritten dismissal flashed in his memory, fixed in green wax—*You do not know me. We have never met. You have no interest in me.*

Oken felt himself go empty and cold. Natyra was not here to rescue him. She was here to watch him die.

CHAPTER TWENTY-SIX

AMBASSADOR AMBROSE LeBrun tried to decide which of the purple maracuyá fruit peeping out from the lush tangle of the vines was the ripest, ready enough for the baby teeth of the toddler he carried on one arm. The boy, his first grandchild, was batting happily at the large, purple-edged leaves in rhythm to his song to the evening.

The vines were thickly woven into the wrought-iron trellis that stood across the southern end of the terrace, providing shade and a certain amount of privacy, setting them off from the central courtyard, and the bustle of embassy staff.

His daughter Sarah sipped at her tea, humming along with her child's spontaneous tune.

"Here you are, little man," LeBrun said as he plucked one that suited him. The child reached out for the fruit with chubby brown fingers; laughing, his grandfather carried him over to join Sarah at the table.

The child gave the selected fruit to his mother and said, "Make little pieces, Mama."

Sarah took it, smiling. "What is the name of this, Zozo? What did Papa teach you?"

The boy squeezed his eyes shut, writhing in his grandfather's arms. "Mama-raky?"

"Try again, Zozo," his mother encouraged him.

"Maracuyá?" the boy tried again.

"Good boy!" his mother cooed at him, and began peeling the purple fruit.

LeBrun set the child in his high chair. "I should be getting back to the office, Sarah. I saw birds coming, flying with escorts, when I crossed the courtyard. The messages will be in by now."

The chimes over the entry to the garden terrace rang with a merry tinkle, making little Zozo clap happily. The ambassador's junior secretary Edward stood on the threshold, looking strained and impatient.

"I'll speak with you after dinner, Sarah. Have a good evening, my dear."

LeBrun patted little Zozo on his head and went to meet his assistant. "You look frightened, Edward. What has happened?"

"I apologize for intruding, sir." The young man held out a small scroll. "This has just arrived from Ollantaytambo." His expression was a note of alarm that rang through the words written on the scroll.

LeBrun read the message through, then read it again in the hope that he had misread something. He made himself take a long, slow breath to calm his suddenly beating heart, and said to his daughter, "Sarah, I must leave at once. Would you send a message to your mother, please? Ask her to have my travel kit sent to the office. If she sends it at once, it will arrive when I do."

"Of course, Father, at once." She gathered up the child and went to the speaking tube, Zozo on her hip, and rang the sequence of chimes for her mother's apartment. Zozo put his little hands around the brass mouthpiece and leaned forward, chanting, "Gram-mum! Gram-mum!"

THE WALK from his daughter's apartment and out of the residential quarters to his ambassadorial suite gave LeBrun time to compose himself. He was reminded most immediately that his brother, the ambassador of Maya Land, while discussing the changing situation in Tawantinsuyu, had said Pachacuti would not last a month as Inca. "The poor man is cracked through and through. The least push, and he will shatter."

If the news Ambassador LeBrun had just learned were true, those shattered pieces were about to fall in a hail of destruction across Tawantinsuyu.

CHAPTER TWENTY-SEVEN

OKEN WAS waked by the peals of dawn. Anxious dreams nagged after him, moonlit pools where serpentine women danced with flames, dragging the darkness out of the night and into the dim morning.

Viracocha was sitting cross-legged before the long wall of the Milky Way. Oken could hear him chanting softly under his breath, reminding him of many morning prayers his mother had taught him.

None of which, however, seemed quite to fit here, and the dream women lingered just out sight, mocking Oken with the guilt he had felt, believing that he had earned Natyra's trust, back in fabled Novgorod.

Mabruke was still asleep. Oken quietly went over to look at the scratches on his face. The swelling was no better, and the wounds looked hot, too red along the edges. He leaned closer to put out his hand to check Mabruke's temperature. Before touching his face, however, Oken could feel the heat. He drew back, frowning.

Oken went over to Viracocha and sank down on his heels beside him.

Viracocha opened his eyes and looked at him.

Oken nodded toward Mabruke. "Fever."

Viracocha stood at once and went to kneel beside Mabruke. He remained very still, gazing at Mabruke's sleeping form, the rhythm of his breathing. Then he stood, moving silently, and returned to sit beside Oken.

"Sleep is the best we can give him," he whispered softly.

Oken agreed.

The two sat side by side, watching dawn grow into bright morning through the figures of the Milky Way.

Mabruke woke when the temple guards opened the staircase entry and put their food inside the attic chamber. He sat up slowly, his good eye blinking. The swollen scratches and graying stubble made him almost unrecognizable. He yawned widely, then shivered.

Oken and Viracocha stood up. Oken went to the water jug and filled the cup for Mabruke, who drank eagerly.

VIRACOCHA STRODE toward the guards with a commanding gesture. The guard with the spear raised the tip, but the threat was lost in the tremor of his hands that made the point waver. Viracocha spoke in clear, commanding words, a long sentence in Quechua. The quavering spear point was lowered, and the guards exchanged unhappy looks. They each gave the prince a curt nod and withdrew. The section of the wall that had let them in swung shut.

"What did you say to him?" Mabruke said. His voice was thick.

"I told him what herbs to bring for your fever."

"Do you think he will?" Oken brought Mabruke a second cup of water.

"If he can get through the security in the passageways."

Viracocha picked up the tray and brought it over to the others. They were just finishing up the last of the fruits, and licking the juice from their fingers, when they heard the mechanism of the staircase opening. Oken and Viracocha stood up at once. Mabruke kept eating.

There was only one guard this time, with no spear. He had a large, plain jug, from which wisps of steam rose, and a fistful of leafy plants that looked as though they had just been ripped from the ground. Despite the man's fierce paint and armor, he wore a desperate and anxious expression. He set the jar and plant down inside the chamber and backed out. His eyes were fixed on Viracocha's face.

Viracocha did not move. He just spoke gently, thanking the guard.

Once the door had swung shut, Viracocha leaped over to the jug and herbs and brought them to Mabruke. The jug held steaming hot water. Viracocha plucked buds from the plants. "Bring me the cup," he said to Oken.

He crushed the buds in his palm, then put them in the cup and poured the hot water over them. He swirled the cup gently until satisfied with the aroma and then held it out to Mabruke.

"What is this called?" Mabruke said as he took the cup.

"*Rawray unquy qura*—fever-herb."

"Lovely fragrance," Mabruke said, breathing deeply of the aroma before drinking it.

Oken found himself heartened by the pungent yet soothing fragrance.

Viracocha, meanwhile, was picking buds and small leaves, grinding them against the stone of the sleeping bench. He dribbled hot water onto the crushed leaves and continued to work the herb with his fingers, then used the edge of the cup to grind the herbs into a paste. "Mama Kusay taught me this," he said.

"Ah, then it will be a potent poultice!" Mabruke said with more of his usual enthusiasm.

Viracocha used a leaf to scrape up the green paste he had created. "To soothe the heat in those scratches."

Oken took the leaf and sat beside Mabruke. "Look at me," he said.

Mabruke turned the injured side of his face to Oken, eyes closed, and let him smear the herb poultice over the scratches. Oken hesitated when Mabruke flinched, then he continued, gently.

"It is helping," Mabruke said. "I can tell. Mama Kusay is wise in the ways of plants and herbs."

"She makes damned fine roast pig, too," Viracocha said, "and she can turn the meanest fish into food fit for Inty!"

"I believe that," Mabruke said. "The Sun himself would step down from the sky to dine at her table."

Viracocha was pleased. "I will tell her that when I see her again."

"I rather hope to tell her that myself," Mabruke said. The unswollen side of his mouth was smiling. He touched his injured cheek gingerly. "Her magic is already working. The heat is fading."

"Your fever?" Oken said, putting his hand out to touch Mabruke's face with the back of his hand. "Yes, cooler—but still too warm."

"After you sleep, Mik, another cup of the tea will do it."

"A nap after such a feast is a fine idea," Mabruke said, pushing the straw together as a pillow. "I shall fall asleep thinking about our next feast in the kingdom of Mama Kusay."

Mabruke fell asleep very quickly. Viracocha returned to his meditations before the Milky Way. Oken sat staring at beast-shaped openings in the wall, thinking, remembering.

MABRUKE SAT up, stretching his long limbs. "Could I have more of Mama Kusay's fever-tea? My faith is in Egypt, but just at this moment, my money is on Mama Kusay."

Viracocha had placed the jug of tea in a sunny patch to hold its warmth, patiently moving it to keep up with the steady march of the sunbeam while Mabruke slept.

Mabruke stretched, then gingerly explored the swollen scratches on his face with his fingertips. "Mama Kusay is a wise woman. I will speak with Lady Nightingale about sending students of the

Sakhmetical School to study with her." His swollen eye was open at last, and the redness had lessened.

"I will prepare another poultice," Viracocha said. "Who is Lady Nightingale?"

"Egypt's Mama Kusay—although I do not think Florry has much experience with frying guinea pig."

CHAPTER TWENTY-EIGHT

THE BELL of Requirement rang at dawn, accompanied by a carillon of lesser bells, closer and more strident. The shrieking of the birds was lost in the ringing echoes. The three princes were already awake, having been roused during the last hour of darkness by that innate sense of impending disaster that had accompanied them throughout the night. They sat quietly, watching the dawn light grow from a pearly luminescence filtering through the stone walls to the full rosy light of morning.

"Will they feed us today?" Mabruke said. His voice was clear, and Mama Kusay's poultice had fully opened his swollen eye.

"Yes. I do not recommend it."

"Why is that?" Oken said, pushing himself up to his feet and stretching elaborately.

"*Teonanactl*," was Viracocha's reply.

"Ah, I see," Mabruke said, also standing to stretch, although less steadily than Oken liked to see. "The sacred mushroom, Flesh of the Gods."

"You know of *Teonanactl*?"

"We have a similar product in Egypt," Mabruke said. "We call it Lotus Dust. We use it during major ceremonies and rituals, for the expansion of conscious awareness of the sacred nature of the eternal dimension. I would not want to be on Lotus Dust while someone was cutting my heart out, so I appreciate the warning."

"As it is meant to be used in our temples as well." Viracocha sighed, a look of amusement almost touching his eyes. "But it is a matter of faith. The sacrificial victim must believe that he is being sent to Court of the Sun instead of Xibalba."

Oken shrugged. "Or just a matter of names."

"*Teonanactl* will be in everything?" Mabruke said, sounding disappointed.

"Knowing Kuchillu," Viracocha said to him, "he probably added dried coca leaf as well, to make the fear more intense."

"Coca would help with the pain, wouldn't it?" Mabruke said.

"Not with *Teonanactl*. Not the way Kuchillu would serve it."

Mabruke heaved an exaggerated sigh. "Well, we will just have to get something to eat when we get out of here." He spoke so matter-of-factly that both Oken and Viracocha broke out into laughter.

Oken was reassured. Concern with filling his stomach was a sign that his friend was sound.

The platter of food brought in by Pomakanchy was, indeed, quite different from their previous meals—a pile of freshly baked pasties, with small bowls of sauce, and three cups of steaming hot tea. The scent of the pasties was maddeningly delicious. Oken actually had to make himself deliberately recall the physical experiences of Lotus Dust to keep himself from surrendering to the demand of his empty stomach and weakened resources. Mabruke was staring at the platter with a look of dismal realization. Viracocha, however, had not moved from his spot, meditating in front of the Milky Way.

The enticing platter remained untouched for the rest of that long morning and afternoon, while the voices of the crowd gathering, the music, the ceremonies, and the game washed over them in rising and falling waves of human enthusiasm. Mabruke slept. Oken, to distract himself from the seductive aroma of the food, watched the games through the grille of artwork. He did not want to see Natyra, yet caught himself searching for her among the crowds on the plaza below. He discovered a keener understanding of Mabruke's decision to retire from the field. There were so many more Natyras in the older man's career.

Inca's team were in blue and yellow body paint, the Maya in red and green. The game was fast and violent, with nothing of the innocent fun he had seen watching Runa's boy at play. The crowd screamed with delight whenever blood was drawn, especially when the player sprayed them with his opponent's blood. The players were lithe and as nimble as dancers inside their elaborate gear. The garishly painted ball flashed back and forth in the sunlight at punishing speeds.

THE HALFTIME bell rang, and the Aklya Kono dancers came out, whirling to the music. Viracocha sat up abruptly, peering out through the grille. "She is there!" he breathed. "She is dancing."

Oken caught a momentary glimpse of her; then the door to their attic prison swung inward, with no announcement. The sunlight dazzled, splashing into the attic chamber. High Priest Ihhuipapalotl stood in the doorway, in full ceremonial dress. Jade panels covered his chest and shins, and he had a kilt and cape of green feathers, with a headdress of plumes that arched over his back. A mask of carved and painted wood gave him a fantastic and remarkable expression, with only his eyes peering through to mark him as human. His personal guards were behind him, iron maces and shields at the ready.

Viracocha stood with a smooth and graceful gesture, in spite of his size and current condition.

"Indeed," Mabruke said. "This must be it."

Incredibly, the high priest's words were not what they expected. "We must hurry," Ihhuipapalotl said to them, "while Pachacuti is watching the new dancer!" He was sweating enough that his makeup dripped in streaks on the jade.

Mabruke clapped his hands once sharply. "Hah! Both hands know what the other is doing."

"Now—quickly!" Ihhuipapalotl said, waving them outside.

Viracocha led them out. They winced at first, adjusting to the sudden brightness. Oken was immediately aware of the fresh taste of the air outside the attic, cooler and keener in his nose.

Ihhuipapalotl led them down a short, narrow stair behind the chapel and through a back door, all the while bubbling over with rapid, almost garbled speech in Quechua. His magical touches at the inner chapel wall, reminiscent of Runa's tiptoe manipulations of solid stone, opened a passage into darkness. They went in, going down a spiral stair with growing speed. There were no guards or gates at the landings. The light was Egyptian crystal, flickering weakly, as though neglected. The air in this dim place was sluggish and dank.

They emerged onto a side plaza at base of the pyramid, through a doorway that then closed invisibly into the wall, leaving them in the shadow of the central staircase.

At the top of the pyramid, Pachacuti's complete attention was on the dancers. His chest piece and collar were gold; his arms and legs wrapped in gilded leather. His sandals were gold, his toes and fingers encased in golden puma claws, with a golden puma helmet, his face framed by its gleaming jaws. The cat's eyes were set with fiery red stones shining as brightly as the gold. He was a blaze of light above them, a second sun in the blue sky.

Ihhuipapalotl waved to the crowd, and—to Oken's complete and amazed delight—Zaydane and Blestyak appeared at the signal. Zaydane and Mabruke greeted each other with a tight hug, their foreheads touching. Blestyak stood back, avoiding Oken's eyes.

"We have horses waiting," Zaydane said, pointing toward the eastern entrance to the plaza, on the far side of the sunken viewing court. "This way!"

The weariness and dismay of their days of imprisonment faded

in the sunlight and the astonishing reality of the rescue team—
even Blestyak. Oken's worldview cleared. Natyra had come to rescue him.

Then the music fell silent, one instrument at a time, replaced by
screams of fear and pain mixed with angry shouting, breaking over
them from the sunken viewing court. Pachacuti's elite squad surged
up the steps from the gardens, pouring in from every side. More
appeared, climbing out of the viewing court. There were scuffles
and mêlées as the villagers and musicians, dancers and singers
perceived the danger and scattered in every direction.

Zaydane's escape plan was now blocked by a wall of Pachacuti's
warriors, maces and shields held at the ready as they advanced.

From atop the pyramid, Pachacuti spied the escapees and shouted
his hatred at Viracocha, brandishing an obsidian axe in one hand
and a jade staff in the other—the emblems of imperial authority.
He kept shouting, vile and powerful curses, his painted features
distorted by passion inside his fierce mask.

Viracocha ran across the plaza toward the stair, climbing back
up to the pink stone chapel atop the pyramid, with the Attic of the
Sun—straight toward Pachacuti.

Oken dashed after Viracocha, his immediate thought being to
intercept him, to pull him away to safety; then, from the corner of
his eye, he caught sight of a gleam, high in the clear blue sky—the
same gleam that had caught Viracocha's eagle eye first. Oken pointed
it out to Mabruke, who in turn shouted to Zaydane and the rest,
ordering them to follow Viracocha.

They quickly reached the middle terrace, where the beautiful little Aklya Kono dancers, the Virgins of the Sun, were looking about
in confusion because the music had stopped so abruptly. The bril-
liance was a spotlight for the tall woman dancing in their midst.
She was barefoot, and wore a garment of silk scarves, the colors of
the rainbow, of earth and stones and water, swirling around her as
she moved. Her headdress was a wild crown of improbable feathers

and fantastic blossoms, which coiled about her bare skull and her long, graceful neck.

Oken almost stumbled into Viracocha, who was standing frozen in place before the dancers, his entire being enthralled by Natyra.

"Scott!" she cried, stopping herself so abruptly that the swirling scarves wrapped themselves, serpentlike, around her before falling still. She stamped her foot at him, hands on hips. "You must escape, you idiot! You must run away—run!"

The other dancers, as if this were their cue, dashed away, disappearing down the steps, squealing in fear as they met Pachacuti's soldiers on the plaza below.

Then Natyra caught sight of Viracocha.

Oken allowed himself to enjoy the sizzle that fired around the pair as they met eye to eye. "Natyra," Oken said calmly, "may I present Prince Viracocha of Tawantinsuyu?"

"Your Highness." She was smiling, her eyes alight.

Zaydane caught up with them. "My lady," he said to Natyra, "Our plans have changed." He pointed to Viracocha. "We must follow this gentleman."

Viracocha leaned back to look up at his brother, raging in the sky above them, a golden puma at the top of the pyramid, screaming in the sky; then Viracocha pointed up, directly at Pachacuti. "There," he said, and he ran, climbing swiftly. Natyra followed, scarves fluttering around her like Quetzal wings.

They reached the top of the pyramid before Pachacuti's soldiers realized where the escapees were, directed by Pachacuti's angry shouting. His troops swarmed up the nearly vertical stair after the three princes. Their legs and lungs were well suited to the effort, and the gap closed at an alarming pace.

A gleaming shadow fell over the Qurikancha as *Mixcomitl* filled the sky. His many wings twitched and tilted, using his jets and the winds of the valley to descend directly toward the chapel. Viracocha's own loyal warriors, in red and gold, stood in the open hatch-ways, armed and ready to defend their prince. Oken could just make out Usqhullu and Runa standing beside Hanaq Pacha in *Mixcomitl's* giant eyes.

Pachacuti's puma headpiece obscured his view of the sky. He could not yet see *Mixcomitl*, or the promise of escape carried on his wings. Pachacuti saw only his own victory—his hated brother rushing to meet death at his hands. His laughter was worse than his curses, dark and vile.

CHAPTER TWENTY-NINE

THEN A new sound, a new voice rose from the plaza below, the voice of the mountain singing. The people were shouting Viracocha's name, urging him on, cheering for him. His name was a battle cry that rose in strength and volume.

"Viracocha! Viracocha!"

From the vantage of this higher level, Oken could see that people were streaming up the Qurikancha steps, coming in from every direction. They carried farming tools, hoes and scythes, and hammers and wooden clubs, held to the ready as weapons, every one of them chanting Viracocha's name. The ballplayers were among them, members now of a greater team. The fans had risen, their rivalry in the ball game forgotten in their sudden participation in a game of national significance.

"Viracocha!"

The people wore no armor, just traditional garb—rainbow-colored skirts atop petticoats, tunics, and jackets, and woolen pants, and black hats with narrow brims, decorated with flowers of every kind. Children were joining them, chanting along with the adults.

"Viracocha!"

More and more of them climbed the steps, watching the drama

unfold on their sacred Qurikancha, shouting in unison, *"Viraco-cha! Viracocha!"*

Pachacuti's men hesitated on the steps, looking back and forth at the Inheritor ranting down at them, the royal Quetzal *Mixcomitl* impossibly overhead, and the people pouring in and filling the plaza below, charging up the steps to challenge them.

Villagers grabbed at the heels of the warriors, risking their own balance to send them plummeting down, screaming, to smash against the steps. Each conquest was met with cheers from the people, their voices growing louder and more strident.

"Viracocha!"

Fights broke out among Pachacuti's men as more of them defected, joining the people, surrendering their weapons, ripping off their armor and throwing it down.

Oken pushed his weary legs and burning lungs to climb faster after Natyra and Viracocha. Zaydane climbed beside him, with Blestyak pounding after.

The voices of the people got louder as they scrambled up the sides of Qurikancha, following their prince.

"Viracocha!"

Oken caught up with Viracocha as they reached the terrace at the top, a narrow expanse of paving where the pink chapel with its ornate attic stood.

Pachacuti waited in front of the chapel with his back to the stone altar. The warrior's calm and solemn face gazed into eternity, ignoring Pachacuti's ranting. Hatred distorted Pachacuti's features, terrible to see, and the hard sunlight flashing on his golden armor made him difficult to look at directly, no longer the son of the Sun, no longer quite human. He waved the axe over his head and thrust it about at invisible enemies, snarling and cursing.

His last loyal man, General Hukuchasatil, ran up to him, arms out to drag him to safety. He snatched a handful of golden armor and pulled his leader around, but Pachacuti used the momentum to spin on his heel, swinging the axe blade in a vicious arc that sliced through Hukuchasatil's throat so deeply he almost severed the spine.

Pachacuti faced Viracocha in battle stance, feet planted, weapons at the ready. The ruby eyes in his headpiece cried bloody tears, and Hukuchasatil's blood dripped from the golden teeth.

Mabruke, Oken, Zaydane, and Blestyak spread out to surround Pachacuti and Viracocha. Viracocha circled, out of reach of his swinging weapons. Natyra kept up with him, slightly behind so as not to tangle his feet, defiant, Sakhmet in her fierceness, a lioness ready to pounce.

Oken kept glancing skyward.

"I just want to leave," Viracocha said to Pachacuti. "Keep your cursed throne! I don't want to rule Tawantinsuyu. I never did. I'm taking *Mixcomitl* to Memphis. This empire is yours!"

"Liar!" Pachacuti swung wildly, snarling in rage as he slashed at his brother.

Viracocha sidestepped, dodging the obsidian blade. Natyra matched his movements, staying carefully out of reach.

"I'm not a god up there in the sky," Viracocha said. "I'm just a man, and that's all I want."

"Liar! King of Liars! I will be free of you. I am the god. I am Inty the Sun—I erase you and your precious Memphis! I erase you from my world!"

Hanaq Pacha had brought *Mixcomitl* as close to the mountainside as he dared. Multiple rope ladders were dropped from the hatches, and Viracocha's loyal guardsmen swarmed down them to the chapel.

Pachacuti shrieked in desperate denial, swinging the axe. Viracocha dodged, and Natyra pirouetted away, leaped behind Pachacuti, and sharply kicked the back of his knee. He staggered sideways and fell, howling, dragged down by the weight of his golden armor. Momentum rolled him over and over, and he only caught himself at the edge of the terrace, scattering his golden fingertips. The jade staff broke as it struck the stone.

Zaydane stepped in, grabbed the obsidian axe away from Pachacuti, and jumped back out of reach.

Pachacuti struggled to regain his feet, hampered by his armor. He was alone, caught between Viracocha's loyal men and the equally loyal and valiant villagers, who filled the steps and terraces, the living and the dead.

"*Viracocha!*" they chanted.

Once he was on his feet, Pachacuti shouted at the crowd, calling them traitors, and worse. "*I am Inca!*"

The people met his words with the same victorious cry, "*Viracocha!*"

Pachacuti howled, throwing himself at Viracocha.

The two men fell, tangled together. Pachacuti had his hands around Viracocha's throat, and spat in his face. Viracocha flipped them both around, pinning his brother to the ground beneath his weight. He pressed down on the puma headpiece so that the lower jaw dug into Pachacuti's throat, holding him there. Both men were breathing heavily.

"Kill me," Pachacuti croaked, forcing the words out past the pressure on his throat. "You've taken everything else from me. Are you too weak to kill—*Best Boy*? Will you make your foreign demons do it for you?"

Their eyes locked for long, tense seconds; then Oken called quietly to Viracocha, "Lucky?"

Viracocha released Pachacuti and stood up and away from him. "Decent, civilized men do not kill their brothers," he said.

Viracocha shouted those words to the crowd in Quechua, making the syllables ring. He pointed to Pachacuti, who was struggling to his knees, and told them that the Inheritor had slain his father, that the Inca was dead.

Then he motioned for the others to follow him, and they ran for *Mixcomitl*'s ladders. Pachacuti pulled himself up to scramble after them. Mabruke, Oken, and Zaydane were already climbing, with Mabruke in the lead. Blestyak was last, blood dripping steadily.

Viracocha and Natyra reached the ladder, and he made her go ahead of him; then he grabbed a rung and began climbing, signaling the winch man to draw them up.

Pachacuti made one final, tremendous effort and hurled himself at the ladder, caught it, and swung up to grab the next rung, and the next, climbing after Viracocha with mad determination. Blood smeared his face, and his breath came in short gasps. He grabbed Viracocha's leg, attempting to pull him free. When this failed, he let go of the rung to use both hands. Viracocha tried to shake free, but Pachacuti clung to him.

Natyra climbed down Viracocha as agilely as if he were a ladder. She held on to him tightly and, using all the power of those wild Cossack thighs, smashed Pachacuti in the face with her feet, forcing him to lose his grip. Natyra smacked his face again, and Pachacuti fell away.

Around that flash of blood and ancient stone, time struck a balance with death and paused for Oken's panoramic view—a golden puma suspended above the splendid colors and ancient stone of Qurikancha, above the Attic of the Sun where he had imprisoned them, above the fields and the gardens, above the villagers who had fought for Viracocha, above those who were dead because they loved their prince.

Pachacuti crashed to the altar with a dreadful and final noise, broken and wrapped in gold.

THIS LONG, stunned moment held; then Viracocha signaled the winch man to lower them back to the ground. When he and Natyra stepped onto the terrace before the chapel, the people shouted, *"Viracocha Inca!"* over and over.

Viracocha went to the altar and the golden corpse. His sharp eyes missed nothing. His rough condition, the damaged, dirty suit, could not diminish him. He was Inca. The people had spoken.

Ihhuipapalotl appeared out of the chapel building, having fled the battle through secret passages. The magnificence of his priestly robes and headdress doubled the intensity of the voices acclaiming their new Inca, happy voices of joy and release. He picked up the largest surviving piece of the jade staff, and Zaydane gave him the obsidian axe he had taken from Pachacuti.

Ihhuipapalotl knelt before Viracocha and offered these imperial emblems to him. "The throne of Tawantinsuyu stands empty, Glorious One." His voice was clear, and joy shone around him. "Your people beg you to take your place as their new Inca, Glorious One. You have freed us from the tyranny of Yupanqui Inca, and the madness of the Inheritor Pachacuti."

Viracocha stepped back a pace. "I did not kill my father!"

"The Inheritor killed the Inca, Glorious One. That is known." Ihhuipapalotl offered the symbols of power again. "Your father and your brother ruled with fear and cruelty, Glorious One. The temples stand with you, to a man."

Natyra slipped her hands around Viracocha's forearm, and whispered in his ear.

Oken, watching from the open hatch on *Mixcomitl,* strained to hear. He did not catch her words, but he could guess the meaning from the way they gazed into each other's eyes. She had chosen him, just as the people had. Viracocha's expression eased. He took the axe and the piece of the broken staff from the priest.

"I accept." He spoke with the voice he had learned from shouting into the wind atop *Mixcomitl,* repeating his acceptance in Quechua, and a cheer rose from below. *"Viracocha Inca!"*

Viracocha walked the perimeter of the terrace slowly and steadily, holding the imperial emblems high, so the people below could see, those who were proved this day to be his most loyal followers. Their cheers and cries of *"Viracocha Inca!"* rose up to the mountains that held Qurikancha and the palace in their arms.

CHAPTER THIRTY

BEING IN the sky restored much of Oken's sense of himself. The ordeal was over, and he looked around at the survivors. He wanted to laugh, but his mouth was too dry. They were in the hold, in the lower belly of *Mixcomitl*, amid bamboo crates with the imperial seal. The crew was drawing up ladders and closing hatches, and he could hear overhead the growl of the engines revving.

Runa dashed about, beaming happily, distributing cold water and hot broth, large mugs of demon's piss from Mama Kusay's kitchen. Mabruke and Zaydane were already deep in conversation, seated on a crate. Natyra and Viracocha went up the spiral stair to the bridge, and Blestyak was carried away to have his wounds tended elsewhere.

Oken wanted to talk to Princess Usqhullu, but then the thought of being clean struck him as the better part of valor. "Runa," he called to her. "Same room, upper deck?"

"Yes, yes! I will take you." She handed her tray to one of the little maids following her about, and took his hand.

Hot water, soap, clean towels, and an endless supply of tasty dishes restored Oken's sense of physical well-being, despite the scrapes, bruises, and aching muscles. He dressed in the oversized morning coat, borrowed from Viracocha's closet, that Runa had set out for him. Flying pumas in golden thread chased after black-faced goddesses with streaming hair, on a sky as red as blood. Oken felt it a fitting image for the imperial family.

Mabruke came in, bathed and shaved, and wrapped in a similar robe. Even without makeup, the professor looked more himself than he had in some days. He said nothing, but stood reviewing the damage to his face in the mirror.

Oken came up behind him, roughly drying his hair with a heated towel. "Zaydane like your new look?"

"Indeed."

Mabruke met Oken's eyes in the glass. "I will recover," he said calmly. "Mama Kusay's poultice is a miracle of the mountains."

"'Miracle of the mountains,'" Oken mused. "We got a mountainful of miracles today, didn't we."

"Speaking of miracles," Mabruke said, "what *was* Natyra doing here? She did not seem the type to follow a man around the world—not even you."

"I said it before. Her reasons are entirely her own." Oken could only smile. "She was here to rescue us." He grinned at Mabruke. "As striking as finding Master Zaydane in the Andes, wouldn't you say?"

Mabruke acknowledged the tease. "Zaydane was following Natyra and Blestyak, as it turns out—which was your suggestion, by the way. Blestyak's connections with the Black Orchid group made him curious. He tells me that Ambrose LeBrun contacted him though the embassy in Urubamba, asking him to help find us. Zaydane is also responsible for bringing Natyra into the rescue plan."

"As a diversion." Oken said.

"I do think Viracocha found her diverting."

Oken had to agree with that. "Which brings us back to the question of why Natyra is here."

"You must ask the lady herself."

* * *

OKEN AND Mabruke ventured down the spiral stair to the bridge. Hanaq Pacha was at his command seat in front of the front windows, with little Runa perched on the edge of a pilot's seat close beside him. They were whispering to each other. When Runa saw them step off the spiral stair, she leaped to her feet and ran over to throw her arms around each of the men in a hug. Oken found he much preferred that to having her bow to him.

Mabruke rested his hands on her shoulders and kissed the top of her head. "My Lady Runa," he said solemnly, "I will tell you again how relieved I am to know that you have been safe here these last days. I trust your son is well?"

Runa nodded happily. "He is helping in the galley, sir. I hope you will meet him soon."

"I will meet him now," Mabruke said. "His bravery in standing by you in these dangerous times should be acknowledged."

"Mik's hoping for a nosh along the way," Oken said to Runa.

She laughed merrily and took Mabruke's hand. "I have just the nosh for you!"

"Where is Princess Usqhullu?" Oken said to her. He had hoped to find her on the bridge, to thank her properly.

"She is tending the wounds of that yellow giant who climbed up the ladders with you." With this mysterious answer, she and Mabruke disappeared behind the tapestry.

"'That yellow giant,'" Oken echoed. That had been his first impression of Blestyak, too.

Then he strolled over to Hanaq Pacha. The rearview glass was up. He stood without speaking, gazing out at the view spread below, magnificent isolation, with tall mountains on the horizon.

Hanaq Pacha said, "Xochicacahuatl, at Quillabamba."

Oken took that to mean their next destination. "Excellent news, Captain—I long for another feast at Mama Kusay's table."

Hanaq Pacha nodded. "I have been away too long myself, sir."

"Ah, that's true. You did not get to linger there as we did that last trip."

The captain twisted around in his seat to look up at Oken. "What happened, if I dare to ask?"

"Ah, so sorry, Captain, of course."

The captain motioned to the musicians to lower the volume so that he could speak with Oken without leaving his post.

Oken decided how far back to begin, then told Hanaq Pacha of his adventures with Mabruke and Prince Viracocha in leisurely detail.

As he wrapped up, complimenting the captain for arriving in good time to whisk them away, Oken realized that Zaydane had been standing silently behind him for a good part of his narration.

"Thank you," Zaydane said. "That was an excellent report."

Oken and Zaydane watched the landscape slide past below. They were at an altitude that showed the little valleys cradled in the mountains' arms, each a miniature Egypt around a toy Nile, held up close to the sky.

Oken said to Hanaq Pacha, "What brought *you* here, Captain? Prince Viracocha told us that Quetzals are not allowed over Ollantaytambo."

"The sacred space has not been violated since the first Quetzal took wing." Captain Hanaq Pacha seemed quite pleased to be able to say this. His Third Eye almost twinkled. "We can only wait to see how the gods will punish us for that." He spoke with such a serene smile that Oken had to laugh.

"Princess Usqhullu and Runa," Captain Hanaq Pacha added. "They made an excellent suggestion."

"It's good to be back in the sky," Oken said with a nod.

"I was also grateful to see this airship appear," Zaydane said. "I do not yet know how Prince Pachacuti got wind of our plan." He sounded less than thrilled with his planning. "I pray they did not harm the horses. They were fine beasts. We are most fortunate that

Princess Usqhullu and Captain Hanaq Pacha had their own plans. Since *we* did not know *Mixcomitl* was coming, the informant could not warn the Inheritor."

Zaydane frowned, making his scar look even more sinister. "I have just sent a bird to Ambassador LeBrun, informing him. A number of people were involved in the cover story that got us onto the Qurikancha grounds. The investigation will have to be thorough." Then he added thoughtfully, "Having Bismarck turn up in the middle of this . . ." He sighed. "I was certain I would find him hiding in the Atlas Mountains. You and Mik have proved I must broaden my view."

"As broad as the Moon."

"Yes. I want to see this place where you found him."

"Do you think he's still there?" Oken said. The thought was most unpleasant.

"That would be too much to hope for."

"Scott?"

Oken turned at the voice. Natyra came down the spiral stair, her feathered headdress replaced by a single green scarf around her bare skull. She stood, regarding him with a stern expression. Oken felt the same electric surge she always inspired in him.

Zaydane acknowledged Natyra with a polite bow, then went to stand beside the captain. The lower volume of the *hara'wi* enclosed them in privacy.

"Talk with me," Natyra said to Oken, walking over to the lounge chairs. She sat down on the divan, motioning for him to sit beside her.

That pleasing warmth of being so close to her spread through Oken. The wild, mad ordeal he had lived through, dragging him through darkness and pain, had nonetheless set him down here, close enough to touch her hand, to feel the fire.

She just looked at him, deciding something about him. Finally she spoke, her voice low and restrained. "When you turned up in

Marrakech, I was terribly disappointed in you. I did not think you would reduce yourself to following me around Europe."

"So you went to Tawantinsuyu?" This was the woman he was sure of, the woman he admired—always, and entirely, her own self.

"I spent months rehearsing that opera, and I made friends with so many of the artists, and that sweet little costume designer— they all lived in Qusqo. They talked so much about the beauties of their world. When Marietta said you were on your way to Andalusia, I decided to see the New World for myself, to run to the other side of the world—to get away from you. The opera went on to Paris, and I took the first flight out of Casablanca—but you were here!"

Natyra hugged herself, refusing to meet his eyes. "Your Nubian prince was all they could talk about." She turned her full glare on him. "They said you were his lover."

Oken did not let himself smile. "He wishes I were."

"You should be. He is a most beautiful man."

"Are you jealous?"

She stood up so that she could stamp her foot at him imperiously. "I have never been jealous of anyone in my life!"

"I can believe that," Oken said quietly, with sincerity. "Why did you agree to help Zaydane with our rescue?"

"I was bored. This country has so few places for the dance—and Zaydane offered me such an audience! To dance before the emperor? I could not refuse."

"I was glad to see you again," he said.

Natyra stood there, arms folded, regarding him with regal dismay; then she relented and lowered her chin, her gaze dropping for just a moment. "I missed you." She tilted her head to the side as she looked at him. "You are trouble, and that is so much more exciting."

"More exciting than what?"

She sat down again, this time gently touching his fingers. "Never mind. I did not come here to scold you, even though you deserve it.

I lied to you, a great lie, the same great lie I have used since I left my village. I was twelve years old, yet I danced like a grown woman, so no one believed that. They thought I lied when I told the truth."

Oken was heartened to see her expression as she remembered the moment of that first triumph. "So you told them you were twenty-five," he said softly. "Of course." He was amused with himself that he had believed her lie so passionately. "Logical."

Natyra smiled with dazzling openness. "When I was a child, they treated me as an adult. Now I am an adult, they marvel how I look so young for my years. I am not forty-eight. I am only twenty-eight."

"You are magnificent at any age, Natyra." Somewhere inside himself, Oken laughed merrily. They were the same age.

"Thank you. I tell you this because I told Viracocha my true age."

"A husband should know such things."

"You know?"

"I was there the first time he saw you, when we were prisoners in the Attic of the Sun, about to die."

"He told me of this moment."

"He told the truth." Oken then described the scene for her, the honesty of Viracocha's passion, how his vision of her had transformed him, had revived them. Oken knew how to tell her, how to give her the moment the way a man felt it, less with words than with the eloquence of eyes and voice, ardor measured in breaths held and sighs restrained.

She listened with equal eloquence, her eyes and her whole being focused on him.

"For such a woman he would live. He would conquer." Oken remembered Viracocha's hushed voice and awed intensity. "He will also accept a throne he does not want," he said, "sacrificing his greatest pleasure in life for you."

"What is that?"

"Flying. He will let the throne clip his golden wings."

"Why?"

"The Inca is not allowed to fly. It is considered too risky."

Oken was thrilled then by the way the lift in her eyebrows declared that this would change. She was already thinking like an empress.

"Thank you." Natyra's smile was solemn and she sat forward to speak seriously. "It is important to me that I know this. You are good to share this with me."

Her green eyes made his heart jump, and he hoped that would always be true.

After she left, returning to Viracocha's quarters, Oken sat there for some time, remembering.

CHAPTER THIRTY-ONE

LORD OKEN used a farscope borrowed from Zaydane to observe Bismarck's rocket base in its little valley. The familiar black pall of soot covering the buildings and grounds seemed doubly ominous in the hard sunlight, layered with memories of pain and dismay. It was too easy to remember the way they had been marched from there to Quillabamba, and the nightmare boat ride after—a nightmare that had gone on for days.

Sunshine on his back was a pleasant sensation, and he made himself focus on that.

Viracocha's warriors were slowly creeping toward the walls of the compound, shielded by pine trees and the scrubby bushes. Oken was impressed by their grace and stealth. Without knowing they were there, he might have overlooked them.

Mabruke and Zaydane were watching silently. Oken saw the captain's signal. He returned the farscope to Zaydane and motioned for them to follow him.

They reached the front gate of the compound and found it standing open, a black silence hanging heavily over the courtyard and the gantry. Zaydane, Mabruke, and Oken followed closely as Viracocha's warriors went in.

Empty.

"Not unexpected," Zaydane said. "Let's see what they left behind."

The command room was as they had last seen it, the deadly red circle around Memphis on the wall map as alarming now as when first seen. There were the black leather chairs with hard arms, heavy and solid as stone, and cushions that never offered comfort. The low ceiling was oppressive, the light harsh. Dishes from a last meal were left on the table, the brown bottles of beer unfinished. The three men spread around the room, taking in the details. Captain Wayta and his men stood by the outer entrance, awaiting further orders.

Mabruke picked up one of the beer bottles and sniffed at the contents. "Yesterday, I would say."

Zaydane stood in front of the map, considering that red circle. "We should take this with us. It's not much, but it is persuasive."

"Stay positive," Mabruke said to him. "This is bound to be Bismarck's undoing, one way or the other."

"Madam does not tolerate failure," Oken said.

"We stopped *this* project," Mabruke said cheerfully. "I will not ask for more than that."

"I will," Oken said. "I have a personal score to settle."

"I'm the one with the scars!" Mabruke said.

"I'm the one who has to look at them." Oken went to the door that he knew would lead to the stairs down to the workroom.

Mabruke did not reply. He hurried to Oken's side, sniffing audibly, and put an arm out to stop him from going down those stairs. He shook his head then with a seriously unhappy look. "Out. Everybody out. Now." However calmly he spoke, there was no questioning the command in his voice. He slammed the door shut with abrupt finality. Zaydane gestured to Captain Wayta to round up his men.

"Now! Quickly!" Mabruke said more urgently, sprinting ahead of them through the coatroom, and out the main door.

Zaydane stopped in the courtyard to speak. Mabruke waved him silent, leading them out the front gate. They had barely cleared the steel line of the gate when an explosion behind them knocked them off their feet, flinging them into the pine trees. Clouds of black dust surged around and into the sky. Oken managed to protect his face with his gloved hands, but spiky branches scraped across his skull. When he sat up, coughing at the dust and shaking his head to clear the buzzing, drops of blood splattered around him.

"Mik!" he shouted, pulling himself to his feet.

Many had landed tangled together. Those closest to the gate were unconscious. Everyone was covered with a layer of soot. Mabruke was helping Zaydane to stand. Wayta sat up, shouting to his men. One by one, they called in response, coughing and wiping their eyes.

Oken went over to his friend, and Mabruke anticipated the question on Oken's face. "I smelled the fuse burning," he said. "It ignited when you opened that door." Then he frowned at Oken. "You're as black as me!" He shook his head. "And you're bleeding."

Oken put his hand up, gingerly feeling the damage. "A scratch. Are you hurt?"

Mabruke said no.

Oken turned to Zaydane. "And you, sir?"

"Unharmed, thanks to Mik and his marvelous nose."

Mabruke tapped the mentioned organ with a fingertip, and the two men grinned at each other.

They then heard the crackle of flames from within the compound, and Mabruke said loudly, "We can't let the evidence in that place burn!" He called to Captain Wayta, who was helping one of his men to his feet. "We have to stop those fires!"

The captain nodded, and gave orders to his men. Those able to move ran back into the compound. The building front was destroyed, blocks tumbled. The explosion had been centered beneath the main room, which was gone, everything flung to the sides. The map wall was shattered. Steel cabinets from the workroom below had been blown upward and lay among the ruins, their contents spilled. Papers were drifting about, some smoldering. Ledger books with green covers were scattered everywhere. The men leaped to these in one motion.

"Wayta!" Mabruke shouted. "Papers—everything—we need this evidence!" As he spoke, he was tying a kerchief around his head to cover his mouth and nose against the soot and smoke. Oken and Zaydane did the same.

Captain Wayta gave orders for his men spread around the ruins, collecting papers and books as they went, beating out flames with their shields.

Oken began stamping out flames with his booted feet, trying to see as many of the crisping pages as possible, for later review. Then, in the midst of the fire, a familiar shape grabbed his attention—a leather scroll-case. He reached down through the flames to snatch it out, beating it against his sleeve. The seal on the outside was scorched but unmistakable, the arms of the Habsburg House of Oesterreich, Albert and Victoria's seal. The rest of the pages before him were forgotten as he opened that case, praying to Sashetah that the scroll inside was unharmed.

In the back of his mind, he wondered if that iron-hard man, Bismarck, had felt the same thrill at a message from his queen that Oken had felt in Novgorod. It was an unsettling thought. It was, at least, a fair thought. Then he scoffed at himself. If Bismarck had felt anything close to Oken's emotion, he would never have left that precious scroll behind.

The wax seal was melted, but the scroll was safe. He unrolled it carefully, feeling a peculiar excitement. He recognized at once the ornamental border on the page from Victoria's palace. Victoria's signature, alas, was the only legible word on the page. The rebel queen was noted for her inscrutable hand.

With an internal curse, he took the scroll over to Mabruke, who was gathering ledger books with the happy intensity of a child at a holiday egg hunt. "Look at this," Oken said tersely.

Mabruke leaned over his armful of ledgers to look at the page. His face brightened. He called to Zaydane. "He's more familiar with her hand."

Zaydane took the scroll with a solemn look, and stood squinting at the handwriting for so long that Oken wanted to shout, then realized he was holding his breath.

"We've got him." Zaydane spoke so quietly and evenly that it rang louder than a shout.

He read from the letter, "'Your blitzkrieg on Memphis cannot happen too soon. I want to hear the explosions here in Vienna.'"

"Weapons violations," Mabruke said, an eager tenseness edging his words. "Bismarck can be legally arrested."

"'That's a prize the Pharaoh will thank us for," Oken said. Bruises, blood, and blackened faces were forgotten. Here was a victory sweeter and more immediate than the Moon.

MAMA KUSAY'S generously filled backpacks were among the missing. Wayta said that was good news. "The leather bears the imperial mark—recognized everywhere. That mark will be reported to the temple."

Zaydane laughed out loud at this. "So we will track Bismarck by the crumbs from Mama Kusay's kitchen!"

Wayta and his warriors remained at the compound, putting out fires and retrieving anything and everything retrievable. Oken, Mabruke, and Zaydane returned to the manor, walking along that too-familiar path beaten into the mountainside. Oken saved his questions for later. Mabruke and Zaydane were engaged in an intense, tersely worded discussion about coordinating protocol procedures between the Atlas, Memphis, and Interpol security agencies in the arrest of Bismarck. Oken listened closely. They would both want written accounts of their dialogue. The hunt was on for real.

CHAPTER THIRTY-TWO

AMBROSE LEBRUN was pressing his signet ring into the wax seals on the last message scrolls as Clarence helped him into his jacket.

"Your travel kit is already on board, sir. You can refresh your makeup once in flight."

"Of course, our makeup must be perfect in the face of disaster."

"We are Egyptians, sir."

LeBrun smoothed his collar and buttoned the jacket. "We are, Clarence." He put the seal into its pouch and slipped that into an inner pocket. "No word from Cornelius?"

"No, sir."

"Let us hope he survived the battle at Ollantaytambo."

Clarence gathered up the scrolls, piling them carefully on the silver tray. "Fly high, sir," he said quietly as LeBrun picked up his walking stick and gloves from the desk.

LeBrun strode away, pulling on his gloves.

Clarence took a deep breath to steady his hands, then hurried out to the aviary. Golden censers looked surprised without their veil of sacred smoke, and the silence in the empty halls filled him with dismay.

CHAPTER THIRTY-THREE

USQHULLU DID not appear until mid-dinner, and she did not come in to join them.

Oken noted the marked change in her appearance, a simple cotton dress with the household emblem on sky blue. She looked as magnificent as ever, but something in her was different, calmer.

Usqhullu explained that General Blestyak was resting from the wounds he sustained in the battle at the Qurikancha. "He is a remarkable warrior."

Natyra laughed fondly. "He is also as thickheaded as a stone wall!"

Usqhullu looked at Natyra with a mysterious smile. "He is. Has he always been so?"

Natyra shrugged eloquently, and the two women smiled at one another.

"How severely was he wounded?" Viracocha was once more sleekly attired in a silk suit, his hair oiled and sleek, his makeup impeccable. The deprivations of the last days showed only in the looser fit of his elegant clothes. His posture, his stance, showed he had accepted and understood the role thrust upon him.

"Not so much as he would wish to brag about," his sister said.

Her quietly spoken words to her brother revealed much: "My husband-to-be has a request of you, a request of the Inca, actually."

Natyra said nothing, smiling around at the men as she took in their surprised looks.

"Really, Hulla," Viracocha said. "So quickly?"

The merriment shining in the princess's eyes told much of the story. Usqhullu smiled at her brother without answering, then shrugged. "I am no less impetuous than you."

Viracocha stood up from the table, put his arms out to her, and brother and sister hugged. He kissed her forehead fondly and said, "What does your next husband request of Inca?"

"Sanctuary."

"Sanctuary? From whom?"

"Victoria."

"This queen has much to answer for. Why does he need sanctuary from her?"

"He has been loyal to her and a spy for her most of his life. I told him he had to choose between her and me." Pride and happiness glowed in her face. "I won."

She and Natyra looked at one another with the eternal understanding of women as Usqhullu said to Viracocha, "It is important to him that he ask you in person."

"Of course."

She turned to the rest of the men. "I think having you gentlemen as witness will reassure him."

The men agreed.

Usqhullu thanked her brother with a quick kiss and went out, returning a few minutes later with Blestyak, who was wrapped in one of Prince Viracocha's crimson robes. Without his uniform, he was quite changed, as though he had shaped himself within its confines, and was only just released. His great bulk was the same, but the stolid, untouchable uprightness of the man had crumbled. He leaned against Usqhullu like an old man. The paleness of his face made his blond hair and mustache as bright as gold. He looked at the floor, unable to meet anyone's eye.

Usqhullu led him to Viracocha, who spoke first. "I am in your debt, my friend. You were wounded in our defense. I thank you from my heart for keeping my lady safe."

Blestyak was taken aback by this, and he glanced around anxiously at the other men, then at Viracocha, and at last found his courage to speak. "Glorious One, I beg sanctuary of you, that I might remain here within the safety of your empire." His voice was breathy and weak.

Viracocha's voice was genuine, enfolding the man in front of him with his warmth. "My friend, on one condition—my future brother-in-law must never again call me 'Glorious One'! You are welcome here."

As though this had taken his last strength, Blestyak sagged against Usqhullu. "Thank you!" he whispered; then he coughed, gasping.

"Back to bed, my love," Usqhullu said to him. "Now."

Oken was too fascinated by this turn of events to pass up the opportunity to observe more, so he stepped forward and gently took Blestyak's other arm, to help support him. The man looked at him with bleak dismay.

Oken said, "Let me help, General Blestyak."

Blestyak nodded, and they took him back to his room.

His room was Usqhullu's room, her bed his bed. The sleek opulence of the suite spoke eloquently of her style and sensibility. It also made clear her love of horses. How fitting, Oken thought, for now she had an officer of the vizier's stables.

Blestyak sat down on the bed and thanked them with breathy words.

Oken stood back, observing the gentle way that Usqhullu held a glass of water out for him, watching him while he drank it, then helped him settle back against the pillows. She smoothed his hair with her palm, smiling down at him. He took her hands in his and kissed her fingers and her palms, then lay back with a sigh and closed his eyes. She kissed his forehead. "Sleep now, my love. The healer will check on you in a moment."

Usqhullu took Oken's hand and led him out. Once in the corridor, she said, "He was struck in the chest by a spear. His lung was damaged, but not punctured. He will recover with rest."

"Not so much as he would brag about," Oken said, repeating her words. "The general is a very lucky man."

"He is a most beautiful creature!" Usqhullu whispered happily. "And he is all the more beautiful to me for being a wounded creature. I will have much more fun with him than I did with my first husband." She winked at Oken. "Someday I'll tell you that story!"

"I look forward to it, my lady."

Usqhullu considered him with that clear-eyed expression of intense regard he had seen on several women's faces in the New World. "The general told me about how he met you." She touched the scar on Oken's cheek with a warm fingertip. "This is from him?"

Oken nodded.

"Natyra came here to follow you?"

Oken shook his head, a smile touching his lips. "To run away from me," he said solemnly. "I am trouble, or so she told me."

Usqhullu nodded, also smiling. "You are, the finest kind. Did you know that I shall be Natyra's lady-in-waiting, when Lucky is Inca? Isn't that wonderful? I know all the names—and *all* the secrets!"

Oken was surprised by the delight with which she announced this. "You are the daughter of Inca, my lady Wildcat!" he said in protest. "Surely lady-in-waiting is too simple a title for you?"

The expression on her warm, lovely face was one of those great rewards for Oken's gift of memory, an expression to keep and to savor. "Oh, my!" she said merrily. "There will be nothing *simple* about the way I play *that* game!" She sighed happily and took his arm, leading him back to the dinner around the table of the moss agate landscape. She was humming softly to herself, a tune of hoofbeats and wings.

CHAPTER THIRTY-FOUR

AMBASSADOR AMBROSE LeBrun arrived in a sleek, official Quetzal, a little black crow that drifted up to his mooring post alongside *Mixcomitl*'s giant gilded condor. Mr. Qusmi escorted LeBrun to the breakfast room, to join Prince Viracocha and the rest at their meal.

Neither the brilliant, sunlit room with its view of the mountains nor the sunny delights of Mama Kusay's remarkable food could brighten the dark news LeBrun had come to tell them.

"On the morning of the *Tlachtli* games, Pachacuti sent orders to his men in every major city—foreigners in the empire are to be seized, and executed." LeBrun kept running his hands through his hair, as though smoothing it could smooth his distress. "The embassy at Chan Chan is under siege, and there is fighting in the streets. Pachacuti's soldiers are on the highways, and we cannot contact them to change their orders."

Viracocha pushed his breakfast plate aside, his eyes sharply focused on LeBrun's familiar face. "I must stop this."

"The embassy has initiated full evacuation across the country," LeBrun said. "Every Quetzal we can commandeer is in flight to get people to safety, but thousands are in danger. This will become a massacre of Egyptians if we cannot stop Pachacuti's men."

"They're soldiers," Natyra said with an offhanded shrug. "Change their orders."

Oken immediately liked her suggestion and spoke up in support. "'From the top to the tip of the country,' remember?" he said to Viracocha. "You've got the fastest ship in the fleet—and you're in charge now, like it or not."

Viracocha nodded thoughtfully. "*Mixcomitl* and I can change their orders. Yes, I must do that—at once."

He looked at Natyra, and his face changed; his eyes took on a different kind of sharpness, a greater light. "You will come with me?" he said to her.

"Of course, I will—my wardrobe is still in Qusqo." She laughed, and kissed his cheek. "We have to impress the troops, don't we?"

Oken could well imagine the effect. The combination of the golden *Mixcomitl* with Natyra's instinct for dramatics and Viracocha's powerful voice, trained by the wind, would have just the right impact.

"From what you told us about the imperial troops," Mabruke said to Viracocha, "they should find it all quite romantic, don't you think?"

"Indeed!" Viracocha said. "Romantic. Yes, *Mixcomitl* and I will talk to them," he said. "That is the Egyptian way, isn't it?"

"That's right," LeBrun said. "The talk-to-me nation. Conversation is more enduring than battle."

Captain Hanaq Pacha folded his napkin, set it aside, and stood from the table. "I will begin flight preparations at once, Glorious One." He bowed to his prince. Viracocha nodded agreement, and Hanaq Pacha left.

Runa watched him go, her brow furrowed in thought; then she ran after him.

"We will have a conversation about a new treaty between Tawantinsuyu and Egypt when I return," Viracocha said to the ambassador as he rose to his feet. "Nothing like the old."

Ambassador LeBrun was greatly cheered by this announcement. "Actually, we could talk on board *Mixcomitl*, if you wish."

LeBrun suggested to Zaydane and Mabruke that they take his embassy Quetzal to Port Zulia, and return to Memphis from there. "The Pharaoh and the Queen must learn of these developments before the story hits the international newspapers," he said to them.

"I do not want you to leave," Viracocha said to Oken and Mabruke. "But Egypt needs you more than I do. Ambrose is here to guide me."

He put his hand out to Natyra. "And you, to guide me," he said to her. "You are an empress now."

"Yes." Natyra took Viracocha's hand, drawing herself up gracefully beside him.

"I would say, then, that you are in good hands," Mabruke said to Viracocha and Natyra, blessing the couple with his radiant smile.

"I do not kiss you good-bye," Natyra said to Oken. "We did that before. I kiss you the next time we say hello."

Oken bowed his head to her in acknowledgment; then the new Inca and his empress left to save their country from further bloodshed. Ambassador LeBrun and his assistant followed them out.

"We can go as soon as our luggage is on board the embassy Quetzal," Oken said.

Mabruke looked down at the dishes on the table, lovingly prepared by Mama Kusay, and sighed with dismay. "Can we finish eating first?"

EPILOGUE

IHHUIPAPALOTL LEANED forward, perched tautly on the edge of his seat. The haeka-glass wall was the only bright light in the control room. A double row of gauges and toggles on the control panel readouts flickered softly in the shadows behind him. He was totally focused on the view in the glass, a wide expanse of red desert soil, packed hard and baking in the African heat. At the far edge of the field was a black-charred gantry, a ceramic and steel tower. Resting inside the webwork of the gantry stood a proud, shining arrow shape, a single design gesture of Egyptian engineering and New World ingenuity, a vision of pure eagerness for flight.

The Sun himself seemed entranced by the importance of the moment, watching from the sky. Ignition was called, and great jets of fire poured out of the rocket's engines, powered by the same noxious brew that burned in Mama Kusay's ovens, grown in swampy vats of compost. Vapor poured away from the gantry and out across the hard desert.

Ihhuipapalotl could not breathe. The silver, shining Moon-rocket hung impossibly still over the billows of flame, then shot skyward. The brighter light of the upper air made the entire rocket glow like gold; then it was gone, vanished in the heavens, a white line of vapor marking its clean ascent.

The cheers were deafening then, men and women dancing wildly about, and laughing, crying, giddy with relief and joy, a dozen languages shouting happily together.

Ihhuipapalotl sat very still, gazing at the white trail piercing the sky. Quietly, he whispered to the soul of his poor old Inca, Osiris Yupanqui, whose lifelong dream of reaching the Moon had been perverted by his mad son. Yupanqui's dream was, at last, a reality.

"This launch, Glorious One, did not fail."

Pronunciation Guide

Aklya Kono (Ak-LEE-yah KOH-noh) Quechua for "Virgins of the Sun." Vestal Virgins of Tawantinsuyu.

Blestyak (BLEST-YAK) General Vladimir Modestovich Blestyak of the horse-guardsmen from Rusland.

Chocolatl (CHOCK-LOT'l) Quechua for the hot cocoa drink native to the southern continent of the New World.

Hanaq Pacha (HAH-NOCK PAH-CHAH) Quechua for "The Highest, Watery Heavens Above."

Hara'wi (HAH-RAH-WEE) Quechua for "sacred music."

Hukuchasatil (Hoo-koo-CHAH-SAH-teel) Quechua for "Mouse Face." Commander of Pachacuti's private guard.

Ihhuipapalotl (Ih-HWEE-pahpah-lotl) "Feathery-Winged Butterfly." High Priest of the Qurikancha Temple Complex.

Ka Egyptian concept of the outer persona, character, charisma, reputation—you as only others can know you. (As contrasted to *ba,* your point of view on reality, your experience of yourself. *Ka* is outer; *ba* is inner.)

Kuchillu (Koo-CHEEL-loo) Quechua for "Slashes with a Knife." Childhood name of Pachacuti.

Mabruke (MAH-BROO-KAY) Professor-Prince Mikel Mabruke, professor of alkhemy and board member of the Guild of Pharaoh's Special Investigators.

Mama Kuna Quechua for the guardian "house mother" of the Aklya Kono.

Mama Kusay (MAH-MA KOO-SAY) Quechua for "Queen of Chefs." The head of the Queen Mother's kitchens.

Maracuyá (MAR-AH-KOY-AH) Quechua for "passion fruit."

Mixcomitl (MEESCH-KOH-MEET'L) Quechua for "Cloud Vessel." Flagship of the imperial Quetzal fleet, and Prince Viracocha's private transport.

Natyra Arkadyena Solovyova (NAH-TEAR-AH AR-KAD-YAIN-AH SOH-LOV-YO-VAH) Dancer from Novgorod, a celebrity known around Europe.

Nayture (NATURE) Egyptian name for the eternal forces, the gods and goddesses, divinity.

Oken (OAK-EN) Lord Scott Oken, fourth son of the Spate Arch of Mercia, Britannic Isles. He is a trained memoryman, and personal assistant to Professor-Prince Mabruke.

Ollantaytambo (OH-LAHN-TAY-TAHM-BOH) "The Resort Palace of Ollantay." Valley of the Imperial Palace, formal residence of the Inca and his Inheritor, as well as his concubines and guests.

Pachacuti (PATCH-AH-KOO-TEE) Quechua name of the current Inheritor of Tawantinsuyu.

Pachamama (Patch-ah-MAH-mah) Quechua for "Mother Earth." The dimension of space/time.

Pharoman (FAIR-roh-man) Generic for the Egyptian Empire founded by Pharaoh Gaius Julius Caesar and Queen Cleopatra.

Ptah-Sokar (p'TAH Soh-KAR) Egyptian divinity of the art of the tomb and the silence of the grave.

Quillabamba (Kweel-ah-BAHM-bah) Quechua for "City of the Eternal Summer." Home of the Queen Mother's estate, as well as the noninheriting offspring of the Inca.

Qurikancha (Kwoor-ee-KAHN-cha) Quechua for "The Temple of the Sun."

Qusmi (KWOOZ-mee) Quechua for "Smoke." The Queen Mother's butler.

Qusqo (KOOZ-koh) Quechua for "The Navel of the World." Mercantile capital of Tawantinsuyu.

Quy (Koo-EE) Quechua for guinea pigs. "Wheek" is the sound they make when excited.

Quyllur Misi (QWEE-lur MEES-ee) Quechua for "Star of the Cat."

Rae (RAY, as in "ray of light.") Egyptian divinity of conscious self-awareness, the eternal source of all consciousness. Rae is the Sun in your mind, lighting your internal world.

Rawray unquy qura (RAW-ray oonk-kwee KOOR-rah) Quechua for "fever herb."

Rimaykullayki (Ree-may-kool-LAY-kee) Quechua for "greetings."

Ripuy (Ree-POO-wee) Quechua for "go now!"

Sakhmetical (Sakh-METI-kall) Egyptian medicine, from Sakhmet, goddess of the healing arts (together with Isis and Thoth).

Satiltzoj (Zah-TEELT-zoj) Quechua for "Face of the Bat." Current President of the United States of Maya Land.

Sobak (SOE-bock) Egyptian god of the neurochemistry of the human unconscious.

Spate (SPATE) The Egyptian equivalent of a state or province, also known as "Nome."

Spinglass (SPIN-glass) fiber-optic technology. Spinglass lamps are "spunglass."

Sunsu Nyakay (SOON-soo-Ny-AK-ay) Quechua name of an abandoned prison compound.

Tawantinsuyu (Tah-wahn-tin-SOO-you) "Empire of the Four Quarters." The empire centered in the Andes Mountains. The emperor is known as the "Inca."

Teonanactl (Tay-oh-nah-NAKT'l) Quechua for "Flesh of the Gods." Native psychedelic mushroom used in religious ceremonies.

Tiwanaku (Tee-wah-NOCK-oo) Quechua for the sacred center of Tawantinsuyu, near Lake Titikaka.

Urubamba (Oo-roo-BAHM-bah) Quechua for "Flat Land of Spiders." Civic center of Tawantinsuyu, site of the main Egyptian Embassy.

Usqhullu (Oosk-HOO-loo) Quechua for "Wildcat." Princess of Tawantinsuyu.

Viracocha Inca Yupanqui XII (Veer-ah-KOH-cha Ink-ah You-PAN-kwee) Current Inca.

Wankakanka (Wank-ah-KANK-ah) Quechua for "Rock Rooster."

Warmi Irqi (WAR-mee EAR-kee) Quechua for "Boy Child."

Wawa (WAH-wah) Quechua for "dear child."

Wayra Wayta (WAY-rah WAY-tah) Quechua for "Wind Flower." Viracocha's personal captain of the guards.

Xibalba (Schee-BAL-bah) Quechua for the Underworld.

Xochicacahuatl (Schoh-chee-kah-kah-HWAHT'l) Quechua for "Flowery Cacao Tree." The Queen Mother's estate.

Yadir (Yah-DEER) Mabruke's maternal grandfather.